Les Tales:

Tempted to Touch

Les Tales:

Tempted to Touch

Skyy, Nikki Rashan and *Fiona Zedde*

www.urbanbooks.net

Urban Books, LLC
97 N18th Street
Wyandanch, NY 11798

ISBN 13: 978-1-60162-413-0
ISBN 10: 1-60162-413-1

First Trade Paperback Printing June 2014
Printed in the United States of America

10 9 8 7 6 5 4 3 2 1

Distributed by Kensington Publishing Corp.
Submit Wholesale Orders to:
Kensington Publishing Corp.
C/O Penguin Group (USA) Inc.
Attention: Order Processing
405 Murray Hill Parkway
East Rutherford, NJ 07073-2316
Phone: 1-800-526-0275
Fax: 1-800-227-9604

Number One Fan

by

Skyy

Chapter 1

Everybody has one—that one celebrity they grew up idolizing. It could be someone from a television show or a sports figure. Either way, you wanted to be them or be with them. You plastered cutout posters from magazines on your walls. You could sing every lyric to their songs, or you watched every episode of their television show. You dressed as them for Halloween and got angry if someone tried to talk bad about them. You dreamed of the day you could meet the person and just let them know how much they meant to you.

Most grow out of that stage. Some realize that celebrities are just people like you and me. Others play it cool when it comes to the person, but deep down they are still just as excited as the first time they ever saw the person. At some age people are brainwashed to think that they aren't supposed to show love to the people who bring them joy in their life. Fanboys are considered weird, whereas fangirls are labeled groupies.

No matter who you are, there is at least one person who makes you wonder, *What would it be like if I met this person?* You might even dream of more. *What would it be like if I could hang out with them for one day?* Or even better, *What would it be like if I could have just one night with them?*

My dream became a reality. This is the story.

I could feel my girlfriend's hands rubbing against my thighs. I frowned as I twisted my body, hoping she would stop. Not only was it four in the morning, but also her hands left much to be desired. I couldn't understand why she thought crusty, callused hands would feel good against my skin. I knew that the state of her hands came from throwing boxes overnight at FedEx, but couldn't she at least wear gloves if she was going to put those paws on me?

"Babe, I do have to be at work in a few hours."

"I thought you didn't have to be in until eleven." She paused, giving my skin a much-needed break.

"Overtime. Remember?"

The grunt she let out let me know she remembered and she wasn't happy about it. Nothing about my upcoming trip made her happy, and I knew denying her sex would be an argument I didn't want to have in the morning.

I placed my hands on top of her head, which she had laid on my thigh. I rubbed the waves in her short hair. I knew she loved it when I rubbed her head. I felt her hand making its way back up my leg. I bit my lip as her fingers opened my lips. I closed my eyes, ground my body against her mouth as she worked her tongue on my pussy with an unusual intensity for after-work sex. Before I knew it, I was actually turned on.

"Let me strap up, okay?" She stopped mid-lick to ask the question.

I hesitated. A little early morning head was one thing, but strapping would require actual energy on my behalf.

"Why are you so energetic? You just got off work." I looked at her big eyes, which were now staring directly at me.

Ciara sat up on her knees. "Can't I just want to please my woman?"

I sighed. It never failed; the studs always had to be dramatic. "Ciara, I have to be up in three hours for work and . . . " I couldn't finish my statement before she was off of me and heading into the bathroom. "Ciara . . ."

"Don't worry about it, Temple. Go back to bed."

She slammed the door behind her. I knew I had a day of attitude to look forward to. I made a mental note to pick up a new video game for her after work and went back to sleep.

Hours later my cell phone's alarm clock buzzed, making me jump out of my deep sleep. This was why I hated when Ciara woke me up when she got off from FedEx. It always threw off my sleeping pattern. I silenced my alarm clock. I needed a few more minutes, but I knew if I closed my eyes, they weren't going to open back up soon, not even for an aggravating alarm clock.

I sat on the edge of the bed. I turned around and looked at Ciara, who could always sleep through my alarm clock buzzing. I smiled. This was the way I liked her the most. The sun's rays beaming in through my bamboo shades lit tiny pieces of her honey-brown skin. I studied her toned arms, which still were one of my favorite parts of her body. Since she'd picked up the second job, her arms had become even more defined. If it wasn't for the beeping of my reminder alarm, I would have stared at her all day.

I took a quick hot shower and threw on a pair of jeans and a cute purple button-down shirt. I opted for wedge flip-flops, even though I knew that flip-flops were technically against company policy. I didn't care. If they were going to send me home over my shoes, I would gladly oblige as I still had a lot to do before my trip.

I grabbed a premixed smoothie out of the fridge, which I had prepared the night before. I had been juicing with various fruits and vegetables for a while, hoping to boost my immune system. The last thing I needed was to develop "con crud," which was the name given to the contagious illnesses that people got while attending large conventions. It was inevitable for many, since being in packed areas meant lots of germs in the air. On a friend's advice, I had started taking a daily dose of Airborne.

I walked back into the bedroom before heading out. Ciara was still sleeping. I thought about waking her up. Maybe a taste of her own medicine would help her to understand why I wasn't a fan of the sex wake-ups. Then I realized an argument would ruin the moment, my chance to watch her sleep. I headed out of the house, closing the door behind me as quietly as possible.

"Temple."

I jumped when I heard someone calling my name. I turned around to see one of my coworkers, Jasmine, staring at me from the seat next to mine.

"Sorry. What's up?" I turned my chair around toward her.

"Where were you just then?"

I smiled. "Girl, my mind checked out of this place an hour ago."

Jasmine shook her head. "You and this damn trip. You better check back in before you get fired before your trip."

I nodded my head. She was right. I had only an hour to go, but my mind was racing. I had so many last-minute things to do before I left town the next day.

"I still don't have the right earrings for an armband." I picked up my to-do list. I had no idea how I was going to get it all done before I caught the Megabus to Atlanta. "Maybe I should just drive myself to Atlanta. That would give me more time to get everything done."

"Yeah, I'm probably not the one to ask, since I honestly don't understand anything that you are doing. I do know the whole purpose of you taking the bus was so you could rest and not have to worry about parking and stuff when you get to Atlanta."

"Atlanta?" Another one of my coworkers, Tina, walked up. "When you going to ATL, girl?"

I never could completely focus on her face, due to the variety of crazy hairstyles she sported on a weekly basis. Today there was some type of giant braid wrapped around her hair with an array of colors braided into it.

"Tina, I have been talking about this trip for months. I'm going tomorrow."

"Oh, for LudaDay Weekend." Tina smiled. "Temple, I have so much more respect for you now. I never thought you would attend LudaDay Weekend." She nodded in approval.

I just stared at her, then said, "I'm not going to Luda-Day Weekend. I'm going to something much bigger and better." I smiled. "I'm going to Dragon Con."

Now Tina was staring at me.

"It's a weekend filled with amazing cosplay and celebrities and parties unlike any you have ever seen before," I explained.

Tina's staring continued. Whenever I started talking about the convention, I received the same confused expressions from my coworkers. I was definitely a different type of girl. While my coworkers saw Labor Day weekend as a weekend to barbecue and party, I considered it a weekend to meet with over thirty thousand other geeks who loved everything from comics to alternative history. I had attended the convention only one time before and had had the best time of my life.

"Temple, you are so weird. I love it." Tina walked back to her desk.

"So, what is Ciara going to do all weekend, while you are at Nerdi Gras?" Jasmine asked as she scrolled through her Facebook app on her phone.

"Hang out with her family and friends, I guess. I'm not really sure. She pissed me off last night."

"Why?"

"Because she just doesn't support me or this trip, and I get tired of her calling me names all the time and mocking me because of the things I like. My two friends I'm meeting up with there are so glad she's not coming. I think my friend Cree is a badass, and she might have beaten Ciara up if she said anything crazy while we were there."

"I'm sorry, hon. It probably is just hard for her to understand." Jasmine finally looked up from her phone. "I mean, it's hard for me to get it, but I can tell you really are into it."

"Yeah, and I get that. But as my partner, I expect her to act more like you do. You don't have to understand it, but you don't have to mock it, either." I sighed. "I tried to explain it by saying, 'What if there was a convention that you could go to and meet Michael Jordan and LeBron James?' I told her I knew she would wear one of their jerseys to show her support. Well, I'm going to get the chance to actually meet the person who was my idol when I was growing up."

I was already stoked about my trip when they announced that the three main stars from my favorite TV series, *Olympus,* a show about the ancient Greek gods and goddesses, would be there. I knew the second they announced that Les Harrison, who played Zeus, Mason Kyles, who played Hercules, and Kirk Mission, who played Aries, were going to be there, I was going to attend. I started planning my costume and decided on a Greek goddess look until I saw the last-minute addition of Ursula Moore. For a young lesbian, there was no one more heroic than the Amazon goddess Ayela. I remembered running home from school to watch the show about the gorgeous, scantily clad warrior who kicked ass in every episode. As an adult, I watched her every week as she plotted evil schemes and had amazing sex as Athena on *Olympus.* I immediately changed my costume idea: I gave up the goddess look in favor of making a replica of one of her famous gowns from the TV show.

I lost Jasmine during my geek rant when her phone rang. I turned back to my desk. I glanced at the to-do list again, realizing that I had way too much to do. I knew the day was gone. I punched out on sick time and headed out the door.

I made a mental note of all the things I needed to get done before I caught the morning Megabus to Atlanta. I knew that I had one more Skype session with my friends who were heading to Dragon Con. They were also dressing up as characters from the TV show. Ever since I met them, we had talked every day about the upcoming trip. Nia was an Atlanta local I met on a Facebook group about the convention. She was known for amazing cosplay and was also a die-hard *Olympus* fan. She introduced me to Cree, who was by far the biggest fan of all. They met when Nia bought an outfit from Cree on eBay. Both women made me look like a bad fan. While I got my costume made, they watched eBay auctions daily to win actual costumes from the show. Nia was going as Athena, and Cree was going as Aphrodite.

I decided to drop by my house first to pick up my costume. I wanted to make sure any jewelry I found matched the red I was wearing perfectly. I pulled up to my apartment to see my girlfriend's car in the driveway. She was supposed to be at work. Immediately, my body started to tingle. I had a bad feeling. I thought about turning around and leaving, but something told me I needed to go in the house.

I could hear music blaring from our apartment. It wasn't her usual Lil Wayne and Jay Z. She was blasting Trey Songz. I slowly put my key in the door and turned the knob as quietly as I could. The smell of sweaty vagina and incense hit me the moment I walked in the house. My body started to tremble. My hopes of finding her sitting in front of the living room television, playing her video games, faded. I took off my heels, because I knew I needed to be quiet. I tiptoed to the back of our apartment, and there I could hear the shower going.

I walked into our bedroom. The bed was a mess. The sheets were clinging to the edge of the bed but were mostly on the floor. Clothes were scattered around the floor. I picked up one of the shirts. It was the same uniform that Ciara wore, but much smaller. My heart began to pound as I heard the water stop in the bathroom. I could hear two people laughing. I wasn't prepared for this. All types of ideas flooded through my head. Was I going to play it cool, yell my ass off, or just commence to kick ass in the house?

"Just get yo' ass back in the bed . . ." I heard my woman say as the door to the bathroom opened. Unable to decide what to do, I just sat on the edge of the bed as I watched the two naked women walk out of the bathroom. Their bodies both froze, and then they stared at me as I sat on the edge of my bed.

"Temple." Ciara's voice cracked. "Temple."

"I think this belongs to you." I threw the uniform shirt to Ciara's naked coworker. I couldn't believe what I was looking at. Standing in front of me was Kelly, Ciara's funny-shaped, trailer park-trash white coworker.

"Temp."

I stood up, walked to the closet, and grabbed my garment bag with my costume in it. "Be out of my apartment by the time I get back."

I couldn't breathe. I had to get out of that apartment. I walked as fast as I could to my car. I slammed the car door closed and called Nia.

Her usual happy voice answered on the second ring. "Hey, *chica!*"

I couldn't speak. I just started to cry. Before I knew it, she had called Cree and had us on three-way.

"What the hell is going on, girl?" Cree's voice was much more forceful.

"In my house, in my bed."

"What?" Nia tried to decipher what I was saying. "What happened in your house?"

I continued to cry. It didn't take long for them to figure out what was going on.

"Please tell me you didn't find Ciara with someone in your house." I could tell it was hard for Nia to get the words out.

I cried harder.

"Oh, hell to the naw!" Cree snapped. "I'm going to kill that bitch! How far is Memphis from Atlanta? Where the fuck is my gun?"

The two continued to console me through the phone. I heard someone yelling my name and saw Ciara running out of the apartment.

"She's coming to my car." Suddenly Cree's spirit jumped into my body. I left the two girls on the Bluetooth speaker-phone as I hopped out of my car.

"Temple, I'm sorry," Ciara said.

"How the fuck could you!" I proceeded to punch Ciara in her arms and chest.

She tried to block my attacks. "It just kinda happened. Please, baby."

"Why is that bitch still in my house?"

"Oh, hell no, that bitch is not still in the house!" I heard Cree yell through the speakerphone.

Ciara became still. "See? That's why this happened. You so busy trying to go be with those girls and that weird shit that you can't even take care of home."

"What the fuck did she just say?" Cree questioned.

"I can't hear," Nia replied.

"That weird shit?" I took two steps back. I threw my hands up. "You know what? Fuck you." I walked back to my apartment.

I walked in to find Kelly standing in the corner. She formed her mouth to say something but quickly changed her mind when she saw the expression on my face.

"Get the fuck out of my house!" I said, and she quickly ran out, following instructions.

I went into my bedroom and grabbed the few things of Ciara's that I could find in the drawer I had given her. She walked into the room after me.

"Temple, please."

"Take your shit." I threw the clothes at her. As she tried to collect them, I grabbed her keys out of her pocket. I pulled my key off of the key chain. "Get the fuck out of my house and never come back."

"Fine." Ciara picked up her cologne off my dresser and walked out of the room.

I followed her out of the house and walked to my car, which was still running.

"Since that's what you want, go be with her," I yelled as I watched her get into Kelly's old Kia.

"Yeah, have fun with your weirdos!" she yelled as Kelly drove off.

I sat in my car and slammed the door. I was fuming; I couldn't think straight. I knew it had happened, but I just didn't want to believe it.

"Honey, are you all right?" Nia's voice filled my car.

It hit me that it had really happened. I started to cry again. "I can't come. I can't."

"Oh, hell no, you are coming!" Cree said, jumping in. "Fuck that ugly bitch. You deserve better. You are going to meet us in Atlanta, and we are going to take your mind off of her mud duck ass."

"Yeah, girl, you need your friends, and we want to be there for you. In fact, I think you should go ahead and take that bus out tonight and come on." Nia was much more sensitive.

"Yeah, I'm flying in tomorrow, and before you know it, you won't even be thinking about her," Cree added.

"But I don't want to ruin you guys' weekend," I sobbed.

"Please! You are going to meet Ursula. Trust me, once you see her, nothing else is going to matter," Cree said.

I thought about what they were saying. I had been preparing for this trip for months and had spent hundreds gearing up for it. This might be the only chance for me to meet my TV idol. I looked at the clock in my car. I had one hour to get to the bus station to catch the last bus to Atlanta.

"Fuck it. I'm gonna catch this bus. I'll talk to y'all later." I hung up to cheers from my friends. Nothing was going to make me miss meeting Ursula, not even a cheating girlfriend.

The bus ride was just what I needed. It was a good thing there were only about ten other passengers on the bus. I got a good seat at the front of the bus, one of the few seats that had a table connected to it. I put on my iPod playlist of emotional songs and spent the whole seven hours crying on and off. We made our final stop in Birmingham before arriving in Atlanta. I knew I needed some time to myself, so I hopped on Hotwire and reserved one night at the Westin Hotel in Atlanta, one of the hotels hosting the convention.

It was unusually cool for a summer night in Atlanta. I walked into the Westin to see WELCOME DRAGON CON signs hanging everywhere. It was like a ghost town in the hotel. I knew that in a few hours the hotel would be filled with costumed men and women, all ready for the convention weekend to start. I was happy for the quiet. I didn't unpack my bags. I took my clothes off and headed to the famous Heavenly Bath the Westin was known for. I got in the shower and let the water hit my hair. I didn't care about letting my natural curls show. I dried off and put on the robe that was hanging in the closet. I sat on my bed and closed my eyes. I just wanted to sleep and forget about my day.

I heard my phone blaring. Cree and Nia were chatting it up in the group FB chat we shared. I turned the notifications off. I knew that starting tomorrow, my overprotective friends weren't going to let me out of their sight. Just as I was putting my phone down, it began to ring. Ciara's face popped up on my screen.

I pressed ACCEPT. I couldn't speak. I held the phone.

"Temple."

Hearing her say my name broke my heart. I struggled to respond. "What?"

"Why won't you answer the door? We need to talk."

"I'm not home."

"Where are you?"

"That's none of your concern anymore."

"Temple, please. I just want to apologize." Ciara almost sounded sincere.

"You already did that. Anything else?" I could feel the anger starting to set back in.

Ciara sighed. "You really want to act like that?"

"Hey, it is what it is. Obviously, you did what you did because you wanted to. There isn't anything to talk about. So, like I said before, you go be with her and I'll be here in Atlanta with my weirdos."

"You're in Atlanta?" Ciara was shocked.

I didn't respond.

Ciara then let out a chuckle. "Well, then, have fun. I won't bother you."

I hung up the phone. I knew there was nothing I could do. I couldn't wrap my mind around why she would chose to cheat, and with someone of such low quality, just because I was into things she didn't get. I was a geek and a fangirl, and I didn't think I needed to apologize for that.

I knew it was something she didn't get, but I had never expected her to cheat on me because of it. I got angrier when I thought of all the things I had put up with from her. I hated the smell of weed, but I had let her smoke it in my house. I didn't understand the fascination with watching every basketball game that came on TV, yet I had constantly watched the smaller bedroom TV when my shows came on, because she needed the fifty-five-inch for her games. I had never made her go to see movies with me, yet I had always found myself at action movies, which I couldn't care less about.

It hit me that I was in a one-sided relationship. I could give and give, but she wasn't willing to give in return. I hated that I had just wasted ten months of my life on a person who didn't deserve ten minutes of my time. I opened the Facebook chat.

Made it to Atlanta. At the Westin, room 1919. Going to bed. See y'all later.

I put my phone on silent and turned the TV on. I flipped through the channels until I saw a familiar face. There stood Ursula in her Greek attire. It was a rerun of one of my favorite episodes of *Olympus*. I knew then that I was where I needed to be. In a few hours I was going to finally meet Ursula, and all would be right in the world again.

Chapter 2

The sound of a man yelling "Whooo, whooo" in the hallway woke me up. I heard someone knocking on my door. I dragged myself out of the bed and cracked the door open. I saw Nia standing there, looking like Princess Tiana from *The Princess and the Frog*. I couldn't help but smile. This was my first time actually meeting her, and she was as flawless in person as she was in her pictures online. The dress was identical to the one in the actual cartoon movie.

"I heard that a little girl was in need of some beignets and a kiss from a prince." She smiled and held up a plush frog version of Prince Naveen. I grabbed the frog from her and walked back in the room. I climbed back in bed, holding the frog.

Nia sat on the edge of my bed. She put her hand on the covers, right where my leg was.

"You okay, sis?" Her soft voice was comforting.

"I'm all right. I guess I should be getting up and heading to registration."

"Yeah, it's crazy out there. I already checked into our room at the Marriott, so we can head over and take your stuff. I can't believe you got this room just for a few hours. You totally could have come to my house."

I forced myself back out of the bed. I gave her back her frog and headed toward the bathroom. "Well, I needed a little bit of alone time."

"I understand. Well, Cree just touched down a bit ago, so by the time we get over to the Marriott, she shouldn't be too far behind."

I popped my head out of the bathroom. "Cool. I might as well take my shower here and at least get some of my money's worth out of the room."

I showered, put on my travel clothes from earlier, and grabbed my bags. We headed out of the room to find the elevator area already crowded with people. Immediately people wanted pictures with Nia in her costume. I snapped photos of her with guys dressed like the Mario Brothers. We got in one of the elevators, which quickly filled to capacity. I looked around to see the Mario Brothers, a fairy, and a guy in full metal armor from the *Halo* video game.

I started to laugh. "Only at Dragon Con would I be in this type of elevator."

The crowd in the elevator laughed, knowing I was right. I knew the weekend was going to be great.

It took longer than expected to walk from the Westin to the Marriott Marquis due to the crowd and the number of people trying to have their photo taken with Nia. I joked that I was her assistant as I held her bag while she posed like she was an actual Disney princess at Disney World. We finally made it to our room, where I set my bags down and proceeded to pull out my Princess Jasmine costume. I knew that the major costumes would be saved for the big panel with the *Olympus* cast tomorrow.

I was working on my Jasmine ponytail when there was a knock on the door. Nia opened it, and I heard a squeal as Cree ran in and dropped her bags on the floor.

"Oh my God. I just saw a bunch of Roman gladiators. I am in heaven!" She hugged Nia. "I'm so excited."

"Oh, that's nothing. Wait till later, when they are all out at the after-hours parties," Nia said as she picked up one of Cree's bags. Cree was the only one of us who had never been to Dragon Con before.

"Hey, girl," Cree said as she hugged me. "You okay?"

"I'm good."

"Well, you look good. Shit. You are wearing that Jasmine costume." Cree started to open one of her garment bags. "Well, since we are doing Disney today, I guess I'll get into this."

We both were shocked and ecstatic to see that Cree actually had a Pocahontas outfit. She had fought us like crazy about doing anything else girlie besides Aphrodite. An hour later we were all dressed as Disney princesses.

We headed toward the registration area, which was at the Hyatt. The convention was being held at a group of hotels in the downtown area of Atlanta. We got stopped by other con goers, as well as by others in town for various events on Labor Day weekend. Not only was it Dragon Con, but Atlanta was also holding host to LudaDay Weekend, two major college football games, a baseball game, gay pride weekend, and countless family reunions. Guys in college jerseys called out to us, trying to get our attention, as we walked to the Hyatt. We made it to the end of the line. Cree was shocked by the line, which wrapped around the side of the building. We quickly let her know that it wasn't as nearly as bad as it would be tomorrow.

The one thing you knew to expect at conventions was lines. Even with the long line, time flew by as we took pictures with other con goers. Cree and Nia made sure to take as many photos with hot guys as possible. It was a little odd being the gay girl with the straight girls, but they made sure to make me feel as comfortable as possible by pointing out all the attractive women they thought I should try to talk to.

After an hour and a half of waiting in line, we finally made it through registration. We got our laminated cardboard membership badges and purchased lanyards to replace the little clips that were provided with the badges. We walked to the lobby of the hotel and sat down to rest a bit before heading back out.

"Did you guys know Billy Dee Williams is going to be here too?" Nia said as she flipped through the schedule book. "Would it be crazy for me to go to the panel just so I can hold up a twenty-dollar bill and ask him if he's gonna make my arm fall off?" We all laughed.

"I think he would welcome questions about anything other than *Star Wars*. Let's add it to our list." I pushed the star on my official app for the convention to add it to my program on my phone.

"Can we discuss something that's actually important, like the fact that I am going to finally get to be eye to eye with Les?" Cree's face was very serious. She was the fangirl of Les more than anyone else. She followed not only him as Zeus, but also a show called *Liason,* which was about being an assassin and which had had its final season a few months earlier. "I can't wait till he sees me in my Lexi costume." Cree was in impeccable shape. On top of winning an actual costume from *Olympus,* she had also won an auction for one of the bodysuits worn by a woman on the show.

"I can't wait to see his reaction, either," Nia added. "We should probably head back to the room so you can get into your costume for his solo panel today."

"I can't wait for the panel tomorrow. OMG, I'm going to see Ursula." I was giddy again.

"Yep, tomorrow is going to be epic," Cree added. "Now, let me go get ready for my man."

As we stood up, my phone began to ring. I looked at it and saw Ciara's face again. I sighed. Cree saw my expression and grabbed my phone. Before I could say anything, she had pressed ACCEPT.

"Temple is busy right now," Cree growled. "What do you want? I don't really care. Look, you sorry excuse of a woman, you don't know my ass. I am from Detroit, and I will come to Memphis and rain hell on your ass."

I grabbed the phone from her.

"What?" I said.

"So you gonna let your little friends talk to me like that? You don't even know those girls like that."

"Ciara, what do you want?"

"I'm coming to Atlanta. We need to talk."

"Don't bring your ass here." I couldn't believe what I was hearing.

"Oh, yes, please bring your ass here. Please do." Cree was pacing back and forth and throwing her hands up as she talked.

"We need to talk," Ciara said.

"Damn it. You have already hurt me, and now you are trying to ruin my weekend too. Don't come here. And I'm not answering your calls anymore, so stop calling." I threw my phone on the chair and stormed off.

Cree and Nia caught up with me. I didn't want to talk about it. I let the convention consume me as we walked back to our hotel. Cree and Nia played along, not bringing up what had happened. I didn't care that I didn't have my phone. I would be just fine not hearing it for the rest of the weekend.

We sat in the room as Cree changed into her catsuit. Nia and I pulled out our seventies vixens for the rest of the day. I let my naturally curly hair poof up in the Afro it got, while Nia opted to wear a blond wig. I had on a multicolored one-piece jumpsuit, while she rocked super-short shorts with a halter top. We added fake guns and looked like we were Foxy Brown rip-offs.

There was an unexpected knock on the door. Nia let us know her friends Carlos and Jason were meeting us to go to the panel. I opened the door to find a six-two, handsome, dark-skinned fellow in a baby blue suit, with an Afro, and a shorter, brown-skinned guy wearing tight bell-bottoms and rollers in his hair.

"Hey, Mama. What's the word?" said Carlos, the taller guy, as he held up the black power sign.

"Hello, Black Dynamite and Cream Corn." I smiled, loving his costume. I knew instantly who he was supposed to be from the suit.

"What's happening, Mama? And you are?" He held his hand out to give me a handshake.

"I am Temple."

His facial expression changed. "Damn, all the fine ones are gay."

I playfully hit him as they walked in the room. They both felt like olds friend instantly. Carlos greeted Nia and continued to talk just like he was Black Dynamite.

"Okay, are y'all ready?" Cree yelled from the bathroom.

We yelled at her to come out. She walked out of the bathroom, and all our mouths dropped. The suit looked like it was painted on her body. The middle was cut out, showing off her abs, which I could only dream of having. She obviously didn't skimp on the wig, either, which hung straight down her back. She was identical to the character on the show.

"Girl, he is going to lose his mind," I said and smiled.

Cree smiled. She was ready to claim what was hers.

The line was shorter than we had expected it would be when we arrived at the ballroom. We knew we would get good seats. We all laughed at Carlos and Jason, who never seemed to break character. People asked to take pictures of us. We all took on personalities, striking various poses, ones you would see on the covers of old seventies movie posters.

"So you are telling me your girlfriend was mad that you like to cosplay?" Carlos asked me as we stood in line.

"Yeah, well, that I like all things geeky."

"I think that's like the best thing ever in a woman."

"You would think that, wouldn't you?"

The usher for the ballroom told us to file into the room. We lucked out, getting seats in the fourth row, but this didn't make Cree happy, because she wanted the front row. We convinced her that she would get his attention better when she asked her question at the question podium.

Once everyone had been ushered in, the moderator for the panel came out in front of the curtain. We all clapped as he introduced Les Moore. Les came walking out, holding one of the prop guns he used on the show. Even I couldn't help realizing how gorgeous the man was. Cree excused herself the second they called for questions. We listened as Les answered stupid questions from people who lacked originality. There were the usual questions, like What costume would he wear if he attended a convention? And Was there anything he looked forward to seeing? He joked about the things he had heard about Dragon Con after dark, and said he hoped to hit a party or two.

We watched as his eyes suddenly widened. He leaned forward in his chair.

"Lexi, it's you!" Les pointed at the person in line.

We turned to see Cree standing there with the microphone in her hand. She held up her gun.

"Oh my God, that is amazing," he gushed. "I mean, goodness, you look more like Lexi than Heather, the actual actress. Goodness, you look like you could kick my ass." The crowd was loving it.

"I'd take that challenge," Cree said, flirting, causing both Nia and me to clap for our friend.

After the crowd calmed down, Cree asked the first good question of the panel. Les discussed his feelings about the final show and revealed how emotional it was to watch the final episode. When he was finished, Cree started walking back toward us. Les stood up and held his arms out, motioning for her to come onstage. We were shocked and the crowd went wild as Cree walked up on the stage and hugged Les. The hug lingered, and he asked her something that made her laugh. She finally came back to her seat.

"OMG. I can't believe that happened," Nia whispered. "I've never seen anyone get called onstage before."

"Me either." I was equally excited. "What did he say to you?"

"He said I looked amazing." Cree couldn't hold back her smile. "I can't believe I just hugged Les."

"You lucky bitch!" Nia hit Cree on her leg. We giggled before finally focusing on the final bit of the panel.

After the panel we headed back to the bar at the Marriott. The Marriott was party central for the crazy after hours of Dragon Con. There were parties in all the ballrooms, not to mention the mini parties that people threw in their rooms. This was the major thing that separated Dragon Con from all the other major conventions. It was a twenty-four-hour party. At night raves lasted till six in the morning. People hung out and drank and took pictures. Also, the costumes got more risqué after hours. A normal Poison Ivy costume would no longer require a leotard, but just some green body paint and ivy leaves. Men rocked crazy getups, some walking around with just towels and nothing else on.

We grabbed our first round of shots. Carlos held his glass up. We all followed suit, holding our glasses up in the air.

"To a kick-ass Dragon Con!" he yelled, causing the rest of the bar to cheer along with us. For some reason in that moment Ciara's face entered my mind. I downed the shot as quickly as I could, hoping the strong tequila would numb all my senses.

"You okay, honey?" I felt hands touch my back. I turned to see Jason standing behind me. "Nia told me what happened. I noticed the look on your face just now."

"I'm okay. Or I will be." I forced the best smile I could.

"Just know you are with family now. We might be as crazy and weird as hell, but we are all family."

"Damn right!" Carlos exclaimed, chiming in. He had obviously overheard what Jason said to me. "We are fucking weirdos. Cheers to being fucking weirdos!" Again, the crowd erupted in cheers. Carlos handed me another shot. I tapped his glass with mine and downed the second shot.

Nia tapped Jason on his shoulder. "I think that you have an admirer."

Jason turned around to see a petite white girl with a terrible nurse outfit on staring at him. He quickly turned back around toward us.

"Tell me she didn't see me."

"Sorry, buddy, but she's headed this way." Carlos laughed.

The nurse walked over and tapped Jason on his shoulder. He rolled his eyes as he turned around to her.

"Um, well, hello there." The nurse was obviously intoxicated, as she slurred her words. "I love your costume."

"Thanks." Jason smiled while trying to turn back around, only to have her grab his arm.

"I was wondering if I could maybe buy you a drink." We couldn't help but laugh as she attempted to flaunt her breasts, which were five seconds away from popping out the too-little costume.

"Um, thank you, but I'm already set." He tried to turn around again, but it didn't work.

"My name is Miley. What's yours?"

"Umm, Jason."

"Jaaaysooon. That's a hot name for such a hot guy."

"Riiight." We couldn't help but chuckle at the blank stare Jason continued to give the woman. "Look, I'm sorry, but we were just about to leave."

"Oh, going to another party?" The nurse perked up, fearing she was about to lose her sexual chocolate.

"Um, not sure. Well, nice to meet you. Bye." Jason started to walk away. We took our cue to follow. We couldn't make it down the stairs before laughing uncontrollably at him. He was, however, not amused.

It was the night that wouldn't end. Nia talked some guys dressed as Spartans into buying us drinks. Two guys wearing togas asked us to dance with them. The dance took a turn for the worse when they started humping on Nia like dogs. Carlos quickly intervened, just pulling her away. We laughed it off, knowing that was just a part of the craziness of Dragon Con. We headed to the main ballroom for the rave that was about to start. A steampunk band was playing as people drunkenly danced to the music. I looked to my right and saw a storm trooper dancing with a fairy. I let the techno music take me away. I danced, never letting go of my drink, which I was, at that point, just nursing.

I noticed two girls, a redhead and a blonde, who were dressed like slutty versions of the Sailor Moon and Sailor Mercury characters. They were dancing together. The liquor in me made me decide to join them. I began to grind against the girls, who welcomed me with open arms. I didn't know what came over me, but I took them both by the back of the head and pushed them closer to each other, and without any hesitation they began to kiss. Carlos, Jason, and many other guys in the area stopped dancing to watch the show. The two girls stopped kissing, and then the redhead grabbed my face and pressed her lips against mine. The blonde didn't want to miss out, so she grabbed my face and kissed me as well. Before I knew it, I was engaged in a triple kiss with Sailor Moon and Sailor Mercury.

I pulled away finally and looked over at my friends, who were all just shocked at what they had witnessed. They all started clapping their hands. I brushed them off, and we continued to dance the night away.

Chapter 3

I could hear the water running, but I didn't want to open my eyes. I finally forced my eyes open and saw Nia dressed in her Princess Tiana costume again. I looked over at the clock on the dresser.

"You are not seriously up this early," I said, noticing that Cree was still dead to the world.

"I gotta get to the lineup for the parade. I didn't want to wake you guys. Especially you, with your drunk ass." She laughed as she picked up her frog. "I'll be back afterward, and we can get ready for the big event."

I soon realized it was the big day. I was finally going to see Ursula in the flesh. Nia left the room, and I turned on the TV. The host hotels had a channel reserved for Dragon Con TV, and it showed nothing but highlights from the weekend, along with panels and exclusive interviews. At that moment it showed people lining up for the parade. I could tell it was a madhouse outside. Something that used to be just for us had now become a favorite for Atlanta residents as well. They no longer had to take their kids to Six Flags to see characters. They could watch a parade filled with characters from cartoons and comics, one with everything Disney, with everything Spartans, and, of course, with *Ghostbusters, Star Trek,* and *Star Wars* characters.

The intro for the interviews came on. I gasped as Ursula appeared on the screen. She was being interviewed in the bar that we were in just the night before. She talked about how excited she was to be at Dragon Con and how she couldn't wait for the panel later on that day. I couldn't believe she was standing in the same area I'd been in a few hours earlier.

"Oh, look. It's your girl." Cree sat up in her bed and wiped her eyes.

"I really hope I don't make an ass out of myself today."

"You will be fine. She's going to call you onstage, just like my Les did for me." Cree climbed out the bed and headed to the bathroom. Deep down I prayed she was right.

Nia returned to our room two hours later, after the parade. We talked about how good she had looked on TV. Cree and I had already had our showers and were putting our makeup on for the panel. It didn't take us long to get in our Greek goddess attire. I put my dress on, and it fit like a glove. The fabric was nice and cool, so I knew I wouldn't get too hot in it.

"I got this for you." Nia handed me a bag. "I knew you didn't have time to go get it, so I got it for you."

I pulled out a gold headpiece and an armband and necklace for my costume. I hugged Nia. My outfit was now complete. The curls of my black wig hung perfectly on my shoulders. I put the gold earrings I had on and gave myself one more once-over. I almost didn't recognize myself. I was no longer Temple. I was Athena.

The fourth row wasn't an option for this panel. We arrived extra early and were in line with only a few older women, who were obviously fans of Ursula's earlier work as the Amazon. I watched as the line swelled with people, most of them wearing T-shirts with her picture on them. People asked to take our pictures and complimented us on how well we matched the actual show. We knew we had it in the bag. The only other people in costume were men dressed as Greek gods. The women there were mostly in Amazon outfits. We were the only Greek goddesses in the line that we could see.

They ushered us in, and we snagged seats in the second row, behind the disability chairs. We were second row, center, and it was perfect. We went over our questions in our heads again. I could feel my body tensing as the time came closer. I was shaking when the moderator walked out onstage. The moderator announced each man first. Cree had a very confident look on her face as Les walked out onstage.

Nia grabbed my arm when Kirk ran out, holding his hands in the air. "Lord, that man is fine."

I could feel the heat rising off her body. Kirk was the sexiest, with his long blond hair and wicked smile. He oozed sex appeal, unlike the other two men, who were gorgeous but didn't sell sex the way that Kirk did.

I held both of my friends' hands as the moderator called Ursula's name. The crowd went wild as she walked out onstage, waving at everyone. I was in shock. She was literally a few feet away from me. I felt like I was watching a slow-motion video. She was flawless, just as I had imagined. Her black hair was straight and hung off her shoulders. Her British accent threw me a bit, owing to the fact that she never talked with a British accent on any of the shows she was on. It was sexy.

The moderator called for questions. We all stood up and headed to the question podium. Just like the day before, the first questions sucked. One obvious lesbian told Ursula that she was her first crush. Ursula talked about how it made her proud to have helped so many lesbians find their way.

Nia walked to the front. We quickly got the attention of the panel. Ursula leaned in.

"I think I see three goddesses," she said to her costars.

"Wow. Three very beautiful goddesses, if I say so myself. Is Atlanta my lucky city?" Kirk said, flirting and causing the crowd to swoon. We all were blushing.

"It certainly can be." Nia came back with this witty response, causing the crowd to clap. The panel loved it. We couldn't believe that came from Nia's mouth.

Nia asked the panel what their favorite episode was. They all responded. Afterward, Cree walked up to the question podium.

"Wait, is that Lexi now a goddess?" Les looked closely. Cree nodded. "Yes, it is."

"Wow! You have to be the best fan ever." He smiled at her.

"I try."

"No, you succeeded." Les bowed his head to her.

She asked the panel how difficult was it having the cast changes for two of the lead characters.

I felt my body tensing up as the mic was handed to me. Out of nowhere Ciara's face popped into my brain again. I suddenly went blank. I couldn't remember my question. The crowd finished clapping for Cree's question. All eyes were on me. I looked directly at Ursula, whose eyes were on me.

"Well, hello there, Athena."

She knows who I am. I felt my hands shaking. The microphone suddenly felt heavy in my hand. I forced myself to raise it to my mouth. Thoughts of all the things that Ciara had said to me about coming to the convention flooded my mind. I could see her with that bitch in my head.

"Hello, Ursula." My voice trembled. "I just want to say that . . ." I couldn't say any more. Emotions filled me, and I started to cry. Cree and Nia both held on to me as I struggled, and I finally got it out. "I am sorry, but I just want to say that you have been the biggest inspiration in my life since I was a child. If it wasn't for you, I never would have come into my own as the powerful woman I am. Well, that I usually am."

The crowd cheered. Some stood up, feeling the same way I felt about her.

"I thank you, love, and I am so glad that I was able to touch your life with my work. As an actress, that's all that we hope for. But I have a feeling that you would have come into your own and been the beautiful and powerful woman I see in front of me right now, anyway. You rock!"

I broke down crying again as the crowd cheered. Ursula stood up and clapped for me as I walked back to my chair. I was filled with emotion. It wasn't the moment I was going for, but it worked just as well. The panel ended with the cast thanking us for our support. We sat there as the crowd dispersed. I had finally regained my composure.

"I can't believe I broke down. I'm such a dork." I put my hands over my eyes.

"It's okay. She loved you. I know it," Cree said.

"No. Les loved you," I responded. "He acted like you were the only person in the room."

Cree paused for a moment, then said, "He kinda did, didn't he?"

"Okay, we need to get over to the Walk of Fame so we can get our autographs," Nia said, trying hard to keep us on schedule.

I shook my head. "Are you crazy? Didn't you see what just happened? I don't want to know what will happen when I am standing right in her face."

"Girl, please. You have to be cried out by now. And it's good, because it's fresh on her mind," Nia replied.

I couldn't get Ursula's face out of my head. I had made a complete fool of myself, and I wasn't looking forward to doing it again. I was sure I would want to jump right off the top of the Marriott if I did one more foolish thing in front of her.

"Okay, how about we go to the Walk of Fame and see the guys first? Then, if you are cool after that, we can go into the VIP room where she is. You know she won't be in the same room with the guys. She's too big of a name." Nia patted me on my back.

I agreed. I could warm up with the men from the show and then work my way up to Ursula.

One of the good things about the convention was the Walk of Fame. Nearly all the celebrity guests spent the time they were not in panels in a large room, meeting and greeting the fans. For a fee, you could get autographs, and some even allowed you to take photos with them. The good thing was that you could just walk up to them and speak for free.

We made our way through the madhouse to the floor that held the Walk of Fame. We flashed our badges and walked into the busy room. Celebrities and their handlers were posted at tables that went around the whole room. The more popular celebrities were right up front. A large banner with Les, Mason, and Kirk on it hung on a wall. Their table was surrounded by women squealing at their beauty.

"Okay, so what's our plan of attack here?" Nia was fully focused on the goal of getting as close to Kirk as she could.

"I say we gorilla those bitches out of the way and get our men." Cree rubbed her hands together.

"Let's just get in line. It's already seven, and the room closes at eight thirty. Plus, once they see us, I'm sure they will at least chat with us." I looked at the line, which was moving faster than expected.

We walked up to the line, only to realize that the majority of the women weren't getting anything signed.

"Oh, look at Les. He's so gorgeous." Cree melted.

"Please look at Kirk. That smile." Nia was in heat, as well. As much as I loved the guys, my mind was elsewhere. I would be no good until I met Ursula.

"It's our goddesses!" Our mouths dropped when Kirk stood up and acknowledged us in the line. "Don't they look lovely?" The crowd cheered in approval.

We couldn't believe what was happening. Two girls gave us dirty looks as we walked up to the table. The two guys were fixated on us. Mason greeted us and thanked us for being such loyal fans. He asked us questions about our costumes. While Les and Kirk mentioned how attractive we looked, Mason kept it on a strictly platonic level.

"So what are your lovely names?" Les asked.

Nia took the lead. "I'm Nia, and this is Temple and Cree."

"Cree, you were an absolutely amazing Lexi yesterday," Les said. He couldn't take his eyes off of Cree. "And today you are just as amazing."

"Why, thank you. You're pretty fantastic as well," Cree replied.

I watched as my friends flirted in moderation with their favorite actors. I noticed the others watching the way things were going down with them. Some women had frowns on their faces, wishing they had received more than a thank-you when they met the guys. Suddenly the handlers were snapping photos of us and the men, because they wanted pictures with the Greek goddess cosplayers for promotional purposes. Others crowded around, snapping photos of us for their large collection of Dragon Con cosplay photos, which everyone had at the end of the weekend.

Not only were the guys total hotties, but they were beyond down to earth as well. Instead of having us leave once the photos had been taken, they asked us to hang around. This was something out of a dream: we were hanging with people we watched faithfully every Sunday night, like we were actual friends. As much as I was enjoying the moment, I still had something else to do, and time was running out.

"Excuse me," I said.

I felt a tap on my shoulder and turned around to see a well-dressed white woman in a pantsuit standing behind me. She looked much more official than anyone else I'd seen, even more official then the facilitators of the convention.

"Aren't you the girl who got a little emotional at the panel earlier?" she said while typing on her iPad.

Mortified, I just nodded my head.

She smiled. "Oh, trust me, it's quite all right. We've seen much worse."

We've? Suddenly my heart began to race. She had to be working with Ursula.

"Thanks. I just wasn't hoping to make a total ass of myself," I admitted.

"Oh, you didn't. In fact, someone would like to meet you."

My heart was now working in overtime. The woman just smiled and nodded her head, already knowing what I was thinking. I tried to remain as calm as I possibly could. Not only had Ursula noticed me, but she had also sent someone to actually come and get me.

"Let me just let my friends know," I told her. Before she could respond, I had walked back over to Nia and Cree, who were sitting in chairs behind the guys as they signed autographs for other people.

"Um, seems Ursula wants to meet me," I announced.

"Oh my God!" they both squealed in unison.

"Go. Go. Go! Text us, and we will meet you when this plays out," Nia said and hit my hand, totally excited by what was happening.

I showed off my overly excited face to them one more time before taking a deep breath and turning around.

The short walk seemed like it would never end. The bigger names, like William Shatner, John Barrowman, and Stan Lee, had been put in a separate room to keep the crowds in better control than they were in the regular room.

To my surprise, the room was practically empty. Ursula was the only celebrity guest left in the room. There was a line of about ten people. I stood to the side with her assistant, who was now talking on the phone with someone about Ursula's schedule for another event. I tried to remain calm, opening my eyes as far as I could, hoping the air in the room would dry any tears that were attempting to form. The assistant was right; I wasn't the only one who got emotional. I watched as another girl completely broke down the moment Ursula shook her hand. Ursula just smiled and rubbed the girl's hand as she blubbered on about how Ursula was the most amazing person on the planet. I did not want to act like that again.

Finally, the last girl left the room, and they closed the door. Ursula spoke with her assistant for a moment before her assistant motioned for me to come over. My feet felt like lead as I attempted to move closer to her. Ursula came from behind the table she was sitting at and met me in the middle. She held her hand out.

"Well, hello there." Her British accent was so cute.

"Hello, Ursula." I could hear my voice trembling.

"So I was sitting in here, signing all these autographs for women, but I didn't see my Athena."

My Athena. She had just called me her Athena. I knew this had to be a dream now. No way was this happening. I had to be losing my mind.

"I'm sorry. I was headed over here, but my friends got caught up with the guys from the show over in the other room. I didn't realize how late it was getting. Not to mention I wasn't ready to make another ass of myself just yet."

Ursula and her assistant both laughed. Ursula's laugh was just like the laugh I'd heard a million times on the *Olympus* show. She touched me on my shoulder, sending a wave of energy through my body.

"You didn't make an ass of yourself. I was quite moved, actually," Ursula told me. "I've seen people cry before, but there was something about you. I didn't get the sense that the crying was just because you were meeting me." Her eyes met mine. It was like she was trying to read my mind through my eyes. I thought about Ciara.

"It wasn't. I, um . . . caught my girlfriend cheating on me the day before I headed here. . . . In my bed." Ursula's mouth dropped, and so did her assistant's. "She didn't understand why I wanted to come here and do any of this, so she did . . . well, what she did."

"What a slag. To cheat on someone so beautiful. . . . She should have her ass kicked." Ursula's expression reminded me of the serious face she had when she was an Amazon.

She had called me beautiful. I blushed. I had no idea what a slag was, but I just smiled while she continued to bash my ex with her assistant. I couldn't believe it. I still couldn't fully comprehend that I was having a conversation with Ursula Moore.

"Well, this has been one hell of a long day. I'm starving." Ursula turned her attention back to me. "Temple, would you be interested in joining me for dinner?" Her lips curled up, an expression I was very familiar with. That smile was usually present when she was up to something on the show or before she seduced someone.

Hell yes! Goddamn right I would! My wide-eyed expression had to let her know my answer.

"Are you serious? Um, sure, I'd love to," I told her.

"Um . . ." Her assistant chimed in. "Ursula, you are supposed to be meeting Jessica for dinner in thirty minutes."

Ursula's lips became very tight. "Oh, I totally forgot about that. I am so sorry, Temple, but I can't cancel this."

I felt my heart break all over again. I smiled and nodded my head. "Oh, it's no worries at all. My friends are probably wondering where I am. We are attending a few parties tonight."

Ursula's bright expression appeared again. "Fantastic. I tell you, this con is really unlike any I've ever attended. I even heard that there are no-clothes parties and furry parties."

"Well, yeah. It's Dragon Con."

"Brilliant."

I walked with Ursula and her assistant toward the door. Two bodyguards walked into the room. The assistant conversed with them, planning the route out of the building.

"Well, will you be at the panel tomorrow, Temple?" Ursula asked.

"Of course." I wanted to shoot myself as soon as the words came out of my mouth. I sounded crazy.

"Excellent. Make your way back here tomorrow night. Tell those guys they can't hog all of your time." Ursula winked at me before leaving the room with her bodyguards.

I stood there, watching her walk off, still completely in awe and in love even more than before.

Chapter 4

I texted my friends and found out they were still chilling in the Walk of Fame room, which had closed ten minutes before. I had to fight with the volunteer working the door before he let me in to meet them. I walked in to see the table merchandise being covered up by the various celebrities' handlers and to hear laughing coming from the area where the guys were. I walked up and found Les and Kirk sitting down with Cree and Nia.

"Ah, look who's back." Kirk's voice echoed through the now empty room.

"Hey, girl!" Nia waved to me while mouthing "Oh my God" at me.

I took a seat next to Cree as Kirk finished his story about one of the fight scenes he had with Les in the show. I could tell the men were genuinely friends by the way they interacted with each other. Since I had read rumors of cast fighting on various blog sites about the show, it was good to see that they actually liked each other.

"I'm sorry to be the party pooper, guys, but the car is here and we have to go," the guys' handler said as he stood there with their two bodyguards.

"Ah, how time flies." Les's Australian accent was the cutest thing ever. "Ladies, it has been an absolute pleasure. We must continue this again soon."

Kirk chimed in like a little boy asking for some ice cream. "I am sure you will be at the panel tomorrow, right?"

"We will be there," Nia assured him and stood up.

"Wouldn't miss it," Cree added as she and the two men stood up. I rose to my feet too.

"You won't be wearing that leather suit again, will you?" Les's dark eyes were fixed on Cree.

Cree shook her head. "I was planning on wearing something else, unless—"

"No good. I need to be able to concentrate on everyone, and not just on you," Les told her. His eyes never left Cree's face. I could see that Cree was trying not to squirm.

"Till tomorrow, ladies," Kirk said, then kissed my and Nia's hand while Les took care of giving Cree a lingering hug.

We followed the guys out of the room. They quickly disappeared into the crowd. As soon as we knew they were gone, we began to scream and squeal like teenage girls.

"I can't believe that happened." Nia hit her jaw with her hands.

"That was fucking amazing. Did you hear what he said to me? I'm about to do extra crunches tonight." Cree couldn't stop jumping up and down.

"Wait." Nia turned to me. "What happened with Ursula?"

The images of Ursula flooded back into my mind. I was smiling harder than the Cheshire cat.

"She was amazing. She called my ex a bunch of names and even invited me to dinner, until her damn assistant reminded her she already had plans."

"Ladies, this night can't be topped." Nia shook her head in amazement. "I mean, what the hell are we supposed to do after that?"

"We are supposed to party!" I exclaimed. "And I'm sorry, but I have a feeling things are going to get a lot better. I can feel it." I gave both girls high fives.

"Damn right things are going to get better. Please, if he thought that catsuit was something, wait until he sees me in my Wonder Woman tomorrow." Cree boasted.

The night didn't end. We decided to party hop. We watched a burlesque show, only to walk out of the room and find a wrestling match going on, which we watched. As we were heading to the first party, we got a text from Jason, telling us to meet him at the Hyatt for a room party that was going on. We headed over to find the suite filled with black people. A DJ was playing hip-hop while people were dancing in their costumes. Some were dressed up as Nick Fury and Jackie Brown, and others were dressed in typical white character costumes. That was another thing I loved about Dragon Con: you could be whoever you wanted to be. We found Jason and Carlos standing against a wall, talking to two girls dressed like Halle Berry's Catwoman. Carlos introduced us, but the two girls were obviously threatened by us and decided to walk away.

"How did you find this party?" Nia asked, just as surprised by it as I was. We had seen other black people at the convention, but never in a big group.

"That guy over there dressed like Flavor Flav gave us a flyer for it. Where the hell have y'all been?" Carlos took sip of his drink. We couldn't help but giggle.

"It's a long story." Nia smiled.

"Um, excuse me," Cree said, then turned around to talk to a guy dressed as Afro Samurai who was standing behind her. "Would you like to dance?"

"Would I? Hell yeah, let's get it," the guy said. We watched Cree disappear onto the dance floor.

"So how about it, Los? Wanna dance with me?" I held my hand out to Carlos.

"See, you lesbians don't know that I am supposed to hold *my* hand out. Come on, girl. Let me show you how to twirk it out."

Nia and Jason followed us, and we all ended up dancing together. Before we knew it, the DJ was playing the Wobble, and we were in a giant costumed Wobble dance line. I felt amazing. I never danced when I went to clubs with my friends at home. I honestly hated going to clubs, period. Even though the music was the same as what I heard at clubs at home, this was different. I was with people just like me. I was surrounded by all types of people who, like me, were professionals in their everyday lives. But for one weekend we could let our geek flag fly without judgment. It was liberating.

Tired after the second line dance, I took a seat on a couch in a corner. I watched my friends, who were now dancing to a song I wasn't familiar with. Ursula's voice entered my head, completely drowning out the music. I could hear her calling me beautiful over and over again. My mind started to get the best of me. She couldn't have been flirting with me. She was obviously just being nice. I tried to shake the feeling I had. There was no need for me to let my imagination run away with me. Ursula was a huge star and an icon, and I was just a girl dressed in a costume.

"Hey, girlie. You ready to head to the next party?" Cree said as she wiped the sweat from her brow.

I couldn't shake the feeling, but I knew I was just being a crazy fangirl. I headed with my friends to the next party, where we partied until five in the morning.

Chapter 5

I couldn't remember how I got into my bed. I sat up, but the massive headache quickly knocked me back down on my pillow. I could hear someone in the bathroom. I squinted my eyes when I saw Nia dragging her body out of the bathroom.

"What the hell did I drink?" she whined as she climbed back in bed.

"If you figure it out, tell me. I need aspirin," I mumbled.

The hotel door swung open, and Cree walked in, wearing yoga clothes and holding a yoga mat. She had a coffee holder in the other hand.

"Rise and shine, ladies. It's a big day!"

Nia and I both growled at her.

"How are you up right now? You drank just as much as I did," Nia declared and threw the covers over her face.

"Because I'm not a lightweight." Cree handed a coffee cup to Nia. "I brought coffee and aspirin."

"Oh my God, you are a lifesaver." I sat up and took my coffee and the pills from her.

The rest of the night was a blur to me. I remembered taking shots, listening to music, and seeing flashing lights, but I had absolutely no idea where we were after we left the blackout party. I couldn't believe it was already Sunday. The weekend was passing by in a flash. This was the last day of panels and parties. I suddenly felt sad. I didn't want it to end, and I didn't want to go back to the reality that was facing me when I got home.

"Well, the panel is at six, which leaves two hours for them in the Walk of Fame tonight," Nia observed. She was coming back to life, already back in planner mode. "I want to do one of the photo shoots. Maybe the cartoon character one, since I'm going as Lana Kane today."

"Oh no!" I jumped out of bed and ran to the closet. "No, no, no!"

"What?" Nia got out of bed and joined me and Cree at the closet.

"I was in such a rush to get out of Memphis, I left my Jem and Jessica Rabbit costumes at home," I said.

"Oh, don't worry. We can figure something out for you," Nia said and started rummaging through her clothes. "I can go back to my house and get something if you need it. I know I have some stuff there."

"Or . . ." We both turned around to face Cree, who was holding a bag in her hand. "You can wear this."

I walked over and took the bag from her. I looked in it, and my eyes popped. "You are kidding me. I can't pull this off."

"Sure you can. With those legs, you can totally pull it off."

I pulled the rawhide and fur out of the bag. The skimpy Tarzan and Jane costume left little to the imagination. I held the top piece up to my chest.

"I can't fit my girls in this."

"Yes, you can. It stretches," Cree said, pulling the halter top around my back.

"Ohhh, and, girl, if you rock my black wig with it and throw on some deep black eyes, you are going to be badass," Nia assured me and started brushing out her black wig.

I shrugged. "Yeah, but who am I supposed to be?"

Both girls looked at each other, then looked back at me.

"An Amazon," Cree and Nia said in unison.

We decided to spend the early part of the day chilling. There were no panels we wanted to see, so catching up on some rest was the best idea. It was the first time I actually got to talk to the girls about things besides the con.

"I'm so glad I met you guys. Seriously, I wouldn't have made it through any of this without you guys." I suddenly felt very sentimental.

"Hell, yeah," Cree said, chiming in. "Nia, if you hadn't bought that outfit from me, I wouldn't know anything about this convention."

"I'm just happy to have two new sisters." Nia smiled. "So do you think the guys are going to treat us the same way today as they did yesterday?"

"I don't see why not. I am still in disbelief." Cree fell back on the bed. "Les was totally flirting with me."

"And Kirk with me." Nia giggled. "But I think we handled ourselves well. After all, we aren't groupies. We are fangirls."

"Damn right," Cree agreed and gave a high five to Nia.

"I think we should just play it cool and not go to the Walk of Fame today. We don't want to come off as groupies. Ohh, look!" Nia pointed at the TV. The announcements on the con television station showed that Ursula was going to be signing with the guys in the regular Walk of Fame room for the day. My heart skipped a beat.

"Well, I guess we will be going to the Walk of Fame," Cree winked at me.

I started thinking about Ursula again. I knew for a fact that the guys had been flirting with Nia and Cree. It was obvious. I still couldn't shake the feeling that Ursula had flirted with me too. I decided to keep my mouth shut. I figured I was just hoping a little harder than I should. My friends were an object of affection for the guys they admired, and deep down I wanted to feel the same way.

As we stood at the elevators later that day, I pulled on my top. I couldn't believe I was actually able to fit into this outfit. My breasts were sitting up, showing off an insane amount of cleavage. The short skirt was cut at an angle to create a tattered look. Bits of fur hung from the skirt and the leg pieces. I couldn't believe I was looking at myself. Even though I felt uncomfortable, I looked hot.

We made it to the lobby, which was already filled with people. There weren't as many costumes as there had been on Saturday. People sat in lines near various ballrooms, some dozing off, trying to get a few extra minutes of sleep before their panels began. Carlos and Jason were sitting in two chairs in the lobby and were not in costumes. Both of them perked up when they saw us.

"Damn. How the fuck did you guys pull off these looks after last night? I'm barely standing," Carlos confessed. He was nursing a cup of Starbucks.

"Willpower," Nia patted Carlos on his head.

We headed over to the hotel where the final panel was being held. The line had already started forming by the time we made it there. Those in line were mostly Ursula fans. A few minutes later a much bigger group showed up, dressed in costumes from the show. We chatted with them about a panel they had missed.

"Since we are standing this far back in the line, there's no way we are getting seats any closer than the tenth or fifteenth row," Nia announced, surveying the scene. "I'm going to go look around for a minute." We watched Nia walk off with determination.

"Oh no." Jason turned his body toward the wall. We saw the white girl from the previous night, the one with the nurse outfit, heading straight toward him.

"Hey, babe." She walked right up to Jason and gave him a kiss on his lips. "Hi, everyone."

We couldn't believe she was that bold. Carlos quickly turned around and walked off.

"Um, hi." Jason looked around, hoping no one else had seen the interaction.

"So we forgot to exchange numbers." Smiling, she pulled out her phone.

"I actually don't have my phone with me." Jason shrugged his shoulders. The girl's smile dropped.

"Oh, here. You can use mine." Carlos walked back over and handed his iPhone to Jason. Jason shot Carlos an evil glare. The girl put her phone number in Carlos's phone. She hugged Jason again.

"Last night was amazing. I'm hoping for an encore tonight," she told him.

"Yeah, um, see . . ." Jason faked a smile.

"Oh, there's my people. See you later." She kissed his lips again before joining a group of other overweight Sailor Moon characters.

We stared at Jason while Carlos's deep laugh filled the air. Jason punched Carlos in his arm.

"What happened last night?" I asked.

Jason shook his head. "You don't want to know."

We continued to laugh at Jason's expense until Nia walked back over to us and motioned for us to gather in a huddle.

"Um, we have seats saved for us." Nia grinned. "Follow me."

We left the line and headed to the ballroom doors. We saw the men's handler standing at one of the doors. We greeted him with hugs, then followed him into the empty ballroom. We took seats on the left side, in the front row.

Jason looked at us. "Maybe we should be asking what *y'all* did last night."

We just grinned at each other.

We watched as the massive group of people started walking in and taking their seats. A few moments later the room was completely filled. The lights went out, and something began to play on a large movie screen. The crowd cheered as clips highlighting the careers of the men played. The crowd went crazy when Ursula's name appeared. They showed various clips from all the movies and TV shows she had been in. The crowd roared when they showed her in her famous battle stance as the Amazon queen. I felt my eyes tearing up as I watched a scene from the show, which was a major part of my childhood. At the end pictures of all four stars appeared on the screen. There was a standing ovation as the group was introduced. Kirk came out with his usual energy. He pointed over at us as he did his signature growl.

I sat up as the moderator announced Ursula's name. She walked out and looked directly at me. I noticed a subtle change in her facial expression when she saw me. She quickly reverted right back to her smile. I didn't know what that was about.

The panel was hilarious. It was obvious they were more at ease with being at the convention. It was the final panel, and everyone was relaxed and silly. Les demonstrated how Ursula would look at him whenever he was caught sleeping with a human. All the men sang her praises, saying how she was the most amazing woman to work with.

Nia got in line to ask a question. Cree and I sat with the guys and listened to the dumb questions people were asking. We rolled our eyes at the obvious lack of true fans in the room. They asked questions that had been fielded at the earlier panel and questions anyone who truly watched the show would know the answers to. One girl asked Les for a date, causing Cree to roll her eyes. Soon it was Nia's turn.

"Since you are all Dragon Con virgins, I was wondering what you thought of our con community. And will we be seeing you guys again in future years?"

Les leaned into his mic. "This has been the craziest experience of my life. I have been to San Diego Comic-Con and some other conventions, but I have never seen anything like this. You people are devoted, and it's awesome. I mean, the costumes are unlike anything I've ever seen before."

"And the parties . . . When do you people sleep?" Mason said, jumping in.

"We sleep when we get back home," Nia joked.

"I swear, I want to put on a mask and party with you guys tonight," Kirk said, making the whole crowd cheer.

"I want to say that I have truly enjoyed myself. I might have carpal tunnel from signing so many autographs, but it was worth it, and I can't wait to come back again. You people are truly one of a kind." Ursula looked directly at me for a second before looking back at the crowd.

Cree squeezed my hand, obviously catching the glance from Ursula.

The celebrities said their good-byes and stood together for group photos for a few minutes after the panel. We noticed the handler heading back in our direction.

"The fellas would like for you to come backstage," he told us. We all followed the handler as the room cleared out.

Before we went backstage, Carlos hugged each of us. "Okay, ladies, y'all be safe. Don't be letting those men get your goodies. *If* you need us, call. We will be at the heroes and villains ball for a while."

"Okay, and for the record, we are fans, not groupies. No goodies will be got," Nia said and rolled her neck at the guys.

"Yeah, right," Jason said, throwing his two cents in before they left.

"Who am I kidding? If Les tries, he will most definitely succeed." Cree affirmed as she high-fived Nia.

We walked backstage, where a few reporters were waiting for the group of celebrities to come off the stage. We stood off to the side as the group came down the stairs. The convention staff thanked and hugged Mason, who walked off with his wife and manager. I watched Ursula talking to a reporter while the guys walked over to us.

"Ladies, thanks for coming today." Les hugged each of us.

"Of course," Cree said. Les hadn't taken his arm from around her.

"So we were thinking that it's the last night and we want to truly experience this convention," Kirk said with his usual sexy, energetic voice. "Would you like to be our tour guides?" We looked at each other. It took no time for us to agree.

"How are you guys going to make it around without a mob?" I questioned as I snuck peeks at Ursula. The jeans she was wearing were giving me a fever.

"Please! We aren't that famous." Les motioned like it was no big deal.

"Well, if you want to, cool. But should we change so we don't look insane with you guys?" Nia said. She had somehow moved from by me to right next to Kirk without me noticing.

"Sure. We have a few interviews to finish up. Here is my number and Levi's number. Call him, and he can tell you where we are." Levi, the handler, nodded his head. "This will be fun, ladies." Les hugged Cree one more time before they walked off with their people.

"Oh my God, I am going to be so damn sexy tonight, that man is going to want to take me back to Vancouver with him." Cree was already planning her outfit in her head.

"Well, hello, ladies." We all turned when the familiar voice spoke to us. We saw Ursula walking toward us. "I haven't had the pleasure of meeting the other two lovely goddesses from yesterday." Ursula was mesmerizing. I couldn't take my eyes off of her. Nia nudged me, bringing me out of my spell.

"Oh, these are my friends Nia and Cree."

"Ah, yes, I heard the men are planning on partying it up with you guys. Watch them. They are live ones."

Ursula winked at the girls. She then turned her focus to me. "Temple, can I speak to you for a moment?"

I walked a few feet away with her without hesitation.

"I truly felt bad about backing out last night. I was wondering if you would like to try dinner again tonight to make up for yesterday."

"Uh . . . um . . . yeah, sure. Of course."

"Great. I need to go to my room and freshen up. I'm staying at the Ritz. I can give you my number, and you can call me. Do you have your phone?"

My face dropped. I realized I hadn't seen my phone since I threw it after the call from Ciara. I heard Nia clear her throat. I turned around to see her holding up my phone. I walked over to her, mouthing, "Thank you."

"Yeah, we figured you might want this back at some point." Nia smiled.

I walked back over to Ursula and watched as she punched her number into my phone. I couldn't believe this was happening. I knew at any moment I was going to wake up and find myself sleeping in my bed, next to Ciara, back in Memphis. Ursula handed me my phone.

"Great. I will call you soon," I said. The words sounded funny coming out of my mouth. I was going to be calling Ursula Moore.

"Great. See you soon." She kissed me on my cheek, sending shock waves through my body. She turned to walk away but quickly turned back around. "Oh, and that outfit . . . very nice." She winked as she walked off with her bodyguards.

I couldn't move from the spot I was standing in. Nia and Cree ran over to me the second we were the only ones left in the room.

"Is this happening? This is really happening." Nia was now jumping up and down.

"This type of shit doesn't happen, right? This is some weird fluke," I said, shaking my head.

"I don't care if it's a fluke or what. Hell, I don't care if those men think that we are easy pieces of ass while they are at a convention. It's up to us to prove them wrong. I say we charm them so well that they want to make us friends instead of possible fuck buddies." Nia stood with her chest poked out.

We headed out of the large ballroom. The lobby was packed as people started to prepare for the night's shenanigans.

"So even if they want to, we aren't going to sleep with them?" Cree questioned, instead of confirming what Nia had said. "Really?"

"Yes, really." Nia held our arms. "We are fangirls. They are going to respect us as such."

Cree frowned. "But it's Les. Did you see how he had his arm around me? It's Les."

"Would you rather give it up now and he never calls, or would you rather spend such an amazing night that you one day get a call to come hang out in Vancouver while he's taping?" Nia asked. "Let's try for long-term friend-ships instead of one-night stands."

"Well, I don't have to worry about that, like you guys have to. I'm just having dinner." I looked over to see the expressions on both their faces. "What?"

"Please, girl, if Ursula wasn't flirting with you, then Les wasn't flirting with me," Cree said as we fought our way through the crowd to the elevators.

"No, she wasn't," I insisted.

"I have to agree with Cree," Nia said. "I think there is something more there than just a dinner invitation."

"You guys are crazy." I got in one of the elevators after it finally cleared out.

"Okay, think what you want, but I know flirting, and there was some extra energy there," Cree observed.

The elevator doors closed, leaving me in my thoughts.

Chapter 6

There were so many scents in our hotel room at one time, it smelled like a Bath and Body Works store. We were dressed to impress. Nia rocked a pair of denim short shorts with a shirt that hung off her shoulders, while Cree had opted for a pair of supertight brown jeans and a matching halter top that showed off her amazing abs. I had tried on outfit after outfit before finally settling on a pencil skirt with a black romper with a lace back. I had put on a pair of black stilettos and had let my hair curl up naturally in a 'fro.

We headed out of our hotel room and back to the elevators. It took forever for an elevator to arrive, which was normal during the convention. We finally made it to the lobby level. The girls were meeting the men at Sear, the restaurant in the hotel.

"Okay, ladies. Behave yourselves," I said as I looked at myself in the mirror on a wall in the lobby.

"You too," Nia said and hugged me. I hugged Cree before heading out of the hotel.

I caught a cab over to the Ritz-Carlton, which wasn't far at all. The lobby wasn't nearly as insane as those in the host hotels for the convention. There was only one group of obvious convention attendees sitting in the lobby. I took my membership badge off and stuck it in my clutch.

I pressed DIAL on my phone. Each ring made my heart skip a beat. Finally, I heard Ursula's voice on the other end. She told me to come up to her room.

The elevator ride was excruciating. My whole body was hot. I just knew I had to be a sweaty mess. I got out of the elevator on her floor and stopped to look in the large wall mirror. To my surprise, I wasn't sweating at all.

Get it together, Temple. I took a deep breath. My phone began to ring. I looked down to see Ciara's face appear. I suddenly felt guilty. I had missed several text messages and phone calls from her since I had left my phone on that chair. I had made the mistake of reading the text messages. Each one had sounded more and more desperate. I then remembered where I was and what she did. I put my phone on silent and headed down the long hallway.

I stood outside Ursula's door. I couldn't bring myself to actually knock. I did the breath test with my hand just to make sure everything was right. Before I could knock, I heard the doorknob turning. There stood Ursula in a red dress in front of me.

"I thought I heard someone outside. Come on in."

I wanted to die. I wondered if she had seen my breath test. The room looked more like an apartment than a hotel room. In the living area there was a table laden with food under silver domes.

"Temple, relax. Trust me, I don't bite . . . usually." Ursula winked as she walked farther into the room. I just knew I didn't hear her correctly. She motioned for me to have a seat at the table.

She obviously hadn't spared any expense, or perhaps the meal was all on Dragon Con. We dined on surf and turf, lobster and steak. After my first glass of wine I began to see her not as the goddess Ursula, but as just another friend. We laughed about the convention. She talked about some of the crazy people she had met while signing in the VIP room.

"I think that's why I found you and your friends refreshing. You weren't dressed as the Amazon queen. Actually, I don't think I saw any other people, except men dressed from *Olympus*. That dress you had on was amazing, and quite accurate."

"I had it made." I blushed. "I actually thought about bidding on the original one, but it's, like, six thousand dollars now on eBay."

"Crazy, I know. I love my job, but I honestly don't know if I could be as dedicated as some people are. I mean, I was just playing a character."

"No." I looked at Ursula. "You were more than a character. You were a revolution."

"How so?" Her eyes locked on me.

"When I was younger, I had no one to turn to. I knew there was something different about me, but I couldn't consider that I could be gay. I'd heard in church how being gay was wrong. I just knew that I was going to hell for the rest of my life." I took another sip of wine.

"But watching the Amazon queen, it made me feel . . . I can't really explain it, but your character made me feel strong."

Ursula wasn't taking her eyes off of me. It was like she was looking inside of me. Her lips were pressed hard against each other. Her eyes were slightly slanted and were making me feel like I couldn't hide anything from her. I just wanted her to stop looking at me before I started crying again.

The room was awkwardly silent. I could hear my thoughts racing through my head. She continued to stare at me, and all my self-esteem slowly started to disappear. I wanted to run out of the room. I knew I had freaked her out. She was probably regretting the fact that she'd allowed me to come to her room.

"I'm sorry," I muttered, hoping to salvage the rest of the evening. "I didn't mean to say so much."

Ursula finally moved. "Oh, you have nothing to apologize for. I should be apologizing to you."

"For what?"

Ursula's eyes locked on me again.

"Because while you were speaking, I honestly couldn't stop thinking of how badly I wanted to kiss you."

Chapter 7

Nia and Cree couldn't stop laughing at Les and Kirk. The guys were so down to earth, the only things that reminded them that they were with celebrities were the Black Cards that hit the table after the meal and drinks.

"So where are we heading to first?" Les looked at Cree.

"Well, that all depends on how far into Dragon Con you want to go." Nia smiled at Kirk. "We can keep it simple by going to a party in a ballroom, or for real craziness, we can hit the bars first, then some room parties."

"I vote for crazy. I want to get real crazy," Les said. He stared at Cree, who wouldn't take her eyes off of him.

The group headed out of the restaurant. To their surprise, the men weren't noticed as much as they had expected. They walked up the stairs to the bar at Pulse, the hotel's bar and lounge. The men were quickly noticed by a few drunk guys, who gave them high fives while offering up their seats at the bar to the group. After they were seated, Les ordered rounds of shots, which they downed quickly.

"This is awesome. I just want to yell something out." Kirk put his arm around Nia.

"Do it. Trust me, it's okay." Nia nodded her head.

"Okay." Kirk stood up on the footrest below his seat. "Dragon Con is awesome!"

Like normal, the crowd cheered and glasses rose in unison. Les stood up, and he and Kirk pounded fists as camera flashes went off. Les sat back down and put his hand on Cree's thigh.

"I'm going to regret this in the morning, when the pictures hit the blogs. What are you two trying to do to us?" he said.

"Nothing you don't want me to." Cree put her hand over her mouth, realizing what she had said. Les gave a devilish chuckle. Cree looked at Nia, who, judging by the expression on her face, obviously didn't approve of the comment.

Les laughed. "You are amazing, Ms. Cree. Simply amazing." He called the bartender over to order more drinks.

I was still in shock. I must have dreamed that Ursula Moore said she wanted to kiss me. I wanted to slap myself just to wake up, because the dream was getting out of hand now. I closed my eyes and then opened them, hoping I would wake up. There sat Ursula, staring at me.

"I am guessing you weren't expecting to hear that," she said.

"Um . . ." I had to take a big gulp of wine. "No, definitely not. I mean, you are Ursula Moore."

"I'm also a woman who is very attracted to another woman." Ursula stood up from the table. She walked over to a smaller table that had a bowl of fruit and two other bottles of wine chilling in silver buckets. She picked up one of the bottles and popped it open. "What can I say, Temple? I was attracted to you the moment I saw you at the panel."

"Why?" I knew it wasn't proper etiquette, but I put my elbows on the table and placed my hands on my head. "I just don't understand."

"How can you not understand that you are an incredibly sexy woman?" Ursula walked back over to the table. Instead of sitting in her chair, she sat in the chair next to mine. She picked up my wineglass and refilled it.

"But I'm a nobody. You can have any woman you want."

Ursula nodded her head. "If that is true, you won't mind me doing this."

Before I could move, Ursula's hand was on the back of my head, pulling me in close to her. Her lips pressed against mine. Her perfume entered my nostrils; I was instantly high off of her. My lesbian instincts were starting to kick in as I parted my lips, allowing Ursula's tongue to enter my domain.

It was happening, after all. There was no way I was dreaming this. I put my hand on her thigh and rubbed it slowly. She was real, in the flesh. The woman whom I'd idolized was giving me the most passionate kiss I had ever had. I didn't know if it was the person I was kissing or the kiss itself that was causing my body to go into overdrive. The confidence I'd been lacking resurfaced as the lesbian aggressive side in me started banging, trying to come out and take over the situation. My aggressive side was fighting a full fight with the fangirl in me, who knew this was crossing a line I couldn't come back from.

"I knew that was going to be amazing," Ursula said in the brief moment she pulled away. She pecked my lips again. "I want more."

The fangirl in me put my hands on her shoulders, blocking her from reaching me.

"Are you sure about this?" I asked.

I wanted to slap myself for even giving her the option to say no. The heat was a full fire, and I knew only one thing would extinguish it. However, I had questions. For one, Ursula had said on tons of occasions that she was not gay, and I could have sworn she had said at one of the panels that she was married. The aggressive side of me didn't give two fucks if she was married or not. I wanted to take her right there on the table.

"The question is, are *you* sure about this?" Ursula stood up and walked over to a table. She picked up a piece of paper. "I would like nothing more than to take you right now. But as you have stated, I am Ursula Moore. I do have certain things to protect."

She sat the piece of paper down in front of me. I picked it up and began to read it. She had handed me a confidentiality agreement. If I went along with it, I wasn't allowed to tell anyone, and if it got out, she could sue me for damages. Suddenly things didn't look so pretty. Not that I would ever tell, but being so legal was a total party pooper. Not to mention I couldn't help but wonder how often she did this. Did she find a fan at every con to make her personal sex slave for the night?

"You want me to sign this?" I continued to read the fine print.

"Temple, I have no doubt in my mind that you would never tell what happens between us. But my manager would kill me if I didn't get it in writing."

"I understand," I muttered, but I really didn't understand. I suddenly felt cheap. The moment I was just cherishing was diminished by a piece of paper.

I could tell that Ursula felt my hesitation. She began to rub my shoulders. Her hands felt magical as they massaged all the tenseness out of me. Who was I kidding? Of course she needed to protect her brand. Just like me, others looked up to her. Asking me to sign something wasn't that big of a deal. I would never tell, anyway. I signed my name on the line.

Before I could cross the *T* in my name, I felt Ursula's tongue brush the nape of my neck, sending chills down my spine. I stood up and turned toward her. I knew it was time. I locked the fangirl deep down inside of me and let the hunter in me come out. If I had to sign that paper, that was going to be the last thing that she had control over. I grabbed her arms and pushed her against the wall. Ursula let out a moan as my lips sucked on her neck and chest.

She ground her body against mine as I kissed her neck, tasting her skin. My hands walked down her sides until they made it to the edges of her tight red dress. I slowly pulled it up as soft moans escaped Ursula's mouth. My hand felt the warmth coming from her thighs. I dove in, realizing there were no panties to remove. I looked at Ursula. Her devilish grin was present.

"You knew the whole time?"

"I knew what I wanted. Not until now did I know I was going to get it." She kissed my lips as my fingers caressed her throbbing clit.

I wanted to taste her so bad. I wanted to know what it was like to taste the Amazon queen, but I didn't go in. Something in me wanted her to beg for it. I didn't know what was coming over me, but I didn't want it to leave.

Chapter 8

Nia and Cree and the guys headed over to the last rave of Dragon Con. All of them were very intoxicated, but they didn't care. The men were having a ball snapping camera-phone photos of people in costumes. Only a few people asked for photos with the guys, which they happily took just to be in photos with various cosplayers. They weren't treated like celebrities by most of the people. Only a few girls squealed when they saw the guys partying with them.

Cree ground her body against Les to the techno playing in the ballroom. Les put his arms around her, pulling her as close as he possibly could. She could feel the erection growing in his pants, but she didn't care. She rolled her hips, grinding and showing him where twirking really came from.

Kirk sat next to Nia at the back of the dark ballroom. They saw people making out in the chairs behind them. One couple was quite possibly having sex in darkness.

"This is insane." Kirk put his hand on Nia's thigh. "A great way to end a long weekend."

"Thank you. Never in a million years did I expect my Dragon Con to be like this."

"Oh, please. I'm sure men are always falling at your feet." Kirk smiled.

"Nah, they might think I'm cute, but the second they find out I'm a total geek, the attraction wears off." They both laughed.

"Well, they are idiots."

Their eyes met. Kirk leaned in, his lips meeting Nia's. Nia couldn't believe just how soft his lips were. Before she was ready, he pulled away.

"I'm so sorry, Nia. I shouldn't have done that." Kirk's usual smile was replaced by a look of worry.

"It's all right." Nia wanted him to come back to her.

"No, I might play that guy, but I'm not that guy. I don't want you thinking I'm trying to make you some type of one-night thing."

Nia suddenly wanted to disappear. She had had Kirk all wrong. He was sexy, but sweet at the same time. She now respected him even more.

"Hey, it's okay. I knew better myself. Liquor and costumes give people the confidence to go for things they normally wouldn't attempt."

Kirk laughed. "Well, trust me, you would have had no attempt under normal circumstances. However, I know you are worth more than that. I told you, you are one of a kind." Kirk kissed Nia on her forehead. They laughed it off and continued to talk and watch the dance floor.

Cree turned around and wrapped her arms around Les. She knew it was wrong, but she didn't care. She was horny, and she had the chance to sleep with the man she had dreamed about every night since *Olympus* aired. She had to go for it.

"So what would you like to do after this?" She smiled slyly.

"It's four in the morning. I think there's only one thing left to do."

"What? An after-hours breakfast joint?" She grinned.

"I can order you pancakes in my room."

Cree took her chance, kissing Les on his lips. He held her body tight in the middle of the crowded dance floor. The erection was full.

"Oh, I'd prefer an omelet."

"Anything you want." Les kissed her again before grabbing her hand and walking off the dance floor.

Cree took her phone out and sent a text to Nia.

Sorry. Had to do it. I'm fucking Zeus tonight.

Nia read the text message and shook her head. "I think our people left us," she said.

"Figures." Kirk stood up. He held his hand out, taking Nia's hand in his. "Let me make sure you get back to your room okay."

I was going to seize the opportunity. Ursula led me to the bedroom. The king-size bed was going to allow us plenty of space for rolling around. I watched her silhouette as she pulled her dress over her head, exposing her naked body. Her golden-brown skin was radiant. There wasn't a hair to be found on her body. She was as smooth as silk, the smoothest I'd ever seen.

Ursula walked over to me and began to unbutton my romper. I grabbed her hands. I was going to be in control of this situation. She didn't seem to agree. Before I knew it, she had ripped my romper, causing the buttons to scatter to the floor. I couldn't believe it. She pulled me closer.

"Remember, I am the Amazon queen." She pulled my sleeves down, squeezing my breasts through my bra. Ursula's tongue danced down my stomach as she pulled the torn romper down to the floor. I slowly stepped out of it and flung my heels to the side of the room. I was still not going to be outdone.

I pushed Ursula on the bed. I grabbed her ankles and pulled her body to the edge of the bed until her vagina was pressed against my leg. I could feel the wetness on my thigh. I ran my hand down the smooth surface of her womanhood. She tried to sit up, but I pushed her back down.

"In here I'm the Amazon queen," I told her.

"I don't think so." Before I knew it, Ursula's legs were wrapped around me. She flipped my body over, and my back hit the mattress. Before I could catch my breath, she was on top of me, pulling my bra up, exposing my Cs. Her mouth nibbled on my nipples, causing them to stand at attention.

I wasn't going to be outdone. I pushed her over and got on top of her. I pushed two fingers deep inside of her walls, causing her to let out a moan, which gave me goose bumps. It was the sexiest sound I had ever heard in my life. I fingered her, covering my hand with her elixir. I pulled out. I had to taste. I sucked her wetness off my fingers. I knew it was going to be good, but I didn't expect it to be hypnotizing. I needed more.

I climbed down and got on my knees. I pulled her ass to the edge of the bed and buried my head between her wet thighs. My tongue fucked her as I stuck my index finger in her asshole.

"Temple!"

My name had never sounded better. I licked, sucked, nibbled, and sucked some more. Her body belonged to me. My tongue fucked her while my finger fucked her ass. I wanted her to feel me for days. Her legs began to tremble from the sensation. That only let me know I needed more. I placed another finger inside her tight asshole as I continued to devour her. She was my surf, turf, and dessert.

"Temple!" Her quivering legs were now having full convulsions. I knew it was coming, and I prepared myself to receive all the nectar her body would give to me.

Suddenly she pushed me off her with her foot. I fell back on my ass. I looked up to see Ursula staring at me. She jumped off the bed and pushed my legs in the air. I felt my lace panties tear as she yanked them with her teeth. Her tongue entered my cave with an animalistic force. She growled as I became her meal. I couldn't stop it. My mouth dropped open. Words couldn't escape, only the short breaths that I managed to take. She wasn't killing me softly. She was murdering me with her mouth. She stopped only long enough to turn around. Her ass was in front of my face as she buried her face back inside of me. I looked at her flower, which was staring at me. A bit of her wetness fell on my lips. I needed it. We submerged ourselves in each other, becoming one.

Chapter 9

"Do the elevators always take this long?" Kirk leaned against the wall.

"It's all a part of the experience." Nia smiled. They had been waiting on the elevators for what seemed like an eternity. For once Nia didn't care. The quicker the elevators came, the sooner her dream night would come to an end.

"I can't believe it's this late and I'm not in the bed." Kirk rubbed his eyes.

"Oh, come on. You have to be used to this." Nia walked over and stood next to Kirk. He shook his head.

"Not at all. On the show most of our call times are super early in the morning, so I'm usually in the bed by ten or eleven. That makes me sound like such a lame." Kirk's smile gave Nia instant butterflies in her stomach. He laid his head on her shoulder, allowing his blond hair to fall on her. She could smell his shampoo, coconut. She liked it.

Just then someone yelled, "Zeus!"

The two looked up to see two guys covered in fake blood walking toward them. Due to *The Walking Dead*, zombies were a popular costume at the event.

"Fucking Zeus standing right here." The same loud zombie hit Kirk on his arm with force.

Kirk smiled. "Yeah, experiencing the con with you guys."

Nia wanted to correct them, as Kirk wasn't Zeus, but she noticed he didn't seem to mind it at all.

"Yeah, and this hottie . . . But that's right. Zeus likes to fuck random chicks from land and not just on the mountain."

"Excuse me?" Nia stood up straight. Kirk grabbed her hand and squeezed it lightly and stood in front of her. She knew it meant he would handle it.

"It's nothing like that. Just having a good time, like you guys," Kirk said.

The other zombie added his two cents in while rubbing his hands together. "I bet."

The first zombie's eyes widened. "Yo, we are headed to this party on the eighth floor. They would fucking flip out if they saw you there, man."

Nia watched as Kirk handled himself like a true man. It wasn't doing anything to prevent her from wanting him more. He smiled, flashing his pearly whites, which she'd grown to love on the TV show.

"Sounds fun, but I have a big day tomorrow, and I'm just gonna make sure my friend here gets to her room all right, and I'm headed back to my hotel. But, hey, thanks for the invite—"

"Oh, we can make sure she gets to her room all right, if you want us to," said the first zombie as he gave Nia a menacing glare, which instantly made her uncomfortable. "Come on. Just stop by the party."

"Thanks, but no thanks." Kirk turned around to face Nia.

"Fuck you, then, asshole!" the first zombie yelled, and then both zombies started cursing Kirk out.

"He's too good for us," said the second zombie.

"Fucking asshole, you suck as an actor, anyway," the first zombie muttered.

Kirk sighed.

"Hey, um, how about you just go? I'll get to my room okay," Nia said. She could see the frustration growing on

Kirk's face. After all, she knew his expressions very well from the show.

"No, I'm okay." Kirk rubbed her hand. "Just ignore it."

"Don't fucking ignore us, bro," the first zombie said.

Nia looked around. Luckily, few people were paying attention to them.

The second zombie added, "I guess he's too busy trying to get some pussy from that whore—"

Kirk's fist met his face, instantaneously knocking the drunken zombie out with one punch. The fall caused the people milling about to finally turn around to see what was going on. Nia grabbed Kirk and pulled him away from the scene before camera phones started to come out.

Moments later they made it to the hotel room and fire escape staircase. It was the only completely empty place in the whole hotel. Kirk shook his head and laughed.

"I'm sorry you had to witness that." He held both of Nia's hands. Nia tried to keep her calm as his gray eyes stared at her.

"No, it's totally okay." Nia could feel the heat growing between her legs. She needed him to stop staring at her before she found herself breaking the rules right along with Cree.

"Damn elevators. What floor are you on again?" Kirk looked up the winding staircase, which seemed to never end.

"Ten." Nia and Kirk both laughed.

"Of course you are." Kirk looked at Nia again. "How about an alternative? I feel that since I fought for you, it's only right that you come back to my room and make sure my hand doesn't swell."

Nia wanted to yell yes so that it echoed throughout the staircase. She smiled. "That sounds great and all but . . ."

"PG rated. I promise." Kirk's eyes were fixed on Nia again.

"Um . . ."

"Look." Kirk took Nia's hand again. "I could make up some excuse, but the truth is that this has been a great night, and honestly, I'm not ready to let you go just yet."

Nia's eyes met Kirk's. She knew she had to be dreaming. How did the little mocha girl have the Adonis from her favorite TV show telling her how he didn't want to leave her? She knew she needed to say no, walk up the insane number of steps, and get in her own bed. But she couldn't take her eyes off of him.

"Well, now, how is a girl supposed to say no to those eyes?"

Kirk squeezed Nia's hand, and they headed out the side door.

Chapter 10

Cree and Les couldn't keep their hands off of each other. The cab ride was like playing a game of seven minutes in heaven.

Les handed the cabdriver money, and then they headed into the hotel. The elevator ride was part two, as Les caressed Cree's back, his hand resting firmly there, and then grabbed a handful of Cree's ass.

He couldn't get the door open quickly enough. Cree didn't notice the lavish suite. She didn't care about the decor or the ambiance. The light from the lamp was all she needed. As soon as they walked in the suite, she had her fingers on the buttons on his shirt, unbuttoning them as quickly as she could.

They kissed nonstop while walking around the suite, leaving a trail of clothes as they went. Les opened the double doors to the bedroom. The king-size bed was made up perfectly. As Cree looked at the bed, everything hit her. This wasn't a game, and it wasn't a dream. She was about to sleep with a man she'd admired on her TV every Sunday for the past five years. Her face dropped.

"Is everything okay?" Les asked.

Cree turned her head to see Les standing a few steps away in his silk boxers. Cree shook her head. It wasn't like the show. His body was ten times better in person. His sun-kissed skin only made his muscles stand out in the dim light. His black hair was still spiked perfectly, just as it was when he picked her up, even though she had run her hands through it in the cab.

"I don't know if I can do this." Cree couldn't believe the words actually came out of her mouth.

"What's—"

Cree cut Les off before he could say anything. "I'm not this girl. I'm not the girl who sleeps with celebrities. Les, I have been a fan of yours since I first saw you. You are fucking brilliant, and if I do this, I will have to live with knowing that the man I am such a fan of will always look at me as just that black chick at Dragon Con that he banged."

Les exhaled, causing his chest to fall some. He smiled as he walked close to her. Les put his hands on her arms.

"That's all I needed to hear." Les's lips pressed against Cree's pouty lips. He pulled her face closer to his with his giant hand. Cree ran her hands up and down his strong back. She didn't want to let go, but she knew she needed to. He finally pulled away, leaving her wanting more.

"Cree, I know you aren't that type of girl. Kirk and I both know you and your friends aren't that type of girl. If you were, I wouldn't have hung out tonight. I would have just brought you back to the room, banged you, and sent you on your way. You are here because I really want you here, and because I am very attracted to you. Even if you weren't one of my fans, I would have come after you. I knew the moment I saw you, I had to have you. Don't deny me."

His deep, raspy voice sent chills through Cree's body. She couldn't say no. She dropped her head as he dropped to his knees. Cree threw her head back as Les pulled her panties down and put her leg on his shoulder. He buried his head in her inferno, which was burning for him. Cree's mouth dropped. Words couldn't escape, only moans.

Cree grabbed his jet-black hair as Les attempted to lick her dry. She knew it would never happen, as his tongue was causing her to get only wetter with every stroke. Les held her hands tight as he stood up. Before she knew it, she was in the air and holding on to him as her legs trembled on his shoulders. He put her back against the wall as he continued his assault on her clit. The muscles were not a mirage: the man was beyond strong. Cree's toes stretched, then curled up. She knew it had to be because he wasn't from America, as no man had ever claimed her with his tongue the way Les was. Cree's legs jerked. She hit her hand against the wall.

Les let out a moan as he grabbed her arms. Cree's back left the wall, and he walked over to the bed with ease with her still on his shoulders. Slowly, Les laid Cree down on the perfectly made bed. Cree watched as he walked over to his luggage, then returned to the bed and slowly pulled off his black silk boxers. Cree couldn't believe the size of his package, which was rock hard, with a curve. She knew she was looking at seven or eight inches with a serious thickness. The curve only excited her more.

Les put a condom on and came closer to the bed. He stared at Cree's naked brown skin. He ran his index finger up her leg.

"Are you sure you want to do this?" he asked.

Cree nodded her head, still unable to form actual words. Les slowly climbed on top, pulling her legs apart. They didn't lose eye contact as he entered her. Cree's mouth dropped open when his tip gave her pleasurable pain. She gasped for air when the curve in his dick found her softest place and hit it over and over again. Cree's fingernails dug into his back. They both moaned as their bodies worked in perfect unison together. He wasn't fucking her; this was something completely different. It was passion at its highest. Cree grabbed his ass, feeling his muscles as they contracted with every thrust.

Cree's lip quivered as Les's hands pinned her down on the bed. She couldn't move. Her body trembled as he nibbled on her nipples, causing them to stiffen. Her body belonged to him, and he knew it and treated it accordingly. Les let out a growl that made Cree's body tremble, and then their eyes locked. There was silence in that moment. They stared at each other as though they were both trying to look into the other's soul. Les didn't take his eyes off of her as he thrust his manhood as deeply as possible. Cree's mouth dropped open as the intensity of the thrusts caused her body to tense.

She felt it coming, pleasure was about to engulf her, but she wasn't ready. All her training and exercise couldn't stop the orgasm from escaping her body. She wanted to hold it in, but that was impossible. Her legs jerked as she held on to him for dear life. She closed her eyes. She wanted to create a mental picture of that moment. She wanted to live in that moment for the rest of her life.

Cree opened her eyes to see Les staring directly at her. Their eyes met again when Les ran his finger across Cree's lips. She licked his finger, closing her mouth around the thick finger. She closed her eyes as she sucked his finger, causing him to moan again. With his left hand he grabbed the side of her thigh. His strokes intensified, becoming faster with each thrust. Cree had already experienced nirvana, but she could feel death creeping back up on her.

"Cree."

Cree loved hearing him call her name. The intensity in his deep voice drove her insane. She could hear him call her name for the rest of her life.

"Cree. Shit." Les pounded his fist on the headboard. He let out the loudest groan, and made the whole bed rumble. Cree watched him climax on top of her. His hard body became limp as he rested against her breasts. Cree ran her hand across his face, wiping the sweat from his brow. He rolled off of her.

It was the moment Cree wasn't ready for. She didn't know her next move. Was she supposed to get up, grab her clothes, and take the walk of shame back to her hotel room? Before she could sit up, she felt Les's large arm grab her. He pulled her body close to his. Their bodies were aligned perfectly. He kissed her on her back.

"That was amazing. *You* are amazing," he whispered in her ear.

Cree smiled, she knew there was nothing she could say to top that. She put her arm on top of his, holding his hand as they both fell asleep, completely exhausted from the best day ever.

Nia couldn't remember the last time she had laughed so hard. The two of them settled into his suite. He gave her one of his shirts to sleep in, and a pair of boxer shorts that probably cost more than Nia's whole outfit. Realizing he had the munchies, Kirk was about to order room service when Nia told him to let her order from a local wing spot that stayed open twenty-four hours on weekends. Twenty minutes later their order of wings and french fries was delivered.

"These are fucking amazing," Kirk said as he ate a hot wing. "I don't think I've had wings that taste so good before." Nia found his excitement, and his Australian accent, cute.

"I'm sure you haven't. They don't make them like this anywhere else in the world. I'm sure of it."

"Those are big words, Madame Nia. Nowhere else in the world?"

Nia sat up and poked her chest out. "I say nowhere else in the world."

"I might have to challenge you about that one day."

They both glanced at the TV a moment later and noticed that the program guide on one of the Starz channels noted that *Olympus* was going to be coming on next. They looked at each other and started laughing. She loved how they just seemed to laugh about nothing at all. Nia reached for the remote, but Kirk stopped her.

"No, let's watch it. Maybe I can see what you guys see in it that makes you want to dress up and stuff."

The show began to play as they settled back in bed, sitting up against the headboard like an old married couple watching their last show before going to bed at night.

"This is one of my favorite episodes, actually," Nia said and ate another french fry.

"Oh, really?"

"Yep. It's where you sleep with Hercules's mom."

Kirk looked at Nia. "What makes it one of your favorites?"

"It's this scene, actually. Your eyes. Man, when I saw this the first time, it gave me chills. You really delivered that monologue well. I felt like I was supposed to go to war or something." Nia laughed, but she realized Kirk didn't. She looked over and saw he was staring at the screen.

"I found out my ex-fiancée was going to die about an hour before I did that scene," he said. He fell silent. The only sound in the room was the one coming from the television. Kirk continued to stare at the screen. From the news and blogs, Nia knew that he had a fiancée who died two years earlier from a drug overdose.

"I was on the set, completely in that bloody makeup, when I got the phone call. I knew what the call was about by the look on my assistant's face. He had never looked so serious before. I really couldn't comprehend what her mother was saying to me, partly because she was crying. I just remember hanging the phone up and walking back to the set."

"I'm so sorry, Kirk." Nia put her hand on top of his.

"Oh, it's all right now. I knew she had problems, but she was my first love, my high school sweetheart and all of that." Kirk smiled, but the usual radiance was gone. "I tried to get her help, but she just didn't want it. It killed me, but I had to let her go. Her mother blames me, of course. She says my leaving her was the thing that drove her over the edge, but I didn't know what else I could do."

"We never know what to do in those situations."

"We?" Kirk looked at Nia. Their eyes met.

"My father." Nia shrugged her shoulders. "He felt that drugs were more important than his only child. So after attempting more than once to get him help, I realized there was nothing else I could do for him."

"Where is he now?" Kirk asked.

"In jail, for at least the next few years. He tried to rob a store when he was high. But, you know, I'm happy he's there instead of out here. At least in jail he has a roof over his head and meals."

The silence entered the room again. Kirk squeezed Nia's hand. She looked at his face. He no longer looked like the actor who was currently on TV, but like just a friend.

"You are something special. You do know that, Nia?"

Nia threw her hair back and smiled. "Well, you know I do try."

They both laughed, and they continued to laugh for the rest of the night, until they finally fell asleep.

Chapter 11

I smiled as I stretched my arms. I had had the best sleep of my life in Ursula's bed.

Ursula's bed.

I quickly remembered that I was in Ursula's bed. The night's escapades started coming back to me, playing like a movie in my head. I had never experienced anything so amazing in my life. I didn't know if it was the age difference that made her such a beast in the sheets or if it was that Ursula was just that bad. I wanted more and hoped for round three this morning.

But I turned over to an empty bed.

I sat up, looked around the room. Her suitcase was gone. I jumped out of the plush bed and ran into the bathroom. Her cosmetics were all gone. I went into the living area, only to see that all traces of Ursula were gone. The room began to spin. She was gone. If it wasn't for the fact that I was standing in a suite I would never be able to afford, I would have thought maybe it was all a dream, after all.

I walked back into the bedroom and began to pick up my clothes. I tried to hold on to the little dignity that I had left, refusing to let the tears forming in my eyes fall. I sat back on my side of the bed. *My side.* Who was I kidding? I didn't have a *side.* I was just the girl who got to sleep with her one night. She probably felt she was doing me a favor, making one lucky fan's dream come true.

I couldn't hold my emotions back. Tears rolled down my cheeks. I regretted the whole thing. Not only did my own woman treat me like I was disposable on a regular basis, but now a person I'd admired since childhood had also made me feel the same way so many in my past made me feel. I continued to cry as I sat there in Ursula's suite, the suite that had erased every trace of her.

I wiped my eyes, wanting to lie back down and erase the whole weekend from my mind. A white card sitting on the nightstand caught my eye. I picked up the hotel stationery and opened it up.

> *Temple,*
> *Had to catch an early flight. Last night was amazing. You are an awesome girl, a girl I will never forget.*
> *–U*

I suddenly felt incredibly dumb. I held on to the card, rereading the words over and over. It wasn't me. She had to catch a flight. She didn't want to wake me out of my sleep, so she just left. This made me feel a little better, yet I still wished things had ended on a different note.

I fell back on the plush pillows on the bed. I put my hands on my stomach and closed my eyes. The night played in my head. I could still feel her touching my skin. I could taste her sweetness in my mouth. I remembered exploring her body, feeling each curve, running my hands through her long black hair. I felt her lips pressed against mine. I felt her breathe her energy into my mouth, rejuvenating my spirit and soul. I could live in those moments forever.

A knock on the door by housekeeping brought me back to reality. This wasn't my room, and I should have been out of here by now. I reluctantly got up out of bed and put my shoes on. I took a final look around the hotel suite. I noticed a single rose still standing in a vase. It had come with the room service she had ordered for us. I smiled as

I picked up the rose and smelled it. I would save the rose with the note as a reminder that I didn't dream this whole experience. My wildest dreams were reality, even if it was only for one night.

Cree felt Les's strong hands pressing against her thighs. She opened her eyes to see him standing over her, completely dressed, wearing a white shirt that hung off his muscles perfectly. His cologne ignited the rest of her senses, as if he were a morning cup of coffee.

"Hey, you," he whispered in his deep voice.

Cree smiled. It was morning, and she knew she had to have morning breath. She got out of the bed and turned away from him as she picked up her clothes.

"Good morning. I see you had an early start. You could have woken me." She walked around the suite, looking for the pieces of clothing she was missing.

"I could have, but you just looked so beautiful sleeping, I didn't want to disturb you. I have a meeting, and then I'm heading back to Canada. I didn't want to just leave while you were sleeping." The statement caused Cree to stop in her tracks. She looked at his chiseled face. He was gorgeous and sweet.

"Well, thank you, but it wouldn't have been a problem. I would have understood. Do I have time to take a shower?"

Les nodded his head. His phone started to ring after Cree disappeared into the bathroom. Suddenly something didn't feel right to Cree. She didn't close the bathroom door all the way and stood there, pressing her ear against the door.

"Hello, sweetie. Oh, it was great. Yeah, I'm headed back today. Yeah. I love you too."

Cree felt her heart fall out of her chest. She pressed her hand against her mouth, not wanting a sound to come out. She scanned her memory, trying to remember if she had ever read anything about him having a girlfriend or a wife. She knew she hadn't. She was positive about it.

Cree turned the shower on and got it. The hot water hit her face. She took a deep breath. Maybe it was a family member. She wasn't going to jump to conclusions too quickly. She took a quick shower and got dressed.

Les was checking over his bags when she walked into the bedroom. He smiled as he walked over to greet her. Les planted a deep kiss on her lips. She wanted to kiss him back but couldn't. He looked at her with his sexy but serious face.

"Is something wrong?" he asked.

Cree took two steps back. She wanted to yell and ask him who it was that he had told that he loved, but she knew she needed to take a more appropriate approach. If she was wrong, she didn't want to make him think he had just slept with a crazy person.

"Nothing is wrong. I just had an amazing time. I hate that it has to end."

Les smiled. "You act as though I'm not going to keep in touch."

"Are you?" Cree's eyes widened. "I mean, because I watch TV, I know how these things usually happen."

Les let out a chuckle. He stepped toward her and kissed her on her forehead. "This isn't TV, baby."

"So this isn't a one-night stand, where you head back to meet a wife somewhere?"

This time Les took two steps back. His smile faded, and his face took on the serious expression Cree knew too well from the television shows. "Okay, Cree, I'm going to be honest with you. Sit down."

Cree took a deep breath as she sat on the side of the bed. She folded her arms, already knowing what was about to happen. Les stood in front of her, rubbing her shoulders.

"Les, do you have a wife?"

"No."

"You don't?" She stared into his dark eyes.

"No, I am not married. But there is someone."

Cree tried to stand up, but Les pushed her back on the bed. He held her arms as she attempted to break free of his grasp. She didn't know what she wanted to do. A part of her wanted to break free and run out of the room, but another part of her wanted him to continue to hold her.

"Cree, it's complicated."

"Complicated? What exactly does that mean?" Cree freed herself, rose from the bed, and took two steps back.

"Exactly what I said. It is complicated, and it's something I'd rather not talk about right now."

Cree felt the tears forming in her eyes. She tried to keep her eyes open, hoping the tears wouldn't fall.

"Cree, please, don't do that."

Les reached out to Cree, but she pulled away. She couldn't stop shaking her head. Her fairy tale was shattering in front of her.

"Cree, it's not what you think, and I promise one day, when the time is right, I will talk to you more about it. But I need you to trust me when I say now is not the time. One day, but not today."

Cree looked at him. She didn't know what she wanted to think. He talked as though they would see each other again.

"So, what . . . ? You want me to be some type of side chick or something?" she said.

Les shook his head. "No, it's nothing like that. I know you are better than that. I would never do that to you."

The words coming out of his mouth were starting to sound like those of the teacher in the *Peanuts* cartoons. She knew she had to get out of that hotel suite. Les followed her into the living room. Cree searched for one of her shoes, but she couldn't find it. She thought about running out and leaving the shoe behind just like Cinderella. Les grabbed her arm and turned her back around to him.

"Cree, I want us to get to know each other better. I want to know more about you, and I want you to learn more about me. I am not happy where I am, and things can always change if the right woman comes along."

Cree felt the wall she had erected breaking down. She studied his face for a sign that everything he was saying was total bullshit. He had a woman. Could this situation ever end well for her?

Les pulled his phone out. He scrolled on it and then held it up to her. She saw a picture of herself from the night before attached to her name in his contacts.

"You are saved in my phone, baby. This is not going to be the last time you hear from me. I can guarantee you that."

Cree wanted to believe it. She had never wanted to believe something so badly in her life. She was staring at the man of her dreams. Not only was he everything she had ever dreamed of, but he had also sexed her unlike anyone before. Now he was standing in front of her, asking to get to know her better.

Cree stepped closer to Les. She put her hand on the back of his head and pulled him closer to her. She pressed her lips against his. Les wrapped his arms around her, pulling her as close as he possibly could. His hands became entangled in her hair as they kissed passion into each other, both with a point to prove. Cree finally forced herself to pull away.

"I'll believe it when I see it." She pecked him one more time on his lips. Then Cree turned around, picked up her lost shoe, and walked out the door.

***

Nia woke up to find Kirk still sleeping like a baby next to her. She grabbed her clothes and headed to the bathroom. She took a shower and fixed her hair as best she could with none of her products. She walked out of the bathroom to find Kirk sitting up in bed, flipping through the channels on the TV. She obviously had fallen asleep before him, because she would have definitely remembered him taking his shirt off, exposing his amazing abs and chest.

"Morning, sleepyhead." She smiled as she walked back over to the bed.

"*Adventure Time* has to be the best cartoon ever created." Kirk smiled.

"I'd say it's up there, but I'd have to give the best cartoon award to something like *Rugrats* or *Jem*."

"Jem." Kirk laughed. "I guess she was kinda cool for a girl's cartoon character."

They both laughed. Kirk stood up. His pajama pants hung off his body, showing the top of his ass. Nia tried not to drool at the amazing specimen in front of her. She didn't see a piece of fat out of place. She knew it was from the workout regimen he needed to follow for the show. He was cut in all the right places and had a smooth body without a lot of extra body hair. She watched him run his hands through the back of his dirty blond hair. His biceps flexed without him knowing it. Nia's heat was rising, and there was nothing she could do to stop it. Kirk turned around to face her.

"I'm gonna hop in the shower real quick. I have an interview to do with Les before we catch our flights back to Canada. But I'm gonna get you back to your room."

"Oh, Kirk, you don't have to worry about that. I can make it back to my room."

Kirk stopped in the doorway of the bathroom. "No, I think I should make sure you make it back."

"Kirk, this is my city. I should probably make sure you make it where you need to be before you do that for me." They both laughed.

Kirk walked over to Nia and gave her a big hug. Nia didn't want to let go.

"You are an amazing chick, Nia. But I think I've said that a few times now." Kirk smiled.

Nia just smiled. She wanted to say more. She wanted to tell him to take her right there on the bed, but she knew it wasn't right. She had had a great night, and she wasn't going to risk messing it up because she couldn't get her hormones in check.

"Well, let me get out of your hair. I had a great night, Kirk. Thanks for everything." Nia smiled at him again.

"No." Kirk held Nia's hands. He stared into her eyes. "Thank you. Thank you for everything. It truly was an amazing night." He kissed her on her forehead.

Nia wanted to scream, but she just continued to smile. She walked toward the door to the suite. She stopped when she heard Kirk call her name. Nia smiled once more, hoping he was about to walk around the corner, rush up to her, and take her in his arms. Kirk appeared in the living room.

"Text me and let me know you made it back safely," he said.

Nia held the smile that was fixed on her face. She nodded her head, knowing she couldn't trust what came out of her mouth if she tried to speak. She walked out the door. She leaned her body against the door for a moment after it closed, not ready to walk away completely.

Chapter 12

I walked into the room, surprised to find it exactly the way we had left it the night before. I knew checkout was going to be soon. I sent a quick text, asking my two friends where they were, then started to pack up all my belongings.

It was the hardest time I've ever had packing. I put my wigs in their bags and folded up my cheaper costumes. I pulled my beautiful Grecian goddess dress out of the closet. I admired its beauty. I felt like I owed everything to that dress.

I paused when I heard someone put a key in the door. I stood there as Nia walked into the room in the same clothes she had had on the night before. I smirked, but before I could say anything, she looked at me with a very straight face and told me there was nothing to tell.

We were both packing up our belongings when Cree finally took her walk of shame into the room. She closed the door behind her, then leaned against it. We just watched as she stared at the ceiling. We didn't know what to think, so we just stood there watching her. She took a deep breath and looked at both of us.

"Well, how was you guys' nights?" She walked farther into the room and plopped down on the bed.

"Shouldn't we be asking you that question?" Nia pressed her lips firmly together. "Details, woman."

Cree fell back on her bed. "That man . . ." She sighed. "God, I love Dragon Con!"

We all laughed.

We listened as Cree spilled all the details from her night with Les. She was glowing. There were moments when she would pause, just because she was lost in the moment. Nia finally broke in, telling us of her uneventful evening.

"Well, at least you know he completely respects you. That's a great thing," I said to Nia.

"I didn't want him to respect me. I wanted him to take me all over that damn room." Nia fell back on the bed. "That body . . . Lord, he gave me a two-hundred-degree fever this morning."

Nia and I laughed.

"I think I would be happier if Les had done the same thing," Cree said, interrupting our laughter. We noticed her stern expression was back again. "I mean, yes, the night was amazing, but I can't help but think that's all it was. Just one night. Now I'm left wanting more."

Nia and I put our hands on our friend to comfort her. I couldn't help but feel the same way. I would probably never hear from Ursula again. The only chance I had of being in her presence again was if I saw her at San Diego Comic-Con or if she came back to Dragon Con again. I had her number, but I wasn't going to call her. I wasn't going to be that chick she banged in Atlanta who won't stop blowing up her phone.

Cree looked over at me. "Temple, what happened with Ursula?"

I was caught off guard. I wanted to open up and tell them everything. I thought about the confidentiality agreement I had signed. In my mind I knew I could trust my friends. They wouldn't do anything to hurt me, but I couldn't be 100 percent sure.

"It was cool. We had dinner in her room. She was very nice."

"Aww, that's awesome, girl. You got to have dinner with your idol. Did she spill any details about the next season?" Nia smirked.

"No, but she was really funny. Just like at the panel the other day. She is just . . . amazing."

The three of us looked at each other. I couldn't help but wonder if they were holding back information just like I was. I wondered if Cree had to sign an agreement like I had to or if that was just something I had been forced to do.

There was a knock on the door, which pulled us from our sister bonding session. Nia opened the door, and Jason and Carlos walked in, dropping their duffle bags on the floor. Both took me off guard as I almost didn't recognize them in regular clothes.

"Do we even want to know?" Nia asked her two male friends.

"Probably not," Carlos said as he climbed in our bed, covering himself with the comforter. "So sleepy."

We all laughed about the weekend as we continued to pack our belongings in our luggage. We compared our signed memorabilia. Cree and I tried to figure out the best way to pack without crushing anything.

We took a final look around the room before heading out. I didn't want to leave the room, and I could tell the feeling was mutual. We grabbed the first elevator we could. I looked out the glass wall of the elevator as we headed down to the lobby. The night before, the hotel was packed with people partying, but now hardly anyone was around, and those people who were there were standing around with their bags, for the most part.

Cree and I watched Nia as she checked us out of the hotel room. I handed her my portion of the room fee. We walked out of the hotel and waited on the valet to hail cabs for us and retrieve Carlos's truck.

"Jason!"

We turned around to see Jason's weekend romp walking toward us. She looked different in regular clothes. Her long brown hair was pulled back in two pigtails. She walked up and hugged Jason with ease. Nia, Cree, and I looked at each other as he accepted the hug without the usual hesitation.

"Hey, you guys. Did you have a good weekend?" she said to us as she put her arm around Jason's back.

"Umm . . . yeah, it was great. I hope you had a good time too," Nia responded for us.

Carlos was amused, as usual, with a smile sprawled across his face.

"I had a blast. Thanks for sharing Jason with me." She kissed him on his cheek.

Jason couldn't say anything. He just stood there like a statue, with his lips pressed tightly together.

"Oh, it was no problem. Right, Jason?" Nia replied as our eyes locked on Jason.

"Right." Jason looked away, trying not to lose his cool.

"Well, it was nice meeting you guys. I need to get home. I'll call you later, babe." The girl walked off and got in the car with the group of friends she had come with.

As soon as her car turned the corner, we all erupted in laughter. Jason stood still, staring at the sky.

"Fuck all of you." Jason shook his head.

"Y'all should have seen them last night. It was so cute. All cuddled up and shit." Carlos put his arm around Jason. "You two make such a cute couple."

We laughed as Jason pushed Carlos off of him.

"And what, or who, did you get into last night, Carlos?" I asked as I nudged him on his shoulder.

"Honey, I got into a few somethings and someones. Hell, it's Dragon Con, after all." Jason smiled, showing off all his pearly whites.

Carlos's truck arrived from the valet. The guys put Nia's stuff in the truck as Cree and I hugged our friend. We said our final good-byes as she started to get in the truck.

"Nia!"

Our mouths dropped open as Kirk came walking out of the hotel toward us. Even the people around us stood in amazement as the gorgeous star came over to our friend. He had a very serious look on his face.

"Kirk, what are you doing here?" Nia said, more surprised than all of us.

Kirk nodded his head, saying hello to us without words. He took Nia by her hand and pulled her off to the side. He lowered his head.

"So I was sitting in the interview and they asked me how my Dragon Con was and I couldn't remember much besides the time we spent together. I realized that I wasn't quite ready for the time to be over."

"Oh." Nia couldn't move.

"I was wondering if you might want to have dinner with me."

"What about your flight?" asked Nia.

Kirk smiled. "There will be others. So, Miss Nia, you showed me Dragon Con. How about showing me Atlanta?"

Cree and I held each other's arms as we watched our friend work her charm on Kirk. We wanted to jump up and down, but we remained calm. I was happy for her, but I couldn't help but be a little envious of her. I wanted Ursula to appear suddenly, and from the look on Cree's face, she yearned for Les to make an appearance as well.

Nia walked back over to us while Kirk talked to the handlers he had had all weekend. She was smiling from ear to ear.

"So seems I have a date, so, um, I will talk to you all later. Girls, call me and let me know you made it home safely." She hugged each of us. "Carlos, just take my stuff to your crib. I'll get it later."

"The fuck I look like? Your personal butler?" Carlos jokingly protested.

Cree and I hugged Carlos and Jason, and they headed off.

Cree and I decided to share a cab. The driver headed toward the Megabus drop-off location for me. I looked over at Cree, who was staring out the window.

"I can't believe it's over." I sighed.

"Les has a girlfriend. He's still involved with his baby's mother."

My head shot toward her. She continued to stare out the window.

"And he told you this when?"

"Afterward."

I rubbed Cree's back to comfort her. "I'm sorry, honey. Are you okay?"

"He said he doesn't want to stop seeing me."

"Um, so, what? He wants you as his side chick?" I instantly didn't like Les anymore.

Cree turned her head toward me. "He said that he wants to start to get to know me and see where it goes. He said there's nothing really serious between them, but they are still involved due to the kid."

"And what do you believe?"

Cree sighed. "I believe that I just had the best night of my life with a man I have been in love with since I first saw him, and I think he just played me." Tears began to flow from Cree's eyes.

I didn't know what to say. I knew that she was probably right. The asshole had used her for sex, and I would be surprised if she ever heard from him again. Ciara entered my head for the first time in a while.

"We aren't going to think like that. We are going to think that he realized that you are an amazing woman and that he's lucky to have spent time with you. I don't think that will be the last you hear from him, but I do think that if you do hear from him, you should resist. You are too good to be a side chick, no matter who it's for."

The cab pulled up to the Megabus drop-off area. I hugged Cree, wishing I didn't have to leave my friend at that moment.

Cree took a deep breath and smiled. "You are right. Please, I rocked his world last night, so he will definitely be calling. But he will be getting my answering machine."

We high-fived. I could only hope she stuck to that. I got out of the cab and watched as she disappeared into the traffic. I turned around to take a look at the line of people waiting to catch the bus. I couldn't help but laugh. It was obvious who my fellow Dragon Con attendees were. We would make eye contact, giving an unspoken hello, as we knew where the other had to be coming from. I saw a few people who were still wearing their badges, not wanting the weekend to be over, just like I didn't want it to be over.

I found a seat at the back on the top level of the double-decker bus. I pulled my iPad out and put my headphones on my head. I couldn't help but press PLAY when I brought up the first episode ever of *Olympus*. I smiled when Les, Kirk, Mason, and Ursula appeared in the opening scene. I shook my head, still finding it hard to believe that I had been with the people I watched all the time. Flashes of my night with Ursula consumed my brain. I felt my stomach knot up. I took a deep breath, trying to suppress the ache I was feeling for her. I couldn't take it. I turned on *Finding Nemo*, trying to think of something less erotic.

Chapter 13

I arrived back at my apartment hours later. I was exhausted. I wasn't sure how I even managed the drive from the bus station to my apartment. I sat in my car, staring at the window to my apartment. It was really over. My weekend was complete, and I was back to reality. I didn't want to go inside. I wanted to turn around, drive back to Atlanta, find a new job, and never come back to Memphis again. It was a tempting thought, but the reality was that I had a mess of a relationship to clean up as best as I possibly could.

I looked over to the side and realized Ciara's car was parked two spots down from me. I knew it had to be someone else's car. After all, I had taken my key back from her. My hands tensed up as I forced myself out of my car and to my front door. I heard music coming from inside my house. I had to be dreaming. She couldn't really be in my house again.

I walked in and smelled Italian food cooking. I headed down the hallway and found Ciara sitting on my couch, playing a video game. She looked up and dropped the control. Ciara stood up, not taking her eyes off of me.

"How the hell did you get in here?"

"Temple, you gave me two keys. Remember?"

"That wasn't an invitation for you to bring your ass back here."

I stormed off to my bedroom. I was pissed. My plan to relax and think everything out was ruined. Ciara appeared in my doorway. I walked up to her and pushed her out of my room.

"Why, Ciara? Why did you do it?" I yelled as I continued to push her farther and farther down the hallway.

"I'm sorry, Tem. I fucked up, and I know it. I just want us to be able to talk about it."

"I don't want to fucking talk to you. I want you to get the fuck out of my house!" I hit the wall with my hand. The pain throbbed through my hand. There was a moment of silence between us as I rubbed my hand against my side.

"If you really want me to leave, I will. But, Temple, I don't want to. I want us to please just talk. *If* you need to yell, then yell. If you want to hit me, do it. Just don't make me leave."

I could see the determination on her face. I could feel her trying to break through the wall I had built up over the past four days. So much had changed in that time period. I thought about Ursula. What would I have done if I had still been in a relationship with Ciara? I knew I wouldn't have had the strength to say no to Ursula. I would have cheated in a heartbeat.

"I just need some time." I walked back into my bedroom. I could almost hear the relief coming off of her.

"So can I stay? I'm making lasagna. I knew you were coming back today, and I wanted to have something ready when you got back."

"Sure. Can you get my bags out of the car?" I sat on the edge of my bed, and Ciara disappeared down the hallway.

I didn't know what I was doing. I didn't know why I was willing to even entertain the chance of us working anything out. I didn't know why I felt guilty. She had cheated on me, and I was single, but the fact that I slept with someone just three days after breaking up with her just wasn't my normal style. If Ursula had been a revenge fuck, I would have felt much better about the situation, but I knew that she wasn't. I knew that I wanted her more than anything or anyone, and if things were different, if Ciara hadn't cheated, I still would have slept with Ursula.

***

Ciara was on her best behavior. We sat down for dinner a while later. She had done her best to go all out, setting the table as romantically as she could with the things I had in the house. She had lit two tapered candles and had dimmed the lights, hoping to create a romantic atmosphere. Her efforts were not working.

"So why don't you tell me about the trip? Did you get to meet that chick?" she asked.

I almost choked on my wine when I heard the question. "Yeah, I met her." I took another large gulp of wine.

Ciara smiled. "Oh, shit. So how was it? Did she like your outfit? Did you actually speak to her?"

I felt my body starting to tense up. The room was starting to feel small. Ciara was staring right at me, and I knew I had to look like a deer caught in the headlights. "Why does it matter?" I snapped.

"Huh?'"

"Why do you care, Ciara?" I felt my anger rising. "You never cared about me meeting her before. Hell, you didn't even want me to go. Now you wanna act like you give a damn."

Ciara wiped her mouth with her napkin. "I was just trying to make conversation."

"Well, why don't we talk about you? What have you been doing all weekend, or should I say who?"

Ciara let out a loud sigh. She sat back in her chair. "Okay, give it to me, Temple. Go ahead." Ciara held her arms out. She pressed her lips firmly together.

"How the fuck could you sleep with that girl in my fucking bed? Ugh. I just realized I have to sleep in that bed tonight." I jumped up from the table and began to pace the floor.

"Temple, I fucked up. Yeah, I did it, and I'm not about to make excuses for it." Ciara rose from her seat and rushed over to me. She grabbed me by my upper arm and pulled me toward her. "I fucking missed you. I was jealous. All you cared about was going to see some chicks you didn't even know a few months ago. All you fucking cared about was that damn event."

"Like you fucking care about those damn video games!"

I pushed away from her and stormed over to the small rack of video games. With little force I knocked the rack over, causing the games to scatter across the floor.

Ciara rushed over and grabbed me by both of my arms. "Stop it, Temple! This isn't you."

Ciara held on to me, pulling me closer and then into her arms. I hit her arms repeatedly. She took each blow without faltering. I knew they weren't hurting her as much as I wished they would. I wanted her to feel the pain I was feeling. I mustered up all the strength in me and pushed my body away from hers. With the strength I had left, I slapped her across her face. The sound rang through the living room.

Ciara stood there, holding her face.

My mouth dropped opened. I covered it with my hand, realizing what I had just done. "Ciara . . ."

She stood there, staring at the floor. I could tell she was past angry. I braced myself. I had seen her this quiet only once, and that had been right before she beat up a girl at the club.

"Ciara, I'm sorry." I took a step forward.

She held her hand out to tell me to keep my distance.

"I'm so sorry, baby," I whispered. I ignored her warning and walked up to her. I wrapped my arms around her. I didn't know what types of feelings were taking over my body. One moment I was angry, and the next moment I just wanted to hold her and make things better.

Ciara turned her head to look at me. Our eyes locked on each other. She took her hand and pulled my head

close, pressing her lips against mine. I watched as her
eyes closed and she kissed me with as much passion as
she could muster. I didn't know why I kept my eyes open.
I never kissed with my eyes open.

Ciara's hands explored my body until they found their
way to my pants. She unbuttoned my jeans and pulled
them down. I grabbed her hands to stop her.

"Please, let me please you," Ciara whispered in my ear
as she pulled my panties down.

I knew it was wrong, but the angry bitch in me didn't
care. I allowed her to lead me to the couch. I pushed her
head deep into my pussy. I wasn't sorry about hitting her
anymore. I knew it was evil, but I only wished she could
taste Ursula on me.

I closed my eyes. I felt Ciara's tongue probing my walls
until she reached her favorite spot. She began to suck on
my clit in a way that was all too familiar. It was the same
thing she always did; there was never a change in her
style.

Ursula entered my mind.

I bit my lip as I pushed Ciara's face down, causing her
mouth to leave my clit for deeper regions of my womanhood. I felt her tongue press against my hole as one of her
fingers entered first.

I could feel Ursula's hair tangled in my hands. I could
feel her skin against mine and her mouth breathing life
into my body.

I began to squeeze my nipples, wanting to feel the
intensity that I had felt the night before. I pushed my
pelvis into Ciara's mouth, grinding against her tongue.

"Strap!" I said.

Ciara sat up and wiped my sticky sweetness from her
mouth. She didn't ask any questions. She ran to the
bedroom to grab her "man." I pressed my fingers against
my clit, rubbing it in soft circular motions, until Ciara

emerged a few moments later, strapped up. She began to mount me, but I stopped her. I stood up and walked to the side of the couch. I bent over the edge. Ciara knew it was her lucky day. She stood behind me and began to slowly enter me.

I wanted it, and I wanted it then. I grabbed the eight inches of rubbery silicone and pushed it into my pussy.

"Fuck me!" I yelled the command.

Ciara didn't know what to think, but she wasn't going to complain. She held my hips as she thrust the strap in and out. I closed my eyes and was instantly back in the suite at the Ritz-Carlton. I felt her soft hands as they pushed me against the wall of the bedroom. I could see her index finger and could feel it graze my collarbone as she made her way in between my breasts. I could see the way she bit her bottom lip in anticipation of what was to come next. I felt my leg graze hers as I lifted it so she could stick her fingers inside of me. I could feel Ursula's mouth kissing and sucking on my neck as she finger fucked me. Flashes of Ursula consumed my mind with every thrust until my river flowed down my inner thighs.

"Damn." Ciara's hands fell off my hips.

I opened my eyes.

I wasn't at the Ritz. I was back in Memphis, in my little apartment. I turned around to see Ciara staring at me in disbelief. She had an unusual smile on her face.

"Baby, damn," she repeated over and over. I looked down to see a large wet spot on one of the legs of her boxers. I had made it rain, and I hadn't realized it. Ciara stood there beaming, like she had just won a prize.

I would let her think that she had something to do with it, but I knew the truth. Ciara was just the vessel. Ursula had fucked me that night.

Chapter 14

Three weeks past, and things seemed to be back to normal. Ciara was starting to spend more and more time at my house, just like before. I would wake up, go to work, and come home like I always did. Dragon Con seemed like ages ago, even though it had been a very short time ago.

I had found things a little difficult in the beginning. All my coworkers wanted to know about the crazy convention I had attended, which only made me think about Ursula more and more. I wanted to talk to her. I would stare at her phone number in my phone. I almost pressed SEND a few times. I didn't want to be the girl who didn't know her place, and I knew I would be devastated if I called, only to be met with a disconnected number.

It was another long day at work, and I was ready to get home and start my weekend. I pulled into my usual parking space, only to see Ciara's car already parked in her normal spot. I rolled my eyes. I didn't want to see her today. I had finally mustered up enough nerve to watch the episodes of *Olympus* I had missed the last couple of weeks. The season finale was Sunday, and I wanted to spend the weekend watching the whole series, including the episodes I'd missed recently due to my inability to watch Ursula on-screen.

I could hear Drake coming from my house. I wanted to scream. I had already received one letter from my apartment office alerting me of the noise complaint. I opened

my door and headed straight for the sound bar. I turned
the music off and turned around to see Ciara standing in
the doorway in just her boxers and sports bra.

"Ciara, do you want me to get kicked out of my apartment? Shit. Why do you have to play it so loud?"

"My bad. I didn't realize it was loud." Ciara shrugged
her shoulders.

I could feel a headache coming on. I tried to think of
a nice way to tell her to hit the road. I had a weekend
planned, and she was not a part of it.

"Oh, something was delivered for you today," she said.

Ciara walked back toward the bedroom. I followed,
wondering what she had done this time. I walked into the
bedroom and saw a large FedEx box sitting on the bed.

"What is it?" I asked as I walked closer to the box.

"I don't know." She sat on the side of the bed.

Curious, I looked at her. She looked as clueless as I
was. I glanced at the address form. There was no return
address on it. I tried to remember if I had ordered something, but I was drawing a blank. I pulled the tab at the
top, opening the box. Inside was a garment bag.

"Did you order another costume?" Ciara rolled her eyes
at the thought of more money spent on costumes.

I shook my head as I held up the garment bag. I pulled
the zipper down. My eyes had to be playing a trick on me.
I pulled the red dress out on its hanger and held it up. My
mouth dropped open. In my hand was a true replica of
Ursula's dress. I laid the dress down on the bed gently,
hoping not to mess up a single piece of the thin silk fabric.

"Seriously, Temple, your dress wasn't enough? You
had to go and bid on that?" Ciara stood up.

"I didn't buy this."

A long white envelope caught my attention. I picked it
up to see my name written across the front. I knew that
handwriting. I had one other note with that exact same

writing on it. My heart began to race. I slowly opened the envelope and pulled out the piece of stationery.

I want to see what you look like in the real one. —U

I felt something else in the envelope. I pulled out a plane ticket, dated for tomorrow. My heart felt like it was going to burst out of my chest.

"So who is it from?" Ciara walked up to me, causing me to jump. I held the envelope tight in my hand.

"Nia. She is insane." I turned and quickly rushed out of the room. I knew if I stayed, Ciara would be able to tell very easily that I was lying.

I stood in my living room, knowing I would have only a moment before Ciara appeared. Ursula wanted me in LA in tomorrow, and I knew I was going. Ciara walked into the living room.

"Why did Nia get you a dress that is just like what you already have?" Ciara questioned while brushing her hair with her brush.

I felt a warm sensation take over my body. I couldn't stop smiling. Ursula hadn't forgotten about me. She wanted to see me, and I was aching to see her.

"Because she is an awesome-ass friend!" I tried to remain calm, but I wanted to jump up and down like Tom Cruise did when he professed his love on *The Oprah Winfrey Show*. My happiness was short-lived. I looked at Ciara. I had to get rid of her.

"I guess the weirdness continues." She shrugged her shoulders and headed back to my bedroom.

I felt like a weight had lifted off my shoulders the second she made that statement. I realized I no longer gave a damn about what she thought. I walked to my bedroom and stood in the doorway.

"Get your shit and get out of my house."

I stood in the doorway with my arms crossed. Ciara sat up in the chair.

"What did you say?" she questioned.

"I said, 'Get your shit and get out.' I'm so over this." I threw my hands up as I walked in the room and began pulling her things out of my closet.

"Temple, what the fuck?"

"I am over this. I'm over you and your stupid-ass comments about the things that I love."

"Oh, come on, Temple. You know I'm just playing." Ciara sat back down, obviously not taking me seriously.

"I'm not playing with you." I pulled her favorite jacket out of my closet and threw it on the floor. Ciara jumped up when her prized possession hit the floor. She looked in my eyes. I saw her face drop. If she had thought I was playing before, she didn't think so anymore.

"You fucking that girl, aren't you?" Ciara huffed.

"What?" I felt my body tensing up.

"Nia! You are fucking Nia!" Ciara was fuming.

"Girl, you would think some shit like that." I laughed. "Unlike you, I don't resort to sleeping with other people."

"Then where in the fuck is this coming from?" Ciara waved her jacket in her hand. "We were just fine. You get this package, and now you don't want to be with me. Something is up, and I demand that you tell me what it is."

"I just don't want you."

I couldn't believe the words actually came out of my mouth. I didn't want to be with her. I hadn't wanted her since I'd walked in on her with the whore. I was over her, and seeing the beautiful red dress just gave me the strength I needed to let go.

"You know what? You are tripping. I'm going to give you some time to think about what you are saying. I'm not gonna take too much more of this bullshit from you." Ciara put her jacket on and zipped it up. She stepped into a pair of her sweatpants and walked out of my bedroom. I heard the front door slam behind her.

I sat there looking at her clothes, which were lying next to Ursula's dress. I didn't have time to think about Ciara. I had a trip to prepare for. I couldn't contain my excitement. I had to call someone and tell them what was happening. I picked up my phone and dialed Cree's number. She answered on the first ring.

"I can't believe what I just got!" I pushed Ciara's clothes off my bed and sat on the edge.

"What's going on?" Cree responded in a low voice.

"Ursula . . . She sent me the original dress she wore on the show. You know, the one that I fashioned my dress after. And she invited me—"

I caught myself. I remembered I wasn't supposed to tell anyone about us. I didn't know how I would explain my way out of getting a random ticket to come visit someone that I was not romantically involved with.

"She invited you where?" Cree turned over in bed.

"Um, just to wear the dress when I watch the finale this weekend."

I hated lying to my friends. I needed someone to share in my happiness with me. I noticed something was different about Cree's voice. She wasn't her usual loud, crazy self. I wanted to kick myself. I was gushing about my gift when I knew she hadn't heard from Les since Dragon Con. Nia and Kirk were hitting it off, talking on the phone all the time while he was shooting in Canada, and now I had this trip with Ursula and the dress, which had just been listed on eBay for over five thousand dollars.

"Cree, I'm sorry. I didn't mean . . ."

"Girl, please, I'm over that. I'm happy for you. Talk about the ultimate thank-you. I think that dress was listed at like five Gs last time I checked the auctions." Cree sat up in bed.

"Yeah."

Cree laughed. She knew I was trying to contain my happiness because of her.

"Temple, I am good. It is what it is. Everything happens for a reason. Now I wanna see pictures, so try that dress on and get to snapping selfies in your mirror."

"Okay, girl. I'll send one. Talk to you later."

I hung up the phone. I knew she was putting on a front so I wouldn't feel bad, and I knew deep down she had to be hurting over Les. She was the biggest fan of all and wasn't receiving any special treatment. I made a mental note to check on her more often but I knew I didn't have much time at that moment. I had a trip to plan for.

"Everything okay?"

Cree turned her head. Les stared at her. She looked at his naked body as he lay in bed next to her. "Everything is fine."

Cree climbed back into bed and kissed her Adonis, as she had been doing for the past two days.

Chapter 15

I called her to thank her for the dress and to question her about the plane ticket. She simply laughed and told me she wanted to see me in the dress for herself. I couldn't pass up the opportunity. I took the red-eye to Los Angeles the next morning.

I arrived at her house in Santa Barbara. I watched as the large gates opened. The driver traveled up a long winding driveway. My mouth dropped open as the villa appeared behind the tall trees. It was something like out of a movie. It was every bit a hidden paradise. The villa looked like it belonged in Europe somewhere instead of California. The trees gave it a very cozy feel, even though it was a huge mansion. I felt my palms start to tense up as I watched Ursula appear in the front doorway.

I managed to contain my excitement as I got out of the car. She walked over and hugged me as the driver pulled my bag out of the trunk.

"Welcome, Temple." She sounded so sweet, like the woman whom I'd admired on the panel at Dragon Con. She thanked the driver and tipped him for his service.

I walked into the house and had to force my mouth from dropping open again. She told me the home was a restored Tuscany villa. I admired the stone floors and walls. She had a very minimalist design theme, keeping to the Tuscan feel of the home. I felt like I was in Tuscany.

I noticed a large painting of Ursula on the wall in the massive living room. I was mesmerized by how realistic it looked. I felt like her eyes in the painting were actually watching me. I felt her hand grab my arm. She turned me around, pulling me close to her. She planted her lips against mine.

She had my dress off in seconds. My body shivered as my bare skin touched the cold stone floor. Ursula didn't say a word as she started to kiss my inner thighs. Her left hand massaged my left breast, caressing it and squeezing my nipple in between her fingers. I closed my eyes when I felt her right index finger feeling the moistness that had already consumed my vagina. She placed her finger inside me, only to pull it right back out. I opened my eyes and watched her suck my sweetness off her finger.

"I've been waiting a long time for this," she whispered. "Temple, my Temple."

Her Temple. . . . My heart skipped a beat as she said my name over and over. I bit my bottom lip as her tongue danced a forbidden dance around my clit. She consumed me, sucking and licking all my sweetness. Her fingers fucked me. She was treating my body like it was her personal playground.

This time I didn't fight back. I let her turn me into her bitch. I didn't want to be in control. I wanted to let her have her way with me, and she did. I submitted to her. I felt death creeping up from my toes and reaching the pit of my stomach. I grabbed her arms as my orgasm escaped my body. Ursula looked up at me. I could see my essence on her face.

"Let's take a dip." She smiled as she stood up.

Ursula took my hand, helping me up off the floor. She held on to my hand, and I followed her outside. Her backyard looked like the set of *Olympus*. Large Roman columns stood around the pool, which looked more like a large lagoon than a swimming pool. The smell of various flowers and citrus filled the air.

Ursula pulled her sundress over her head. I watched as she dove into the water like she was a pro diver. I knew I couldn't do that. I sat on the edge of the pool and put my feet in the water. To my surprise, the water was rather warm, but still cool enough to enjoy.

"Come on in," Ursula said before disappearing under the water again.

I didn't know how to tell her that I wasn't that great of a swimmer. I watched as her silhouette came closer and closer to me, until her head popped up out of the water right in front of me. She smiled, placing her arms on my legs.

"You do know how to swim, right?"

"Yes, just not really well."

"I won't let you drown, I promise." She winked at me.

I let my body fall into the blue water. We went from fucking in her living room to playing around in her swimming pool like we were two big kids, and this was all within the first hour of my arrival. I had no idea what to expect from the rest of the weekend.

We got out of the water, and she led me to a guest room in her house. I took a long warm shower and washed my hair. I pulled my curly mane back into a ponytail. I opted for a simple blue maxi dress with three large tulips printed on the side.

I took a moment to try to take it all in. Then I walked out on the balcony attached to my room. I could see the beautiful backyard, which was covered in twinkling lights. The pool was illuminated, making it appear electric blue. I took a deep breath; this was the way to live. It surely beat my little apartment.

I heard a ringing sound coming from my room. I realized it was my phone. I dashed inside and scrambled to find it, only to roll my eyes when I saw Ciara's face pop up on the screen. I pressed IGNORE. She was the last person I wanted to talk to. Moments later the phone began to ring again. I knew she would just keep calling, so I pressed the SEND button.

"Yes," I said in the driest tone I could muster.

"Where are you?" Ciara sat in her car, staring at my front door.

"I'm out."

"Don't fucking play with me, Temple. Where the fuck are you?"

I could hear the anger in her voice, but I didn't care. I wanted to tell her I was in a lavish mansion, getting pleased by a real woman, something she could never amount to, but I knew I couldn't.

"I went to Atlanta."

There was silence on the phone. I just held the phone, waiting on a response.

"So you had to go be with her, huh?" Ciara's voice cracked.

"There you go. For your information, I'm not even with Nia. She's not even in town herself. I just needed to get away for a minute, so I came here."

"You needed to get away from what?"

The hurt in Ciara's voice actually made me feel bad. This time I took a long moment before speaking. "You already know the answer to that."

I knew the words had to hurt her, but I was past the point of caring. She had hurt me, and I wasn't over it. On top of that, I was in the mansion of the woman I'd fantasized about and idolized most of my life. I knew Ciara could never compete with that. What we had would never be the same. I wondered how I would ever date another woman after experiencing Ursula. How did you go backward after being with the best?

I heard Ursula call my name. The silence on the phone just further solidified my decision. Ciara wasn't putting up a fight at all, which bothered me for some reason. A piece of me wanted her to yell at me and tell me that she wasn't going to let me go or give up on us. Another part of me wanted her to just realize that she had messed us up and that we would never be the same again.

"Well, you just continue to do you, Temple?" Ciara said, breaking the silence. "Let's hope I'm still here when you decide you are ready to come back."

She hung the phone up, leaving me speechless. Another reality set in. What if I did want her back one day and she wasn't there? I didn't have time to worry about that. I knew what I wanted, and she was waiting on me. I knew this type of opportunity came only once in a lifetime, and I wasn't going to let it pass.

Cree watched Les get dressed. She loved watching his muscular frame flex with the smallest motions, such as pulling up pants or buttoning the buttons on a shirt. While women lusted over his body, she got to experience it now on a regular basis. As much as she loved watching him dress she also hated it simply because she knew it meant that he would be leaving her soon.

"Watching me dress again?" Les smirked.

Cree sat up in bed. "Maybe." She winked at him.

Les crawled across the bed. He grabbed Cree's face and pressed his lips against hers. She loved his rough touches. He manhandled her just the way she liked it. She wrapped her arms around him, pulling him down on top of her.

"Um, no, not again." Les shook his head. "I'll never get back to Toronto if I let this happen."

"Fuck Toronto." Cree giggled. "I think this is just as enticing as a stupid TV show filming." She opened her legs, exposing her Brazilian-waxed vagina. Les let out a deep groan that rumbled through the room.

"It is far, far more enticing." Les touched her smooth skin. "Maybe just a little taste."

Cree giggled as she pulled his T-shirt over his head. Les entered her with his tongue. Cree pushed his head deep into her walls. She wanted him to savor it. She wanted him to relish it so much that he couldn't leave. Les moaned as he ate her like she was the last meal he would ever have.

Les's phone started to ring. Cree knew that ring well. It was home and usually meant his daughter was on the other end. Les moaned, then stopped his feast by laying one final kiss on her clit. He got up and reached for his phone.

"Hey, bumblebee."

Les disappeared into Cree's living room. Cree hit her hands against the bed. Her body was in full heat, and the distraction meant she would not find a release unless she finished it off herself. She got out of bed and grabbed her robe.

Cree walked into the kitchen and pulled a bunch of fresh fruit and veggies out of the refrigerator. She used the NutriBullet Les had bought her and created his favorite smoothie. She poured the smoothie into one of the large disposable cups she had bought just for him. Cree walked into the living room, where he was still talking on the phone with his daughter. She handed him the smoothie. Les grabbed her and pulled her onto his lap. She sat there with her arms around him as he told his youngest daughter he would see her soon.

Cree now knew the reason why her time with Les was limited. His wife had died about a year earlier from breast cancer, leaving him with two daughters to raise alone. The youngest was too young to comprehend what had happened, but his oldest had taken the death hard and was now overprotective of him. He had witnessed firsthand her dislike of his dating when she thought that rumors of him sleeping with a costar had started in the rumor mill. He decided he wouldn't get serious with anyone until he knew his daughter was 100 percent okay with it.

Cree didn't like it, but she understood that for now they couldn't be more than what they were, a weekend romance. Les had flown her out to every city he was in except for Toronto, where his daughters were currently staying with him during filming. Even though she knew the situation, her feelings were starting to grow deeper for the man she had already been in love with before ever meeting. She struggled to keep her emotions in check; the last thing she wanted to do was lose him.

"Is everything okay?" she asked the moment he hung up the phone.

"Yes, everything's fine. Of course, Piper is annoying Cherish, but that's what little sisters are supposed to do." Les kissed Cree on her cheek.

Although the sex was amazing, it was the smaller things that were causing Cree's feelings to develop. They were open and honest with each other about everything. They would spend hours talking while he was on the set and was waiting for scenes to be set up. He tried to spoil her, but she wasn't into the things that most women wanted. The only thing she wanted was time, and she knew she couldn't have nearly as much as she wanted.

"This is great," Les said, taking another sip of the smoothie. "Thanks, baby."

Cree felt her heart melting. She stood up and walked into her bedroom, knowing that her emotions were about to get the best of her. Les knew something was up. He always knew something was wrong when she walked away without saying anything.

"Cree."

"I'm sorry. I really am. Just give me a minute." Cree wiped the tears forming in her eyes.

Les walked up behind her and wrapped his arms around her. She touched his bulging biceps. She held on as they looked at each other in her bedroom mirror.

"Is this becoming too much for you? I understand if it is," Les said.

"I'm okay. Really, I am." Cree forced a smile to appear across her face. She knew he knew she was lying by the sullen look on his face.

"Cree, I don't want to hurt you. I know I've asked a lot of you, but I—"

"Les, I'm all right. Yes, I would like us to become more, but I understand. I know what I signed up for."

Les didn't know what to say. He kissed her on the nape of her neck. The kiss sent chills through Cree's body.

"I want you to buy yourself something nice." He pulled a stack of hundreds out of his pocket. Cree tried to say no, but he wouldn't accept it. He left the wad of bills lying on her dresser.

Cree stared at the money lying on her dresser. Les's phone rang. She watched through her mirror as he answered his phone. She knew it had to be the car service there to pick him up. After he hung up, there were no words. She handed him his bag, fixed his tie, and kissed him one more time before he walked out the door.

Chapter 16

This had to be what pure bliss felt like. I had fucked Ursula in every room of her villa, in some rooms twice. We couldn't get enough of each other. I could say officially that I'd had every inch of Ursula and she had had her way with every part of my body as well. We sat on a blanket in one of the gardens. Ursula picked up a piece of papaya. She allowed the juice to roll down my thigh. She licked the sweet trail off my leg while I ran my hands through her long black hair.

"This has been insane," I said. I kissed her mouth, taking half of the fruit that was hanging from her lips.

"It has been a pretty amazing weekend, if I say so myself." She winked.

I didn't know what it was about her. She was like the sun radiating warmth into me with every smile. Whenever she gave her devilish grin, I would be instantly ready for her to take my body as her personal prisoner.

"I don't want this to end. How can I go back to work after this?" I fell back on the blanket, and Ursula rubbed a piece of fruit around both of my nipples. Her mouth soon found its way to the sweet spots.

"Well . . ." She paused as the tip of her tongue grazed my hard right nipple. "All good things do have to come to an end at some point. I have to get back to Toronto to shoot the show you love so much."

I didn't want it to end. I knew if she asked me to right then, I would devote the rest of my life to fulfilling her every whim. I was hooked on her; she was everything that I wanted and then some. I didn't know how to go back to the real world after living in paradise.

I watched Ursula's naked body as she stood up. She reached her hand out and took mine, helping me up off the ground. We held each other as she planted sensual kisses on my mouth, cheeks, and neck.

"I don't want to go. I really don't want to," I muttered.

Ursula stopped kissing me. She looked in my eyes with a very serious face.

"You aren't going and getting serious on me, are you, Temple?"

The question caught me off guard. I took two steps back. I didn't know how to answer it. I could not fathom how she could think this was anything less than love happening between us. Even though it had been only one weekend, there was no way a person could do what we'd done to each other without feeling something for the other.

"Um, I don't really know how to answer that question."

It was Ursula who took a step back this time. Her usual smile turned into a straight-faced expression. I couldn't take my eyes off of her. I was searching for something to let me know I wasn't crazy for having feelings for her, even if our time together had been brief.

"Temple, I don't know how to say this, but I thought you understood that this is just us having fun. This is not, nor will it ever turn into, anything more than that." I couldn't believe how her voice went from sexy to professional so fast.

"I'm not saying I expected a relationship, but I thought there was something a little bit more than a casual romp going on here."

"Well, if I gave you that impression, I am very sorry." Ursula picked her robe up and began to put it on. She turned away from me and started to head into the house.

My head was spinning as I stood there, naked, in her garden. I picked the blanket up and wrapped it around my bare skin and followed her.

She stood there in the kitchen, pouring a glass of wine, as though she hadn't just burst my dream bubble. I couldn't speak. All the things going through my mind sounded dumb. I wanted to go off, but what right did I have? I wasn't her girlfriend, and she had never made a single statement to let me know she wanted something more with me. I should have known better. Why would she want something more with me when I'd let her have all of me without hesitation? I could hear my mother's voice echoing in my mind. *Why buy the cow when the milk is free?*

"Ursula . . ." My voice trembled like the first time I asked a question at Dragon Con. "I didn't think we were in a relationship or anything, but you flew me here, you gave me the dress. We've been doing . . . well, what we've been doing all weekend. I just figured this was a little bit more than playing around."

Ursula shook her head in a condescending manner. I had never felt so dumb before. She walked up to me and put her hands on both my upper arms.

"Sweetie, I wanted you here because I wanted to do exactly what we've been doing all weekend, having fun together. I like you, and I like what we do together, but, honey, that is all it is. Two adults having a good time together."

"So that's all I am? A fuck buddy?"

"I'd like to say it's more than that, but if that's what you want to call it . . ." Ursula's face didn't change.

I'd never been so offended before. I had never in my life been a fuck buddy. I had never had a one-night stand until Dragon Con. I'd let her turn me into something that I had never in a million years thought I would be.

I nodded. "Well, okay then."

I didn't know what else to say. I felt tears wanting to form in my eyes. I couldn't let her see me cry. I couldn't let her know I felt like the biggest fool on the planet. I walked as quickly as I could to the guest room where my things were.

I closed the door behind me and headed straight to the bathroom. I ran the water to drown out the sound of my crying. I heard her knocking on the door. I wiped the few tears from my face and began to fan my eyes. Was it really all in my head? Did I make something out of nothing just because I was fully satisfied sexually and starstruck? She knocked on the door again. I suddenly realized that she was right. She didn't owe me anything. I had allowed her to do what she wanted to me, and I didn't regret it, because I knew I had wanted it to.

A sense of anger mixed with a wild ego took over my mind. I opened the door to the bathroom. Ursula took two steps back as the door opened. I looked at her. She looked concerned. I didn't want her pity. I wanted her body.

There was a loud thud when I pushed her thin frame against the bedroom wall. Ursula looked at me. She didn't know what to think. I didn't know what to think of myself. A side of me had come out, a hunter of a different kind. I didn't need to talk. I needed to show her why I was more than just a fuck buddy.

I yanked the sash from her robe, then yanked the robe off of her. I picked her right leg up with my right arm. Ursula let out an excited whimper as I sucked her neck and pushed three of my fingers inside her with as much force as I could muster. She moaned as I fucked her with an intensity I hadn't shown her before. She begged for more, and I no longer took my time or went easy. Her wetness covered my hand. She was enjoying every bit of it. I bit her nipple until she squealed. Then I sucked on it, giving her both pleasure and pain. My thumb entered her ass as I continued my assault on her. I wanted to leave my mark. I sucked right above her breast, leaving a swollen red area, which I knew wouldn't disappear for a while.

Ursula yelled my name over and over. No longer was I her sex slave. This time she belonged to me. I felt her walls tighten around my fingers. Suddenly her body convulsed, until she began to rain down on my hand. I took my hand out and pushed two of my soaking wet fingers into her mouth. She sucked her sticky sweetness off my fingers like she was Super Head.

I wasn't sure how we made it to the bed, but before I knew it, I had Ursula's face buried in my pussy. I was in control. I pushed her head down as far as I could manage. I pulled her hair, getting it tangled in between my fingers. My body ground against her tongue while she licked me like I was her favorite ice cream. I wrapped my legs around her. I wasn't going to let her go until I was ready. I felt her fingers inside of me, and my body quivered every time she hit my spot.

I could feel my orgasm flooding through my body until my essence covered her mouth and hand. She didn't stop. She wanted to take every drop of my essence. My chest rose and fell with my heavy breathing. It was as if all of me, all my energy and all my emotions, came out with my release.

I unwrapped my legs from around Ursula. She crawled to the head of the bed, then put her arms around me as I turned over on my side. I couldn't look at her. I wasn't ready to look at her. She kissed me on the nape of my neck.

"See? Fun," she whispered in the sexy voice I was used to hearing.

I had a lot of words for what we did, but fun was not one of them.

**

I woke up earlier than usual. It was Monday, and my weekend was over. I called my job and let them know that I was sick. I wasn't lying. I really was sick. I was sick from knowing that this was my last day with Ursula.

I tiptoed out of the guest bedroom, where Ursula was still sleeping. The cold floor awakened my few senses that were still sleeping. I didn't bother to get dressed. I walked through her lavish villa in the nude. I opened the door to the backyard. The grass was moist from the morning dew. I stood at the edge of the swimming pool. The lights hadn't turned off yet with the arrival of morning. I crossed my arms and jumped feetfirst into the water. It was much colder than I had expected. I realized the heater hadn't been turned on.

I opened my eyes while still under water. All I could see was blue. I could hear the water from the waterfall hitting the pool. I stayed under until my lungs couldn't take any more. I swam back to the top and put my hands on the side of the pool. I didn't know if it was the lack of oxygen, but I suddenly had a clear head.

I walked back into the guest bedroom and took a long hot shower. I put lotion on my body, slowly caressing my oversexed body parts. I brushed my thick hair back into a ponytail. I packed up all my toiletries and took one final glance around the bathroom to make sure I had everything.

I walked back into the bedroom to see Ursula sitting up in bed. Her breasts looked amazing even in the dim light. I put my toiletry bag in my suitcase. I pulled out my last dress, a black and blue maxi dress, to put on for my flight home.

"It's early." Ursula's sultry voice rang through the room.

I closed the suitcase and turned around to face her. "Yeah, I called the airline, and they have a flight in three hours that I can take. I called a cab. It should be here soon." I pulled the dress over my head. It fit my body well, clinging in all the right places.

Ursula got out of bed. She put her robe on and walked over to me. "Are you sure you are ready to go?" Her voice alone made it hard for me to answer the question. She wouldn't take her eyes off of me.

"Yeah, I need to get home. I'm already missing one day of work."

"I think I can give you a few reasons to miss another day or two." Ursula tried to reach for my face, but I quickly turned away.

"No. I need to get home."

Ursula stood in that spot. For the first time she was speechless. "Temple, are you sure about this?"

"I'm sure." I heard my phone ring. I knew it had to be the taxi waiting on me.

Ursula walked out of the bedroom. I grabbed my suitcase and headed to the living room. Ursula buzzed the taxi driver into her gate. I tried not to look at her, but I could feel her eyes burning the side of my face. Unable to take it anymore, I turned and saw that I was right. Her eyes were fixed on me.

"Thank you for an amazing time. I truly did enjoy myself," I said. Now I was the one who sounded professional.

"Did you? Because leaving like this makes me wonder if you did."

I didn't know how to take her attitude. For a person who wanted only to have fun, she sure wasn't acting like she didn't care about me. I put my bag down and walked over to her. I pressed my lips against hers. I had to kiss her one last time. I needed one more kiss, in case it was my last.

I didn't want this kiss to be erotic. I wanted it to be the most sensual and romantic kiss she'd ever experienced. I tried to show all my feelings in that one moment. I wanted Ursula to know what she could have with me, something real and a person who would love her forever. After all, I had already loved her most of my life. I finally let go of her. I could tell from her expression that she was surprised by the kiss.

"Stay. . . ."

"I can't."

"Stay, Temple." Ursula lowered her head. Now she couldn't look at me.

A piece of me wanted to stay. A large piece of me still wanted to do whatever she wanted me to do. I walked out of the villa, leaving Ursula standing in the doorway. I looked only at the trees as the driver made his way back down the long driveway. I watched the iron gate open. I forced myself not to look back. I felt like looking back would turn me into a pillar of salt. I put my shades on as a single tear fell down my cheek.

Chapter 17

The apartment I had once loved looked more and more like a shabby piece of shit each time I came home from a trip. I rolled my eyes as I walked into the small living area. I was missing Ursula terribly already. Nothing seemed right. I didn't know why my apartment felt so different to me. I pulled my rolling suitcase into my bedroom.

My eyes immediately noticed that a drawer to my dresser had been pulled out farther than it should have been. I realized it was Ciara's usual drawer. I walked over and looked in it. The drawer was empty. I walked over to my closet and saw a large gap in the middle. Ciara had taken all her things. There wasn't a single trace of her left. I walked into my bathroom. Even her toothbrush was gone.

I walked back out of my bathroom and sat on the edge of my bed. Everything was sinking in. I had walked away from my dream woman, and I had finally pushed Ciara completely away. I felt empty inside. I wanted to be held, but I had no one to hold me. I was completely alone for the first time in over a year.

I thought about drinking the emptiness away, but I knew it wouldn't work. I decided to immerse myself in work. I cleaned my apartment from top to bottom. I washed clothes that didn't need to be washed, and cleaned out my refrigerator. With nothing left to clean, I decided to cook. I made a full meal, including steak, baby potatoes, and vegetables. I baked a fresh batch of

Toll House cookies to go with the pint of vanilla ice cream
I had in my freezer. I blended a batch of strawberry
daiquiris and poured some into a large plastic martini
glass I had gotten at a Cinco de Mayo party.

I sat the food on my coffee table. I sat down and
turned my television on. I scrolled through the plethora
of channels, unable to find anything I wanted to watch.
I felt a sharp pain in my side. I didn't know why I did it,
but I pressed the DVR button on my remote, displaying
the final episode of the last season of *Olympus,* which I'd
missed while sexing the star of the show. I pressed PLAY
and sat through the episode.

I couldn't eat. After the daiquiri in the glass disappeared, I decided to drink straight from the blender
container. Ursula looked amazing. Even in her vengeful
states on the show, she looked amazing to me. I watched
as she kissed Les, who played Zeus. A ton of memories
of my kissing her flashed in my head. It was complete
torture, but I didn't care. I wanted to feel the pain. I
needed to feel it so I didn't call her or answer her call if
she ever called me. I had to get her out of my system, or I
knew I was doomed.

Cree couldn't take it anymore. It had been two days,
and she hadn't heard anything from Les. She didn't know
why he was avoiding her calls. She couldn't get their last
meeting out of her head. She knew she had ruined it with
her silly emotions. She had a feeling she'd pushed him
away.

She had to get her mind off of her situation. She headed
to her job at the bank. It felt like it had been ages since
she had been in the office, although it had been only a few
days. Before long, the bank was so busy, she didn't have
time to think about her failed relationship.

"Excuse me, but are you Cree Lancaster?"

Cree looked up from her computer to see a petite white woman standing in her doorway. The woman smiled. She didn't look like the usual women who walked into her bank branch. She reeked of money.

"Yes, I am. How can I help you?"

The woman walked into the room and closed the door. She sat down, placing her Birkin bag on the empty seat next to her. Cree noticed the diamonds in her ears. Cree sat straight in her chair as the woman continued to look at her. The woman extended her hand to Cree.

"I'm sorry. Where are my manners? My name is Sybil. I'm Les's fiancée."

"Excuse me?" Cree's back straightened up completely. She noticed the diamond ring on the woman's finger. Cree could feel her body starting to tremble, but she forced herself to remain calm.

"Yes, you heard me right. I'm his fiancée and the mother of his children, or as your kind might call it, his babies mother, or whatever you wish to call me."

Cree held on to the arms of her office chair. Sybil smiled, not losing one inch of her cool. She pulled her hand back when it was clear that Cree wouldn't shake it.

"Look, I'm sorry, but I didn't—"

"Oh, don't worry, Cree. I'm not here on something malicious. I've been with Les for so many years, I know him like the back of my hand," Sybil said, cutting Cree off. "I know he cheats, and honestly, I usually don't care. Hell, men will be men, and men love new cunt."

"Wait a minute now." Cree felt her blood starting to boil. A woman she hadn't even known existed was confronting her, and now that woman was calling her names.

Sybil put her hand over her mouth. "Oh, I'm sorry. I wasn't referring to you. See, this is the reason for my visit."

Sybil stood up and began to pace the floor in front of Cree's desk. "You see, Cree, I'm used to the random girls. They come and go. Usually, he meets the little groupies, fucks them, and never speaks to them again. But now, all of a sudden, he has other things going on. He is gone every weekend. He has a new pep in his step, something that has been gone from our relationship for a very long time. This made me suspicious."

Cree watched as Sybil finally stopped pacing in her red bottom stilettos.

"So I had to do a little investigating, and I found out that Les has been spending all his weekends with a little black Pop-Tart from Chicago, of all places."

"Look now . . ." Cree put her hands on her desk. "I understand you might be upset. Trust me, I'm not the happiest camper right now, either. But you aren't going to come in my place of business and call me names."

Sybil stared at Cree. She knew that Cree was not playing. She put her hand over her mouth again. "I apologize. Let me sit." Sybil sat back down in the chair in front of Cree. "So, anyway, this thing you have going on with him has to stop. We have children to think about, and no woman is going to come between what I have built."

Cree sat back in her chair as she watched Sybil pull out a checkbook. Sybil began to scribble on the check.

"So how much is it going to take for you to disappear?"

"Are you trying to buy me?" Cree was insulted.

"Oh, come on. We both know why you are messing with him. It's what all you women do. If you think I'm about to let some girl come in and ruin the future I've been building with him, you have another thing coming."

Cree shook her head. She couldn't help but laugh. Sybil looked up from her check.

"What exactly is so funny?" Sybil questioned.

"You are, actually." Cree folded her arms. "Here I am about to feel really horrible about what I have been doing, and then you come in here at me the way that you have.

For the record, I didn't know you even existed. You're his fiancée, but you surely aren't featured in any articles and you don't make an appearance at any premieres or anything else."

"We like to keep our relationship private."

"It sounds to me like he likes to keep you hidden, and obviously, for a reason."

"I beg your pardon?" Sybil's voice cracked. "How dare you . . . ?"

"No! How dare *you* come into my place of business, calling me names, because your man prefers to be with me over you! Maybe if you were handling your business at home, he wouldn't be flying me all over to be with him."

"Do you think I give a damn about where he flies you? I am only looking out for my relationship." Sybil hit Cree's desk.

"No, it sounds to me like you are only trying to look out for your finances. You don't seem to care at all that your so-called man is sleeping with me."

"I'm not going to sit here and take this." Sybil jumped up out of the chair. "Trust and believe me when I say that Les is never going to be with you. He's not going to lose his daughters or me over some fling. You, my dear, can have his little penis. I have everything else, and I'll be damned if you or anyone else comes in between that. So I hope you enjoyed him while you could, because he won't be back."

Sybil put her shades on. She picked up her expensive bag and walked out of Cree's office. Cree's whole body was shaking. She picked up her phone and sent a text to Les.

Just met your dead fiancée. Go to hell.

Cree took a half day and headed home. She cried the whole way to her apartment. She couldn't stop crying. She couldn't bear to hear from Les. She missed twelve phone calls from him before she turned the phone off. She wanted to call Temple and Nia, but she knew they had no idea she had been dealing with Les this whole time. She didn't have anyone to turn to.

A loud knock woke Cree out of her sleep. She realized she had fallen asleep on her couch. She walked over to the front door and peered out the peephole. There stood Les, with pain etched in his face.

"I can hear you, Cree. Open the door." Les's raspy voice was deeper than normal. "Please."

Cree stared at the doorknob for a minute before finally unlocking the door. She walked back into her living room as she heard the door open.

"Cree." Les dodged the wineglass that came flying toward his head.

"Dead? You told me she was fucking dead!" Cree yelled.

"I'm sorry." Les lowered his head.

"How could you do this? To me?" Cree picked up a book from the coffee table and chucked it, hitting him in the arm.

Les rushed toward her, grabbing her arms. "I didn't know what to say. I didn't want to lose you."

"So you tell me that she's dead. What type of sick shit is that?"

"Cree, please. She *is* dead to me. She's been dead to me for a long time."

"Oh, really? The ring on her hand says something completely different!" Cree hit Les on the arm, hurting herself in the process of trying to hurt him.

"The truth is that I am not with her anymore. I left her a long time ago, but she has been making my life a living hell. She extorts money from me and threatens to keep my children from me. The only time she ever cares about anything is if she thinks it's going to come in between her and my paychecks."

Cree looked at Les. She could see the hurt on his face. He looked sincere, but he was an actor. He was supposed to be able to deliver a line.

"I can't. I can't do this." Cree pulled away from Les, throwing her hands in the air as she walked away.

"Cree, don't you know how much I care about you? Don't you know that she would have never come to you if she didn't know that you were someone special to me?"

"I know that. I could tell she was a piece of work the moment she started talking." Cree paced the floor.

"Then why are you still mad?"

"Because you fucking lied to me!" Cree yelled as she pointed at Les. "You broke the trust between us. Don't you know I would have been there? I wouldn't have cared about some crazy baby mama. But you lied. You took my choice away from me! You lied to me!"

The room became oddly quiet. Les held his head down like a child in trouble. Cree looked at her hands. They were trembling.

"Please. How do I fix this?" Les's deep voice didn't seem so masculine anymore. He sounded more like a wounded child.

"You can't." Cree walked over to the front door. She opened it and then stood next to it. "You need to go."

"Cree—"

Cree didn't respond. She held the door open, but Les stood in the same spot. The Mexican standoff continued for minutes, as neither of them planned on moving. Realizing she wasn't budging, Les finally gave in. He stopped at the door. Cree didn't want to look at him. She knew if she looked at him, her resolve might break. Les turned Cree's head toward his.

"I'm not giving up on us," he said, his voice trembling. "I'm not."

Les walked out the door. Cree slammed it behind him. She stood there fuming. Her lower lip began to quiver. Tears began to swell in her eyes. She fell to the floor, crying against the door she had let the man she loved walk out of.

Chapter 18

Days turned into weeks, and then two months passed. I hadn't heard from Ursula since leaving her home. A glutton for punishment, I watched her Twitter and Instagram for any clues to what she was doing. She posted only about working on the final season of *Olympus* and shared pictures from the set.

My life was getting back to normal. My days became routine again. I spent my days listening to my coworkers talk about the gossip they'd read about random celebrities and what was going to happen on the reality shows they all watched.

I was working on a friendship with Ciara. She had known something was up when I left town. I couldn't tell her the truth, but I did tell her that I was seeing someone I met at Dragon Con. I assured her it wasn't Nia or Cree, but I still could tell that she questioned the friendship we had.

Nia and I were both shocked to learn that Cree had been sleeping with Les the whole time. We got text messages telling us to get on Skype two days after I got back from the trip to see Ursula. We both gasped when we saw Cree's face. She didn't look like our sister. She was broken. She tried to hold her emotions in, but as soon as she said Les's name, the tears started to flow down her face. We had never seen her like that. She wasn't the one who cried. We were. She was usually the one telling us to suck it up. Concerned, Nia and I both decided to take an emergency trip to Chicago that weekend.

132   Skyy

It was good to see my friends again. Nia and I did everything we could to take Cree's mind off the situation she was going through. Nia and I both needed answers about Les, and Nia was able to get those answers easily out of Kirk. He confirmed the whole story. Les was battling with his babies mother over custody. Les had made the mistake of falling for a gold digger and having children with her. When he realized that she was only out for money, he broke the engagement off. Angry, the woman used their children against Les on a regular basis. She really didn't care about Les. She just didn't want to see him happy with anyone else. Being a private man, Les didn't want his personal business splattered all over the tabloids, but Kirk made Nia aware that Les seemed to be so affected by what had happened with Cree that he was looking into legal ways to protect himself and his daughters.

We hesitated about telling Cree what we had learned from Kirk, but we finally gave her the information he had provided. We sat on her bed as she lay under the covers, and told her what Kirk had said. We couldn't tell what she was thinking. Her eyes were blank, and her face was dull. She took a while to process everything we told her before finally raising her head and looking at us.

"This doesn't change anything. He still lied, and I can't forgive that," she declared.

Nia and I both looked at Cree as she put her head under the covers. We both knew there was no coming back from this. Cree had always said that lying was the one thing she would never tolerate after her last relationship ended so badly due to a lying cheater.

Nia was the only one who seemed to have a positive experience happening from our convention weekend. She was still seeing Kirk, and things looked really good for them. We knew Nia was trying to hide her happiness for the sake of Cree. Finally, at lunch on Sunday, before we headed to the airport, Cree took Nia by the hand and told her that she was ecstatic about the way things were going for her and Kirk, and that she didn't have to hide her happiness. Cree was right. Seeing my friend happy made me happy, even if my own personal life was in shambles.

My situation didn't hit me again until I got back home late Sunday night. That was when I realized I was alone again. I didn't have anyone I could confide in. I had no shoulders to cry on, because I couldn't tell anyone about the secret rendezvous that I had shared with Ursula. But as the days went by, the fact that I had to deal with everything alone just made me stronger. I realized I didn't need a shoulder to cry on. I could take care of myself. I knew I would hate it if my friend's trash-talked Ursula the way we had originally talked about Les. I was glad no one knew about the affair. I didn't want anyone's opinions about what I did. I had enough opinions of my own to last a lifetime.

I was snuggled up on my couch, watching *Scandal,* which was my newest fangirl obsession. I couldn't help but admire the fact that Olivia Pope made being a side chick seem okay. Even Cree joked from time to time that she easily could have been Olivia Pope with Les.

There was an unexpected knock on my front door. I paused the DVR, refusing to miss a single minute of the show. I opened the door without looking through my peephole. My body froze when I saw Ursula standing there in a pair of jeans and a black sweater.

"Can I come in?"

I hadn't realized how much I missed her sultry voice. I opened the door, allowing her to walk into my house. Ursula walked all the way into my living room. She glanced around my apartment before focusing back on me.

"So I was leaving New York when I realized I had a layover here in Memphis. Somehow I ended up missing that flight."

"You missed your second flight? How?"

I was standing against my kitchen bar. I couldn't walk into the living room. I couldn't be that close to her.

"Okay, so I purposely missed it." Ursula smiled. "I figured I'd take the chance and come to see you."

I felt my heart skip a beat.

"You could have called."

"That did occur to me, but I didn't think you would answer my call." She sat on the edge of my couch. "And besides, I wanted to see you."

I couldn't believe she had just taken it upon herself to show up at my house. I knew the old me would have thought it was a romantic gesture, but the new, stronger me saw it as her acting so arrogant that she didn't think that I would have company.

"Ursula."

"I miss you, Temple." She stared at me with her big brown eyes. "I miss you a lot."

I felt the wrecking ball trying to break down the wall I had built around my heart. "Ursula—"

"I know that you probably find that hard to believe, but I do. I miss you. I miss what we had."

"What we *had?*" I walked closer to the living room. "Ursula, you said yourself we didn't have anything. It was just two adults having fun."

"Well, I miss that fun," Ursula whined, like a teenager trying to get her way. "You can't seriously say you don't miss it too."

She was right. I missed everything about it. I missed the way she felt against my skin and the way she tasted. I missed my hands getting tangled in her hair and the way she bit her lip when she was ready for me to taste her. But

more than anything, I missed lying in her arms. I missed
the late-night laughing and the early morning fucking. I
missed her.

"I miss a lot of things, Ursula. But what I don't miss is
feeling like I'm just a piece of meat."

"You weren't—"

"Ursula, I had some amazing times with you, and I
wasn't even able to share them with the two people who
could have helped me get you out of my system. I don't
want to be the dirty little secret that you take out of the
closet when it suits you. I'm worth more than that."

"So you really wish to say I treated you like a dirty
little secret?" Ursula snapped. I could hear the change in
Ursula's voice. She was getting angry. She stood back up.
"I invited you into my home and gave you complete ac-
cess to it. I tried to get you to stay, but you chose to leave.
I never made any promises to you that I didn't keep."

The words hit me like a ton of bricks.

Ursula went on. "You want to know why I invited you
to my room to begin with? Temple, I invited you because
I thought I saw something genuine in you. I knew you
were a fan, but there was something more there. I didn't
think you would be a person who only saw me as the
Amazon queen or a fucking Greek goddess. I wasn't going
to have you sign that bloody agreement. That was my
management who made me do it, because they didn't
know if you were legit or just a fan trying to get a picture
to sell to a tabloid. I knew you wouldn't, but I have a
brand to protect. I made the mistake of thinking that you
saw past that."

In that moment I realized just how wrong I had been.
Ursula hadn't led me on or filled my head with thoughts
of a relationship. I had allowed myself to turn nothing
into something. I wanted to kick myself for being so
foolish. She had been right all along. What should have

been just fun had turned into more for me, but that was because it was more to begin with.

"Ursula, I have admired you my whole life, and being with you was just more than I could handle. I let my love and admiration for you cloud my mind. But understand that wasn't the reason I caught feelings. I caught feelings because I couldn't believe that someone as amazing as you actually wanted to be with me."

Ursula said nothing. We didn't take our eyes off each other as we stood there in silence. We didn't know what to say to each other. The truth was out there, but neither of us knew what to do with it.

Ursula finally broke the silence. "Temple, I like you. I want to still see you. But I can't and never will be able to do more than what we were. Can we just live our lives and go back to having fun with each other when the time permits?"

I wanted to say yes. A large piece of me wanted to take her right there in my small living room, on my old couch, which probably cost less than a single pillow in her villa. I wanted to just feel her one more time. But I knew in my heart that it wouldn't be one more time. I would allow it to keep happening simply because I loved knowing that I had someone as amazing as Ursula.

"See, the thing is, now that I've experienced something so amazing, I don't want to go back to less than I truly want and deserve. I can't be your weekend lover. I want more out of a relationship, even if that means not being with you."

Ursula let out a sigh. "Impossible woman, you are."

Ursula walked over to me and reached out her hands. She hugged me. I put my arms around her, hugging her tightly.

"If you ever need anything, you have my number. Keep in touch, kid." Ursula winked at me.

I walked her to my front door. She planted a sweet peck on my lips before walking out my door. I watched as she got in the back of the town car. A piece of me couldn't believe I had let her go. But the majority of me knew it was the right thing to do.

I knew it would be the last time we shared an intimate space. I knew I'd let her go for real this time. All I had now was my memories, my signed mementos, and a dress that I couldn't wait to cosplay in.

Chapter 19

Saturday, August 31, 2013 . . .

Cameras flashed as Nia, Cree, and I stood in an iconic pose from the *Olympus* television show, along with thirty-seven other people dressed in cosplay from the show. We were the largest group of cosplayers for the show, and we had gathered together to show our support for the show's final season and for the final *Olympus* panel of Dragon Con. This year Nia, Cree, and I were surrounded by people dressed as every Greek god and goddess from the show. Some were even dressed as mortal characters from the series.

After the picture taking, we all laughed and talked about our costumes and how we had made them. Cree and Nia met people whom they had never seen before but whom they had cursed out many times for winning eBay auctions that they had bid on. Everyone looked amazing, but I had a secret weapon that made heads turn. I had the dress.

Other women dressed as goddesses were completely in awe of my dress. I told everyone that I had won it in an auction. The only people who knew where it came from were Nia and Cree. The moment they laid eyes on the dress, they knew something was up. I couldn't lie to my friends. I told them that Ursula had sent it to me as a gift. I knew they wanted more answers. After all, why would a person send such an expensive gown to someone for no reason at all? I simply said that she had promised to send it to me at dinner and she had actually come through for me.

The doors to the ballroom opened, and people started filing in, trying to nab the best seats possible. The *Olympus* cosplay group was able to secure the third and fourth rows for us. We sat as a unit to show our support and love for the show.

I knew she would be there. It had been announced months earlier that the majority of the cast would actually be attending this Dragon Con. It was a big deal to get so many of the stars at anything besides San Diego Comic-Con, which was the only convention that was known for always having A-list celebrities.

Cree grabbed my hand. I knew she had to be just as nervous as I was, or even more so. Les had tried to talk to her for months after the breakup. He had sent her flowers and presents of all kinds. He had called constantly, leaving message after message. She had wanted to respond, but she hadn't been ready. I knew that there was more to it than just being upset that he had lied. One day Cree had finally told me the truth.

"I don't think I could ever truly trust him, even if this hadn't happened," she'd told me about a month after the split. "He's the most beautiful man I have ever seen, and I would always wonder if I am the only one. I'm not a strong enough woman to be with him. I know I'm not."

It was a hard reality to face, but I knew exactly what she meant. We were fangirls, a rare breed of true fans who were devoted to the actors and the work they created. But the truth was, for every fangirl, there were thirty groupies and gold diggers at every turn. People mostly didn't understand us, or they automatically put us in the groupie category. But we never needed or cared to sleep with the objects of our fandom. We just wanted to support them, let them know that their work meant a lot to us.

Even after the whole situation with Ursula, I was still the fan I was before. I still admired her and the work that she brought to life. She was still the Amazon queen who had helped to shape me when I was a young person, and I would always love her as a person for that.

The moderator walked out onstage, causing the room to go crazy. One by one he called the actors to the stage, starting with the supporting cast. Cree, Nia, and I sat in anticipation when he got to the last three names.

"Introducing the god of war. Give it up for Aries, Kirk Mission!"

We nudged Nia as Kirk ran out onstage, holding a sword in his hand. The crowd went wild, and Nia face turned red from blushing.

"And he's the one and only Zeus. Give it up, Dragon Con, for Les Moore!"

I jumped as Cree's fingers dug into my skin. Les didn't make the grand entrance that Kirk had made. He bowed his head to the crowd before sitting down. He looked up as he sat down. His eyes went directly to Cree, and his face dropped. Cree's nails dug into my skin again, until I finally had to hit her to make her stop. They made eye contact before he pulled his gaze from her and focused it on the moderator.

"And we know her as Hera, but some of you know her as the mighty Amazon goddess. Give it up for the flawless Ursula Moore."

My heart was racing as Ursula walked out onstage. Her hair was no longer black. She had lightened it to brown with some blond highlights. She stood in one spot as the room gave her a standing ovation.

Once everyone calmed down, the moderator addressed the actors.

"Well, we are so honored to have you all here at Dragon Con. I know that Mason, Kirk, Les, and Ursula were able to experience our little freak show last year. We are surprised you came back."

The crowd and the panel laughed.

Mason leaned into his microphone. "What do you mean? I love Dragon Con. These are my people!"

The actress who played Aphrodite chimed in. "He's right. He's the biggest nerd on the planet. He has more video games than my son."

"That is true. Where is the gaming room this year?" Mason looked around the room as various guys stood up and yelled out the location of the gaming room.

"Well, Kirk, I heard you had a very good Dragon Con last year." The obviously gay moderator smiled. Kirk's dimples appeared as he began to blush. Les hit Kirk on his arm.

"That is true. I actually met the love of my life here last year," Kirk revealed.

The whole room began to swoon. Nia lowered her body down in her chair.

"Really? Yes, we heard you fell for one of us," the moderator joked. "Where is she?"

Les nodded his head. He began to scan the audience.

"Well, I tried to convince her to come backstage, but she refused. She's actually out there in cosplay with you guys." Kirk stood up and scanned the room until his eyes reached us. He smiled and pointed at Nia. "There's my little goddess."

The rest of the cosplay group was shocked when Nia finally stood up. The whole group cheered as people patted her on her back. She made a facial gesture at Kirk that indicated that she was going to kill him for outing her in front of everyone.

"She's going to kill me later." Kirk laughed.

"That has to be the most romantic thing ever. See, people? You can find love here at Dragon Con." The moderator's high voice was humorous.

The moderator then made the announcement that they would take questions. I noticed a very determined look on Cree's face.

"I'm going to ask a question. Come with me," Cree said and stood up. I noticed the way Les followed her with his eyes.

The questions were mostly dumb, as usual. Most of the questions were aimed at Ursula. She smiled and answered them, making the crowd laugh as much as she could. I could feel my body heating up with each one of her smiles. One of the first guys in line asked about the final episode of *Olympus* and how the atmosphere was on the final day of shooting. The room was silent as the panel talked about how emotional it was to say good-bye to the show.

I noticed the clock on the wall. The hour had flown by. There was still one girl in front of Cree, and I didn't know if she was going to get to ask her question.

"Since Kirk found love here, I was just wondering if any of you would be interested in trying your luck as well. Maybe you, Les." The tall, slender girl batted her fake eyelashes at Les. Cree wanted to kick the girl.

Les smiled. He looked at the girl, but for some reason, I felt he was looking through her instead of at her. "I actually did try my luck last year, but it didn't work out as well for me as it did for Kirk here." Les put his hand on Kirk's shoulder.

"Oh, well, I bet that bitch is kicking herself," the moderator said and laughed.

Les shook his head. "No, I am the one kicking myself, actually."

The room fell silent, and all eyes were on Les.

"But who knows what might happen this year? I mean, it is Dragon Con, right?" Les smiled, causing the crowd to go wild.

"And on that note, I think we are going to bring this to a close—"

"Wait!" Les yelled, stopping the moderator in mid-sentence. "This is the last time. We would like to take a few more questions."

The crowd cheered, and the rest of the panel applauded. The handler handed the microphone to Cree. The room fell silent again as Cree held on to my hand.

Before Cree could ask her question, Ursula spoke into her microphone. "I remember both of you. You are the Greek goddesses from last year, right?" Ursula glanced at me.

I took the microphone out of Cree's hand. "Yes, we are."

"Your dress, darling. That is an amazing replica." Ursula's devilish smile showed off her deep dimple. My body no longer belonged to me. I was instantly under her spell.

"It's actually the real one," I said.

I could tell the crowd was stunned by the whispering I could hear floating around me.

"Oh, wow. You must be a really dedicated fan," Ursula replied.

"I'm your number one fan." I threw my smirk at Ursula.

"I have no doubt that you are." Ursula applauded while nodding her head up and down.

The crowd applauded along with Ursula as I handed the mic back to Cree. I turned to walk away, but Cree grabbed my hand again. I stood there and watched my usually strong friend try not to lose all her cool in front of the hundreds of people in the room.

"This question is for Les." Cree cleared her throat. "Your character Zeus, and many of the other characters, had some amazing monologues during the show. I know I, as a fan, have felt many of them to my core. Well, piggybacking on the previous girl's question, Les, if you could say one thing to the girl from last year in hopes that it will get her back, what would you say?"

You could hear a pin drop if it fell in the room at that moment. Les lowered his head and then leaned into his microphone.

"Ohhh, that is a good question," Les said.

The moderator stood up and walked over to Les with his mic. "Les, if this mystery woman was sitting in here right now, what would you say to her? And, men, listen up, in case you have to say something like this one day to a girl."

Les paused for a moment as the crowd prepared to hear his answer. He looked up at the moderator, then back at the crowd.

"Talk about pressure." Les shook his head, and the crowd laughed at his comment.

Les lowered his head for a moment. Then he pulled the microphone close to his mouth. Cree's nails dug into my hand, until I had to pull away due to the pain. Les's dark eyes were fixed on Cree.

"I get to play a man who has many words, but that's all I am doing, playing a role. I can only wish to have the words that the writers write for us to say, but sadly, I don't. So in saying that, truly, all I can say is that I am deeply sorry and a day doesn't go by that my heart doesn't ache for you. I didn't realize what I had, and if I was given another chance, I would spend my lifetime trying to make up for it. If not, I will spend my lifetime regretting the mistake I made."

Oohs and aahs echoed through the room before the crowd gave a standing ovation. Cree's hands were trembling.

"I think that's the sweetest thing I have ever heard," Kirk joked, acting like he was wiping a tear from his eye.

His humor was a much-needed break from the intensity of Les's public declaration.

"That was beautiful. If that girl is in here, you better forgive this man." The moderator put his hands on both of Les's broad shoulders. "I think we are going to take one more question."

The handler gave the microphone to me. My mind went blank. I said the first thing that came to my mind.

"That last one is hard to come after, but I want to keep it simple and just say if you each had one thing to say to all your fans, what would that be?"

Each star gave a brief statement. Most wanted to thank the fans for their support of the show. Some made more inspirational comments.

"I also want to say from the bottom of my heart, thank you all. And I want to thank this amazing cast for giving me some of the best years of my life. And when you find that someone special, hold on to them," Mason said and then bowed his head while the crowd clapped for him.

I couldn't take my eyes off Ursula as she pulled the microphone close to her face again.

"There really isn't much that I can say that my amazing cast mates haven't already said. So I will say, find things you love and do them as often as you can. Life is made to be lived, and live it to its fullest!"

Kirk was next. "I would just say thank you all so much for everything. You guys rock, and I can't wait to party it up tonight. Dragon Con, you rock!" Kirk jumped up, throwing his hands in the air. His comment caused the crowd to go wild.

"And on that note, we will say good-bye," said the moderator. "Thank you again, and, everyone, give it up for the cast of *Olympus!*"

You could hardly hear the moderator's final statements due to the cheering of the crowd. The cast stood together while people took final photos. Cree and I sat there while Nia answered questions about Kirk from people standing around her. She had taken on the celebrity girlfriend role like she'd been dating celebrities her whole life.

As I watched Ursula with the others, I started to think about the final time we were together. She didn't offer me what I was used to, but I couldn't help but wonder if that was what I needed or wanted. My past relationships were playing in my head. All the women I had known had given me a traditional relationship, yet none of them had called forth the feelings I had felt in those few moments I spent with Ursula.

The room cleared out quickly when the cast disappeared backstage. We knew it would be a matter of moments before the convention volunteers started to tell us to leave.

"Okay, so do you guys want to go backstage or head out? I just need to let Kirk know what we are going to do," Nia said.

"Backstage," Cree replied, then walked off before we could respond. We followed her backstage.

"Les!" Cree suddenly exclaimed. She stood taller than I'd seen her stand in a while.

We watched as Les completely abandoned the members of the press whom he was talking to. There were no words. Cree opened her arms, and Les wrapped his arms around her. They embraced, kissing as if it was the first time. We couldn't believe it. The press was eating it up, snapping photos of the reunion.

Suddenly, it hit me like a ton of bricks. I was denying myself the pleasure I'd always wanted, just because I wasn't going to have the title of girlfriend. Ciara had given me the title of girlfriend, and it had meant absolutely nothing in the end. For almost a year I had been missing the one thing I wanted more than anything, all because she wouldn't be my girlfriend.

"Well, that's beautiful. Don't you think?"

The familiar voice sent chills down my spine. I turned around to see Ursula standing directly behind me.

"Good to see you, Temple." Ursula gave me a hug. It wasn't like her hugs normally were. It was distant and professional.

"Ursula?"

"Yes?"

I didn't know if it was the right thing. I didn't know if I would regret it in the end. I didn't care. Life was meant to be lived, and I was ready to live it.

"Can we possibly have a drink later?" I didn't take my eyes off of her. I could tell she was surprised by the invitation.

"Are you sure?"

"I've never been so sure of anything in my life."

It didn't make sense, but matters of the heart rarely did. Cree knew it would take time, but she couldn't spend the rest of her life wondering if she had missed out on the man of her dreams. I knew that anything that happened between me and Ursula would be just for fun. I didn't know what the future would hold. All I knew was that in that moment I was going to do what I wanted to do—what my mind, soul, and body wanted to do—and that if anyone should be with her, it was me.

I was her number one fan, after all.

Crossing Layne

by

Nikki Rashan

Chapter One

The first time I heard her voice, I knew I was in trouble. It was light but serious, adolescent like in tone yet confident. And her enunciation of each syllable in every word she spoke was quick but clear. She sounded out of breath, like she was in the middle of a race against a fast-paced treadmill. I heard the pounding of her feet and the whirring of the belt beneath her.

"Hello?" She panted into the phone.

I gathered my composure and prepared to speak to the woman whom, until two months ago, I had known nothing about. I hadn't known her name or her address, her age or zodiac sign. I had had no idea where she worked, where she grew up, if she was a wife, mother, or if she had siblings. I simply hadn't even known she existed.

What I did know now was that every morning, after I left for work, my wife, Layne, had called her. At least once a week they had had lunch at Le Colonial, a place I had once recommended to Layne that we visit. Layne had quickly dismissed the suggestion, as if merely speaking the words had been a waste of my energy. Now I knew why. Could she actually take her wife to the meeting spot to which she regularly took her mistress?

Her name was Nina. And she had successfully filled in the gaps in Layne's heart that I had been unable to reach, places that I had yearned to occupy but that Layne had shielded like a cocoon, protecting her unspoken feelings.

"Hello, Nina. This is Taryn."

She was silent. The breathlessness I had previously heard halted; there was the sound of a short beep and then nothing but dead air.

"Are you there?"

"Hi, Taryn. I didn't expect you to call so soon," she told me.

My head tilted sideways, and I immediately started toying with the crystal paperweight on Layne's office desk. Layne had been a professor of English at a well-known university in Chicago, where we lived. Layne had adored language; her passions had lain in words and books. On the walls of her office were shelves of textbooks, famous literary works, and history and autobiography books. She still had the first encyclopedia collection her father had purchased for her when she was a child among stacks of dictionaries; she bought a revised dictionary every year.

During our years of marriage, I had entered Layne's office frequently. I'd bring her a cup of coffee on a Saturday morning while she pored through online newspapers and magazines, or I'd wake her for bed when she had fallen asleep reading papers. What I hadn't known were the secrets Layne had kept in her office. Locked in one of the drawers of the grand wooden desk were journals she had hidden underneath school papers. She'd locked the drawer with a small gold key. I found the key in her wallet. It took weeks for me to figure out where the key belonged.

I sighed, stood up, and peeked through the cream blinds at our backyard and the inground swimming pool. The water was cloudy, covered with strewn grass clippings and drowned insects. I hadn't been swimming in two months. I pictured them there, Layne and Nina, making love against the concrete steps at the shallow end. Layne had written about the experience in a journal, one of eight I had found that recounted the last twelve years of her life. Of those twelve, she had documented seven years of indiscretions that I had known nothing about. Since Layne's unexpected death two months ago, I had learned that the woman I had believed was the love of my life hadn't had those same feelings about me. Behind my back, she had explored dark, explicit sexual affairs that I knew nothing about.

On the lined pages of the journals, in her sporadic handwriting, Layne told tales of erotic adventures with Nina. She wrote about nights they visited underground swingers clubs and engaged in voyeuristic exchanges with other couples, male and female, gay and straight. Layne wrote in loopy curves, accentuating a capital *B* or a lowercase *l* when her spirit was calm and unnerved. Her penmanship slanted when she was stressed, the ink imprinted deep into the paper. And when filled with excitement or elation, she wrote in carefree, quick scribbles, her words crossing lines frantically.

"Are you there?" Nina now asked me. I closed the blinds and returned to Layne's leather chair.

"I'm here." I hesitated with my next statement. "I'd like to see you."

"When?" Her voice left no indication of concern, as if she had already prepared herself for the day we would meet.

"Today."

"I can be there in an hour."

"Let me give you the address," I offered, as I would with any guest venturing to my home.

"I know where you live."

Of course she did.

"I'll see you then," I told Nina and hung up Layne's desk phone.

I rubbed my temples, my eyes closed. I knew that what I was doing was strange and that it was unnecessary to meet Nina. Why would I want to meet the woman who had been an accomplice to the greatest betrayal I had experienced in my life? Yet I couldn't help it. I had to meet her. She had been privy to details about Layne that Layne had not granted me. What was it about her that had allowed Layne to open up in ways she hadn't to me, her wife of eight years?

I left Layne's office, closing the door behind me out of habit. Layne had always insisted on keeping her door closed, and I had never been allowed to enter without first knocking. In the kitchen I started a pot of coffee. While it brewed, I mentally attempted to prepare what I had to say to Nina. What did I want to do? My first instinct leaned toward the hereditary blood of my father that ran through my veins. He was an abusive man; he had a tendency to kick anybody's ass at any time, usually my mother's. This thought intrigued me most, as I assumed it would any woman in my predicament. I pictured myself opening the door and punching Nina in the nose before she had a chance to see it coming, the same way my father had done to my mother on more occasions than I cared to recount.

More than anything, I just wanted to see her. The portrait Layne had scripted of Nina had begun to con-sume my every thought; I felt vulnerable to her. And for my own emotional fulfillment, I wanted an in-person comparison. In her writings, Layne had described me as a flawed gemstone and Nina as an impeccable diamond. Did she truly not have one imperfection?

Upstairs, I showered and then lathered myself with Layne's favorite perfumed lotion. Silly it might be, but I wanted a part of Layne with me during the meeting. I wanted Nina to feel like a stranger in my home and not the invited guest in our lover's arms. I wanted to take back ownership of what had been involuntarily and unknowingly stripped from me, even if it could not be tangibly reclaimed.

Over my hips I pulled on stonewashed jeans and then I donned a cream turtleneck. Despite the unexpected warm October weather—the temperature was seventy degrees—I felt cold. I brushed the silken strands of my hair into a ponytail and twisted the loose hairs into a conservative bun. On my lips I applied a clear coat of lip gloss, and then I swept mascara through my already lengthy lashes.

Back downstairs, I contemplated whether or not to put on a CD. What music best illustrated my mood and accompanied the introduction that would soon take place? Classical had been Layne's preferred genre of music. Many evenings we'd lounge in our family room while sipping wine and listening to the sounds of a gentle violin or a calming piano. Layne had relished educating me in the arts, whether it be music, theater or, of course, literature. At least I had thought she took pleasure in awakening my attraction to the creative. In reading Layne's journals, I had learned that she had grown indifferent to nurturing my cultural awareness. She had begun to resent that I had a less refined background than she had. Now I, after reading her journals, resented nearly everything about her.

The phone rang just as I was retrieving two coffee mugs from the cabinet. I checked the caller ID and saw that it was Jenna, my daughter.

"Hi, Mom," she said before I could speak. "How are you?"

Layne died on July 8, several weeks after Jenna completed her sophomore year at Spelman College and arrived home for summer break. We had just enjoyed a weeklong family getaway in the Virgin Islands, where we lounged by the ocean, the three of us bikini clad under the penetrating sun. Daily, Layne would consume her maximum intake of tropical drinks; she granted herself hard liquor on vacations only. We allowed Jenna just one drink, while I was permitted one glass of wine with dinner each night. All day long we took photos of one another, my favorite being one of Layne nestled in a hammock, peering at me over a book she was reading. Her wedding band sparkled against a ray of sunlight. She looked peaceful and rested. Her smile appeared sincere. She seemed happy. How was I to know she was a lying, cheating, deceitful wife with a hidden life she concealed so cleverly?

The Monday following our return home, I woke early for work. Layne stayed in bed, her vacation extending several more weeks. Before I left, I bent to kiss her tanned skin and tousle her short hair. She opened her eyes.

"Got any plans today?" I asked.

She repositioned herself comfortably under the sheet. "No. I'll be home. I want to finish that book."

"Good. I'll see you tonight." She went back to sleep. Or so I thought.

Three hours later I received a phone call from an officer, who informed me that Layne had been struck by a vehicle that had flipped over a median into her car in a North Chicago neighborhood. She died instantly.

"I'm sorry, ma'am," he muttered unsympathetically before mumbling additional information on Layne's then whereabouts. I was left with a trembling phone in my hand, a shattered heart, and an unanswered question: what was Layne doing miles from our home just hours after she told me she'd be in all day? I hadn't known at the time, and still had no confirmation, though now I assumed she had been headed to see Nina.

Jenna was heartbroken when she returned to school in late August, leaving me in such an overcast state. I hadn't shared with Jenna what had suddenly shadowed my spirit. She assumed my introverted demeanor was solely due to Layne's sudden passing, not the discovery of the double life Layne had been leading.

"I'm okay, Jenna. I'm okay," I told her now.

"You don't sound okay," she rebutted.

I had had Jenna twenty years ago, at the tender age of sixteen, the same age at which my mother had had me. It scared me at times, the mirrored lives my mother and I almost led. I grew up on the South Side of Chicago, in my grandmother's house, the same home where my mother was raised. My mother and father lived in the upstairs unit of the house, and I had a room downstairs with Grandma. Gangs and crime riddled our neighborhood: purses were snatched during the day, and gunfire crackled throughout the night. Young men succumbed to the seduction of their environment, while young women surrendered to the temptations of those same young men. My mother and I fell into that category.

At fourteen both my mother and I lost our virginity to boyfriends who were four years our senior, and at fifteen we each became pregnant. Grandma, who refused to allow me to become the high school dropout my mother had been, cared for Jenna during my junior and senior years so that I could finish my courses. She wanted me to "be somebody." In my family, unfortunately, the pinnacle of success at that time was a stroll across a platform stage in the gymnasium to accept a document for obtaining a minimum education.

After high school I waitressed full-time in a nearby restaurant, where, above my minimum wage pay, I'd take in tips from sweet old gentlemen who came in each day for coffee while they read the newspaper, and from hustling twentysomething fellas who wanted to give me more than just their order. In the evenings Grandma and

I would place my tips in a container box hidden in the corner of my closet; she didn't trust "big ole banks." Every two weeks I would cash my check at the local convenience store, buy an outfit or two for my growing Jenna, and save the rest. I knew then that somehow I'd escape my dark surroundings.

At twenty I met Jimmy Sharpe. Jimmy was a young alderman with dreams of mayoral service. He had come into the restaurant, soliciting, on a late spring morning. I was off that Friday but had walked over with Jenna to pick up my check. If it hadn't been for the perfect timing that day, I'm not sure what course my life might have taken.

Jenna, always an eye-catcher with her youthful, round face, cinnamon skin, and reddish-brown eyes, caught the attention of Jimmy, who was busy chatting with Chucky, the owner of the restaurant, about flyers he wanted to leave at the counter where patrons paid their bill. He was a visionary with a plan of rebuilding broken neighborhoods and saving our youth before they got sucked into the "ghetto mind-set," as he put it.

"Look at this pretty little girl right here," he had said to Chucky, pointing at Jenna when she and I left the back office with my check. "We can't have this young baby ducking and dodging bullets and unable to play jump rope outside her house. We can't have our young men locked up while our babies are having babies. It's time for us to rally up and get our neighborhoods in check. Come on, Chuck," he'd urged. Jimmy was allowed to leave his flyers.

I was about a block away from the restaurant, with Jenna's hand in mine, headed back to Grandma's, when he called to me.

"Miss! Excuse me, miss!"

I tended to ignore men who called to me, most often in terms that suggested we were more than strangers who were simply passing one another on the street. But Jimmy seemed different. When he caught up to us, he paused a moment to take in a breath while straightening his bow tie. He wore a suit, and with his oval-framed glasses, he resembled a member of the Nation of Islam community, one you might see pushing fruit and newspapers on the corner.

"You didn't take a flyer." He smiled and handed a white paper to me.

"Oh, thank you." I smiled back and then started to browse the flyer. Jimmy was part of a group of men and women looking to renovate and reopen a neighborhood center for our youth. His flyer described it as a place of refuge and safety. He wanted to present our young people with the gift of opportunity and growth, and he needed volunteers to bring his dream to life.

"This is your daughter?" He nodded to Jenna, who tightened her small fingers around my hand.

"Yes. This is Jenna."

Jenna waved bashfully, then covered her face to conceal a shy giggle.

"How old are you?" he asked me.

"Twenty."

"And how old is Jenna?"

"She's four."

Jimmy's expression softened. "So you understand our need."

I nodded without a word.

"I'll see you at the meeting, then?"

I thought of Jenna and her future. *Our* future. I thought of Grandma and her desire for me to make something of myself. I knew I could start by helping others to make something of themselves also.

"Yes."

Over the next several years my life changed dramatically. I continued to waitress while I saved money. On weekends, Jenna and I would walk to the developing center so I could help clean, paint, and organize donated supplies. For the first time in my life, outside the grim walls of Grandma's house, individuals with a passion for life and betterment surrounded me. They had the ability to see more for the woman in the grocery store with a patterned scarf on her head, walking in slippers, with a baby on one hip and another latched to her leg. They saw a person who possessed the ability to become anything she wanted to be if given the chance. I was drawn to their desire to uplift.

A year and a half after the beginning of our venture, the project was complete. Jimmy's dream was manifested when the We Are One Neighborhood Center opened its doors, offering such services as after-school care and tutoring for elementary through high school students, and recreational venues, including a small basketball court and a game room. The center operated primarily through the efforts of kindhearted and attentive volunteers. The staff was minimal, and Jimmy wanted me to be a part.

"Join us," he said one day, after we had locked up the center. "We need a front desk person. Someone as sweet as you to welcome everyone in. I'm sure we can match whatever you make with Chuck. Jenna is about to start first grade. Surely, she can come to the center after school. Come on, Taryn," he urged with the same tone he had used with Chuck the year prior. I was honored, and I welcomed the change. We Are One had been my place of employment ever since.

Jimmy and I continued to work closely together, and I began to learn the mechanics of a nonprofit organization. And as the center's programs expanded, so did my duties. Jimmy told me I was naturally gifted in business. He complimented the creative ideas I shared with him regarding new services and programs the center might offer, and he trusted my task-oriented mind to help see them through to fruition. He flattered me with praises of my ability to connect with the kids who entered our doors, some timid and shy, and others aggressive and obstinate. Though I remained fairly reserved in demeanor, with the children, I thrived. I had unknowingly found my calling.

Grandma died when I was twenty-four. She left her home and a small life insurance policy to me, which pissed my father off, as he was convinced my mother would be the beneficiary. He didn't take his anger out on me; he had never vented his frustrations in my direction, only in my mother's. As they grew older, their fights became less frequent, sparked only by events that involved money, such as the loss of Grandma's inheritance. Jenna and I took over the first floor of the home, and while I considered kicking my parents out, I didn't. I loved my mother, and at the time I couldn't bear leaving her alone in my father's hands. Though most of my life we remained distant, thanks to a cracked ceiling against a creaking floor, my heart soared when I'd catch her in moments of happiness. Her smiles sprouted like sporadic rainbows after a storm. You didn't expect them, yet nonetheless you marveled at their beauty.

One day two years later, when I was twenty-six, Jimmy and I were preparing the conference room for a meeting with the board of directors. That evening we expected three new members in attendance, all of whom Jimmy had met and whose bios I had typed and prepped prior to their arrival. There was Benjamin Thompson, a personal injury attorney, Marcie Wells, a real estate agent, and Layne Jackson, an assistant English professor.

Layne's profile stood out the most, particularly her statement that she wished to be a part of an organization that helped individuals who had grown up less fortunate than she had. I had studied her photo, a professional shot of her in a navy business suit, and I had wondered how differently this thirty-year-old's life was from mine. She wasn't attractive or unattractive, yet she was strangely alluring, nonetheless. She had a full, round face, large, heavy eyes, and a flat, but straight nose. Her lips, wide, pouty, and shiny, led to her smile, which I felt was her best feature. She had the straightest, whitest teeth I had ever seen. Her relaxed, confident expression exuded happiness and enthusiasm, sentiments I rarely saw in any adults aside from Jimmy.

I was still in the conference room, alone at that moment, when Layne arrived first. Jimmy had retreated to his office to take a call prior to the meeting. I was in the rear and had just poured myself a cup of water before I planned to go greet attendees at the front desk.

"Hello," she said with my back to her.

"Hi," I replied, startled, spilling a few drops of water. I turned around and went to shake her hand.

"Layne Jackson," she told me.

"Taryn Dawes."

She peered at me, as if attempting to extract my thoughts via telepathy. I stared at her too, though I learned later that we had been intrigued for entirely different reasons. Layne tried to analyze if I was interested in her, while I was more curious about her background. I had asked Layne over the years why she felt I could have taken a liking to her in five seconds' time. She had assured me that attraction was instantaneous; it was there or it wasn't. We had never agreed on that topic, as we hadn't on many.

"What do you do?" she asked.

"I work here."

She appeared surprised; her expression shifted to curious. On board meeting days I wore something from my usual casual wardrobe. She eyed my above-the-knee black skirt and white blouse and then studied my shoes.

Understanding swept over her face when she realized my black pumps came from a low-end department store, in contradistinction to the designer heels on her feet. She nodded subtly, but I caught it.

"What's it like to work here?"

"I love my job. It's a wonderful feeling to give to the community and to help these kids." My response was shorter than I preferred as it looked like Layne had already lost interest in my answer. "I read that you're a professor," I stated, turning the attention to her.

"I am." She shrugged casually, a weak attempt at modesty, not a drop of which, I eventually discovered, existed in her list of qualities.

I checked my watch. We still had six minutes before the meeting officially began, and though I wanted to greet members up front, as I always did, Layne's arrogance aroused me in an unfamiliar fashion.

"Tell me more," I said.

It was as if Layne had committed her speech to memory. She rattled off her life résumé, first informing me that she was born in a wealthy and prestigious Chicago suburb. As a child, she already knew she wanted to follow in her mother's footsteps and enter the field of education. Her father, who had then recently retired, was a successful managing partner with an insurance company.

Layne attended private school and excelled in her courses, receiving honors and awards in English. She prided herself on winning her first spelling bee at age six. At twelve, she ventured into sports. She was a talented member of her school's volleyball team, and in high school, she was the star player on the softball team. She received both her undergraduate and graduate degrees from well-known schools on the East Coast and had been back home in Chicago for the past three years, pursuing her doctoral degree in education. All those details Layne spewed in the matter of four minutes. When she finished, she stood straight and proud, as if awaiting my applause.

One might think I would have found Layne intimidating, considering the severe differences in our backgrounds, hers in the upper class and mine in the poverty-stricken streets of South Chicago. If anything, I became more intrigued. She was unlike anyone I had ever met.

"You've been fortunate, Layne. You'd be an inspiration to the kids at our center. I look forward to you serving on our board," I told her sincerely. I checked my watch again. The after-care program down the hall would be closing soon, and I needed to grab Jenna. "I have to get going. I'll see you next month."

"I hope so." She smiled.

The following month Layne again arrived early. We chatted in the conference room, and that time she inquired about my background. I felt comfortable with her and opened up to her about my experiences growing up with Grandma and the abusive nature of my parents' marriage. I told her how I met Jimmy, and informed her that I had a ten-year-old daughter, who, like Layne, had a fondness for reading and English, her favorite subject.

A few days after the meeting I received a package at the center. Inside were two books. The first was for me, an impressive and thoughtful fictional story about a young mother who overcame the adversities of her upbringing and soared as a successful businesswoman. The second was for Jenna, a Mark Twain classic. When I called to thank Layne for the gifts, she invited me to lunch. After lunch, she asked me to dinner the following night. Then she wanted to have lunch the next day and dinner once again. I had no idea Layne was flirting with me. I didn't recognize her gentlewoman behaviors as anything other than kindness. She opened doors for me and helped me order from exotic menus at the restaurants we visited.

She surprised me with a pair of strappy summer heels with the same designer logo as hers.

Over a two-week time frame she introduced me to my first spa, for a massage, manicure, and pedicure, my first taste of wine, and my first Broadway-style musical in the theater district downtown. Before Layne, my life and my world had centered mostly on a five-mile radius on the South Side of Chicago. Maybe I should have known she was courting me, but I had nothing to compare her actions to. I had never seen a man woo a woman. My boyfriend-girlfriend experiences were limited to frequent walks to fast-food joints, followed by trips downstairs to a basement mattress, when I was fourteen and fifteen.

I had had sex with a few neighborhood men before I got pregnant with Jenna. Though Grandma loved me as my primary caregiver, no one in our house, especially not my parents, concerned themselves with my whereabouts, and I was able to come and go as I pleased.

It was Marcus with whom I enjoyed sex the most. He was the only guy who slid his tongue between my legs before sliding his curved penis inside me. Secretly, I had always hoped he would skip penetrating me, because the only thrill I received was when he held what he referred to as my "pearl tongue" between his fingers and sucked and licked with his fat tongue. I hadn't been intimate with anyone since Jenna was born, and although I knew same-sex relationships existed and women did exactly what Marcus had done to me, I was oblivious to the fact that Layne was pursuing me.

I didn't consider this possibility until Ms. Sheila, an older woman who volunteered at the center and cared for Jenna when I needed a sitter, suggested it to me as I prepared for another evening out with Layne.

"That woman is liking you," Ms. Sheila told me in a tattletale tone.

"Layne? What do you mean?" I picked up my purse and retrieved my lip gloss to do a reapplication.

"She's a homosexual, honey. Don't you know who the homosexuals are?" Ms. Sheila eyeballed me behind her bifocals.

I laughed. "Ms. Sheila!" I didn't know what else to say.

"I have a surprise for you tonight," Layne told me after I got into her car and settled into the cream leather seat.

I smiled like a schoolgirl. No one had ever taken such time and energy to make me feel special the way that Layne had. She drove us to her condo near Lake Michigan, where we had a catered candlelight dinner on the balcony overlooking the water. It was one of the most spectacular moments of my life.

"This is beautiful," I told her. "I don't want this night to end."

Layne gazed at me, her dark eyes flashing a delicate brown against the light. "Would you like more wine?"

I was already buzzed, though I told her I wanted another glass. She poured. It was the only time she granted me more than one drink.

"Taryn?"

I sipped. "Yes?"

"Will you dance with me?"

I giggled. "Sure."

She stood up and reached for my hand. She pulled my body to hers and placed her other hand at the small of my back. I inhaled quickly. She was so close. She was so warm. I was so intoxicated by both her and the libations.

"There's no music," I pointed out.

"We don't need any. Just move with me," she instructed. Layne moved slowly, her linen pants pressed against my cotton summer dress. We fell into a silent groove. Her thighs guided my thighs left and right, ever so gently. I closed my eyes, laid my cheek on her shoulder, and rocked with her sway. Her grip tightened.

No one had ever held me so affectionately. Or held me so tenderly. Not my mother or father, and not even Grandma. Jenna clung to me like a child did to a mother. I was her security. I was her protector. I was her warrior. The kids at the center hugged me every day; I was their support when no one else was there for them. But Layne's embrace was different. Layne held me like she loved me. I didn't know what that love and affection felt like until that very moment. It was surreal. I almost started to cry. But then I laughed.

"Layne! Layne . . ." I said, slurring. Then I laughed. "Ms. Sheila said you were one of the homosexuals!"

Layne chuckled and pulled me into a tight hug until both our giggles subsided. Slowly, she released me and planted a kiss on my forehead. Another, then another on my nose. And a fourth on my lips. She pulled away to look at me. In my flats, we were the same height.

"Does that prove Ms. Sheila right?" she asked.

I didn't respond, too enamored by the tingles her lips had left on mine.

"Come inside."

Layne led me to her oversize sectional and laid me down. I melted into its comfort.

"Taryn . . . ?"

"Hmm?"

She straddled my hips and bent to kiss me again. "You know I really like you."

"You do?"

"Yes."

I stared into her yearning eyes. "Why?"

"Because I do," she stated firmly and then kissed my neck.

"Okay."

I closed my eyes again as she devoured my skin with her lips. My body responded instantly. I was aching, like an adult woman being made love to for the first time. Layne sampled every angle of my body with her mouth, and when she lifted my dress to touch me where no one else had since I was a teenager, I nearly passed out. The feeling was foreign. It was neither my own hushed middle-of-the-night fingertip exploration nor streams of warm water from the detachable showerhead nozzle while I sat on the edge of the tub. It was real. It was fascinating. It was dizzying. And the deeper she went and the faster she moved, the more I knew she liked me. Just because she said she did.

That was ten years ago, and over the years, when Layne told me she loved me and I asked her why, she never gave me a different answer. She simply repeated, "Because I do." I accepted that because I wanted to believe her. I went along with it because I didn't know better. I surrendered to it because I had never known what real love was supposed to feel like.

"Mom?" Jenna said now, pressing.

I grabbed a wooden serving tray, placed the mugs on it, and poured my and Nina's coffee. "I'm here."

Jenna sighed. She was concerned.

"Don't give yourself a headache worrying about me. If it comes down to it, I'll book a flight and come see you in a few weeks." I hoped to pacify her.

She laughed lightly. "I'm not eight anymore. You can't appease me so easily."

I laughed in return. "I wouldn't lie to you. If I need to get away, you'll be the first and only person I go to, okay?"

"Okay. Hey, maybe we can catch a new movie while you're here. Or go shopping, hint, hint," she teased. Only, I didn't laugh with her. From the kitchen window I saw a black car winding its way slowly up our curved driveway. She was here.

I rushed Jenna off the phone. "Jenna, honey, I have to go. I'll call you later."

"Are you okay?" Her tone exhibited worry again.

"I am. Don't worry. Talk to you later." I hung up before she could reply.

The Mercedes parked outside the front door, and through the tinted windows I could not see her. The car idled for minutes. I wondered if she was contemplating leaving. Perhaps she felt just as crazy as I did at the prospect of meeting the wife of her dead lover. What was the point? What did we have to gain?

I turned my back to the window. If she left, maybe it was for the best. She could be saving us from sharing mournful sob stories about Layne. Two strangers united to grieve the death of the woman they both loved. How pathetic.

I was almost expecting to hear the tires squeal as the Mercedes drove off in the opposite direction when, instead, the doorbell rang. It was a light chime, pleasant and welcoming. At that moment, though, it sounded more like a strike of lightning had pierced the home, cleaving it in two. My heart jolted. I smoothed my hands over my jeans and then my hair. I exhaled deeply before walking through the family room to open the front door.

When I looked at Nina for the first time, I knew why Layne had loved her. She smiled weakly. I softened. It seemed Layne had been right all along.

Attraction really could be instantaneous.

Chapter Two

Her name is Nina. We met today through the dean of science and mathematics. When I looked into her eyes, it was like I took my very first breath. . . .

Nina and I stood for a moment, I, uneasy and suddenly awkward.

"May I come in?" she finally asked.

"Yes." I stood aside, and Nina walked in.

She wore a lightweight, classic black trench coat, which was buckled tightly around her waist. I wondered if she, too, felt the same solemn chill I did. She looked about the foyer and toward each room connected to it. Her eyes seemed to take in all that was familiar, including the photos on the mantel in the living room to the left, and the crystals in the curio cabinet to the right. She peered toward the family room, down the hall, and finally at the looming staircase behind me, which led to the master suite. It seemed that Layne had intentionally barred Nina from the upstairs master suite. I had found no evidence in Layne's writings that suggested Nina had been in the most personal haven of our home. Was that some form of respect? With all the lies Layne had told—with the lie she had lived with me every day—did it even matter that they hadn't slept in our bed?

Nina gazed back at me.

"Let me take your coat," I offered.

Nina removed the trench coat to reveal a solid black, fitted dress with a plunging neckline. Her breasts, round and small, were braless; her nipples, pronounced through the fabric that clung to her skin. I imagined them, brown, firm, and erect, pinched between Layne's clenched teeth and fingertips, or squeezed by metal clamps, as she had described in the journals. On Nina's feet were recognizable black stilettos, an obvious gift from Layne, as I had the exact same pair in my closet. It was like a long-distance slap from the grave. The first of many, I guessed, though I had willingly invited the assault.

I hung Nina's coat in the foyer closet. "I made coffee," I told her.

She took a step forward toward the kitchen before I could, and then stopped, realizing the inappropriateness of her action. I moved in front of her. She paused while I retrieved the tray from the counter, and walked behind me to the table. We each took a warm mug before we sat next to one another, I at the head of the table, she at my right. She stared into her coffee without moving.

"Cream and sugar, yes?" I murmured and went to the cabinet. We remained silent while I scooped spoonfuls of sugar and poured creamer into the set. Now that she was here and now that I had seen her, I tried to calm the complicated feelings that swirled within.

I brought the small porcelain set back to the table and placed it in front of her. Though I usually preferred condiments as well, at the moment black coffee seemed most fitting. A few more moments passed before I spoke.

"Layne kept journals. Years of journals." I looked out the window and then back at Nina. "That's how I learned about you."

She acknowledged my statement with a slow nod and looked out the window herself. "I didn't know about you," she confessed.

My eyebrows rose, and my breath stopped. I had received another sharp slap from the dead. Layne had cheated on me for seven years, and as absurd as it might sound, I hadn't even been given the honor of being mentioned?

"She waited," Nina continued, her words accelerated, her thoughts conjoined into long run-on sentences. "She waited until I began to question why she couldn't stay the night and why she didn't accept my calls during late hours and why she seemed to disappear for extended periods at a time. Then she told me she had you, a wife." Her expression dimmed.

"You stayed, anyway," I stated. I questioned, really.

Nina sensed my agitation. She warmed. Small red blotches formed just above her breasts and crept like paint splatters up her neck and spilled into the cheeks of her oval face. *When she blushes, it's like a dozen roses blooming. . . .*

"I did," she acknowledged.

"How long had it been?"

"Two years."

Two years with no recognition and then only when cornered. *Ouch.* I was insulted again.

We stared at one another. Her appearance and demeanor matched that of her voice, gentle but intense. She sat in a professional manner, erect, her bare legs crossed, which, I assumed, was natural for her given her high-powered position as director of the Office of Communications and Marketing. Her wide forehead led to the smooth edges of her black and wavy shoulder-length hair. She wore it in no particular style, though it was wildly in place. Her ebony eyebrows and long dark eyelashes contrasted with her neutral makeup. I was curious if her brown eyes really did darken when she was serious and reveal hazel glints when she was excited, the way Layne had described.

"I know," she said in response to my exposed feelings.

"You know what? What it's like to be cheated on for seven years? No, you don't know."

"Actually, I do," she said, disagreeing with me. "I know what your shoes feel like."

"So if you've walked in my shoes and you know how much it hurts, why would you torment someone in the same manner?"

"It wasn't planned," she told me softly. "Like I said, for two years I didn't know Layne had you and had a family."

"And yet you both betrayed me for five more years."

"That's true," she admitted. "If it helps, Layne and I weren't in love. I loved her, yes. I loved the way she made me feel, the energy and excitement we shared, and the sex." She almost smiled. A dimple on each cheek became imprinted and then quickly vanished, as if she realized her ill-timed flashback of sex with Layne was impolite. "It was you she loved, Taryn," Nina offered. "I know she did. She talked about you and Jenna all the time."

My body flinched at the way Jenna's name so casually flowed from Nina's mouth. I was, again, instantly aggravated and next frustrated by the uncontrollable medley of emotions that kept surfacing in her presence. I could imagine that over seven years Layne shared details about our life with Nina, but again I felt slighted. Bitter that I was an invisible shadow to their union, only an attachment that silently loomed behind their every move.

Nina leaned forward. Our elbows touched briefly before I drew my arm away. The ripples of irritation began to subside due to her nearness. She smelled so good. Like the aroma of the sweet and sweaty deepest sensual part of her had been dabbed behind her ears and between her breasts. With each inhale I took, her scent clouded my thinking. No wonder Layne had been powerless against her.

"I suppose you don't want to hear that from me," Nina stated.

"Look, Nina, don't bring Jenna into this. She has no idea about you and Layne. I haven't the heart to tell her."

Nina almost appeared offended, as I had been earlier, when I learned Layne had not mentioned me for two years.

"I understand." Nina sat upright once again, resuming a stiff, composed position, though I noticed small beads of sweat glistening around the mound of her cleavage.

Her body is warm and sweaty, her skin wet and slippery against mine, when I fuck her from behind.

I saw them in my mind, Nina's body spread and exposed, her arms bound with rope, her legs wide while Layne thrust a dildo deep into Nina's ass, satisfying the voyeuristic pleasures of the onlookers they entertained.

"Is there anything you'd like to know?" she inquired.

"Yes. I want to know why you couldn't find someone else to have sex with. Why you continued to choose another woman's wife."

I feared her answer, although I already knew what it was. It was Layne who couldn't let Nina go, not the other way around. Layne was putty to Nina and to the lifestyle Nina wanted for them. It had taken no coercion or sweet talk; Layne had accepted Nina's invitation without resistance.

Why hadn't Layne sought those pleasurable intimacies with me? Even before Nina, my and Layne's lovemaking had been one-sided. She hadn't allowed me to reciprocate the simple pleasures she delivered to me. From what I had learned over the years, and particularly through reading Layne's journals, our sex had been tame. It had been mild and inflexible. Though I had hungered for her body and had craved to delight her in any way she wanted, she had seldom requested anything of me. If I asked, I was usually denied. I had begun to feel like her set of encyclopedias. I was there for her to marvel at and to run her fingers across, to open and tour at her leisure, satisfying her thirst to explore, only to be placed back on the shelf to admire until she once again felt the urge. I hadn't known that for most of our partnership she had been dedicated to Nina, whom she explored freely, fervently, devouring her like a book she never wanted to end.

"I doubt that any answer I give will suffice as a justifiable explanation. There's nothing I can say that will make all of it okay. I know that."

Internally I agreed. I was disgusted by their deceit, mostly by Layne's disgraceful behavior. In hindsight, I realized she had told me multiple lies every day.

"How was lunch with your fellow professors?" I'd ask her. She'd respond with an elaborate tale about how one or the other was doing, when in actuality, she had spent lunch fucking Nina in one of their offices, in a car, or in the bathroom of a restaurant. It seemed they thrived on being watched, and if they were not, they thrilled at the mere possibility that someone might see them.

"How's Sandy doing in class?" I would ask her. Layne always had a student who needed her help in the evenings. It could have been Herman, Matt, Melissa, or Jane. It didn't matter. They *all* requested her guidance. She was preoccupied a couple of nights per week, returning home only when I was already lying in bed with a book.

"So-and-so is still struggling," she'd explain while she undressed in the walk-in closet. I learned that in truth, those were the nights she and Nina went to after-work social and happy hours at swingers clubs. Sometimes they would sit and watch other couples engage in sexual activities, and other times they would strip nude and participate in orgies. When I thought about the level of deception and the length of time it had gone on, I hated Layne, and I wanted to hate Nina, except I didn't. As she sat before me, I had to admit that Nina was every adjective and metaphor Layne had described. It pissed me off and intrigued me at the same time.

"No, there's nothing you can tell me to make this all right," I told Nina. We fell silent again. I was suddenly uncertain about how to continue the conversation.

"Well, I knew you'd find Layne's journals, and I knew you'd call me. There must be something you'd like to know," Nina continued.

"She told you about the journals?"

Nina stared once again out the window, toward the oak tree on the side of the house. The journals were yet another piece of Layne that Nina had been granted access to and I had not.

"Yes, I knew. She told me she chronicled almost everything about us."

"What else did she tell you? About her, about me, and about our family. I was with Layne for ten years. Why couldn't she confide in me?" My voice rose and trembled with anger toward Layne. I slammed my palm against the table. "Why didn't she take me to the fuck fest places she took you?" Finally, I had grown irritated, like any betrayed woman should be from the start. Nina almost appeared satisfied. Her bottom lip suddenly dipped inward, as if to conceal a smile.

"What exactly do you mean?"

"I mean, it seems like the two of you weren't engaged in just sex. It's like you were her confidante. You, not me, were the one woman she worshipped above anyone else."

Nina lowered her gaze. Her long, thick false eyelashes created brief dark halos beneath her eyes.

"I do believe you've misinterpreted what Layne and I had," she told me.

"I read the journals. I read every thought she had about you. You . . ." I struggled to come up with the proper comparison. "You were her Aphrodite."

She smiled generously. "And you were her beloved Hestia," she explained, as if we had discovered the answers to my questions about Layne. "We fulfilled two different needs in her. Don't you see that?"

"No, I don't see that. Because in real life she committed herself to me. She committed herself to taking care of me and Jenna."

"She did that. Layne was meticulous about ensuring you and Jenna wanted for nothing," Nina affirmed.

"She should have been that particular with my heart." I sipped my now chilled coffee.

"Taryn, I think you and I both know Layne wasn't devoted to anyone's needs more than to her own. Sure, she'd make sure you had the best. She'd always make sure she had better."

Nina was correct. There had rarely been an occasion over the ten years I had known Layne that she hadn't utilized to recognize herself, even celebratory moments for others. Even during our courting stage, Layne had shown signs of the preferential treatment she bestowed on herself, and it outweighed her generosity toward me.

When she treated me to my first theater experience, the show wasn't a well-known production. Though I was mesmerized by the costumes, the singing, and the dancing, the musical was second-rate. The week after, she and her parents saw a play that had been sold out for months, well before its arrival in Chicago. Layne had even trumped me with our wedding rings, mine a 3.5-carat emerald-cut solitaire, hers a 4.0-carat. I never minded Layne's personal extravagances. As a woman who grew up without even one concert attendance and only costume jewelry, who was I to complain?

"So, what? Are you the *better* that she treated herself to?" I asked in response to Nina's comment.

Nina placed a pecan-colored hand on mine. Her skin was warm. I didn't move away that time.

"I'm not better than you, not in any way," she said, trying to comfort me.

"This still makes no sense," I blurted, unable to understand Layne's betrayal, Nina's presence next to me, and why I liked her touch.

"Right now I know it doesn't. Maybe in time it will," she offered.

Nina's words were no consolation. I had hoped she could offer details about Layne that I hadn't known. My most pathetic of inquiries was whether or not Layne had ever truly loved me. Even though Nina had promised that Layne did, I realized it proved nothing. Nina could declare that Layne cherished our love and commitment, and still that made no sense given the fact that Layne cheated on me for seven of our ten years together. She could have deceived me for the rest of our lives, and I wouldn't have known about it. The only solace I had was I had read every single page of each of Layne's journals, and her last entry was the only hint that her years of double-crossing might have been coming to an end. I wondered if Nina knew what Layne had written the night before she died.

"Nina, when was the last time you talked to Layne?" I asked.

She hesitated before she spoke. Her breathing seemingly halted once again, as it had when I stated my name on the phone with her that morning. Finally, she sighed, and my stomach began to tighten with nervousness.

"She was on her way to my house when she was hit by the car." Nina's voice shook as she spoke, her tone suddenly unsteady and her words seemingly uncertain. "I've felt so guilty for so many reasons. For having the affair in the first place, for taking her away from your family, and if it weren't for me, she'd still be here."

She bit her bottom lip to control its shaking. A tear fell from each eye and created identical droplets on the wooden table surface. With the answer to that one question, Nina had flipped from abetting mistress to guilt-ridden sinner. Was I, the pained, confused widow, supposed to console the fascinatingly beautiful philanderer at my side?

I had to admit, I couldn't control the pendulum sway of emotions that dominated my being while she was there. I wanted to despise her and be repulsed by her presence, though silently I was intrigued by all that she might be able to offer me: an after-the-show, behind-the-scenes peek into Layne's curious obsessions and passions. Maybe at the same time Nina would lead me to the unwritten climax of Layne's story: the vacant journal entry she had yet to write. The one she would have written in oversize, loopy penmanship, as her spirit might have been lighter and freed at that point.

"Nina, I'm afraid I forgot about something I must tend to," I told her. "I would, however, like to see you again, if that's okay with you."

Like piercing sun rays through clouds on a dim day, golden glints sprouted throughout her dark brown eyes. "Yes. I'd like that."

We both stood. I tasted her, that musky part of her, through the breeze in her movements as we walked to the foyer. I retrieved her coat, which she draped in the bend of her arm. The house seemed warm once again, no longer swirling with chilly, melancholy memories of the dead, but rather the heated thrill of a chase to solve an unsolved mystery.

Nina abruptly turned to face me before she stepped outside. The skin above her top lip perspired lightly. "When should I expect to hear from you?"

"Soon."

The left side of her open mouth twitched, and an anxious grunt escaped her lips. She covered it with a delicate smile. Her eyes, still highlighted by light bronze speckles, revealed her piqued interest. "Yes, soon, okay.

As odd as it may sound, it's been a pleasure to meet you, Taryn." Nina stared into my eyes. "You are exactly as I had imagined."

"Have a good day, Nina." Slowly, I began to close the door, forcing her to step outside. I wasn't yet prepared to confess that she was everything I had imagined and dreamed about so many nights after reading Layne's journals.

"Same to you."

Nina took the five concrete stairs carefully, the horseshoe-shaped muscles in her calves accentuated with each step. With the front door closed, I watched her through the peephole. The lights on her Mercedes flashed when she unlocked the door via remote. Nina opened the door wide, tossed her coat onto the peanut butter-colored leather of the passenger seat, and sat sideways in her own seat before placing her right and then left leg inside, graceful and trained, like she had attended etiquette school. She retrieved black sunglasses from the overhead built-in holder and placed them over her eyes before she started the car and closed the door. I could no longer see her through the heavy tint of the windows. Slowly, she drove away, exiting opposite the entrance to the half-moon-shaped driveway.

I turned around and leaned my back against the door. After several minutes of internal debate about what to do next, I returned to the kitchen and retrieved my cell phone from the counter.

"I need to see you," I told him when he answered.

"I'm always available for you," he responded.

"I'm on my way." I hung up the phone, then took the stairs to my bedroom, where I grabbed Layne's journals. I stuffed them all inside a tote, snatched my car keys off the dresser, and left my suburban home for the South Side of Chicago.

Chapter Three

He was the only friend I had, and next to Jimmy, he was the most significant man in my life. Layne hadn't known about him. I had not mentioned the friendship in order to protect him, not in an effort to deceive Layne. To guard his identity, our meetings remained in the neighborhood in which I grew up.

I drove the dusty, busy streets of some of Chicago's most dangerous communities until I reached my destination. I pulled into the near empty parking lot, which would be congested with everything from old Cadillacs to shiny new BMWs on Sunday. The smell of freshly cut grass greeted me when I exited my Jaguar with the tote bag of Layne's journals in my hand. I admired the perfectly lined grass edges as I walked to the large, front doors made of bronze-tinted glass.

Inside the air was fresh, as cleaners were prepping the church for services the next day. I headed toward the pastor's office. His assistant, Cassandra, was making copies at the large printer.

"Ms. Dawes, good to see you. He told me to let you right in."

"Thanks, Cassandra."

She led first down the short hall to his office. A large painting of him hung just outside his door. She knocked, opened the door, and closed it behind me after I stepped inside.

He stood up from the leather chair behind his desk, dressed in light gray pants and a matching vest with a blush-pink oxford shirt underneath. His presence was an attention grabber. He was noticeable at six feet four, he was still fit from his former track days, and he always dressed in expensive tailored suits. His thick black hair had begun to gray around the edges over the past year, whitening since the day Layne and I took Jenna to Spelman for her second year. Ron had sat across from me, Jenna, and Layne in a restaurant as we had brunch the morning before we left. He was just another patron at the restaurant to my family, an elegantly dressed man at our side. Only I knew the reason he sat at a nearby table, sipping coffee with one of his deacons.

"Taryn," he called as he walked toward me. He greeted me with a firm, full kiss to my cheek.

"Hi, Ron."

"Here." He pointed to one of the seats in front of his desk.

Ron and I had reconnected nine years prior, after ten years of silence. He had been a tricky young man, too handsome and clever for his own good. He had never fallen prey to the streets of our neighborhood, because he had been too busy preying on girls and women.

Ron had known at the time that I was pregnant with Jenna. He had seen me once as I entered my third trimester, my stomach round and swollen like a bubble. I had bumped into him at the corner store on a run to buy Grandma a bottle of vinegar for the douche bag she left hanging in the bathroom. Ron had had his arm wrapped around the shoulders of Sade, a bubble gum-popping junior I went to high school with. He left her at the counter and approached me as I searched the shelves.

"I see you knocked up." He took a swig of the pop Sade had just paid for.

I rubbed my belly. "Yep."

He cocked his head sideways. "So who's the daddy?"

I had wanted to throw every bottle of vinegar at his head after that question, but that was too much like my father and I knew better.

"It's your baby."

He peeped over his shoulder to be sure Sade hadn't overheard. "You sure, shorty?"

"I was only with you when I got pregnant."

He rubbed the stubble on his chin. "All right then. Let me know when you pop. I'll bring some milk and bottles and diapers and shit. Cool?"

I accepted Ron's offer, but I was too shy to follow up with him after I gave birth. One day, when Jenna was three months old, I was sitting on my front porch with her on my lap. She was drooling and her small, delicate fingers were balled into wet fists when I saw Ron turn the corner onto my street. He was driving a Pontiac Grand Am, a hand-me-down from his parents. With his window rolled down, he and one of his buddies, Eddie, peered at me and Jenna sitting on the creaky wooden porch. Ron held up his first and second fingers in a "V" peace sign formation and rolled past us without a word. After that, I never saw him on my block again. Grandma had insisted I didn't need "that nothin' boy," anyway.

He became a pastor at a young age, when he was thirty-one, and it was soon after that that I stumbled upon him in Jimmy's office, while they discussed how the church could be of service to the community center and vice versa. Initially, he didn't recognize me, but I knew who he was, and as the father of my beloved Jenna, I saw her features in his face instantly. As the three of us talked, I noticed his demeanor quieted and he stared at me intently. He broke into an uncontrollable cough the moment he realized who I was.

He was relieved when Jimmy told me I would be in charge of developing the program that would serve some of the troubled youth in his congregation. He handed his business card to me. "Please call soon," he requested, urgent desperation in his voice. Because of the center's partnership with the church, my meetings with Ron had never come off as questionable or suspicious.

Ron was head pastor of one of the largest, most influential churches in the city. He had married a woman slightly older than him and had a family of his own. No one had ever found out that Ron had fathered a child as a young man, at least no one aside from Grandma, my parents, and the two of us. I had never sought any aid from him, and even if I had wanted to early on, I wouldn't have known where to find him. By the time we met again, I was with Layne, living the same high-class lifestyle that he was.

During our first one-on-one meeting, Ron delivered a plethora of apologies. He explained that he hadn't forgotten about me and Jenna and had often wondered how we were. I showed him pictures of Jenna, which brought tears to his eyes. He immediately began sending monthly payments to me, which I kept with the inheritance I had received from Grandma. Ron assured me he would assist me in any way, but he never offered to meet her. We decided to keep Jenna the secret she had always been. Ron, still a new pastor, with a toddler and a newborn at home, feared the repercussions should he bring a bastard daughter into his home and church family.

It might have been selfish to withhold the identity of Jenna's father from her and from Layne, but I acquiesced to the fact that Jenna never seemed to miss having her father in her life. And when Layne and I moved in together, we agreed that we would be the only parents Jenna could ever want and need.

"How is she?" Ron asked, referring to Jenna, as I sat across from him in his office now.

"She's doing fine. She's settled comfortably back at school."

"Let me see a picture."

Whenever I saw Ron, he always wanted to see the most current photo of his daughter, or he would ask me to play a voice mail from her so that he could hear her voice. I used my cell phone to show him a picture Jenna had sent to me via text, one of her and her sorors dressed in pink and green, with erect pinkie fingers. He held my phone in his hand and stared at the screen.

"Glory to God, she gets more and more beautiful." He placed his hands behind his head and leaned back in his chair. "How are you holding up?"

"I'll show you." I opened the tote bag and placed the stack of Layne's journals on his desk. "These are Layne's. Twelve years of her life are documented right here. I found them after she died, and I've read every single one."

Ron looked at the stack, his breath held behind tightly pressed lips. "Pandora's box," he said, exhaling.

"You said that right. This morning I met the mistress she had been cheating on me with for the past seven years unbeknownst to me."

I assumed that as a pastor, Ron had been privy to the confessions of those who had coveted their neighbor's wife, and I thought little would shock him. And yet his gaped mouth and furrowed eyebrows displayed surprise.

"Layne had an affair you never knew about it, and you met the woman this morning?" he asked, repeating what I had just told him.

"We had coffee in my kitchen."

"Are you crazy?"

"Maybe," I admitted. "I had to meet her."

"Why?"

4

"The way Layne described her, she is the epitome of beauty and sex and all things womanly. This was no normal affair they had. The things they did, and the places they went . . . I don't think I know the woman that I married."

Ron placed his forehead in his palms. Each gold and diamond pinkie-finger ring left imprints on his skin when he lifted his head back up.

"Taryn, I'm sorry. Certainly a person like you didn't deserve that kind of treatment. Seven years? Not to come off callous, but how did you not know?"

"Hindsight is twenty-twenty, right? With all her late nights out and not answering calls, I should have suspected something, but I never did. It was too convenient for them, anyway. They saw each other every day at work."

Ron sat forward in his seat. "She works at the university?"

"Yes. Nina is her name."

"Jesus, Taryn." Ron coughed and reached for the bottle of water on his desk. "I don't know what to say," he said after taking several gulps. "I can't imagine how you feel."

"I found the journals two months ago. I was hurt. I was mad. I cried every day for weeks."

"I wish you had reached out to me. We could have prayed through this. God is a healer."

"Yes, I know, and I hope He's forgiven me for taking matters into my own hands." I picked up Layne's last journal from the pile and opened it to her last passage. "I can't let go of what she wrote the day before she died." I handed the journal to him. He picked up a sleek pair of black- and red-framed glasses, and he began to read.

Layne had written this passage midway through our vacation, during an afternoon when Jenna and I had gone inland to shop. In it, she detailed the closeness she had felt to me and Jenna during the ocean dinner cruise we attended the prior night. Both Jenna and I had worn lightweight gowns, and Layne a white pantsuit. After dessert we had walked on deck, arms linked together, and we each had wished upon a star. Layne had wished for peace and forgiveness.

Eerily, Layne also wrote that she was tired of leading a double life. *It hurts to hurt those I love,* she wrote, pressing hard, making deep indents into the page. Yet in the next sentence she stated that she didn't want to let either of us go. She wrote that she adored Jenna and indicated she'd be more devastated if Jenna uncovered her betrayal than if I did. And still, she continued, she couldn't imagine her life without Nina. And finally, simply, she documented that she loved me. Even in her most personal writings she didn't explain why.

Perhaps it was her confusion—the seeming sudden rupture of the stitches that held her dual lives together—that had somewhat appeased the anger, agony, and resentment that had mounted in me with each journal I read. I had wondered, after I closed the last book, if maybe her weariness had led her to make a decision. I couldn't help but speculate that she was preparing to end her split life, only which relationship she might have ended had remained unwritten. It was the idea that maybe she would have chosen me over Nina that lingered about my heart, and although I hated Layne most days, in some way her last journal entry had soothed the hurt, even if it was like nursing open heart surgery with a Band-Aid.

"Not that it'll change the past at all, but I want to know who she would have chosen, me or Nina."

"Why?" he questioned, confused, his hands in the air and shoulders shrugged. "Even if she was going to leave Nina and recommit to you, does it matter after all those years of deceit?"

He had a point. Layne had already gotten away with her infidelity. To imagine that even if she had chosen me in the end, I would have been oblivious to her acts—and to the fact that she had loved someone else for over two-thirds of the time I had known her—sickened me. But Layne was dead, and her only chance of redemption was a posthumous profession of love for me.

"Yes. It would help me in some way to believe she really did love me, after all. Even though I'll never have the chance to know what it feels like for her to love me totally and completely, I would know that at least she wanted to try. That for once she chose me over herself."

"And you think Nina can help answer that for you?"

"Maybe she can, or maybe she can't. I have to try."

"What about you? Does she describe you in the same ornate way she describes Nina in all these?" He tapped the journals, opening and flipping through the pages of a few of them.

Layne's earlier journals, the ones penned prior to her affair with Nina, were less detailed. She documented her transition from the East Coast, her home, to Chicago after receiving her graduate degree, along with the pressure and intensity of earning her PhD. Regarding me, she noted that she had become a part of the board at We Are One, and stated that she had met a "nice young lady who is nothing like me."

"Her descriptions of our dating phase include none of the loving, delicate metaphors and similes she devoted to Nina," I answered sadly.

He leaned back again. "This sounds crazy. You may uncover some things you may not want to know."

I placed a hand on top of the journals. "What could be worse than reading, in her own words, my wife's profession of her love for another woman?"

His eyes, the color of a russet canyon at sunset, the same shade Jenna had inherited, appeared sad and distressed. "I don't want to see you get hurt further. It's obvious what this Nina is capable of. She couldn't possibly mean any good to you or for you, Taryn. You should leave this alone."

"I can't."

"You mean you won't."

"Just tell me you support me."

Against his honest feelings, Ron gave me his blessing. "If you need me for anything, just call. I'll be praying."

I placed Layne's journals back inside the tote. "Thank you. I will."

Ron hugged me tightly, his body temperature warm through his clothing. "May God bless you," he whispered.

On my way out, Cassandra handed me a card with the names, addresses, and phone numbers of five boys and five girls from their church. Ron must have had her prepare the list as a cover for the real purpose of my visit.

"Pastor wants to know if these kids can volunteer at the annual fund-raising game," she explained.

"I'll be in touch first thing Monday," I told her before leaving.

I was close to home, having just turned left on the smooth tar-black road of our upscale community, when I saw a black Mercedes about a quarter of a mile in front of me. Red brake lights struggled to shine against the fall sunshine as the car halted in front of my driveway. The tires turned right, and the car disappeared behind the tall, orange and yellow leaf-filled trees shielding the drive. I sped up, my heart banging against my chest as I raced to meet Nina's car just as she was parking in the same spot she had that morning. We exited our cars together.

"Nina," I said, unsure about what had brought her back, and nonetheless thrilled that she had returned.

She stood before me, her fitted black dress clinging to her body like her own skin. Her emotions showed: red spirals circled her damp chest like a spider-spun web. "I thought of something, something I didn't mention earlier today, that maybe you should know."

My head dipped to the right, and I readjusted the tote on my arm. "About Layne?"

"Yes. About our conversation the morning she died."

"Come in, please."

Nina followed closely behind me as I walked up the stairs and into the house. She observed the tote bag I held.

"Is that them?" she asked anxiously, softly.

We stared at the stack of journals, the newest journal on top, less tattered, worn, and dingy than the ones beneath it.

"Yes, these are Layne's."

Nina stared into the tote bag, her expression solemn and intrigued, her mouth flat, her eyes wide, as if attempting to extract the words from the pages.

"You took them somewhere? Has someone else seen these?" Her calm tone faltered slightly.

I didn't want to tell Nina that someone other than the two of us and our dead lover knew of their affair. Especially with that one person being Jenna's father, the man whom Layne had known nothing about.

"I went to the park to read. Sometimes I reread them to see how I missed what was right in front of me," I replied accusingly.

I also didn't want to confess to Nina that I had become obsessed with the journals, and enchanted with and drawn to her before we even met. By the time I had finished reading about year three of their relationship, I no longer had the desire to burn the pages I read, but instead I had curled up on the couch or in bed with the journals day and night, seduced by Nina through Layne's words. It was absurd and embarrassing, and yet it was true.

I set the tote bag down on the table in the foyer and took off my coat. Nina's eyes lingered in the direction of the tote.

"Come," I told her and led her into the family room, to the couch. We sat comfortably facing one another. "What happened to you and Layne the morning of the accident?"

"Before Layne died, I had a feeling she was going to end our relationship. Before you all went on vacation, she told me she didn't think she could do it anymore, said she couldn't grow old loving two women in her life."

It hurts to hurt those I love. . . .

Nina went on. "She told me that in my office, and the look in her eyes wasn't convincing that it was me she wanted. The morning she died, she called and said she needed to talk to me. I assumed she had made a decision while on vacation with you."

"What exactly did she say?" I wanted to know. Maybe Nina would solve the mystery sooner than later.

Nina clasped her fingers together. Her thumbs twiddled and circled over and under one another. She spoke rapidly. "The truth is, I had taken the day off because we were supposed to spend it together. Her tone seemed off, she was not her usual self when she called, and she didn't seem to be interested in the plans we had previously made for the day. She told me that you had just left for work and that she needed to talk to me. That's all she said. I told her I'd be waiting at home for her, and she never showed. I knew not to call her when she was late or didn't show, so I didn't know of the accident until the next day at school."

Nina slowly moved forward until our knees and shins touched. I fought to keep my eyes off the skin of her exposed thigh.

"What would have happened when she got to my condo, I'll never know. *We'll* never know," she added, as if she was mimicking me, as if she experienced the pained craving I had inside to understand what felt like Layne's last will and testament of love to one of us. "Maybe, Taryn, there is something for you and me in all of this," she suggested.

"Such as?"

Nina explored me with her eyes. She reviewed my feet, a small seven against my long legs. She studied the crease of my jeans that accentuated the triangular shape that led to the place that ached for attention. Finally, she met my gaze once again, and I saw in her eyes the look I had both yearned for and feared.

"I think you're a good person, Taryn. Better than me and Layne, actually, and I'm sorry for what we did to you. I'd like to make it up to you."

I snickered involuntarily. "How can one make up for seven years of lies?"

"I'm not sure I can fully heal the hurt you have. But I'd like to be there for you in any way I can. If you let me."

She's irresistible, as enchanting and sinister as the sweetest forbidden fruit. . . .

"Yes, okay. I'd like that," I answered, surrendering foolishly, but still aware of my actions and intentions.

She smiled delicately. "So you will be calling me, then?"

"I need to visit the university next week," I replied. Layne would soon be honored with a memorial, an honorary plaque that would hang in a hall at the school, and there was some paperwork I needed to return. I had decided to return the forms in person. "I would like to visit you then," I told her.

"My office? I'd love that," she responded. She rose. "Until next week."

I stood next to her. "Until then."

We walked to the front door, I behind Nina, inhaling her fragrance as it swirled in front of me. She left the house, and again, I watched her enter her car and leave my property. I absorbed the quiet, the lifelessness of the house, as I had most days since Layne's passing. I was alone again. Since Jenna had left for school, there had been no one to talk to, no one to laugh with or watch a late-night movie next to on the couch. Mostly, there had been no one to hug or kiss or to satisfy my womanly desires. I felt lonely and in need. I went back for the tote, dug for the journal I had read more than the others, and returned to the family room.

I inserted a CD of old songs that brought back intense childhood memories. It was the music my mother and father would play the evenings he planted a kiss on my mother's cheek over a fist. Sometimes after Grandma went to bed, I'd creep up the back staircase to their unit and watch my mother on her hands and knees while my father thrust into her from behind. Over the music I could hear her scream, but then she'd smile her extraordinary smile, and I was happy. Unlike the usual embarrassment I felt at those particular flashbacks, in that moment I felt only a connection. I felt the rush of their passion—pain masked by frenzied lust. I was indeed my mother and father's child.

Standing next to the couch, I removed my turtleneck and lowered my jeans until I was able to step out of them. I unsnapped my bra, took off my panties, and then released the bun that held my hair together. It fell down my back. I lay on the couch and opened the journal to a page I had folded over. That page began an entry in which Layne documented one of her and Nina's sleaziest, most passionate exchanges. I had read the scene many times, as it had become one of my many favorites.

I envisioned a crowd of men and women surrounding a metal table upon which I lay, my arms bound above my head with chain-link cuffs. I was completely naked, as Layne had been, my legs spread, my moist middle ready for Nina. With my first and second fingers, I patted my stiff, swollen pleasure spot the way Nina had gently swatted Layne with a leather flogger. Layne, skeptical, had doubted Nina's ability to bring her to orgasm in that manner, but Nina, focused and skilled, had proven Layne wrong. Up and down Layne's body, Nina flogged softly and forcefully, bringing Layne to shivers. My hips rose from the couch, my body hungering for Nina's slaps against my breasts, my waist, and my wetness. I screamed at climax, the way Layne had described her own cry of ecstasy, curious if I had become my own sadist, inflicting both pain and pleasure upon myself.

Chapter Four

"I never liked her."

Next to me sat Ms. Sheila, in her early seventies now and still a volunteer at the center. She was expressing her disdain for Layne while we both sat in Jimmy's office the following Wednesday. We had been discussing my wish to leave early for the day so I could go to the university.

Ms. Sheila was a wide-hipped woman who covered her full-figured body with colorful dress-like smocks and sweatpants every day. On her feet she wore white orthopedic-style shoes. Her daily attire was most fitting for a day-care center or nurse intake role. Today she had on a red Mickey Mouse print.

"She always came in here acting so proper and arrogant, like she couldn't stand to touch the table or sit in the chairs, and snubbing everybody, like we were beneath her. Lucky you're a pretty girl, Taryn, or I doubt she would have looked twice at you."

"Sheila, I think that's enough. A bit inconsiderate, don't you think?" Jimmy squinted his left eye, while the right opened wide into an awkward, intimidating stare behind his glasses, a tactic he artfully used on disruptive kids to quiet them. Ms. Sheila shrugged her meaty shoulders like she didn't care but said nothing further.

"Layne was very good to the center while she served on the board. She was wonderful with Jenna too," he affirmed. I noticed he had omitted me from his statement. "Thanks for letting me know you're taking off early. Never a problem."

I stood to leave, and just as I reached the door of his office, he addressed me again. "Taryn, Cassandra called and asked if there was room for the list of kids she gave you to volunteer at next Friday's basketball game. I didn't know you and Pastor Ron had a meeting." He shot me the exact bullying gaze he had just dished out to Ms. Sheila.

The list. How had I forgotten? After Cassandra gave it to me, I had tossed the piece of paper in the tote bag with Layne's journals and hadn't thought about it again.

"Yes, we had a short meeting Saturday afternoon."

"On the weekend?"

"Yes. I had come to the center to grab something I forgot in my office when I remembered Ron had mentioned kids volunteering at the game. Because I was on this side of town, I went by the church."

"I was here Saturday. I didn't see you." His right eye stretched open even farther.

"Oh, I was in and out so fast."

"What time?"

"Around one," I said.

Jimmy acknowledged my lie with a low grunt.

"I'll arrange it all and reach out to Cassandra and let her know there's room for the kids. Thanks," I said, then hustled out of his office before he could question me further.

I wondered if Jimmy had ever noticed Jenna's resemblance to Ron: their matching brown hue, their stunning reddish-brown eyes, their similar mannerisms, even though Jenna had grown up without Ron's presence. When Jenna laughed, she released the same loud bellow from her belly as her father, and both of them rocked and slapped their right knee when elated. Had Jimmy figured out Jenna was a mini, female replica of Ron?

At my desk, I logged off of my computer and retrieved my purse and keys. As I approached Jimmy's office while exiting from the rear of the center, I overheard him still in conversation with Ms. Sheila, who had remained in his office. I slowed and listened outside his door, where they couldn't see me.

"No matter how you feel about Layne, there's no need to mention this to Taryn," he told her in a hushed tone.

"I'm telling you, that woman wasn't good enough for Taryn. She may have had all the money in the world, but that don't mean a thing with a hollow soul."

"It's too late to be bringing this up, don't you think? Let it go, Sheila. We're talking about a dead woman. Let her widow live the rest of her life in peace."

"Okay, but it's hard to look her in the face these days, knowing what I know."

"It would be harder if you broke her heart."

I bit my bottom lip while tears warmed my eyes. How many people knew of Layne's secrets? I wiped my eyes, lifted my chin, and walked past his office.

"See you tomorrow," I called to both of them, without slowing my strut or glancing inside.

Inside my car, I questioned how Ms. Sheila could possibly have any inside information about Layne's indiscretions. They lived in two different realities, worlds apart. If Ms. Sheila had had information regarding Layne's betrayal while Layne was alive, wouldn't she have told me? We had never been best friends, but we'd been close enough over the years at the center that, I wanted to believe, she wouldn't have knowingly watched my wife betray me. Was I the only one who had been naive about the dynamics of my and Layne's relationship, she the queen, free and reigning, and I her pawn, limited in mobility? What would they think of my actions now if they were aware that I had befriended the woman who had made love to my wife for seven years without my knowledge?

After I parked in a visitor stall inside the university parking structure, I walked past what used to be Layne's assigned space. It had been granted to someone else now, a Ms. Pierce, the sign read, and her conservative Ford Focus rested where Layne's flashy 735i used to sit. It was the place where she and Nina had daring sex right under the nose of campus security and against campus policy.

I walked toward the main campus hall, where both Nina's office and the office of Charles Henry, the faculty dean, were located. Layne's former office was several blocks across the campus, in the English building. It was now my understanding that a couple of times a week, rain or sunshine, one of them would trek to the other's office, where they would either have sex or connect or confirm their evening plans at a secret location. They never sent text messages or e-mails; the only written documentation of their affair lay in Layne's journals.

I was walking down the hallway in the direction of Dean Henry's office when suddenly both he and Nina appeared after exiting another room. They headed toward me, in conversation with one another, leather portfolios in each of their hands, which suggested that they had just left a meeting. The expressions on all three of our faces altered when they saw me. I bit my bottom lip, my worst nervous habit, unsure about whom to greet first. The smile on Nina's face flattened, and the grin on Dean Henry's lips disappeared, flipping to form a sorrowful curve.

"Taryn," he said as we approached one another. When we stood face-to-face, he reached for my hands, held them in his, and kissed my cheeks. Dean Henry was old. He was fragile and pink faced, with sparse white hair. I imagined that before the wrinkles, in his younger years, he had been handsome. "How are you doing?" His aging blue eyes showed concern.

Nina stood still next to him, fascinating in an azure dress with a squared neckline. Her breasts again sat high, like two ripe apples awaiting my bite.

"I'm okay, Charles. Thank you," I answered. "I wanted to bring the papers for Layne's memorial to you." I reached inside my briefcase and handed a manila folder to him. He flipped through the pages quickly, his face dented with wrinkles as he read. He closed the folder.

"Looks good."

"Layne would be so happy to know the school will be honoring her."

"Of course. She was one of our best." His voice cracked. "Did you come all the way down here just to drop these off?" He checked his watch. "Come to my office. Let's chat awhile. This here is Nina Nelson." He turned to Nina. "I do believe you were a friend of Layne's, correct?"

Nina cleared her throat. "Yes, yes, I did know Layne," she answered and then looked at me with her hand extended. "I'm so sorry for your loss. . . ." She paused when my hand rested in hers. "Your name again?"

"Taryn. Layne's wife." I shook her hand hard.

"Come, ladies." Dean Henry walked in front of me and Nina as he headed into his office. Behind him, she and I glanced at one another briefly before we sat on the love seat near the back of his office, which seemed more like a mini library, with shelves of books and comfortable seating. Dean Henry sat in a matching single chair to my right.

"How are things at the center?" he asked.

"Well, thank you. Seems like we continue to grow with each year, thanks to the support of so many in the community and throughout Chicago."

"It's been some time since Layne sat on the board, but perhaps the school could make a donation on her behalf." He opened his portfolio and jotted a note on the yellow pad.

"That's a generous offer. Thank you."

"It's no problem. Nina, how well did you know Layne? I thought I saw the two of you together from time to time. Or maybe it was this old man's eyesight playing tricks on me." He gave a throaty chuckle at his corny jest.

Nina responded with an exaggerated laugh, her breasts jiggling. "Oh, Charles, you are a funny guy. About Layne . . . yes, we met years ago and became good friends, and I agree with what you said earlier. She was one of the best."

I turned my head to Nina, annoyed by her sly implication, and her eyes met mine. She continued talking.

"Layne was incredibly dedicated to the school and to the students. She talked about her love for teaching all the time."

Charles's head wobbled in agreement. "She would work the longest hours. Her students meant the world to her."

"She was focused on giving all that she had to what was important to her," Nina said, chiming in again. "Her late hours . . . You know, she never wanted to leave anyone at the school dissatisfied."

"You seem to have known Layne well. Funny she never mentioned you to me," I interjected.

Nina grinned. She appeared happy that I had acquiesced to playing the private game she'd started. She waved my comment off with the flip of her wrist. "I'm certain that wasn't intentional. I mean, why mention a friend at work? There wasn't much to tell."

"She talked about work at home a lot." I turned to Charles. "She adored you," I told him. To Nina, I said, "I know the names of all the people she was close to here at the university, and still, you are unfamiliar."

"Interesting. Surely, there were no secrets with us," she teased. "I'm glad you came today. I just remembered there's something of Layne's in my office. It's a pen, one she said she treasured. She left it just before . . ." She paused for emphasis. "Before the accident. Come to my office. I'll give it to you. Charles?"

He waved a hand in our direction. "Oh, sure. You two young ladies go ahead."

We all stood.

"Again, so good to see you. You'll receive information regarding Layne's memorial from Beth, my assistant, via mail," Dean Henry told me.

"That sounds great. Thanks," I said.

"I'll get back to you, Charles, on the meeting we just had," Nina told him on our way out. "This way, Taryn."

I followed the heel-to-toe click of Nina's shoes to the end of the hall. Her office was tucked around a corner to our right, cove-like. One would have thought it was a janitor's closet were it not for the nameplate on the door.

The air in her office was warm, despite the swirl of cool air that blew in from the crack of a window. Nina closed the door behind me. Her space had minimal detail. Her walls were sparse, with nothing other than framed accolades in her favor. Behind her petite desk were a few shelves of books. There were no personal pictures of her with family or friends. It was nothing but a bare-bones, polished, crisp, clean work space with one window. Outside, a concrete path less than five feet away connected the buildings to the left and right, and the main atrium stood straight ahead.

"Do you see that woman right there?" Nina asked me.

We stood at the office window while she admired a woman walking across the courtyard. She walked alone, carrying a warm drink in one hand, her smartphone in the other. She was tall, with fluffy, layered blond hair that bounced with each energetic step. She wore black-rimmed glasses perched on a thin nose. Her lips, colored burgundy red, stood out.

"Who is she?"

"Her name is Amber. She's the only woman I would have given up everyone for." Nina turned to face me. "Everyone."

"By *everyone* you mean Layne?"

Nina turned back to Amber, catching her backside before she entered an adjacent building. "Yes. Remember when I told you I've been in your shoes? I ran miles in them for her. We used to be a couple. We had an undercover, secret relationship, and she refused to come out of the closet, with her family name and all. She gave in to the pressure to settle down and marry, and I didn't know that about three years into our relationship, she began seeing a man. Even when I found out, I stayed with her." Nina sighed. "Everyone has their weakness, Taryn, and she's mine."

"Did Layne know about her?"

Nina took a seat behind her desk. "Yes, she knew Amber and I were once a couple."

"Did the three of you ever . . . ?" I didn't finish my question, afraid of what she might say.

Nina frowned. "No, we didn't. I would never share Amber with anyone else."

"Layne's gone, so is there any chance the two of you can be together?"

She snorted. "Are you kidding? Charles loves me, but he doesn't love me that much."

"Excuse me? I don't understand."

"Amber is Dean Henry's granddaughter."

"You had a relationship with his granddaughter, and he doesn't know about it?"

Nina shook her head from side to side. "To this day, he has no idea that his cherished Amber is the love of my life." She fiddled with a lone piece of paper on her desk. I took a seat in front of Nina as she reminisced, her eyes lowered to her desk.

"Amber is the one who introduced me to voyeurism. During our time together we were monogamous, but she loved to watch and be watched. I fell in love with it from my first experience. There's nothing like it. You'll see."

"How are you so sure about that?" I asked, though I did not doubt her words. She ignored me and continued her story.

"Once she got engaged, she ended our relationship, but she didn't want to let go of the sex. I was devastated, but I agreed." She lifted her eyes to me. "I needed something else to do, and I needed somebody to occupy my time, so I pursued Layne intentionally to make Amber jealous."

"Did it work?"

"No. Amber thought it was cute, my desire to make her feel like she was missing out. She continued to flaunt herself in front of me and taunt me with her presence. Still, after all these years, she can call and I'll drop anything."

"So you're still friends? More?"

"We have lunch every couple of months in my office." Nina grinned.

I understood and wondered how many women besides Layne and Amber had laid their bare asses across Nina's desk. "Did Layne know?"

"No. That's one secret I kept from Layne. She didn't know Amber and I were still intimate. You know, Taryn, I would have chosen someone else had I known Layne had a wife," she confessed, thoughtful for a moment.

"Yes, well, that's neither here nor there, is it? What's done is done. Anyway, I take it there's no pen." We were opposite one another, she still behind her desk, leaning forward with her palms flat, exposing a small gape between her breasts.

"There is no pen, no," she confessed. "I had to get you out of there sooner than later, or Charles would have had us in his office all afternoon." Slowly, she walked around her desk and sat on it in front of me. "Plus, you came to see me, not him."

I stared into the alternating bronze and brown mutations in her eyes. "Yes, I did. So tell me . . ." I walked to the window and looked out at the students. A few were sitting on benches with open books and chatting with one another next to the waterfall. Some sat alone with their eyes closed, headphones on the ears, while others walked back and forth between buildings. "How did you do it? How did you two manage not to get caught with so much activity all around you?"

"It wasn't always easy. There were some narrow escapes, times when we had only seconds to get ourselves together. It was dangerous, and that's what made it exciting." Nina's desk creaked as she got up to stand behind me at the window. "Once, I was standing exactly where you are, blinds up, everyone right outside this window. For those who walked past, it appeared that I was simply looking out at the space, enjoying the view. No one could see that Layne was on her knees behind me, tossing my salad, as people like to say," she told me casually.

My stomach turned, and my throat tightened around the acid that rose to the back of my mouth. I didn't know what had gotten into me. Maybe it was the conversation with Jimmy and Ms. Sheila, combined with Nina's sideways antagonism, but I had begun to hate Nina, and I hated her more with each second that ticked by.

"It was a game. It was fun. It was a constant test of our limits and what we were capable of. I smiled at a female student as I came that day, and she had no idea."

I turned to face her. "That's disgusting."

"Is it? I don't think you really believe that, not by the glow of excitement I see in your cheeks." She studied my face, mistaking my flushed agitation for foreplay. Her face had brightened in hue as well. "Look, I know that everything about this situation is unusual. Bizarre, even. You and Layne, me and Layne, and now you and me. Tell me again. Why are you here?"

"I'm here to figure out why my wife couldn't love me the way she loved you," I answered, with half the truth.

"I thought we were getting past that, Taryn. And you might want to rephrase that question and ask yourself why your wife didn't fuck you the way she fucked me." She stepped closer. "Isn't that what you want to know? Why night after night she chose me over you? Even Charles knows she spent more time here than at home."

My right hand twitched involuntarily. I had always been one to maintain control of my emotions, and even in my moments of deep aggravation, I had never acted impulsively. That quality of passivity I had inherited from my mother. In that moment I could feel the shedding of those layers, to reveal another part of me.

Nina searched my face for an indication of my thoughts. I showed nothing. That skill I had learned from my father. He had never allowed my mother to know if a punch was on its way. I balled my hand into a fist to control the spasms.

When I didn't answer her, Nina returned to her desk and removed a handheld mirror from one of her drawers. "Come here and tell me what you see."

I walked over to her and stared at my usual reflection in the mirror, touching the strands that led to the bun at the back of my head. Layne had cherished my hair like a young girl would the synthetic strands glued to the vinyl scalp of her Barbie doll. My hair was long and straight, and nothing more to me than a reminder of my partial Native American heritage. I had wanted to cut it many times, but Layne would never let me.

"What do you mean?" I asked Nina.

"Look at yourself. Tell me what you see. Tell me *who* you see."

"I see myself."

"Anything else?"

What did she want me to say? "No," I answered impatiently.

"That's the problem, then. That was both your and Layne's problem. I see otherwise."

She handed the mirror to me and stepped behind me. She removed the bobby pins that carefully held my bun in place. It unraveled, like a loosened ball of yarn, and then she released the band that held all the hair together, slowly tugging it down my back. She spread her fingers against my scalp, rubbed aggressively, and shook my hair, creating a longer version of her own sporadic strands.

"Look at yourself. You're wildly beautiful. Don't you know that? There's more to you than what meets the eye. I see it, even if Layne didn't. I want you to do something for me."

"What?"

"Let go."

"Of?"

"Let go of the woman you think you are, and release the alter ego you have inside. She's in there," Nina commanded. "We all have one. I do, and your wife sure did." She walked to the window, closed it, and lowered the blinds.

She taunted me as she walked back to her desk. "Are you really a woman who lets everyone walk all over her, who lets her wife fuck somebody and then come home and lie next to her? What kind of weak woman does that?"

Nina laid her body flat against the wooden surface of the desk and lifted her dress above her waist to reveal bare, panty-less hips. I inhaled the scent that radiated from between her thighs and became light-headed. In front of me Nina blurred into two and then three clouded figures, and her hungry eyes multiplied and crossed one over the other, staring at me with desire and provocation. My skin prickled, from the follicles in my scalp down to the soles of my feet. Inside my chest, my heart pounded louder than it ever had, its drum sound clogging my ears. I couldn't see and I couldn't hear properly, but I could breathe, and it was heavy and hard.

Layne's journals suddenly rushed to me, the words hammering against my brain, smashing my outer shell, cracking and breaking it to reveal the storm inside. I tried to resist the energy that poured through my veins and electrified my skin, but I couldn't. I felt alive. The air engulfed my skin and heightened my sensitivity. I walked toward Nina and ran my fingertips along the desk. Its grain sent sensations from my hand, up my arm, and into my chest. Onto the desk I crawled, my coat grazing Nina's bare legs. She turned her head to the left and buried her face in my hair. She inhaled the strands that swept across her face.

Beneath me, her eyes were low, her eyebrows relaxed, and her lips wet. I wanted to taste their sweetness as Layne had described. I kissed her, and her mouth was warm and salty with sweat.

With my right hand, which was still pulsating, I stroked her thighs, gripping her creamy skin between my fingers. I whispered delicious words in her ear and bit the lobe tightly between my teeth. I grazed her neck with an open mouth, leaving her to guess where I would bite next. I rested at her jugular, sucking at it and digging into the skin around it. She winced in pain. I asked Nina if she liked it. She muttered yes through clenched teeth. In hushed, fast-paced words, she sputtered her delight. She moaned with pleasure and murmured my name repeatedly. I lost myself. Every kiss, every lick, every grope, and every bite became more forceful.

Without warning, I thrust fingers into her, which her body enveloped anxiously. I moved fast and hard until Nina was a blur underneath my body. With my left hand around her neck and the other penetrating her deeply and aggressively, I showed her that I was in control and that I wasn't the weak woman she and Layne thought I was. That I could be just as intentional in hurting the woman next to me as Layne had been each night she crept into bed with me after having sex with Nina. I squeezed tighter and thrust harder until I became dizzy with exhaustion, and still I didn't stop.

In my mind I replayed every lie and every deception and released my pain on to Nina. For every time they made love behind my back, I dove deeper, my fingernails clawing at her sensitive insides. For every unanswered call, late lunch, and missed dinner, my grip became stronger. Only when Nina's sounds changed from moans to gasps for air did I slow my pace and then release my fingers from her throbbing tender space. I stared into her fearful eyes and felt vindicated. Inside and out I smiled, the same smug smile my father gave to my mother when he dared her to respond to his actions. Nina's face was the color of cranberry, and her eyes were glazed with unfallen tears. She had both her hands around my wrist, and I realized I hadn't yet loosened my hold around her neck. I clutched the ridges of her throat once more and then let go.

Nina grabbed her neck and rolled over and coughed, inhaling and exhaling with effort to regain her breath. It took several minutes, but the color in her face returned to its golden-brown hue, and she finally calmed and took in air at a controlled pace. Her eyes, now dry and light with hazel glints, looked at me.

"Yes," she muttered, her voice strained and ragged, a perverse grin on her lips. "Yes, I knew she was in there."

Above Nina, I smiled, wiped my fingers across her chest, and then lifted myself off the desk. I straightened my coat, picked up my purse, walked to her closed office door, and placed my hand on the knob. I imagined my hair was a tossed mess, damp with sweat around the edges, and I didn't care. I opened the door, breathed in the cool air about the hallway, and left. As I, flushed and in disarray, passed well-dressed employees of the university, I continued to smile to myself. Whoever I was becoming, my mind was both fascinated by, and afraid of, what she was capable of.

Chapter Five

Layne hadn't allowed me to drink often. When she was alive, I would partake in libations with her and her friends, all a bunch of uppity, pretentious men and women who celebrated their successes through raised glasses of Dom Pérignon during private yacht parties or in a secluded room in Chicago's upscale restaurants. Even at those events where Layne and her counterparts inhaled drink after drink, Layne would always restrict me to just one.

Even at Layne's repast, which had been as stuffy and stiff as her friends, I had found myself abiding by Layne's rules, limiting my intake to one glass of wine, although I had craved more. At that time I had still loved Layne and had wanted to honor her and represent her properly from six feet above. Her friends had been gracious, kind, even, paying attention to me for the first time. I wondered what those friends would think if they knew of Layne's truest feeling about them, how she had scrutinized their careers, their homes, their clothing, and the schools their children attended. Layne, with her superiority complex, had defamed her counterparts, though they had done nothing but adore her. They, like me, had been clueless about the person Layne really was.

I was in the master bathroom Jacuzzi, listening to an R & B and rap station, which Layne would have scolded me for if she were alive. As further retribution, I was sipping my second glass of full-bodied red wine. I leaned back

against the bath cushion and closed my eyes, remembering how diligently I had wanted to follow Layne's wishes
for her funeral. She had documented every detail with
her attorney in advance, unbeknownst to me, and I was
merely handed the paperwork the day after she died.

We held the service at the funeral home of a wealthy
friend of hers. Everyone in attendance wore designer
dresses and expensive suits. It was a boring service,
nothing like the spirited funerals I had attended as a child
for family members of my father. Layne's parents spoke
about her upbringing and the successes she achieved
from grade school until she died. Jenna and I talked
about our family life, reading from a script Layne had
written herself. I learned that every two years she had
provided her attorney with a revision.

Layne had selected which family members and friends
would be allowed to speak. There was no allotment for
anyone else to express their grief. The only moment
they had was just before the service ended, when all the
attendees walked to the front to say their final good-byes
to Layne's closed casket.

My eyes shot open, and I sat upright in the bubbly
water. "She was there," I whispered.

I remembered seeing her now. She'd worn a simple
black dress, with a veiled hat covering her face. Nina had
stopped and rested her hands on the white casket before
kissing it. Then she had turned and glanced at me and
Jenna through the lace, and her eyes had darted ahead
when my eyes met hers.

"Un-fucking believable."

I picked up the wineglass and threw it across the stark
white bathroom. Dark burgundy droplets splattered the
wall, and glass crashed on the floor. I grabbed the bottle
off the ledge of the tub, turned it upright over my lips,
and swallowed until it was empty. I couldn't believe Nina

had had the audacity to attend the funeral. But, after she had fucked Layne for seven years, should I have expected anything otherwise from her?

My phone rang, disrupting my thoughts.

"What?" I answered angrily.

"Oh my God, Mom. What's wrong?" Jenna sounded panicked.

"Nothing."

"You sound mad."

"I am."

"About what? Are you okay?"

"Enough with the questions. I'm fine, all right? I'm relaxing in the tub with wine."

"Have you had more than one glass of wine?"

I became more agitated. Even my own daughter had been trained to maneuver Layne's puppet strings in her absence. "Is it your duty to monitor my drink intake?"

"No, it's just that I know how you get when you drink."

"Is that so? Tell me, how do I get?"

"Well, Layne once told me that you act like Grand-mother when you drink, and that's why you're allowed only one glass of wine."

"Excuse me? When did she tell you such a lie?"

"Years ago, Mom. You had fallen asleep one night after dinner, and I was helping Layne clean the kitchen. She told me how Grandmother had gotten into a lot of trouble with Granddad one night after drinking too much. She told me you were the same way, flirting with one of her friends after too much wine. She said in order to keep us a family, you weren't allowed to drink more than one."

"And you believed that shit?"

Jenna was silent for a few seconds. In twenty years she had never heard me curse. When she was a young child, I had refrained from using poor language around her.

As Jenna got older, Layne had forbidden me from using profanity in front of her.

"I was, like, twelve years old," she went on. "I didn't have a reason not to believe her. Plus, I remember living downstairs with Grandmother and Granddad, and if drinking is what caused their fights, I wanted to make sure that didn't happen to you and Layne."

I knew which story Layne had told Jenna. My mind backtracked to when I was age nine. It was the first and only time the police had been called on my father after a night of partying gone wrong. They had been out with my aunt Chelon, my father's sister, celebrating her boyfriend's birthday. My father, apparently, had perceived my mother's friendliness toward this man as excessive and unnecessary. Why did she have to hug him like that? Did she have to sing "Happy Birthday" so loud? She must have wanted to fuck him, the way she was smiling at him all night. These rhetorical questions and allegations I heard as my father punched and kicked my mother on the floor above me. I was lying in bed, hugging my favorite doll, when my mother eventually came screaming into our kitchen downstairs. Grandma, who normally "stayed out of grown folks' business," even that of her abused daughter, had already called 911, and by the time my father came banging on our now locked door, the police were at the front.

Grandma had advised me to stay put in my room, but I was curious despite my fear. Although Grandma might have saved my mother from hospitalization or even death, I watched my mother, in hysterics, curse and fuss at her mother after my father was handcuffed and taken to the county jail. With a warming black eye and an oozing bloody nose, my mother insisted my father hadn't meant any harm, and pleaded with Grandma for bail money. She whined and fussed and threatened Grandma with suicide and even with burning down the house. It was only when my mother flaunted her birth rights and threatened that she'd take me away that my grandmother reached inside her housecoat and tossed a handful of twenties to my mother. My mother was gone without a "Thank you" or a "Good-bye," raw face and all.

"Taryn!" Grandma had caught me peeking from my door and scooted me back into bed. Even though I hadn't seen the physical effects of my parents' abusive relationship before that night, I didn't cry, even with the visual of my mother's battered face. I hurt for my mother, but not for her physical pain. I wanted only to see her happy, and if being away from my father hurt her, which clearly it did, then I wanted them together. I accepted her joy in any form, despite Grandma's warnings.

"When you grow up to be a lady, don't let no man treat you the way your daddy does your mama. People show love in funny ways, but that's not love, baby."

If Grandma had been watching the flow of my and Layne's relationship, would she have thought Layne's psychological control and betrayal any different than the abuse my father inflicted on my mother? I shouldn't have been shocked by the exaggerated story Layne told Jenna, but I was. What other lies had she fed my child?

"I've never lost control under the influence," I told Jenna now. "As a matter of fact, I didn't even drink until I met Layne. I resent her for fabricating that story to her advantage. You should know me better than to believe that kind of story from her."

"If I didn't know better, I'd say she was right. Listen to you."

"What did you say, young lady?"

"You're acting so different, so aggressive."

I knew I sounded unlike my usual self. I had already heard the change in my tone. It was heavier, sultrier even, and pissed off.

"Why is that a problem?"

"I guess I'm just used to Layne being the vocal one."

"It's a new day, and it's just me and you now, so get used to it."

"It doesn't have to be," she said softly.

"It doesn't have to be what?"

"Just be me and you. I do have another parent somewhere, don't I?"

"What are you saying?"

Jenna hesitated before she spoke. "Well, I joined this group here at school. It's a bunch of us girls who grew up without our fathers. We're fatherless daughters."

My heart pounded quickly. "And?"

"We talk about our experiences and how we grew up. Everyone knows I've had two mothers for the past ten years, and for the most part, no one has much to say about that. Except it reinforces everyone's idea that I should know who my father is."

Jenna waited for me to respond.

"Well?" she said, pressing, after I said nothing.

"You just lost one of your parents. Is that where this is coming from?"

"I miss Layne, but no, this isn't about her."

"I don't want to talk about this right now, Jenna."

She groaned; her breath sounded like static in the phone. "When is a good time to talk about it?" she asked in the sassy tone that she used when she was frustrated with me, and that I had always ignored.

"Later. Let's discuss this during your next visit home."

"Fine. I'll be coming home the week before Thanksgiving," Jenna said, though I had stopped listening. After twenty years, why had she now decided to find out her father's identity? I couldn't do this now. Not now, not with everything else I was dealing with, not with everything else I wanted to explore and learn about myself. How could I also handle her sudden need to know her father?

"So is that all right?"

"What?"

"Coming."

"Whenever, Jenna. Come anytime. I'm here."

"Okay, the twenty-second. I'm going to book the ticket on your card now."

"Sure."

"I'm going to let you get back to your wine, Mom. Don't have too much," she advised, as if Layne had left her with a list of what I was and was not allowed to do.

"Good-bye." I hung up the phone and rested against the tub, allowing the pulsing water from the jets to prod and soothe my muscles. However, I couldn't relax and shake off the conversation I had had with Jenna. Within a few minutes, I lifted the outlet knob, and the water started its twirl down the drain. I grabbed a towel, dried off, and walked naked to the kitchen for more wine.

Chapter Six

The building was gray and dull, like a slab of concrete had been dropped between two buildings. It was surrounded by busy, lively bars and restaurants on a main street just west of downtown. I had passed the location on a few occasions on my way to the Magnificent Mile and had never noticed it.

"This is it?" I asked Nina over the Bluetooth speaker in my car.

"Yes."

The club we sat in front of was one of three that Nina and Layne had frequented.

It was 6:00 p.m. on a Thursday night, and most passersby crept past the building as if it weren't there. Only a few people, a trio of two men and a woman, stopped in front of the slate and iron door and sought entrance.

"Are you ready?" Nina asked me.

"I am."

Although I had been perturbed by the realization that Nina had attended Layne's funeral, it hadn't overshadowed the newfound power I felt after the near choking episode in her office. I had replayed the incident repeatedly in my mind, on an ego trip, envisioning that if I hadn't snapped out of my daze, I might have killed her.

I drove another block to a public parking lot and paid the fee. We exited our cars, each of us bundled under wool coats, as the temperature had dropped from above to below average Midwest numbers. Together we walked, both of us well dressed, our heels tap-dancing against the sidewalk. We looked like two friends on our way for after-work cocktails and casual conversation, not the taboo lovers we had become, preparing for my introduction to an evening of unrestricted voyeuristic pleasure.

At the door Nina knocked twice, and the cover to a small rectangular peephole slid sideways. Bland blue-gray eyes surveyed us before the cover closed once again. The door buzzed, and we were granted access. A bulky male, muscular in the arms and fat around his midsection, stood before us. I saw recognition dawn between him and Nina, though they didn't acknowledge one another. It felt like a scene from one of my favorite crime shows, like the clubs they showcased, the ones with secret back-alley entrances and passwords to disclose for admission.

"Identification, please," he requested.

Nina had already advised that I leave my wallet behind, so in my pocket I had only my driver's license and eight twenty-dollar bills. The bouncer took both my and Nina's ID and went into an office. Through a small window we could see him quickly scan and print copies of our licenses, then place the papers on top of a small pile. He returned to us.

"For our records only," he informed me prior to handing me my license.

"Protocol," Nina echoed.

From the small space in which we stood, we moved through another door into a dim hallway. Light fog circled about the air as we walked toward yet a third door. Nina paused before opening it, glancing back at me again and asking if was I ready. I nodded to her. Inside the next room, I didn't know what to take in first, the porn playing on the big-screen televisions, the bar filled with people making out, or the couples freely engaging in sexual acts on the couches to our left.

The room smelled of spice. And sex. It smelled like Nina and that part of her I craved to devour once more. Nina led us toward two empty stools on the opposite side of the bar from the entrance. My legs shook with nervousness as we walked past a man and a woman leaning against the bar. He was performing body shots from her cleavage, and his thick pink tongue licked salt, lemon, and tequila from her skin. Beyond them was another couple, and they kissed and groped one another.

"Hey, sexy," the brunette woman whispered to me as we walked past, before placing her tongue back in the man's mouth.

As we rounded the bar, I stopped, caught off guard by a man who sat on a stool, his zipper open, a blond woman's head bobbing up and down between his legs as she sucked his manhood. He puffed a cigarette and winked at us as we took seats next to him. I tried not to look, but they were right next to me. My eyes locked on the man's veined, pale penis, and I noted how it disappeared into the woman's mouth every other second. She sucked hard and fast, her cheeks caving and filling with each up-and-down movement. A few minutes later, the man placed a hand firmly on top of the blonde's head and released a few grunts. The woman swallowed, taking deep gulps, stoop up, wiped the corners of her mouth with a napkin, and took the man's cigarette and began puffing on it herself.

Finally, I turned to Nina, who had placed our drink orders. I removed my coat, which Nina took and placed with hers on the stool beside her.

"Seriously?" I mouthed to her, unsure how I felt about what I had just witnessed. Maybe I would feel differently if it had been two women.

"Have you ever?" Nina asked.

"Only once," I admitted. "With Jenna's father." I recalled the incident and told her about it. "I was fifteen.

We had just left White Castle and had walked to one of his friends' houses. The place was filled with guys, all older than me, and girls about my age. Everyone was smoking and drinking. I didn't do either."

Because of the effect drinking had on my father, I had refrained from alcohol as a teenager and had never had any until I met Layne. I had smoked weed once, but Grandma had smelled it on my clothes and had told me that I was too good to smoke reefer and that it would turn my lips black.

"He smoked with his friends and then took me into a bedroom," I continued. "We had already had sex a couple times, and I thought that's what he wanted again. I started to take off my shorts, but he told me no and asked me to take off my shirt instead. He sat on the edge of the bed and told me to get on my knees in front of him, so I did. He pulled his penis out and asked me the same question you did. Had I ever sucked dick? I told him I hadn't. He liked that. He instructed me to lick my lips and open. Then he stuck it in my mouth."

I paused to accept my drink from the bartender.

"He told me what to do. Lick, suck, and stroke. The whole time he pinched my nipples. I coughed and gagged when he came, but he held my head down and made me swallow it. The taste . . ."

"Bitter."

"Yes. I hated it and never did it again. We had sex a few more times before he moved on to another girl."

I took a sip of the rum concoction Nina had ordered for me. It created an immediate buzz, not surprising considering my body was accustomed only to wine.

"There was a man many years ago, when I was much younger, who wanted nothing but for me to give him head," Nina told me. "I don't hate men at all, but I have never wanted to be with one since him. Women, now

that's my specialty, even though I still like to watch
straight sex and gay boys. This place is the best of all
worlds. It's for those who want to be free to do whatever,
wherever, and however they want to. There's no pressure.
Most people come with people they plan to have sex with,
but there's no requirement to have sex, either. You and I
can sit here all night long and watch with no questions."

Nina cocked her head to the side. I followed the direction in which she was pointing and saw a man seated in
a reclined chair, stroking himself. "Some people come
alone and masturbate their evening away. It's like a
lovefest. People who are alone, couples, or groups, all
are welcome. Even the bartenders indulge from time to
time," Nina went on. "This one here, one night she fucked
herself on top of the bar with a beer bottle."

I looked at the middle-aged woman, who appeared to
be a mother, judging by the scratchy stretch marks that
scarred her belly. She had full breasts and wide hips, and
her loose thighs suggested that she hadn't exercised in
years. She was average looking, and with clothes on, she
could be the woman picking fruit next to me in the grocery
store, or a fellow shopper I said hello to as we passed one
another while browsing in a department store.

"We're no different than everybody else," Nina explained, reading my thoughts. "We get up and go to work
each day, some of us have families, we're young, we're
old, and we're single, married, gay, straight, bi, black,
white, Asian, whatever. We come from every color of the
rainbow."

Nina had identified nearly every characteristic of the
horny people around us. A twentysomething Hispanic
couple sat in the far right corner, and a bare-assed male
was seated on the couch, a woman straddling and bouncing on him, her ass smacking his groin with each thrust.
An older lesbian couple lay next to them, and the woman

with short, cropped hair had her face buried in the bosom of the voluptuous lady beneath her. There was a group of individuals who were dry humping each other on the small dance floor, and there were many like us, who drank and watched the activities about them.

"You came here with Amber as well?" I asked.

Nina leaned forward and wrapped her arms around my waist. "Yes." She lifted my shirt and kissed the skin around my navel.

I leaned my head back and allowed her tongue to dive into the small peephole of my stomach. "I'd like to meet her."

Nina stopped. "Amber?"

"Yes."

Nina sat back, biting the nail of her index finger, deciding. "She would like that. I am protective of her, you know. You can look, but don't touch."

"I'll try to keep my hands to myself."

"You better."

"Let me know when you plan to meet again. I'll stop by."

Nina smiled. "You sure learn quickly. Me, you, Layne, Amber, and all these people around us, we have one thing in common—pleasure. We've all been blessed with these beautiful bodies that respond to others visually and physically. I watch that couple over there, and I get wet." Nina stroked my lips with her index finger. "I touch you, and I get wetter."

I took Nina's finger inside my mouth and sucked it. She moaned as my tongue licked her skin and under her smooth fingernail. Suddenly she stood, took my head in her hands, and thrust her tongue deep into my mouth. We kissed hard, angrily and passionately, our teeth clicking against the other's. She bit my tongue, and I bit hers back. I tasted blood and kissed deeper, again feeling frenzied at the thought of hurting her. I felt a hand on my behind.

"May we?" the gentleman next to us inquired.

Nina and I broke apart. Breathless, I wiped my mouth. Nina smirked. "No, not my specialty. Sorry."

"Well, what about her?" he asked. The blond woman grinned excitedly.

"Let's see." Nina walked over and leaned the woman's body against the bar. "Take off your panties," Nina instructed and held out her hand.

The woman lifted her short, faux leather skirt and stepped out of a white lace thong. She gave it to Nina, who placed it over the man's head. The crotch area rested on his nose.

Nina ran her hand over the woman's brown, stubbly pubic hair. She reached lower and, judging by the woman's sharp inhale, placed fingers inside her. The woman's head rolled backward.

"If you want it, you have to get it," Nina told her. She then placed her left foot on the rest that circled the bar and leaned her left hand against the bar. The woman began to grind and circle her hips over Nina's fingers. "That's it."

Nina then turned to me and tilted her head in a "Come here" gesture. I moved to Nina's right side.

"Lift her shirt," Nina instructed.

The woman wore a white T-shirt with a ragged-cut V-neck. I raised her shirt and unhooked the front clasp of her bra. Her large, heavy breasts fell against her rib cage. The woman continued to rub against Nina's palm, her legs bent, the muscles in her thighs flexed. She lifted her head again; her green eyes were half closed.

I positioned myself so I could assist Nina. I leaned forward and placed a pink nipple in my mouth. The woman responded with a soft sigh, and then a pleased exhale escaped from her lips. I felt moist. Layne had rarely permitted me even that simplest of acts, and here a stranger, a woman whose name I didn't even know, wanted me to have her. I licked her areola, my tongue tracing the outer circle. I opened my mouth wider, taking as much of her fullness inside as I could. She rocked her hips, fucking Nina's fingers, while I stimulated her breasts. She panted and moaned and squealed high-pitched, nasty words of delight.

"Yeah, yeah, fuck my pussy," she repeated.

Nina's breath was hot against my ear. She too was panting and whispering her thoughts. She called the woman a bitch, which the woman accepted, informing us she was "about to cum all over" Nina's fingers. Her body stiffened, and then she collapsed against the bar. Her head hung limp, and her eyes were shut tightly. She never reopened them while we were there.

Nina released her fingers and wiped her hand with a napkin. The man, with the panties still on his head, had unzipped his pants again, and his exposed penis rested in his sticky hand.

"You're welcome," Nina told him before she turned to me. "Let's go."

We put our coats back on and exited the building just as a woman and a man were entering. The woman's face was familiar, like that of someone I had seen in passing on more than one occasion. Her expression showed that she had recognized mine as well, and then I realized she was a client at the salon where every two weeks I got my hair washed, deep conditioned, and flat-ironed. I turned my head and pulled the hood of my coat over my face.

"What happens if you run into people you know?" I asked Nina, feeling panicked during our walk back to my car. "Does that happen?"

"It does from time to time, and there's nothing to do but acknowledge the fact that we all were in the club together. We all keep one another's secret. At least that's the silent code."

"Who have you run into?" I wanted to know.

"Now, Taryn, that would be defying the code, wouldn't it?" She chuckled.

"Yes, I suppose it would." Inside, I had become paranoid about the woman we saw. Would she tell my stylist? I hadn't considered the possibility of encountering someone I knew, not during my first visit, given the fact that Layne had escaped recognition for seven years. Or had she? Were the exhibitionists bound that tightly by the code of confidentiality?

"So tell me. What did you think?" Nina asked.

"It was almost everything Layne described, but nothing compares to being there. I see why Layne got hooked," I admitted. "I can't wait until we visit the next place."

"That was a two-star hotel we just left. Where we're going next time, that's a five-star resort. You'll fit right in."

We reached our cars. "Come over?" I asked. My body was too hot for the night to come to an end. I needed more.

"I'll follow you," she agreed.

We reached my home in thirty minutes, good timing considering Chicago's never-ending traffic jams. Once inside, I wasted no time. I knew exactly what I wanted.

"Follow me."

I headed toward the staircase. Nina remained still, and only when I turned around did she start to follow me. She moved carefully, slowly, like she had been forbidden from entering this territory. I guessed I was right in my assumption that Layne had intentionally kept Nina out of our bedroom. That meant that I would have her in a way that Layne hadn't, which gratified me further.

Upstairs, Nina walked behind me down the short hallway to my bedroom. I placed a hand on each handle of the white double doors and paused. Nina was quiet; her breath had halted with anticipation. Finally, I opened the doors to the massive room, whose decor was sleek, modern, simple, and all white. Before us, waiting, was the king-size bed. I threw our coats on a chair, took my shoes off, and nestled comfortably against the pillows at the head of the bed.

"Lie with me," I requested.

Nina took small steps to the edge of the bed and crawled onto the side on which Layne used to sleep. We faced one another.

"I've never been in here," she stated, her eyes devouring the space.

"I know. Can we finish what we started at the bar before we were wonderfully interrupted?"

Nina's bottom lip dipped inward into a sheepish smile. I was learning firsthand that she was sexually flexible, playing passive and shy when preyed upon, and dominating and forceful when in her voyeuristic element. She seemed to like it both ways.

"Take your pants off," I instructed her in the same tone she had used when making demands of the blond woman.

Nina unbuttoned and unzipped her slacks and slid them down to her feet. She used her toes to peel them from her ankles. Again, she wore no panties.

She's sweet. She's salty. She's my palate's favorite flavor. . . .

"I want to taste you." I raised my arms and removed my wool sweater, then unbuckled the belt around my waist. I lifted my hips, lowered my pants, and tossed them on the floor. Next to Nina, I lay in my pink lace bikini panties and bra. She removed her blouse to reveal a satin black bra with a diamond setting in the center. Nina stretched her body into a receiving position, placing her arms above her head and opening her thighs to me.

"It's yours if you want it," she eagerly conceded.

It had been years since Layne had allowed me to touch her, and at times I felt like a novice in the art of pleasing another woman. But I had been an attentive apprentice and had taken mental notes of the way Layne's tongue sweet-talked my body into a climactic surrender.

I positioned myself over Nina, anxious to graze her with my lips. I first touched her knees, showering delicate kisses on their bony ridges and alongside the caps. From what I had read, Layne and Nina never made love. They fucked. They had aggressive, forceful, daring sex in reckless places. I wanted to have Nina like Layne hadn't, coupled with her tenderly and gently, making love to her on Layne's side of the bed. Nina yielded to my wishes.

When I finally tasted the sweet tang that fell against my tongue, I laid eyes on the black-and-white photo of Layne and me on the night table at Nina's side. Layne gazed at me with her round eyes and watched the woman she loved wrap her legs around my neck. Nina's hips swayed into a slow grind beneath me, and as she clutched the pillowcases and murmured "Taryn," I stared back at Layne, satisfied, superior even, having savored her woman in a manner in which she never had.

Chapter Seven

Ms. Sheila and I stood together outside the center's gym to greet players, parents, volunteers, and spectators from the community as they arrived at the fund-raising basketball game. It had been a busy week of finalizing details to ensure the night went as smoothly as in prior years, as the game was one of the center's most popular annual events, attracting hundreds of people.

I had noticed that Ms. Sheila had been short with me ever since our conversation in Jimmy's office. While she remained cordial when we saw one another, her old eyes scrutinized me. She looked me up and down with the same demeaning gape she had accused Layne of perpetrating. I didn't know if her shortness had anything to do with her words in Jimmy's office and the private conversation I had overheard.

"We haven't had an opportunity to talk and catch up," I said casually to her after welcoming a group of teenage girls. "How is everything with you?"

"I'm fine. Blessed to see each day."

"How's Mr. Robertson?" Mr. Robertson was her husband of fifty-one years.

"He's better now. Finally, after all these years, got himself saved at church this past Sunday."

"That's good for him. You both must be happy."

"Yes, child, we all need saving of the soul." Her eyes popped wide behind her glasses. "How have you been?"

"I'm healing. It's getting easier day by day to deal with Layne's passing."

"Uh-huh." She clicked her dentures with her tongue.

I pressed her to find out what she disliked about Layne. "What was it about Layne that you didn't care for? She was far from perfect, I know. What had she done to you?"

Ms. Sheila peered at me as if she couldn't believe I didn't know.

"I ain't tryin' to start no mess."

I became anxious, though I continued to smile as each attendee passed into the gym. "What do you mean? What is it?"

Jimmy appeared in his annual getup, a black suit with a white shirt and a white bow tie. The black leather loafers on his feet shone from a fresh polish. He interrupted our conversation. "Taryn, time to start the game."

Ms. Sheila looked relieved.

Before the game started, I took to the center of the gym, and with a microphone in hand, I welcomed the guests and thanked them for their attendance and support. I reminded them through their participation at the game, whether a ticket purchase or an additional donation, they were supporting various programs that benefited the center and the community as a whole.

We Are One's drill team performed a dance routine before Sabrina, a sophomore high school student who assisted with some of the younger kids, sang the national anthem. Ms. Sheila had disappeared to the concession stand, where she was assigned to monitor the volunteers. During the first half of the game, Jimmy and I sat courtside with some of the city's well-known supporters, including several politicians, the mayor, two Chicago Bulls players, and Sugar, a famous homegrown talent, who was set to perform one song at halftime. After Sugar's performance and few words spoken by some of the honored guests, all the well-known supporters left, missing the second half.

With five minutes left in the fourth quarter, Ms. Sheila met me again at the gym's exit. I had hoped she would then confess her angst about Layne, but she had brought a young man named Lewis back with her. Lewis was one of the young people from Ron's church who had volunteered to sell hot dogs, chips, soda, and snacks at the concession counter.

"How'd it go, Lewis?" I asked him.

"A'ight." Lewis was a short guy, about five foot four, and he wore washed-out jeans and an oversize navy-blue Polo T-shirt. He was fidgety, bouncing his feet from left to right, kicking the heels of his white Nikes together.

"A'ight?" I said, mimicking him. "What is that?"

"I mean, I had a good time. Thank you, ma'am."

"Now, that's better." I patted him gently on the shoulder, and he jumped. I had learned years ago that some of the kids were unaccustomed to affection, as I had been while growing up, and reacted to touch differently. Some were hostile; some welcoming. Lewis looked at me as if I had offended him, but he quickly softened, casting his eyes downward and biting his bottom lip.

The buzzer soon sounded, signaling the end of the game.

"I gotta go," Lewis told me and Ms. Sheila.

"Thanks for helping out tonight. We'll see you again?" I asked him.

Without answering, Lewis vanished in front of the crowd of people that began to exit the gym. Ms. Sheila and I repeated "Thank you" many times before we heard gunfire about two minutes later. There were two loud pops back to back. The noise caused the many people who were exiting to run from the gym into the already packed hallway. Security guards rushed past frightened individuals while I grabbed my cell phone from my pocket and called 911.

Jermaine, one of the guards, and I managed to escort Ms. Sheila into one of the small janitor's closets, and I told her to wait there. Jermaine and I then tried to keep the panicked crowd under control on our way out to the parking lot. Everyone outside was screaming as they stood around a boy who lay on the ground. By the time we reached the limp young victim ourselves, several police cars had already arrived, sounding their horns and sirens to break through the thick crowd. Teenagers yelled obscenities, damning the shooter. Others cried for the victim.

"It was Lewis! It was muthafuckin' Lewis. We gon' get his ass!" a young man named Harold yelled.

"No! I can't believe this. Not Eddie!" Sabrina cried.

The officers jumped out of their vehicles and swiftly took control of the crowd, backing the stunned and angry gapers away from the body. They then began their investigation by interviewing the witnesses. For several hours, the center was on lockdown. Some of the attendees were questioned, and Jimmy and I did our best to keep a growing number of antsy and impatient people calm. By the end of the night, we learned that there had been a squabble between Lewis and Eddie. The word on the street was that Eddie had been bragging about having sex with Lewis's younger sister, who was just thirteen years old. Lewis had had his friends meet him outside to give him a gun and then to drive the getaway car.

Over the years, the center had had its share of fights and troubles and had taken careful precautions to keep the kids safe. We hadn't, however, experienced an escalation in violence as severe as a shooting. The media got wind of the shooting, and in response, two reporters arrived to take statements, which Jimmy handled.

Before locking the doors to the center, Jimmy and I sat in his office and completed an incident report, one that we kept on file for the center's records. We also sent an e-mail to Ron, informing him that we needed to meet with him the following week and asking that he adjust his schedule to accommodate our request.

It was almost 4:00 a.m. by the time I got home. After a hot shower, I got into bed and stared across the room at an outfit hanging on the outside of the door to the walk-in closet. After the night's chaos, I was ready to unwind, and that ensemble and what came with it would provide me all the release I needed.

Chapter Eight

Nina described the mansion as a hedonist's paradise. It was located in a secluded, discreet location, buried at the end of a dark two-mile road in an upscale suburb on the far west side of Chicago. It was midnight when we pulled up to the dimly lit, massive modern-style home. The windows were draped in black coverings, with only a peek of light creeping through the corners. The sight was ominous, yet alluring, I had a feeling of anticipation and trepidation, like one might expect when approaching a dark haunted house.

Men in black tuxedos greeted us after we reached the top of the driveway. One on each side of the car opened our doors. An olive-skinned man with eyes the color of nutmeg took Nina's keys. She handed him a fifty-dollar bill, and he placed a small ticket in her hand.

Nina wore a calf-length sable fur coat, and I, a red-leather trench. We both wore five-inch black platform stilettos, which pounded against the ground as we ascended a lengthy number of steps until we reached large doors with stained-glass windows. Two new tuxedo-wearing men opened the doors and then took our coats, along with the ticket Nina had been given by the valet. Right after that, a woman wearing an elaborate Mardi Gras-style mask approached us with a tray of dry martinis. We each took a glass and began our venture into the party.

I hadn't seen Nina's outfit until now, as we had gotten dressed at our own homes. She wore a tight, strapless black leather dress, short enough to reveal the hump and curve of her ass cheeks from the back. Around her neck was a spiked collar, and she had on matching spiked wrist cuffs made of leather. Her hair was in a gorgeous state of disarray, with wavy curls scattered about her head.

I wore a red and black bustier and a short leather skirt, with a sheer G-string beneath. At Nina's request, I had spent hours putting spiral curls in my hair and following an online makeup tutorial to create intense smoky eyes. Neither technique was I familiar with, yet I was pleased with the transformation. In no way did I resemble the stereotypical conservative, librarian-like woman I saw in the mirror each day.

Nina and I walked across a marble hallway that led to an open, sunken room filled with white leather sofas and silver and glass tables. Dim pink lighting created an intimate vibe throughout. Contemporary jazz poured through speakers at a low volume.

Men and women casually mingled about, talking and drinking, socializing as if they were at a dinner party. The only giveaway as to the nature of the evening was our attire, or a lack of it for most. Many men and women were dressed like me and Nina, with bare-chested guys in leather chaps and women in leather catsuits or tight-fitting dresses. Other women wore lingerie: sheer chemises, lace camisoles, and bras and panties with garters. Everyone was beautiful, like airbrushed magazine cover models with high cheekbones and pouty lips. Everybody was fit, toned, and shapely.

"There is no sex in this area," Nina explained. "This is where guests come before they venture down either of the halls." On each side of the room was a long hallway. "The rooms to our left are for orgies." All the doors down that hallway were closed. "You'll see what the right side is for later," she teased.

We sat on a love seat and were soon approached by a woman who had been standing alone near the bar. She was an Egyptian beauty, with a golden-tawny complexion against midnight-black hair. On her slim figure she wore a sparkling gold bra and panty set with black fringes that swayed with her every step.

"Hello." She stood in front of me and introduced herself. "I'm Clarissa."

"I'm Shelley," I lied. Nina had informed me that although names were rarely exchanged, I should be ready to provide a fake one if needed. She had told me that many women used cliché, alter ego stripper-like names, such as Diamond, Precious, and Tasty, and had recommended that we invent the opposite.

"Do you mind if I sit?" Clarissa asked me.

Nina scooted to the side to make room for three. Clarissa placed herself next to me, her legs stretched outward, with the right over the left. She rested her arm behind my head.

"I couldn't resist speaking to you." She tousled one of my curls between two fingers. "You look amazing."

I blushed and felt nervous, unsure if Clarissa's presence was an invasion, considering I had arrived with Nina and expected to follow her lead. "Thank you."

"I am alone tonight," Clarissa announced. "Would you mind if I accompany you?"

I didn't have an answer for her, unaware myself of what the rest of our night entailed.

"You are more than welcome," Nina answered on our behalf. "Come."

The three of us got up and walked to the hall at our left. On the handle of each closed door hung a red or green sign. I heard moans and groans and words of pleasure from behind each door.

"Clarissa, you know what this means, don't you?" Nina asked.

Clarissa's red lips arched upward. "I do."

"Please explain to Shelley."

Clarissa leaned close to my face. Her skin smelled fresh, with the light scent of jasmine circling about her.

"Behind these doors lies a variety of fantasies. Red signs mean that no additional guests are allowed."

We continued to walk until we reached the fifth door, where Nina stopped and put her hand on a gold handle with a green sign.

"The green means more are welcome," Clariss told me.

Nina pushed the handle and opened the door. Inside the small room were four naked women, a brunette, a blonde, a redhead, and a silky smooth woman with luscious chocolate skin. The redhead stood at the edge of a high bed, her hands at the waist of the blonde, penetrating her from behind with a strapped dildo. The African-American woman kneeled on the bed, her ass pressed against the face of the blonde. She cooed oohs and aahs as the woman's tongue dove into her coffee cheeks. The brunette sat on a corner chair, her legs spread wide over the armrests, masturbating with a vibrator. Nina closed the door behind us.

The three of us leaned against the wall and watched. For a woman who had never experienced the environment I was in, I felt comfortable. I was aroused. I was wet and wanted to relieve the throbbing that instantly pulsed between my legs.

I directed my attention to the woman in the chair. She had been watching the women on the bed, but her eyes now turned to mine. She increased the speed of the tiny purple vibrator and rubbed it aggressively against her clit. Her murmurs increased in volume as she climaxed, and her pink lips opened and shut with each pleasurable spasm. She rested a moment, her arms at her sides, then got up, walked up to us, and stood in front of me. She took my glass and sipped. She kissed me next, her tongue warm and tasting of expensive vodka.

"You are a beauty," she told me.

So was she, with tanned skin, dark brown layered hair, and lust-filled blue eyes. She looked at Nina, assuming I belonged to her. "May I?"

Nina gave her permission to touch me. "Yes."

The woman stroked the moisture between my legs, and her slim finger grazed my lips. "Oh, yes." She turned to Nina. "I'll tie her hands."

She opened a small box on the floor next to the bed and pulled out a rope. She stood in front of me and took my hands, placed them behind my head, and tied my wrists together. Next, she loosened the strings at the back of the tight-fitting bustier and released it. She ran her hands down my chest until she reached my abdomen. She caressed me, then continued to rub her hands down my thighs until she spread my legs. She lowered herself to her knees, unhooked my skirt, and slid it down my body. With her teeth, she removed my panties. She tossed them into the small box after I stepped out of them. Her tongue suddenly darted out, and she licked my hungry lips.

"You are in for a treat," she told Nina after she stood. Then she and Clarissa took several steps backward and allowed Nina to take control.

With her left hand, Nina grabbed my throat and squeezed, choking me as I had her that day in her office. With her right, she pinched and rubbed my clit. I struggled for oxygen, while enjoying the pleasing sensations the tips of her fingers brought me. I neared climax quickly, and she stopped, releasing the grip around my throat and abruptly ceasing the pleasure. She got on her knees and, with a warm tongue, aroused me once again. Repeatedly, she brought me close to orgasm, only to stop before the actual release.

I was sweating, my heart was beating fast, and my knees quivered. I was near tears with desire. The woman had returned to her chair, masturbating while watching us.

"Beg me," Nina demanded.

"Please," I cried desperately.

"Please, what?"

"Let me cum," I pleaded.

Nina licked the wetness around my lips and on my upper thighs, continuing to tease me. "Not yet." She turned to all the women. "It's showtime, ladies."

With that, they all stopped fucking and stood up. One of them, the redhead, retrieved a collar from the box, untied my hands, and placed it around my neck. Another grabbed a chain and attached it. She handed the chain to Nina, along with a whip.

"Hands and knees," Nina instructed.

I lowered myself to the floor and waited. The women used white towels to blot themselves dry, and then Nina opened the door. Nina lashed the whip against my ass and told me to go. On my hands and knees, like a dog, I entered the hallway. Across the shiny floor, she led me back through the lounge area and down the other hallway. All the guests, every single one of them, followed us to the last door at the end of the right hall. I entered first, with Nina at my side and the four women, plus Clarissa, in tow. The room was large, with dark gray cement-like walls and a poster bed in the middle of the floor.

"Get on." Nina unclasped the hook of the chain from the collar.

I crawled onto the bed and lay on my back. Men and women sat in chairs and stood around me with drinks in hand. Some kissed, some ground against one another, but mostly I was the center of their attention. At least fifty sets of hungry eyes devoured my body. I was sweating with anticipation of what was next.

The four women each took an arm or a leg and tied it to a corner post. The scene was almost as I had pictured it the many nights I touched myself while thinking about it. Nina stood at the foot of the bed, with Clarissa at her side. Nina then nodded to the redhead, who then crawled onto the bed with a black leather flogger in her hand. She rested her body behind my head and ran the flogger over my face, down my lips, and between my breasts, caressing my nipples. She slapped one, then both, darting the leather left and right. I arched my back, wanting more. I wanted her to go lower, to help me release the pressure I had inside. She stroked my stomach with the flogger and finally tapped my clit. She danced it around and around until again, I was ready to break free. Nina told her to stop. Upon command, the woman got off the bed and stood at the top right post.

The masturbating brunette was next. On top of me she positioned herself in a sixty-nine position, and with her rouge ass in my face, she buried her tongue deep inside of me. I screamed uncontrollably, and my legs shook. She fucked me with her stiff tongue, and within seconds, I was ready to burst. She stopped. It was the most pleasing torture I could have imagined.

Then the blonde crept onto the bed, placing herself at my ankles. I felt her tongue lick the top of my foot, slow and then fast, making circles on and tapping my skin, and then with her lips she made strong sucks up my shins to my knees and thighs. She never stopped kissing.

At last, the dreamy cocoa woman crawled snake-like onto the bed, her long legs slithering across the silver sheets, and straddled my chest. She lowered her waist onto my left breast, stroking her clit against my erect nipple. Between the kisses to my thighs and the moans from the woman pleasing herself, I wanted nothing more than to squeeze my legs tight and cum with her. But, with my legs separated, I couldn't. Instead, I focused on the way her lower lips swallowed my nipple, which was becoming increasingly wet, sliding against my skin. With the limited experience I had exploring a woman's body, I had never considered an orgasm possible in that manner. When the woman squeezed her knees tightly around my body and let out one final cry of ecstasy, I yelled with her, repeating the flurry of curse words that escaped her full lips. Her aroma remained even after she removed herself from on top of me.

Nina, who hadn't moved and had stood to watch each woman's performance, walked to each post and untied the rope that bound me to it. At the right side of the bed she positioned herself and raised her short leather dress. The redhead handed her a tan-colored rubber penis. My eyes grew wide. Layne and I had never used toys in lovemaking. I was unsure what to expect. Nina watched me as she attached it to the straps of the leather holder around her waist. She smirked deviously as she got onto the bed with me.

"Ladies and gentlemen, the grand finale," Nina announced.

Nina approached me on her hands and knees and surprised me by lying down and flipping me on top of her. She saw the fear and desire in my eyes.

"Ride it, Taryn," she instructed me softly, so only I could hear. She guided me to my knees, over her, until the tip touched my soft wetness. "Come down slow."

My lips slid onto the dildo and flooded the empty space that had been craving attention. I gasped from the twinge of pain and the simultaneous pleasure as the dildo rubbed against and filled my inner flesh.

"Yes, that's it," Nina whispered. "Rock with me."

Nina rolled her hips beneath my body, and I felt the pressure of the dildo deeper inside. It found an untouched place, a small womb that nestled every hidden fiber of pleasure I had not experienced. With each stroke, I came down against Nina, the dildo grazing my insides, my clit brushing against the heated leather. My flesh gripped and pulsated around the dildo as my climax built. My ass smacked against Nina's upper thighs, and the look on her face was stern, as she was intent on bringing me to wild orgasm. The ripples intensified until my body tensed from the strength of the orgasm, which had been escalating for an hour, and a rush of juices streamed down the dildo, ejaculating onto the leather.

My head fell forward, and I collapsed against the leather of Nina's dress. She didn't stop, though. She sat me upright and kept fucking me until I came again. She placed me on my hands and knees and fucked me from behind. She sat on her heels and fucked me while I straddled her hips. "Just like that," she said, guiding herself with her hands wrapped around my ass cheeks.

I rubbed my sweaty face against her wet skin and stuck my tongue into her mouth. We kissed while I continued to ride her. I noticed that several couples and groups in the room had started an orgy around us. Groans and moans and screams of pleasure surrounded us and filled the room, with us as the ceremonial highlight of the evening. Finally, exhausted, I lifted myself from the dildo and lay on the bed. Nina took me in her mouth, deliciously licking the remnants of our sex, soothing my throbbing pussy. I closed my eyes and allowed her to bring me to one final, delicate orgasm. The room broke out in applause.

I opened my eyes once more as Nina guided me off the bed. My legs wobbly, I stumbled in the black heels I still wore on my feet. The clapping continued as we exited the room. Nina walked me into an adjacent black-and-white bathroom, where she warmed a washcloth and placed it between my legs. She wiped gently and then dried us both off with another towel. Clarissa was outside the door when Nina opened it.

"I enjoyed watching you this evening. I hope to see you again," she told me boldly. She glanced at Nina, then turned and walked back into the grand pleasure room.

Nina and I walked toward the front of the mansion, where two men were already waiting with our coats in hand. We wrapped ourselves in them and stepped outside into the cool air. Nina's Mercedes sat idling, waiting for us. My thighs tensed as I sat inside.

"You were marvelous," she told me as we pulled away and drove down the dark driveway.

I smiled at all I had experienced, reveling in the memories Nina had just created for me. Although I had read Layne's detailed journals and had pleasured myself to her words, the mansion had more than met my expectations.

"Thank you."

"Seven years . . . seven years and Layne never fucked me the way you did. I told you, you're a natural. Layne didn't know what she was missing."

I was flattered. "No, she didn't. I guess there is more to me than what meets the eye. You'll see."

We rode quietly to my home, my mind wandering back to the mansion, my body still warm with sensations from the new encounters. I had completely surrendered to Nina and to what I had hoped to experience with her.

Nina waited until I was inside before she pulled off. I took the stairs up to the master bedroom, feeling like a different woman, powerful and carefree. I wondered if that was how Layne had felt after outings with Nina. I opened the French doors to the room and imagined Layne lying in bed, asleep, as I had so many nights when she arrived home in the early morning hours. I took off my shoes and dropped my coat to the floor. I crawled in bed and gathered large white pillows in my arms, simulating the way Layne would cuddle me those nights. I pitied her, as she was so naive and was unaware of what I had just done without her knowledge.

Before closing my eyes, I reached for the black-and-white picture of me and Layne, and I laid it facedown. With a sleepy, satisfied grin on my face, I turned my lamp off.

Chapter Nine

The following Monday I sat in my office, taking back-to-back calls from parents who were worried and upset about the shooting. Some were concerned about the center's protection of their children in after-school programs and threatened to transfer their children to day-care centers. I had already spent three hours reassuring parents and caregivers that the shooting was an isolated incident and that the center was a safe place for their children.

Jimmy and I met in my office at 11:00 a.m., at which time we briefed one another on what we had covered that morning. I presented Jimmy with the idea of hiring a second security guard. Before we began a budget review to determine if that was feasible, Jimmy shared that he and Ms. Sheila had something to tell me.

I picked up my phone and dialed the front desk extension. I asked Myesha, the receptionist who had taken my place many years ago, to locate Ms. Sheila. "Have her come to my office, please."

A few moments later Ms. Sheila opened the door and took a seat next to me. She shifted uncomfortably, tapping the thick black sole of her shoe rapidly against the linoleum floor.

"In light of what happened Friday, I thought it best we all talk," Jimmy told me, but then they remained silent.

I turned my head back and forth between the two of them. "What's this about?"

Ms. Sheila reached in the pocket of her blue and orange smock and pulled out a small device. She handed it to me. I turned the little black square in my fingers and set it on my desk.

"What is that?" I asked.

"It's a camera, Taryn. She spied on you every day," Ms. Sheila blurted.

"What? Who spied on me?"

"We assume Layne did," Jimmy answered.

"Where did you find it?"

"The electrician found it the day he came to check the wiring, back when you were on vacation at the start of summer. I knew what it was as soon as he showed it to me. It's just like the one I keep in my house to watch all my grandkids coming in and out. Can't trust everybody, especially the folks we love. Them kids might take some of my precious jewels," Ms. Sheila mumbled.

"There are no hidden cameras here at the center. We don't hide who and what we're watching with the security cameras we have around here," Jimmy noted. "The only explanation for this is Layne. The question is, why would she want to spy on you?"

"'Cause sneaky folks always thinkin' somebody else is sneaky, that's why," Ms. Sheila said, jumping in. "She could have been watching you at any time, and if there were any secrets told in your office, she knew about it. Like I said before, I wasn't trying to be up in no mess—"

"Thank you, Sheila," Jimmy said, cutting her off. "I planned to share this with you the day you returned from vacation. Unfortunately, Layne died that day, and it didn't seem right anymore. We didn't want to cause you any distress by sharing it afterward. With the recent security issues and the extra measures we might take, I had to tell you. This camera is a breach not only of your privacy but of the center's as well."

I didn't know how much more I could handle. Not only had Layne cheated for years and told my daughter lies about me, but she had also spied on me while I was at work? I tried to recall when Layne had had an opportunity to place the camera in my office. Once she resigned from her four-year service on the board, she rarely visited the center and hated driving on Chicago's South Side. She had picked me up from work only once after resigning, and on another occasion, about a year ago, she had dropped by the center unannounced while I was in a meeting with Jimmy. I didn't know she was there until I found her waiting for me in my office. Had she installed the camera then?

"I don't know why Layne would put this camera in my office. All I can say is, I'm learning the woman I married isn't who I thought she was," I admitted.

"Uh-huh," Ms. Sheila murmured.

I took the small gadget in my hand again and got up. "Thanks for telling me about this. Jimmy, you understand if I take the rest of the day off?"

"Of course," Jimmy responded.

Ms. Sheila and Jimmy left my office, with Ms. Sheila continuing to mumble unflattering remarks about Layne. I ignored her, gathered my purse, and then left the center. Once I got home, I took the tote with Layne's journals into her office. I set it on the floor, sat in her chair, and stared at the closed laptop that remained on top of her desk. Since her passing, I had been unable to access the computer, as it was password protected. I hadn't spent much time trying to decipher the password, previously trying only the words *Layne*, *Taryn*, and *Jenna* to gain entry. Now I wanted to know if she really had been spying on me and what she had seen.

I opened the laptop and powered it on. When the password box appeared, I typed in the word *Nina*. I was denied.

I tried *English,* but again, no entry. I tapped my fingers on
the keyboard, entering a blur of letters and unintelligible
words. I got up and strolled past the shelves of books on
Layne's walls. Given that Layne was as anal as she was, the
books were organized by subject, like in a library. I passed
a section of autobiographies and African American fiction,
then reached a shelf of books on Greek mythology.

"You were her Aphrodite," I had told Nina, aware of
Layne's fascination with mythological persons. Nina had
smiled in response, as if Layne had also told her that.
I typed *Aphrodite* into the password box, and Layne's
desktop appeared. The backdrop was a picture of silver
handcuffs. Folders covered most of the screen, their
titles predominately related to her work at school. In the
bottom left corner was a file with my name. I moved the
arrow over it and clicked.

There wasn't much in the folder, a few pictures and
tax documents. But there was another folder within the
file titled "The Office." Inside were tens of videos, their
still shots capturing the desk in my office. Anxiously, I
watched the first one, which was dated late August of the
previous year. There was no sound to the video, only a
streaming view of my desk from above.

For over an hour I watched videos, fast-forwarding
through much of the footage. The activity in my office was
minimal. I spent most of my time on the phone or away
from my desk. Jimmy and I held a few meetings, some
of my coworkers stopped by to drop off paperwork, and
occasionally one of the kids would visit me. However, I
was usually alone. Then Ron entered one day.

He greeted me as usual, with a hug and a kiss to my
cheek. I watched us, silently, interact across my desk. I
remembered the meeting. We talked about Jenna and
how emotional he had been sitting in the restaurant
with us, so close to her, but unable to speak. I pulled

out my phone and showed him pictures of all of us upon our arrival at Spelman, then of us helping to get her settled into her dorm along with her roommate. Ron then pulled out an envelope and handed it to me. Inside were five one-hundred-dollar bills, the exact amount he had been handing me monthly since we reunited at the center. Over the years, Ron had given me over a hundred thousand dollars, none of which Layne knew about. At least I thought she hadn't.

The footage with Ron started just after we dropped Jenna off for her second year. To be precise, it was almost a week after Jenna had left for Spelman, and only a day before she left, Ron had sat near us at brunch. Had Layne noticed the two times Ron and I caught each other's eye in the restaurant, diverting our eyes a mere second after they connected?

I continued to watch the videos, including two more that included scenes of Ron giving me an envelope again. The videos stopped just prior to our summer vacation. Perhaps the camera had continued to roll, but Layne had been unable to download further footage. I couldn't figure out what she planned to do with it, had she lived.

Before shutting her laptop, I changed the password to *Taryn*.

"Ha," I said to no one, pleased that I had gained access to Layne's laptop. I was also pissed at the discovery of Layne's additional deceptions, more proof of her obsession with controlling me.

I reached in the tote and emptied Layne's journals onto the desk. I flipped through the pages of several until I found the entries I was seeking. At the printer across the room I scanned the pages I needed and placed the copies in an envelope. I then placed the journals in Layne's drawer where I originally found them, and left the office, defiantly leaving the door ajar, with the envelope in hand.

Chapter Ten

It was a bleak, cloudy November afternoon, the Friday before the week of Thanksgiving break, when I walked the pathway toward the main campus hall. The snow that fell a few days prior had melted, and only muddied patches remained scattered about the grass.

Before I headed to Nina's office, I stopped to visit Dean Henry, who was expecting me. We chatted for five minutes before I headed down the long hallway and around the bend that led to Nina's office. Nina and Amber were inside when I arrived. I closed the door and leaned against it, my ankles crossed, arms behind my back, my hands around the doorknob. I locked the door.

"Hello," I said.

They were sitting casually next to one another in the chairs in front of Nina's desk. I entered during a conversation about a new program being implemented in the math department. The last words Nina spoke were about their need to work together during the process. How convenient it had been for all of them to get laid in the same place they got paid. Nina smiled at me.

"Amber, this is Taryn, Layne's widow."

Amber stood and walked toward me, removing her glasses during the process. She positioned her tall, full body before me. "This is your Layne's wife?" she asked Nina, her eyes on me.

"Yes."

"My, aren't you luscious." She bit the tip of the frame of her glasses between her teeth.

"Thank you," I said.

"She's here to watch," Nina announced.

"Ah, so that's what you were waiting for. I was getting anxious." Amber chuckled. "You're in for a treat," she told me.

Amber took two steps back and began to unbutton her white blouse. She opened it to reveal a nude-colored lace bra over her full, freckled bosom. With her fingertip she caressed her nipple. Slowly, Nina rose and met Amber in front of me. Nina ground her hips against Amber's body, as if dancing to a funky, slow groove only the two of them could hear.

Nina's hands ran up and down Amber's clothing, and then she gripped her skirt in bunches between her clenched fingers. Amber moaned. Nina perspired. I stroked my cleavage. Amber peered at me seductively, then turned to Nina.

"I like the wife better already," she told her.

Together, they took additional steps back until they reached Nina's desk. Amber scooted her ass onto it, raising her skirt in the process to reveal matching nude lace panties. She held on to the edge of the desk and circled her hips against the smooth surface. I watched the flesh between her legs rise and then slowly disappear beneath her.

"Ahh," she hummed.

I ran my hands down my slacks and mimicked her grind against the palm of my hand.

Nina positioned herself between Amber's legs, stroking the lace with her middle finger. I saw Nina's finger dip inside Amber's panties and disappear between her pink lips. Nina penetrated Amber deeply. Her finger dove in and out of Amber's flesh, while her thumb caressed Amber's clit. I watched them lose themselves in the pleasure of the moment, neither performing for me nor seemingly aware of my presence.

There they were before me, Amber's skirt above her waist, her creamy ass against the desk. My heart raced with excitement from watching them together for a reason of which they were unaware. Amber's long blond hair hung back, and her mouth was agape, her red lips in an O. Nina was flushed, and sweat ran down her hairline, as she focused on bringing Amber to climax. As Amber's grunts and moans intensified, and her soft whispers became audible words of pleasure, I walked to the window and leaned against the ledge.

Amber's belly began to quiver. "Yes," she murmured.

I placed my hand on the opener to the blinds.

Amber's legs began to shake.

I wrapped the string around my hand tightly.

Nina pumped Amber three more times, until Amber burst into cries of delight. "Nina, yessss."

I opened the blinds.

Sunlight lit up the room. Only three feet outside the window stood Dean Henry, his old lips in the same O formation Amber's had been. He clutched his chest with a wrinkled hand.

In the midst of orgasm, Amber fought the pleasures she felt while she struggled to comprehend what had just happened. She sat upright, her breathing heavy, and her blue eyes squinted toward the window. Nina's eyes widened, and the sweat on her face glistened against the glare that shot through the window.

Students began to slow their pace, and two of them caught Dean Henry as he lost his balance. He hadn't taken his eyes off of Amber and Nina. A small crowd formed outside the window until finally Nina released her fingers from Amber and ran to close the blinds.

Amber scrambled off the desk, lowering her skirt, no longer exuding the sultry confidence she had fifteen minutes earlier. "Oh my God, my grandpa," she whined.

Amber continued to cry as she straightened herself up. "My husband . . ." She wiped sweat from her forehead. "Did you set this up?" she suddenly asked Nina.

"Amber, no, baby, no. I'd never do anything to hurt you." She reached for Amber's arm. "You know I love you. Please don't go," Nina begged.

"You've ruined us both! He'll never forgive us!" Amber shrieked at Nina before she opened the door to find Dean Henry standing outside. He was somber and angry, with tears that left the corners of his eyes and rolled over the crevices of his wrinkled face.

"Grandpa." Amber grabbed the lapels of his blazer and buried her face in his chest. She cried like a young girl who'd been caught kissing a boy behind a tree. His frail arms pushed her away from him.

"Go to my office now," he ordered. Amber hustled around the corner and disappeared. His eyes then met Nina's. "You're fired," Dean Henry barked at Nina, his thin lips trembling.

"Charles, wait." Nina ran to him, pleading as Amber had, clutching his jacket. "We can work this out, can't we? I'll do anything," she told him, her lips only inches from his. She stroked the white collar of his shirt and caressed his cheek. He grabbed her wrist and, with all the energy it seemed he could gather, pushed her away. "You've got to be kidding me. Don't you have any morals? I want you out of my building in ten minutes, or security will be here to escort you out." Dean Henry held the folder I had given him twenty minutes earlier in the air. "Taryn, thank you. The memorial is over. It's not going to happen." He turned and shuffled away.

The papers I had given Dean Henry on my way to Nina's office were the copies of entries from Layne's journals that I had made the day I found out about the hidden camera in my office. While reading the journals, I had come across numerous entries in which Layne had slandered everyone she knew, including Dean Henry, even suggesting she would be a better fit in his role than he ever had been. I had made those copies while setting up the perfect opportunity for vengeance against both Layne and Nina at the same time.

If Layne loved only one person in her world, it wasn't me or even Nina. It was herself. Nothing was more important to her than her name and the image she projected. To most hurtfully cross Layne, I had to smear her character and discredit the picture-perfect appearance she had falsely presented to almost everyone she knew. I hoped Layne's skeleton turned over in its grave at the realization that the university would delete her from its database, as if she had never taught one class.

Nina grabbed the edge of the door and leaned against it, her head resting against the wood. She closed her eyes and bit her bottom lip, her forehead bent into a confused and worried frown. She then opened her eyes and glared at me. "What have you done?" she screamed, enunciating each word slowly.

I smoothed my hair, smiling triumphantly at Nina. I walked toward her and pushed the door closed behind her. "You know, Nina, when I first read Layne's journals, I wanted to hate you. I hoped every beautiful word Layne wrote about you was a lie." I took a step closer, until I stood only a couple of inches from her face. "They weren't, though. You are just as fascinating as she said you were." I stroked her lips with my index finger. "You're irresistible."

I turned around and sat on her desk as she continued to lean against the door. "You've shown me parts of myself I didn't know existed. Like you said yourself, there's more to me than what meets the eye. But did you actually think you could have it all, Layne *and* me? Did you really think you could fuck my wife for seven years, and I'd fall right into your arms to carry on where she left off?"

"What? I thought we had something."

"We did. And now we don't."

"How could you destroy my career like this? It's all I have."

I adjusted my purse over my shoulder. "The same way you destroyed my family. It was all I had."

Nina charged at me angrily, gritting her teeth out of fury. She raised her right arm in the air, her palm wide open, to slap me, but I caught her wrist and pushed her back against the door. My left forearm pressed firmly against her esophagus, and my right hand curled into a tight fist, which I lifted over her face. My response was innate, an inherited reflex passed down from my father, as it was the grip he used on my mother when she regretfully tried to fight with him. Nina's eyes turned fearful, widening and then shutting in preparation for the punch I was ready to deliver.

My knuckles hovered over Nina's eye, the momentum of the swing halted as I contemplated whether or not to surrender to yet another part of me, the aspect of myself I had fought to ignore. In Nina's frightened state, I saw my mother, tense with fear, awaiting my father's wrath. I recalled the common saying "The apple doesn't fall far from the tree." Was I capable of inflicting physical pain like my father had on my mother? I had glimpsed my potential only weeks earlier, nearly asphyxiating Nina when I lost control on her desk.

Slowly, I lowered my arm and lightened the pressure against Nina's neck. I had accomplished what I wanted, and didn't want to impose further damage on both of us. Nina reached for her neck and rubbed it with shaky hands.

"Think twice before fucking somebody else's wife," I warned her. "It may cost you more than just a job next time."

Nina slid her body down the door and crouched into a ball on the floor. "Yeah, well, you should have thought twice about having secret meetings in your office." She peered up at me. "She knew about Pastor Ron, and she was going to tell Jenna once she put it all together. The money . . . she needed proof with the money, but for once, only once, you were smarter than her. She couldn't find it."

Grandma and her fear of big ole banks had come in handy. The money—all of it, both the proceeds from her life insurance policy and Ron's payments, a total of $175,000 in cash—was split between several designer shoe boxes in my closet and had been right under Layne's nose the entire time.

I tapped Nina's thigh with the heel of my shoe. "Better hurry. You have eight minutes left."

I opened the door and walked out.

Chapter Eleven

Ron and I sat next to one another in Jimmy's office during the first meeting we had called since our initial gathering after the shooting at the center. Ron was professionally attired, as usual, in black slacks and a blazer with a white shirt and a mustard- and black-striped tie. His demeanor was somber yet aggressive.

"I have to apologize again, Jimmy. I didn't know there would be a problem with Lewis. Cassandra and I tried to pick the best-suited kids to volunteer at the game."

"I understand you had no way of knowing," Jimmy responded. "So far, we've done a good job at reassuring the community that the center is a safe place for their kids. People were worried. Your comments to the media were helpful. We appreciate you standing up for us."

Ron had used his name and his clout to help ease the tension surrounding the center. He had invited journalists and reporters to attend his mega-church following the incident, and during that service he had prayed and had urged the community to continue its support of the center. We Are One had built a reputation as a premiere institution for youth, and it had even been compared to some nationwide services, like the Boys & Girls Clubs, and Ron refused to allow the incident to discredit the center as a trustworthy place.

"Where are we with Lewis?" I asked Ron and Jimmy.

Ron responded, "As you know, Lewis's mother contacted me to ask if the church could post bail for him, and

I had to tell her no, she'd have to raise the funds on her own. Her family wasn't able to get the money, so Lewis has been in jail since the shooting. He's being charged with attempted murder. The church will continue to pray for his family."

"And Eddie?" I asked.

"He had surgery to remove the bullets, and his organs have suffered severely. The prognosis is better," Jimmy answered, removing his glasses and rubbing his tired eyes. "He lost his ability to use his right arm, but he was finally able to go home over the weekend."

"We will not give up on that young man, because our God is a healer. The church is praying for him too," Ron added quickly. "Taryn, Cassandra and I will continue to work closely with you through this."

We all jumped out of our seats, alarmed by the sound of a door slamming down the hall.

"Where is she?" a recognizable voice yelled.

"Right this way, baby," Ms. Sheila said.

We heard scurrying outside Jimmy's office before the door sprang open, though no one knocked.

"Look who's here," Ms. Sheila announced.

Jenna, dressed in jeans and riding boots, with a multi-colored poncho draped over her upper body, darted into the room with her hands on her hips. Her cheeks flared red from anger.

Ron coughed, cleared his throat, and hacked again. He stumbled backward two steps, and I jumped up to catch his stuttering feet. Nervously, he smoothed his hair.

"Jenna, what are you doing here?" I questioned. Jenna had come home for Thanksgiving break the prior weekend, and before I left for work that morning, she'd told me she would be having lunch with one of her high school friends.

I looked to Ron, who, with his eyes closed, was in prayer. A repetitious litany of "Jesus" and "God" escaped his lips.

"Is it true?" Jenna screamed.

Jimmy walked from behind his desk and grabbed Ms. Sheila, who was propped against the door frame, by the elbow on his way out. He closed the door.

"Is what true?" I said.

"What Nina told me. Is it true?"

"Nina?" My stomach curled as I felt Layne's familiar, faraway kick from the grave. "How do you know Nina?"

"I never met her until two hours ago, when she showed up at our house, telling me my father is a big-time pastor here in the city, and worst of all, she told me that you know him and that you've kept it from me." Her words came fast. She was winded, heartbroken as she released them from her mouth. "Please tell me you haven't been lying to me all these years."

"Jenna . . ." I reached for her, but she pulled away.

"Oh my God, it's true, isn't it? She knew everything about us . . . Layne, you, me. How did she know all those things?" she cried, her voice high-pitched, resembling the screams she would wail at two years old, when in the midst of a temper tantrum. She retreated behind Jimmy's desk, her back to me.

"I can explain," I offered.

"Explain what? That you're a liar?" She didn't turn to face me. "Nina said Layne was so shocked and hurt that you kept this from both of us. How could you?"

The fast-paced events unfolding before me began to come clear. Nina, spiteful after I had exposed her and Amber to Dean Henry, causing an end to their affair and her career, had sought revenge by twisting the truth and exposing the one secret I had kept from Jenna all these years.

"That's not entirely true. There's more to the story," I told her, only she continued to throw questions in my direction.

""Did you really accept money to keep me a secret?" Jenna turned around and looked to Ron, as if noticing him for the first time. She absorbed Ron's features, a partial mixture of her own, until her eyes coated with tears. She bent forward, her arms wrapped around her stomach. She heaved, but nothing came up.

"You've got to be fucking kidding me," she muttered. "She said you would be here."

"It's just a coincidence that he's here, Jenna. He's helping to repair the damage after the shooting we had at the center."

"The shooting you told me all about, except for the part about *him* helping? Him being my father? How could you do this to me?" She turned to me, disgusted. "I just asked you about my father and you acted clueless."

I reached for her across Jimmy's desk. She jerked away, then leaned against a small window, her arms wrapped around her body in a protective hug.

"I didn't tell you I didn't know who your father was. I told you we'd talk about it later. You caught me off guard. I didn't know what to say."

"How could you keep this from me?" she demanded again.

"We thought it was for the best."

"To deny me my father! How is that the best?" she challenged.

I struggled to provide the proper explanation. "We had a family. Ron had a family. We didn't want to disrupt either household." My eyes pleaded with Ron for assistance.

He finally spoke. "Jenna, don't blame this on your mother. We both made this decision."

Her anger turned to pain, and more tears fell from her eyes. "How could you know I existed and not want to know me? How could you ignore your own daughter?"

Ashamed, he lowered his head. "I don't have an answer that would satisfy you. Here, have a seat." He led Jenna to the chair he had been sitting in before she arrived. "I knew this day would come. I just didn't know when. I should have been more prepared."

He sat down next to her.

"Your mother is a beautiful woman who has raised you the best she could. You must understand that. Your life would be unbelievably different had she not had the will and the skill to make a better life for both of you. For over half your life she did it without any help from me, and to her I am grateful for that. Your mother and I met again here at the center when you were eleven. By that time I was a pastor, married, with two young children at home. Your mother had dedicated her life to Layne, and we agreed it was best not to mingle the households."

"What? You're no better than her. You call yourself a man of God and you have a secret bastard child no one knows about?"

He tried to hold Jenna's hand in his, but she snatched it away. "I'm sorry. I wish I could change this."

"No, you don't. You've had years to make this right, and you didn't."

"I know this isn't easy," he said, attempting to understand.

"Easy for who? You? Mom? You don't know anything. You're just mad because you two got caught."

Ron's eyes met mine. The natural reddish-brown color of his eyes had darkened. He returned his focus to Jenna. "I know because I know someone this has happened to." His forehead crinkled into deep indents. "My own father had a daughter I didn't know about until I was around your age. She grew up quite troubled, tossed from foster home to foster home after her mother died young. Even though my father knew she existed, he didn't reach out to her. At around sixteen she found a family that adopted her and got her on a good path. They helped her find my father a few years later."

Jenna, still angry, with heavy breathing and frowning eyebrows, listened quietly.

"My mother and father had been married twenty years when my siblings and I met my sister. She showed up at our house one day, announced who she was, and demanded an explanation from my father. Like me, he had failed at doing the right thing when he had the chance. He said he didn't know what to do."

"This sister . . . do you still talk to her?" Jenna asked.

"My sister decided not to stay in contact with us. She was still too hurt that my father hadn't sought her after her mom passed, so she moved on with her life. Every now and then we cross paths, but for the most part, we don't hear from her."

"How could you make the same mistake as your father?" Jenna wanted to know.

"I should have learned from my father's mistake, but I didn't. I'm asking for your forgiveness. From both of you."

Jenna looked to me and then Ron with red, tear-filled eyes. "I'll try," she said softly.

"There are still many unanswered questions for you," Ron continued. "Your mother and I will do our best to answer all of them. Taryn, forgive me for not being man enough to step up and be a father to Jenna the way I have been to the children I have at home. We made the decision together, but I should have stood firmer in doing what was right, because I knew better. I have hurt all three of us by lacking that courage to speak up when I should have."

"I don't want to be like your sister," Jenna suddenly stated, her disposition shifting from anger and sorrow to an eagerness to connect with Ron. "I want to know you. I want to know my siblings. It's not too late, is it?"

Ron's expression was strained. I knew that not only was his congregation unaware of Jenna's existence, but so too was his wife, Georgeanne. Ron stood and took Jenna in his arms. "No, it's not too late at all." They hugged until they both opened their arms to me. I welcomed the warm embrace. The three of us cried together, for our own reasons, all of us shocked by the sudden, unplanned meeting between Jenna and Ron.

"With God, we will get through this," Ron affirmed.

Jimmy rapped on the door and let himself in. He stood before all of us with his hands on the hips of his plaid slacks.

"What have I missed here?" Jimmy asked.

I broke from Ron's and Jenna's embrace and flung my arms around Jimmy's neck. More tears ran onto his shoulder. Jimmy had been a godsend when I was twenty years old and had remained a consistent source of support in all the years I had known him. I regretted having kept the secret from him, as well as from Jenna.

"It's a family reunion," I whispered to him.

Stunned, Jimmy grabbed my shoulders, holding on to them but separating us. His eyes danced behind his glasses as he looked from me to Ron and Jenna. "I had no idea," he eventually said, his normally strong voice soft.

"I'm sorry for not telling you sooner. No one knew," I confessed. "Until now."

"Is that what the camera was about?" he asked me.

I nodded.

"What camera?" Ron questioned.

"We're going to head to my office," I told Jimmy. "We have some things to talk about."

"Of course." Jimmy shook Ron's hand and slapped his shoulder. "You're a good man, Pastor Ron. These ladies need you now more than ever."

"No way can I live without them," Ron said. The two men smiled at one another.

We left Jimmy's office and entered mine down the hallway, where we sat talking for three hours. Ron and I answered Jenna's questions, which ranged from what we were like as teenagers to what happened the day we reconnected, to how a woman she had never met knew about her father when she didn't.

Jenna broke down in tears once again when I told her about the day Ron saw her in person for the first time.

"It was a little over a year ago. We tried to remain inconspicuous, but it seems we were unsuccessful. Layne placed a hidden camera in my office shortly after, and from that, she confirmed that Ron was your father."

Jenna nodded. "The money?"

"I have every dime of it, and it's all yours," I assured her.

Jenna shook her head between her hands. "I still don't understand where Nina comes into all this."

I sighed, unsure how to answer, wanting neither to condemn Layne for her affair with Nina nor to admit that I had one with Nina also.

"Nina is a woman Layne and your mom knew," Ron stated. "I'm old school, Jenna. The rest is grown folks' business."

Jenna laughed. "I remember Grandma used to say that when I was little."

Ron checked his watch. "Before I go . . ." He reached into his pocket for his wallet. "This is Ron Jr., and this is Shonda." He handed Jenna pictures of her siblings just as Jenna's senior picture slipped out of his wallet. She smiled at all the photos.

"We kind of look alike. I can't wait to meet them."

Ron stood and opened his arms for another hug, which Jenna accepted. "I love you," he told her.

"I love you too. I can't wait to tell my group I'm no longer a fatherless daughter."

He kissed the top of her head. "Never again, my child, never again."

Chapter Twelve

Jenna and I sat in the second row of Ron's church and listened as the choir serenaded the congregation with its third uplifting and tearful song. Jenna and I hadn't been to church since we moved in with Layne, and Jenna, perhaps moved that we were in her father's church, appeared touched by this sentimental moment. After announcements were read by a perky teenage girl with braces, Ron rose from the pulpit and approached the podium. He wore a black robe over his suit, and his waxed shoes shone against the bright lights above him.

Ron leaned against the wood, his face stern, his sideburns glistening with perspiration. He looked at me and Jenna, then at his wife and children, who sat in front of us.

"Today I want to talk to you all about confession," he finally told the congregation, his voice low and serious. "There comes a time in all our lives when our past catches up to us. Now, I'm not saying that in a negative way. I'm saying that God has a way of bringing to light everything that's done in the dark. I have to admit, ladies and gentlemen, that I'm not a perfect man. I am a man of God and strive to live in a way that honors Him. Sometimes even I fail. That is why today I must confess my own imperfections. John said, 'If we confess our sins, he is faithful and just and will forgive us our sins and purify us from all unrighteousness. If we claim we have not sinned, we make him out to be a liar and his word is not in us.'"

Ron looked to me and Jenna. "As a young man, just shy of twenty years old, I fathered a child."

Chatter erupted throughout the congregation as church-goers began to speculate and gossip about his unexpected revelation. Since Jenna and I were new faces in the crowd, an elderly woman next to me eyed us curiously, wondering if Jenna was the child he spoke of.

"She's a beautiful young lady who I'm proud to call my daughter." Ron opened his palm in our direction. "Please stand." Jenna and I rose. "My daughter Jenna. You see, ladies and gentlemen of the Lord, God has a purpose in everything, and one of my life's greatest purposes is to be a father."

Ron continued with his sermon, a personal profession of his sorrow for not owning up to his responsibilities the way that he should have. He asked the congregation for forgiveness and acceptance of his new, expanded family. His wife, Georgeanne, gorgeous but with a stale personality, sat under a large angled hat, her stiff smile failing to undermine the grimace on her face. Ron Jr. and Shonda, who were fifteen and nine, wiggled in their seats, twisting around to wave and say hello to us.

After service, members of the church flocked to me and Jenna, hugging us and telling us we were welcome at the church anytime. Not everyone was friendly, particularly the members of Georgeanne's entourage, who flocked around her and stuck their noses in the air as they stood at her side. It was Georgeanne's duty as first lady of the church to exemplify the forgiveness Ron had asked for from his congregation. She hugged me, barely, her arms floppy against my backside the brief moment she held me.

"We're happy to have Jenna join our family," she told me. She embraced Jenna next, her hold tighter, which suggested she felt empathy for Jenna given the wayward manner her parents had handled the situation.

Afterward, Jenna and I began to exit the church. On our way out, I glimpsed a woman who sat still in the last pew. As I got closer, I saw that it was Nina, bare faced, her naturally unruly hair pulled back into a bun similar to mine. She gazed at me and Jenna, her eyes dark and flat and her lips pursed. She got up and left with the crowd before we reached her.

Jenna and I walked into the corridor and stood near a picture of her father and Georgeanne, which was enclosed in a glass case. Jenna, who was taller than me, standing at five foot nine, stared knowingly into my eyes.

"I may be young, but I'm not stupid. I can put two and two together," she said.

"What exactly do you mean?"

"Layne and Nina. And you . . . ," she said, trailing off. I didn't have a response for Jenna, and before I could prepare one, she pulled me into her arms and hugged me hard. "Is it wrong of me to be glad she died?" she whispered in my ear.

"I've wondered the same thing myself lately."

We had linked arms and started toward the glass exit doors when we heard someone call Jenna's name. We turned around to find Ron Jr. approaching us.

"My dad . . . *our* dad," he began, correcting himself. "He wants to know if you can have dinner with us." Ron Jr. was a well-dressed, smart young boy, and spoke like the privileged kids he attended private school with. "He said he'll drop you off later."

Jenna turned to me. "Mom?"

"Of course. Have a good time."

Hurriedly, she kissed my cheek and left with Ron Jr. I was putting on my gloves when a woman spoke to me.

"Shelley?"

My head shot upright, and I spun on my heels to face Clarissa.

She extended her hand to me. "Or is that not your real name?" Clarissa smiled delicately, slight crow's-feet registering about her eyes.

"I . . . um . . . Hi," I stammered, looking around to see who saw us engaged in conversation, as if we were still partially naked at the mansion.

She leaned forward and whispered. "It's okay. You're safe here." She winked.

I didn't know what to say.

"Thank God for church. My prayers have been answered." She lifted her arms in the air like she was in worship. "I had hoped to see you again. You're just as beautiful as I remembered."

"Thank you."

"Walk with me."

Clarissa led us out of the church and into the parking lot. We trod slowly, careful not to slip on the iced-over snow.

"So. Nina . . . is she still your lover?"

"You know Nina? You know Nina's real name?" I questioned.

Clarissa laughed. "Yes, I know of Nina. Once upon a time she was Nancy and I was Connie. All the newbies come up with fake names until they've acclimated." She faced me. "So tell me. What's your name?"

I hesitated before answering. "Taryn."

We approached a brand-new black Range Rover. Clarissa stopped next to the driver's door. "Taryn, I would love to meet for a cup of coffee."

"Clarissa, I appreciate the invitation." I stared at the snowflakes that had begun to fall. "I've been through a lot lately. I don't think I'm ready for what you're looking for."

"You don't know what I'm looking for until I've offered it," she told me. "Let's start with coffee and take it from there. Come on. Who doesn't love a good cup of java?"

I kicked ice with the pointy heel of my boot. "Okay. Yes."

Clarissa reached into her designer bag and handed me her card. "Wonderful. Call me." She pushed the remote to unlock her door, got inside the car, and drove off. Only once I was inside my own car did I look at the card. Clarissa Benson was a vice president at one of the nation's most renowned accounting firms. I slid her card into my wallet, smiling to myself. Nina was right. Voyeurs were everywhere, at every turn, and you never knew where you might bump into one.

Jenna and I had decided to travel for a portion of her Christmas break. She had returned home before our scheduled flight to New York City, where we would enjoy a seven-day vacation. I was finishing packing the night before our departure when I realized I needed more baggage. I went into the guest bedroom to retrieve another piece of luggage. My heart stumbled in my chest when I picked up a carry-on bag. It hadn't been used since our family trip to the Virgin Islands, and my mind recalled seeing it draped over Layne's shoulder as she brought it from the car into the house the night before she died.

I returned to my bedroom, placed the small carry-on on my bed, and began filling it with scarves and hats, the same accessories I'd choose for Chicago's weather. When I opened a side pocket to stow my jewelry, I found an envelope. On it was my name, written in Layne's handwriting. I flipped the envelope repeatedly in my hands, caressed the lettering, my finger tracing the large, loopy *T* at the beginning of my name. Finally, I sat on the bed and slowly opened the cream paper.

My dearest Taryn,

I write this letter to you as our annual family vacation comes to an end. It is with a heavy heart that I begin this note, as I am unsure how to express what I have to say. For the first time in ten years, I will try.

I love you. Oh, how I love you. I have loved you since the moment I laid eyes on you. You have done nothing but love me unconditionally and unselfishly, and yet I cannot tell you I have mirrored the same love for you. I have wronged you in unimaginable ways, and I beg you in advance for forgiveness. At last, my eyes have opened. You will see a change in me once we're home. I recommit my vows to you and promise from this day forward to love you as you have always deserved.

For years, you asked why I loved you. Let me tell you. . . .

Taryn, you are the sunshine peeking through the clouds on a rainy day

The star I wish upon on a moonlit night, filling me with hope.

You are a butterfly grazing my skin with delicate kisses against my lips,

The nectar of a flower whose sweetness I crave,

My favorite melody played softly in my ear.

You are an orange sun grazing the horizon, shedding light on my day,

The treasure found at the end of my rainbow,

A treasure so golden, so precious, and so rare.

You are forever locked within the walls of my heart,

And the key only you shall hold.

As long as my heart beats, it beats for you.

And even once it stops, know that I love you.

Always. Forever. Layne

With the back of my hand, I wiped the salty tears that streamed down my face. Jenna knocked on the door and peeked her head inside the room.

"Mom, you okay?" she asked after noticing my tears. She sat next to me on the bed and stroked my hair, which I had begun to wear down regularly.

I sniffed. "Yes." I placed the letter back in the envelope and set it on my lap. "It's from Layne. She wrote it the day before the accident."

"What does it say?"

Another tear escaped and fell onto the envelope. I wiped it gently with my index finger. "It says everything I always wanted to hear."

Jenna leaned forward and kissed my cheek. "I love you."

"I love you too."

"I'm going to bed. I'll see you in the morning."

"The car will be here at seven. Meet me downstairs."

We hugged tightly before she got up and left. I set the envelope next to the carry-on, and then I continued adding personal items to it. When I finished packing, I positioned the luggage upright at my door and retrieved the small gold key from a dish on Layne's nightstand. Before I left to go downstairs, I pulled my hair into a tight bun, securing it with several hairpins. I took the letter into Layne's office, closing the door behind me. I sat at her desk and used the key to open the bottom right drawer.

I removed all of Layne's journals and tearfully replaced them with the letter. At last, I had what I had always wanted from Layne: a declaration of her love for me. In that moment, as I took Layne's journals to the shredder, I realized that I was and always would be the fruit of my mother's labor, the reverential offspring who clung to the roots from which she had sprouted.

Page by page, I erased the truth of Layne's past, my mind and heart focused solely on the future we'd never see.

With all that had happened since Layne's death, I wanted to act on the new woman I thought I had become: strong, independent, and carefree. And yet at my core I was my mother's child, a woman who wanted only to be loved in whatever form it came. I accepted Layne's profession of love with a sense of liberation, because in the end, Layne had wanted a new beginning with me. She might never have shown me, and now she would never be able to prove it, but I believed she loved me, just because she told me so.

Honey and Absinthe

by

Fiona Zedde

Chapter 1

Chloe Graham used her hip to shut the door of her green Honda Civic. She tripped over the sidewalk and cursed, almost falling over her small suitcase.

"Shit!" she muttered under her breath as she grabbed the handle of the suitcase and wrestled it up onto the sidewalk. Then she picked up her duffel bag and yanked it up to her shoulder.

In black stilettos, a short yellow skirt, and a barely there sheer blouse that exposed her black bra and diamond belly ring, she was definitely not dressed for moving. But it was what she felt like wearing. It had been a real hell of a week, and she wanted to feel at least a little pretty to counteract some of that. Never mind the fact that it was October in Atlanta and what she could actually feel was the bite of the wind on just about every part of her skin.

Shivering, Chloe quickly made her way up the driveway, past a gleaming black convertible, to the light green, three-story house that belonged to her mother and stepfather.

Even with the wind, the mid-afternoon sun warmed her arms and shoulders, sinking into her halo of natural coils and into her scalp as she hurried up the drive. She was tired and sad. But she didn't want to look like either of those things, hence, the stilettos and tiny skirt. They were her armor against all the bullshit the world had recently thrown at her in the form of an unfaithful girlfriend and the need to move back home at the ripe old age of twenty-three, just because she lost her high-paying, straight-out-of-college job to said ex-girlfriend and side chick drama.

She'd already had a long day, having dropped off in a storage unit nearby the meager possessions she'd gathered in the five years of living away from home. With the U-Haul returned and her car off the tow dolly, she felt a bit more like herself. More free.

She clattered up the front porch with her bags and fumbled to unlock the door, nearly dropping the keys twice in the process. As she pushed open the door, the smell of fresh baked bread flowed out to meet her. She heard raucous feminine laughter, Goapele's light and sensuous voice on the stereo singing about angel wings fluttering. Stepping into the bright living room of her parents' home, which was like a page from *Southern Living* magazine, Chloe immediately felt an unburdening, a sense of everything being better with the world. The familiar feeling of belonging whenever she was in Atlanta.

"Honey!" Her mother jumped up from the couch with a wide and welcoming smile. "I didn't know you were coming today."

Kai, the other woman sitting on the couch, crinkled the corners of her eyes but did not stand.

On the coffee table were the remnants of a pumpernickel loaf and two glasses of hot apple cider. Her mother, a gourmet caterer and personal chef, must have just baked bread and invited her friend over to sample it.

"Surprise," Chloe said, weakened by her mother's happiness and Kai's unexpected presence. She had barely dropped her bags on the floor before her mother swept her up in a tight hug, kissing her cheeks. Her eyes tingled with the tears she hadn't shed the entire time her ex-girlfriend, Jerica, had been tearing her life apart.

"If you'd told me you were coming today, we would have helped you."

Her mother, slender and beautiful with her short silver hair and a knee-length orange sheath dress, spoke automatically for her best friend, who only leaned back farther on the couch to watch them.

"Hey, Little Bit." Kai greeted Chloe with a widening of her smile, calling her the nickname she'd used for her since she was a child.

Kai was coolness itself, as evidenced by her masculine sprawl in her corner of the couch. As she tilted her head at Chloe, her waist-length copper locks caught the sunlight pouring in through the windows on both sides of the room. The multicolored scarf she wore over the thin cotton shirt she'd paired with loose jeans fit her sinfully well. When she was younger, Chloe often teased her that she was like a female version of Lenny Kravitz.

"Hi, Mom. Kai." Chloe smiled despite the exhaustion of the day. And despite the knocking in her chest at the sight of her mother's best friend. "You know I had to do things on my own. Everything's already been put into storage. This is all I have with me until I sort out the job in New York."

Her mother tugged at a long coil of Chloe's hair. "What on earth are you wearing?"

"Clothes." Giving her mother a devilish look, Chloe pulled away and waited for Kai to approach her.

Light flickered in the depths of Kai's green and gold eyes as she took in all of Chloe. Moving with her typical lethargic grace, she rose from the couch for her hug. She never rushed to do anything, even when she was supposed to be in a hurry.

"You used to dress like this back in the day, Noelle. Don't even act." Kai pulled Chloe into her tall body.

Warmth. The smell of the spicy-sweet cinnamon and rose body oil she wore. The strong arms that always seemed like they could handle anything. As they hugged,

Kai's necklace, a fire opal set in silver and hanging from a silver chain, pressed into Chloe's collarbone.

"Thank you, Kai." Chloe allowed herself to cling briefly to the other woman and breathe deeply of her scent. "It's good to see you."

Chloe was in love with Kai, completely and unequivocally.

This unrequited love was the reason she'd left Atlanta to go to Los Angeles for school. Even though she would have loved to go to Spelman, her feelings for the older woman in her last few years of high school had been out of control. The only way she knew to get past them was to run to the other side of the country. And now here she was again.

Chloe bit the inside of her cheek and pulled back from Kai, even though she longed to lean on her until the exhaustion in her body went away, along with all the problems that had plagued her in the past year.

"Kai and I were about to go grab a bite at The Flying Biscuit. You should come with us. We'll buy you lunch, and you can tell us all about the drive from California."

"That's the last thing I want to talk about." Chloe made a face. "But I will take you up on lunch, though."

"Good." Kai glanced at Chloe's high heels. "You may want to change your shoes. We're walking down there." The restaurant was less than half a mile from the house.

"Okay. Just give me a sec." Chloe reached for her duffel bag, but before she could lift it, Kai took it from her.

"I'm surprised you didn't break your shoulder carrying this thing." Kai lifted the bag to her shoulder. "What do you have in here? Weights?"

"Just a few books, shoes, and clothes." Chloe shrugged. Plus, her vibrator and spare batteries.

"Like mother, like daughter." Kai strode ahead of her with the duffel bag, her steps long and graceful as she headed for the stairs.

Her mother grabbed Chloe's suitcase. "Let us at least do this for you." She turned to follow Kai.

Chloe stepped into her bedroom in time to see Kai drop her duffel bag on the bed. Her entire body prickled with awareness of the other woman—all five feet, ten inches of muscled flesh and confident beauty—who seemed at ease no matter where she was. How often had she dreamed of having Kai in her bedroom?

She slipped past Kai to unzip the duffel bag, trying to act naturally as the woman turned to leave the room. Behind her, she heard her mother curse softly and drop the suitcase.

"Grab this bag for me, please, Kai. My cell phone's ringing." Her mother ran back downstairs.

"I can get it," Chloe said a moment before Kai brushed past her to pick up the suitcase.

"Maybe next time, Little Bit," she said with a grin.

She rolled the suitcase into the room and against the far wall while Chloe dug into her duffel for a different pair of shoes to wear. Maybe even different clothes. She was suddenly self-conscious with so much skin on display in front of Kai.

The older woman hesitated in the doorway, hands in the pockets of her jeans, the patchwork scarf bringing out the fierce green in her eyes. "Everything okay, Little Bit? You don't seem like yourself."

Chloe grabbed a pair of red Converse from the duffel bag, then, after a pause, sat down on the bed to take off her stilettos.

I wish you wouldn't call me Little Bit. I'm not a child anymore.

"Things are okay now," she said instead. "My last few months in LA were a mess. It's good to be home, though."

"If you ever want to talk about it, you know I'm here."

"I do. Thanks."

Kai nodded once, then slowly left the room. Chloe let out a deep breath.

Yes, Kai was there.

She couldn't forget that if she tried. Even now, her unsteady breath reminded her of the many daydreams she'd had about Kai, the times she'd touched herself to thoughts of the other woman simply kissing her. Chloe's fingers trembled as she searched her duffel bag for a pair of jeans.

Kai was the most handsome and most beautiful woman Chloe had ever known. Her mother had often teased her about how, when Chloe was a baby, Kai was the only person she would allow to hold her without fussing or crying with enough lung power to wake the dead.

If anything, her childhood adoration for her mother's best friend had grown only deeper. Her feelings had grown from an infatuation to a teenage crush to this deep and troubling desire that threatened to incinerate her from the inside out. She'd tried so many times to kill her love for Kai, to tell herself that it was wrong and that it could never bear anything more than rotten fruit. But her heart wanted what it wanted. And it wanted only Kai.

The only good thing about being bombarded by memories and her desire for Kai was that it distracted her from what she had just gone through with Jerica. The pangs of her ex's betrayal were already less than when she'd walked in the house. If Kai kept up this palliative effect, Chloe would be over all her ex drama by the next week. Hopefully.

She smiled wryly at herself in the mirror before quickly changing into a jacket, tight jeans, and her Converse.

Downstairs, she met Kai and her mother at the door.

"I'm ready," Chloe announced.

They left the house and took the winding sidewalk toward the Candler Park neighborhood, strolling shoulder to shoulder through the fallen leaves. Chloe drew in a deep breath of the autumn air, enjoying the crispness of it in her lungs. This was nothing like LA, and she was grateful for that.

"That looks much better," her mother said, eyeing Chloe's outfit. She looped her arm around Chloe's.

"Or at least warmer." Kai's bright eyes skimmed over Chloe's body in a casual appraisal. "But you look beautiful no matter what you're wearing."

Chloe nearly stumbled at the unexpected compliment, far used to the other woman being more sparing with her praises. She found herself staring at Kai, then forced her eyes away when her mother asked her how long she planned on staying in Atlanta.

"I'm here only for a little while. A month, maybe less. Once that job comes through in New York, I'm gone again."

"That's so soon. I thought you'd at least be here through Christmas," her mother replied.

Chloe shook her head. "Definitely not that long. If it hadn't been for Jerica, I'd probably still be in LA at Creative Faces." She named the special effects studio where she had worked until her ex-girlfriend's antics in the parking lot got her fired.

She had loved that job, had taken pride in being able to call her mother and say that she'd done the monster makeup for a movie showing on TV. Most days, Chloe mourned the loss of her job more than the girl who'd cheated on her.

"I told you Jerica was bad for you," her mother said. "You were much better off with that other one. What was her name? The artist who did nude paintings of you . . . Khaulah, I think her name was."

Chloe exchanged a laughing glance with Kai. "You know very well that was her name."

Her mother had liked Khaulah for Chloe only because she had had a minor straight-woman crush on her. The curly-haired artist had been profane and funny, perennially sexy in a V-necked shirt, with whiskey-colored eyes that laughed before her mouth did. But Khaulah had wanted important things that Chloe hadn't, at least not yet—children, a home, marriage—so they had to go their separate ways.

Her mother looked at her with mischievous eyes and squeezed Chloe's hip. "She was such a little devil. She would have made your life so interesting."

Chloe swore that if her mother hadn't been happily married to her stepfather for over fifteen years now, she would have made a play for the light-skinned artist.

"I don't need *interesting*, Mom," she said with a faint smile. "Jerica gave me plenty of that, and I'm so over it."

Chloe nodded in greeting as they passed other people making the Saturday afternoon walk down to the little strip of restaurants and independent shops. The day hummed with the sound of the wind through the trees, the rustle of fallen leaves stirred up by passing cars, and the faint rattle of the MARTA train nearby.

"If you need anything regarding the job, just let me know, Chloe," Kai said, breaking the comfortable silence. "I have some contacts in New York who might be able to help you."

Chloe nodded, thinking the last thing she needed was to create any sort of connection with Kai in New York. Especially when she was trying to run away from her attraction to the woman. "Thanks, Kai. I'll let you know if I do."

They continued down the hill toward The Flying Biscuit, chatting about inconsequential things. The Southern food restaurant was one of her mother's favorites and a place Chloe had practically grown up in. The staff and the signature T-shirts had changed over the years, but the menu had, thankfully, stayed the same. She was addicted to their wheat biscuits and apple butter.

Over lunch, she caught her mother and Kai up on the latest drama in her life, including Jerica's latest stunt, which was the last straw. Not only had she come to Chloe's job acting a fool so many times that the police were called and Chloe was eventually fired, but Jerica had also broken into Chloe's apartment, begging for a second chance at the relationship, swearing that Chloe was wrong and that there was no other woman. Chloe knew Jerica had been telling the truth about that one thing: there had been no other woman. There had been *dozens* of women. So many that Chloe was embarrassed that she hadn't realized the sheer magnitude of Jerica's infidelity.

Jerica, a merchant banker, had been sleeping with three of the tellers at the bank where she worked, a neighbor in Chloe's apartment complex, even one of her old professors at UCLA. It had been humiliating. Then Jerica had had the nerve to try and play her for a fool again, telling Chloe that there hadn't been anyone else, when the evidence had slapped Chloe so hard in the face that she practically got whiplash. When a woman approached her with Jerica's cum-stained panties, explicit text messages and tit-for-tat crotch shots, Chloe didn't even have the luxury of disbelief.

But Jerica had been a player when Chloe met her. *Chloe* had been the fool for trying to change someone who was obviously still enjoying the way she lived her life. To be honest, though, the most beguiling thing about Jerica was that she looked like Kai.

"And that's who you left Khaulah for?" Her mother shook her head.

"Noelle," Kai said with a squeeze of her best friend's hand as they sat around the lunch table. "That's not what she needs right now."

"Sorry, honey." Her mother took a bite of her shrimp and grits, her dark eyes flickering with a wicked humor that Chloe had never quite gotten used to.

"Noelle is just kidding," Kai said. She sliced into a fried green tomato and brought a piece to her mouth.

"No, she's not." Chloe wrinkled her nose. "Anyway, I know I made a mistake with Jerica. That's in the past now. I have New York and a new life to look forward to."

"Darling . . ." Her mother grew serious. "You know I tease you sometimes, but I just worry you won't find the right partner for you. Someone who loves and cherishes you like you deserve." She squeezed Chloe's hand. "By the time I was your age, I already had Duncan in my life."

Chloe tugged back her hand to sip her mango iced tea. "Kai's still single, and I don't see you worrying about her."

"Oh, I do worry." Her mother glanced at Kai with a grin. "But you're still not old enough yet to hear those conversations."

Kai chuckled. "Shit, *I'm* not old enough."

The two friends shared a smile.

After lunch, they went back to the house. In the foyer, Kai announced that she was about to leave and give the two women time alone.

Chloe hugged Kai good-bye, the familiar feeling of longing mixed with relief sitting in her chest. She wanted Kai near but knew that she shouldn't. Every time she'd thought over the years of declaring her love for her mother's best friend, she'd forced herself to remember what the two women were to each other.

Noelle Williams had gotten pregnant in high school, when she was much younger than Chloe. She had barely known what to do with a child, as she was still one herself, a smart sixteen-year-old with a formerly bright future in front of her.

Kai, her best friend since kindergarten and an out lesbian all their lives, had been supportive of her friend throughout her entire pregnancy and the birth of her child, standing in place of Chloe's father, who had been a high school senior at the time and had run as far from the responsibility of parenthood as his Harvard scholarship could carry him.

Even when Kai left for college, and eventually a job in New York, she remained a constant in her best friend's life, helping to soothe her worries when Chloe came out as a lesbian, assuring Noelle, who was worried that her daughter would cut off her hair and start dressing like a boy, that if Chloe hadn't shown those proclivities before, it was unlikely she'd start doing so now.

"She's a femme who likes makeup and clothes," Chloe remembered overhearing Kai say to her mother once.

And quietly, Chloe had said to herself that she was a femme who liked girls who dressed like boys. Much later— once Noelle had calmed down about Chloe's compromised future entailing a house, a husband, and two-point-five children—she'd asked her daughter if it was because of Kai that she wanted to be a lesbian. Did the older woman glamorize her gay life so much that it made Chloe want to be her?

Chloe could only say no. She didn't feel it was okay for her, as a fifteen year-old, to say that she didn't want to *be* Kai, but that she wanted to be *with* her. No. Her mother would not have appreciated that at all.

While her mother walked Kai to the door, Chloe sat on the couch and waited out their good-bye. She leaned back and listened to the sound of Kai's quiet steps in the loafers that she preferred, her feet barely making a sound against the wooden floor compared to the click of her mother's high heels. Chloe took a deep breath, trembling, as she thought again of Kai's body. Her easy confidence and the way she moved with a slow, coiled energy made Chloe wonder how she would be in bed.

Her mother came back into the living room and sat on the couch next to Chloe. "Okay. What aren't you telling me?"

Chloe shook herself from her daydream of Kai's body. "What do you mean?"

"There's something going on with you. You haven't said anything, but I can see it on your face. Kai senses it too."

Chloe forced herself to relax beneath her mother's penetrating stare. "Your senses might be a little off. Everything's fine."

Her mother held her gaze for a long while. "Just because you're almost twenty-four doesn't make me worry any less about you. And it doesn't make you too old to confide in me." Her mother propped her elbow against the back of the couch and faced Chloe. "Please keep that in mind."

"I will."

Her mother drew a deep breath. "Okay. I understand if you're not ready to tell me what it is. Maybe you can talk with Kai."

Chloe automatically shook her head, recoiling at the mere idea of sharing her secret with the object of her desire. "No."

"Ah, then there *is* something." Her mother looked both pleased and worried. "That's what I thought. And that's fine. I hope you can resolve it while you're here. Whatever it is."

Can I make this attraction disappear in the next few weeks? She plucked at the knee of her jeans, avoiding her mother's eyes. "I hope so too."

A slender hand tapped Chloe's thigh. "Well, if you're going to mope around the house, you might as well help me out in the kitchen." Her mother stood up. "I'm baking scones for a client."

"Almond butter?" Despite her recent meal, her taste buds perked up. "If I didn't know any better, I'd think you were trying to distract me."

Her mother squeezed her waist, surrounding her with the scent of skin-warmed patchouli. "But you do know better, don't you?"

Chloe smiled and leaned into Noelle Graham's shoulder, grateful for her love and perceptiveness. Just then her cell phone chimed.

"Excuse me a sec," Chloe said absently as she plucked her cell from her back pocket.

"Hey, girl," a warm and Southern sweet voice sang in her ear.

It was her friend Zahra, who still lived in Atlanta. They had grown up together in the same neighborhood and had taken divergent paths after high school. Zahra had decided to stay in Atlanta and go to Spelman College, while Chloe had left for LA. But they had remained close during the five years they had spent on opposite coasts.

"What's up?"

"You made it home yet?"

Her mother gave a little wave, indicating she was heading to the kitchen. Chloe nodded and propped her hand on her hip, slowly crossing the living room while talking to her friend.

"Yeah, about two hours ago. I just got back from lunch with Mom and Kai."

"Oh, yeah, that hottie Kai." Zahra laughed, a husky and filthy sound. "When are you finally going to get a piece of that?"

"Stop it!" Chloe hissed, flashing a panicked glance at the doorway her mother had just disappeared through. "Don't say that."

"As if you haven't been thinking it for the past two hours."

Chloe squeezed her eyes shut, regretting the day, drunk and horny from cheap Southern Comfort, she had confessed her Kai crush to Zahra. It was something that her friend had never allowed her to forget, bringing it up at the most inconvenient times, so she barely had a chance to forget about her foolish and impractical desires.

"I haven't!"

"Liar!" Zahra chuckled. "Anyway, I didn't call to torture you about your fantasy lover. My boss gave me free tickets to the fair for next Saturday. I think you should come with me."

"I think I *will* come with you." Chloe grinned.

She and Zahra had gone together to the fair as kids, but some of her best memories were from being there with her mother and with Kai, a girls' day and night out that usually started with brunch and ended with hot cider in front of the crackling fireplace.

"Good. I'm glad I didn't have to work too hard to convince you to come with me."

Through the phone, Chloe heard the sound of glass tapping glass, the gurgle of liquid, as if Zahra was pouring herself some wine.

"I know you don't like to work for it," Chloe said.

"Damn right."

Chloe laughed again. "Just text me what time you want to go, and I'll be ready."

"Sounds like a plan," Zahra said. "Now, go back to baking cookies, or whatever *Cosby Show* shit you and your mom are about to get into. This vibrator is about to start screaming my name."

"Too much damn information." Chloe hung up the phone at the sound of her friend's laughter.

It was good to have someone who knew her that well. Someone to tease her about her childhood crush and the fact that she and her mother always baked together. That was one of the things she'd missed out in LA, with only strangers around her, for five years. It was good to be home.

Chloe went to bed that night with that same feeling of contentment at being home and with her family. After a long hot shower, she slipped between the sheets, Diana King's latest album playing on her iPod.

Now that she was away from the warm smells and the beautiful chaos of her mother's kitchen, the memories of what she'd been trying to escape by leaving California came flooding back to her. Jerica. The lover who had been the most like Kai. So much like her that Chloe had even convinced herself that she was in love with her. At least for a little while.

The sheets rustled as she turned over in the bed, a pillow pressed to her stomach.

Jerica, younger than Kai by almost fifteen years, was arrogant and self-consciously sexy. But at the time Chloe saw those things as simply confidence. Jerica was aware that she looked good, with her long, wavy hair, seductive brown eyes, and athletic body. But she had no idea everything about her was a pale copy of another woman. A better woman.

There were nights when they made love and Jerica's fingers gripped Chloe's hips while she took her from behind, the splendid friction of their strap-on sex and the doggie-style position allowing Chloe to imagine that it was Kai who was fucking her. Kai stroking her so deeply with her detachable dick that Chloe felt the heat of it in her throat and her tightening nipples. Her head flinging back as she bit her lip and barely stopped herself from crying out the wrong name.

She stirred restlessly in the sheets, her thighs sticky with the remembered pleasure of those nights. She pressed her fingers between her legs and hissed in arousal. It was easy to let go of the specter of Jerica and reach for the preferred fantasy of Kai, the pain and betrayal of what she'd endured in California floating away as she called up the ready image of her dream lover. Kai's mouth on her pussy, the glittering beacon of her eyes guiding Chloe toward orgasm.

She moaned and quivered in the bed.

Chapter 2

Late evening sunlight draped over the large fairgrounds, haloing the Ferris wheel, the cotton-candy carts, food stands, and the scarlet big-top tent that loomed above it all. Chloe leaned against the wall leading to the public restrooms, waiting for Zahra. To pass the time, she watched the other fairgoers wander past, talking and enjoying themselves, some carrying large stuffed toys they'd won. The smells of barbecue, freshly popped kettle corn, and roasting corn on the cob laced the air.

A woman walked in Chloe's direction to go into the restroom, then did a double take when she saw Chloe. She nearly slammed into the wall as she tried unsuccessfully to walk and stare at the same time. The woman, a pretty femme in a maxi dress, with a lush Afro, smiled at Chloe, blushed, then disappeared around the wall toward the restroom.

Zahra came from the restroom, brushing a hand down the front of her tight jeans. Her long straightened and colored hair fluttered around her face as she shook her head. "Remind me never to take that sixty-four-ounce lemonade challenge again."

Chloe laughed. "I already told you not to do it."

"Yes, but did you see that hot stud behind the counter? I swear, she was eyeing me."

"You swear that everybody is eyeing you."

"Aren't they?" Zahra stuck a pink lollipop in her mouth and struck a pose. Ass out, D-cup breasts on display in a low-cut gingham blouse, pouty lips fastened to the sticky candy.

With her thick hair pressed out around her shoulders and down her back, her big black eyes, and a mouth that had brought many women to their knees, Zahra was absolutely gorgeous. Her body was stacked in all the right places, and she never hesitated about showing it off.

When the two girls had met in middle school, Zahra had introduced herself by saying they either had to be best friends or enemies for life, since Chloe was the only girl at school as pretty as her.

"Girl, come on!" Chloe rolled her eyes and grabbed her friend's elbow.

They had been at the fair for more than two hours, most of the time spent eating the ridiculous fair food, including doughnut hamburgers, and staring at the pretty *young* stud behind the counter at the lemonade stand. Although she was having fun with Zahra, Chloe was ready to do something else.

Zahra bumped her hip. "Let's ride the roller coaster next. I feel a need for a good long scream."

Chloe grinned. "Is that why you've been trying to get that young girl from behind the counter of the lemonade stand?"

"Oh, that's a very good idea." Zahra's black eyes twinkled, as if she'd never thought of it. "Let's go by there one more time and give her one last chance to ask me out."

Before Chloe could protest, her friend was dragging her toward the bright yellow lemonade stand, which already had a long line in front of it, mostly what seemed to be thirsty femmes waiting for a taste of that same stud Zahra wanted. But the girl wasn't behind the counter.

Her friend made a sound of disappointment. "Damn! She probably already went home for the day."

"I'd like to go home with you, though."

They both turned around at sound of the low feminine voice. The stud from behind the counter at the lemonade stand. The girl had changed her clothes—she was definitely a girl, probably still in college by the looks of her. Before her short locks had been pulled back from her face with a headband, but now she wore her hair loose around her face. And instead of a stained white apron, she wore a striped polo shirt, a bow tie, and skinny jeans. Very queer boi.

"Damn, you clean up nice," Zahra said. She approached the girl, looking predatory and femme sexy with her blouse-popping cleavage and dark, wet smile.

Chloe could see the night was going to end with the hard piece of jailbait sitting in Zahra's passenger seat instead of her. It was a good thing that she always traveled with enough money to get herself back home, no matter where she was.

"Hey." Chloe nodded at the girl, who gave her a lingering glance and a quick hello, before turning back to Zahra. "I'm going to take a look around the grounds for a while, Z," she said.

"Are you sure?" Zahra looked like her mind was already in the girl's pants. "We could all just hang out together." The tone of her voice said something else entirely.

"No, I need to walk off all the food I just ate," Chloe said. "Besides, there's a watermelon-judging contest I want to see that started . . ." She glanced at her nonexistent wristwatch. "About ten minutes ago. If I hurry, I can catch the seedless entries."

"Oh, okay." Her friend's voice was distracted. "I'll see you later. Text me if you need something."

And why would I do that? "Sure." Chloe turned and left them.

Although Chloe loved Zahra dearly, she knew her friend was a sucker for a handsome girl with muscles. They'd gone out together countless times, only to end up taking separate cars at the end of the night because Zahra had found a girl she wanted.

Chloe wasn't worried. She was in the town she'd grown up in and at a fair she had gone to over a dozen times. She had money in her pocket and pepper spray ready for any emergency. Still, although she enjoyed the fair, it wasn't necessarily a place she ever wanted to be by herself. But if she had no choice, then she would make the most of it. She paid for a ticket to ride the Ferris wheel and climbed into one of the cars alone.

The lush curtain of evening was falling, the sunlight already turning a darker gold in the sky. She squinted behind her sunglasses as the wheel swept up with a lurch and a squeak, carrying her slowly into the sky. Chloe leaned back in the car and looked out over the fairgrounds. At the people, the clowns, the brightly colored tents, and the roller coaster, which rippled like the outline of a mountain range on the other side of the park. She wasn't a big fan of roller coasters and had gone on one only once, on a dare from Kai when she was a teenager. It had been terrifying, and she hadn't done it since.

Kai. Even with all the distractions of the day, the older woman hadn't been far from her mind. While she'd watched her friend flirt with her stud, she'd thought about Kai. Wondered what she was doing. If she was dating anybody. What it would be like to share something as simple as an evening alone with her.

Useless thoughts.

She shook her head, holding on to the metal bar of the Ferris wheel car as it swung down, slowly descending back to earth. The attendant, a pimply boy with braces, unlocked her from the car and helped her step down.

"Thanks."

She turned away, adjusting her purse under her arm.

"You want to go back up again?"

The sound of Kai's voice took her by surprise. "Hey! What are you doing here?" It was like she'd conjured the other woman from her daydreams.

Although, not even in her dreams had Kai looked that good. She wore scuffed cowboy boots, jeans that clung to her firm thighs, a faded Angela Davis T-shirt with a ripped collar, and a brown leather jacket. Her locks were pulled back from her face, showing off her bright eyes and firm lips. Chloe frowned at the hint of tension around the other woman's mouth.

"I'm here with a couple of friends." Kai waved absently behind her. "But I was walking back from the turkey-leg stand when I noticed you up in the air all alone." Kai glanced behind her, as if she expected someone to materialize behind Chloe. "Who are you with?"

"I came with Zahra, but she met up with someone else." But as the words fell off her tongue, she thought they sounded a little pathetic. "Not that I mind," she rushed to reassure Kai. The last thing she wanted was for the other woman to feel sorry for her.

"I'm sure you don't," Kai said with the barest smile. "You've always been pretty independent. Noelle and I always loved that about you."

I wish you could love me the way I love you. Chloe stared into Kai's eyes as the crowd moved around them, unable to look away. Then she cleared her throat, forcing herself to get a grip. "So, are you going to go back to your friends now?"

"No. I think they can fend for themselves. Despite your independence, I don't like the idea of you being out here on your own."

Chloe frowned. "I'm twenty-three, Kai. Not thirteen."

"I know very well how old you are, Chloe." She glanced up at the Ferris wheel. "So, how about that repeat ride?"

Chloe shrugged. She didn't have anything else to do. "Okay."

The ride on the Ferris wheel was different with Kai at her side. Chloe was more aware of everything—the sun's heat on her face, a deeper chill in the fall air as the day retreated, Kai's particular scent. She shivered with awareness in her corner of the car, her stomach dipping and swaying with her nervousness. The other woman smelled differently today, like cinnamon and cloves. The spicy fragrance twined in her locks and in her clothes, inviting Chloe's nose closer. She deliberately stayed on her side of the car.

"What kind of incense do you burn?" she asked suddenly.

Kai glanced at her, an eyebrow raised in surprise. She knew that Chloe didn't like incense, that the smoke irritated her nose. "A few kinds," she said. "Depending on my mood."

"Oh. Whatever it is you burned today smells good." She'd been to Kai's place countless times in her life. The downtown Decatur condo, with its view of the square and the quiet area Chloe had always loved. Kai's condo was as charming and lovely as Kai was and always smelled like some sort of incense or fragrant oil.

"I didn't burn any today."

Chloe tightened her hand on the bar across her lap, realizing that it was the other woman's body oil that made her smell so delectable, a sweet scent she wanted to sniff the source of and burrow into. Had she rubbed the oil on her breasts? Were there traces of it between her thighs? Would the oil be sweet to the taste or bitter, like forbidden fruit?

Jesus!

She savagely bit her lip to curb her lustful thoughts.

"It's okay, you know," Kai said.

"What do you mean?"

"Just relax with me. You don't have to worry about whatever is on your mind so heavily these days. Look at this beautiful day. Let it ease into your spirit and take you away from all your troubles." Her soft voice drifted around them.

The Ferris wheel car creaked as they climbed higher into the air. A cool wind brushed against Chloe's face, stroking her lips.

"Are you taking the same advice?" Chloe had noticed a faint tightening around Kai's mouth, which was unusual for her. A sign that she was worried about something.

"I'm doing my best." The older woman flashed a smile, although muted shadows lurked in the green and gold depths of her eyes. "But things will unfold as the universe determines."

Chloe couldn't hold back her smile. Despite Kai's corporate job, she was a bit of a hippie. She had an altar at home, where she burned candles and honored her ancestors. She loved festivals like the Michigan Womyn's Music Festival and Burning Man. And she had never seen an incense cone she could resist. But she also loved to make money, and she enjoyed skiing and everything else that her six-figure job afforded her. Chloe loved those contradictions.

People saw Kai as this tough dyke in charge, with her long copper-colored locks, intense eyes, and a face that was almost too handsome to be real. But it made her feel special to know that under all that, Kai was a kind woman who'd rather lie in a hammock and listen to Tibetan chants than watch TV. That she had a laugh so big and wide, it invited others to join in. That she was the perfect partner to a woman who could appreciate her.

"Yes, they will," Chloe said, responding to Kai's comment about the universe's will. "For better or for worse."

"Baby, in the end it's usually for the better."

Chloe shivered at the endearment. Was this the real reason she had come back to Atlanta? To hear Kai call her "baby" and to bask in the older woman's company? To get more of the real thing before she went off again on a search for a suitable imitation?

But I don't want another imitation. I want the real thing. "Are you seeing anyone these days?"

"Why do you ask that?"

"It's a question." Chloe shrugged. "We're two grown women having an adult conversation, right?"

Kai's gaze flickered down Chloe's body. "Yes, we are." She tightened and released her hands around the car's safety bar. "No, I'm not seeing anybody right now. I'm actually in my second year of celibacy."

"Celibacy?" Chloe didn't bother to hide her shock. A woman like Kai was walking sex. Inspiring a thousand wet dreams with her long-legged and loose-limbed stride, that sexy smile, and that finely muscled body, which made women want to drop to their knees in worship. "Why?"

Kai laughed. "Don't look so surprised. It hasn't been a hardship," she said. "Sex is not that much of a big deal to me." Then she clamped her lips shut. "I can't believe I'm talking about this with you."

"If it was not me, then whom?"

The older woman chuckled again. "Are you quoting Trina, the Baddest Bitch?"

Chloe was surprised again. "What do you know about that?"

"I may be almost forty, but I'm not dead."

"Ha! That's very true." She snuck another look at Kai's heart-stopping body. "Maybe you and I can hang out, after all."

The older woman flashed a wicked grin. "I'm not sure you're ready for that."

Chapter 3

The Ferris wheel swept them high in the air once again, and Chloe simply relaxed at Kai's side, sharing laughter and bathing in the liquid sunshine of her smile. It felt peaceful and right to be with Kai at the top of the world, with no one else around.

With a deep breath, she savored the sounds: the determined cheer of the carousel organ, laughter and conversation rising from the people below, the rattle of the roller coaster and its passengers shrieking in fear and delight.

"Thanks for coming over to see me, Kai," she said, looking over the fairgrounds, only half expecting to see Zahra and her date. "I'm glad you did."

"You're welcome." Kai's voice wrapped around her like sun-warmed winter fleece.

Earlier, being with Zahra had made her feel like a kid again, bubbling with irrepressible, irresponsible energy. It had felt good. But with Kai, she felt all of her twenty-three years, all the yearning and desire she'd stored up since she'd fallen in love. She wanted to be a grown-up and a mature woman for her. But why, when Kai was not *for* her? Chloe twisted the strap of her purse, trying to push those unwanted thoughts out of her head. She needed to leave for New York ASAP.

When the ride ended, Kai helped her from the car with a warm hand around her waist. The other woman's leather jacket brushed against Chloe, bringing with it the smell of Kai's condo, making her think about Kai's bedroom.

Her bed. The two of them making love. A tremor darted through her.

They left the field with the Ferris wheel, their footsteps muffled on the hard dirt ground, arms lightly brushing. The sun was both dark and bright at the horizon, burning away the last of the afternoon and leaving behind trailing ribbons of golden clouds.

"It's been years since I've been here," Kai said. "Noelle told me you were coming here with your friend, but I had no idea it was on the same day Tanya and Tori wanted to go." She mentioned friends she'd known since college. Partners in business and love. "The place hasn't changed one bit."

Chloe shoved her hands in the pockets of her jacket. "I know *you* haven't changed."

"You're probably right." Kai seemed thoughtful. "I look at all these people around us—a lot of them I grew up with—and realize it's true. They have husbands, wives, kids, gray hairs. And I'm still the same." Her eyes flashed to the crowd on the path with them, some obviously coupled, others with friends. "Alone."

"I didn't know you wanted . . . that."

Throughout her life, Chloe had seen Kai with many women. Gorgeous women whom she sometimes brought around Chloe and her mother, and whom everyone seemed to know about. Glamorous women who'd just never stayed around.

"Everyone wants companionship, Chloe. That's why I was so happy when your mother found Duncan. It's not just about having someone to raise a child with. It's also about having someone to keep warm on winter nights and to tell secrets to. Someone who understands most things about me."

She had never heard Kai talk like this before. "Are you just saying that because you're hanging out with Tanya and Tori today?" She knew the two women were deeply in love and had an identical glow of absolute contentment when they were together. It was both sickening and enviable.

"Partly," Kai said. Some of the tightness she'd had earlier around her mouth returned.

"Well, you know that hanging out with a couple will make anyone feel like a third wheel." Chloe gently bumped the other woman's shoulder. "Plus, it's cuffing season. This cold weather makes everyone want to hook up."

Kai guided her around a trio of giggling girls who'd stopped in the middle of their path. "It's about more than hooking up. I can have that anytime I want."

Wasn't that the truth? Kai could get it right there at the fairgrounds, under the setting sun, with the carnival sounds wailing around them and Chloe on her knees, begging for a taste.

Stop. It.

"It's good to know you don't suffer from low self-esteem."

"True." Kai laughed. "That was never one of my issues."

Yeah. She had always been confident. Something else Chloe had always liked about her. She smiled to herself. She loved Kai for that and so much more. The woman was an important part of her life, one that she didn't want to lose. And she couldn't afford to let her infatuation blind her to that.

She put on a determined smile and hooked her arm around Kai's. "Come, Helen of Troy. Let's see if you can win me a prize."

They made the rounds of the fair as the day drew to a close and the sky darkened enough to allow the fair's lights to glow brilliantly against the somber sky. Kai won Chloe a gigantic panda at the ringtoss; then Chloe bought her boiled peanuts as a thank-you. They were

Kai's favorite thing to eat at the fair, but she didn't treat herself often.

The night glimmered around them as they talked about everything from Chloe's experiences in LA to Noelle's celebrity clients to the next meeting that Kai had out of town. The latter was a trip to New York that promised to be incredibly informative in parts but also incredibly boring.

"You should bring someone with you," Chloe said. "Don't the other execs bring their wives and husbands?"

"They do, but you're forgetting I have neither one."

Chloe hugged her panda tighter as she squeezed between two groups of posturing teenage boys. "You could always get an escort and have her be your companion on the trip."

Kai's eyes widened. "What?"

Chloe laughed. "Get your mind out of the gutter. You don't have to sleep with her."

"I don't need an escort, Chloe." Kai scowled at her.

"It's not what you think." She smiled again at the other woman's shocked face. "My first roommate in college was an escort. Sometimes guys would pay her to just fly with them to a meeting or a family event. She got a free flight, meals, and gifts. And all they wanted was a pretty girl who would listen to them and be there if they got bored."

"Jesus." Kai shook her head. "Just don't tell your mother about this ex-roommate. She'll have a damn heart attack."

"Mom and Stacia got along."

"But I bet Noelle didn't know how she was paying for her tuition."

"You're right about that." Chloe shrugged. "She invited me to come along with her on a few trips."

"What?" Kai stopped in the middle of the crowded path. People bumped into them, shooting annoyed looks at Kai, who refused to move or even acknowledge them. "Tell me you didn't go with her. Those so-called sexless trips can change at the drop of a dime, Chloe. Those men are nothing to play with on their own territory."

Chloe toyed with not telling the truth. But she'd never lied to her mother or Kai about anything. Kept things from them, yes, but never lied. "I went with her."

"Are you serious?" Kai's eyes snapped. She grabbed Chloe's arm, giant panda and all, and dragged her out of the path of traffic, seeming to be aware for the first time that they were obstructing the path. They stumbled to a halt near a paddock, where a pair of horses lazily fanned their tails against flies. "You could have been—" She bit off whatever she was going to say. "Tell me what happened."

"Stop treating me like a child." Chloe tried to shake off Kai's hold on her, but the other woman was strong, her fingers biting into her skin, even through the layers she wore. "It was years ago. And nothing happened. I went with Stacia on a trip to Dubai to see some guy. Everything was cool. He fed us, told us to sleep in the same bed, came in the room to talk with us every night and watch us in the bed. Then he took us back home to LA. End of story."

Hectic color flooded Kai's cheeks as her hands tightened around Chloe's arms. "Why the ever-living fuck would you do something like that?"

The curse shocked her. "Stop acting like it just happened a few weeks ago. It was freshman year. I'm obviously unscathed from the whole experience."

"This is serious." Kai's eyes snapped again. Her mouth thinned. "He could have raped you or shared you with his rich friends, then dumped your bodies in the desert. What the fuck?"

Chloe could feel Kai's hands trembling, feel the waves of anger rolling from her body. She took a deep breath to keep herself calm.

"It's okay." She pressed her palms against Kai's chest through her leather jacket. "I haven't been that stupid in a long time."

"Noelle and I worried enough about you being so far away." Kai's fingers tightened even more on her arms. "We never dreamed you'd do something like that."

"It was something I did in college to make some extra money. I won't do it again."

Kai narrowed her eyes. "Did you sleep with any of these guys?"

"Of course not. I went with Stacia only a couple of times. It was fun, and nothing happened."

"A couple of times . . . ? Sweet Jesus." Kai abruptly released her arms and stepped back. "Chloe . . . I think you're giving me a heart attack." One of the horses in the paddock nearby snorted.

"Stop living in the past, Kai." She tried for humor and a smile. "I made it to the ripe old age of twenty-three without anything happening to me."

Chloe remembered once telling an old girlfriend about her adventures with Stacia. The woman, another Kai clone, had reacted in much the same way Kai was now.

Chloe treated Kai the same way she had treated her girl then. She twined her arms around her neck, allowing the stuffed panda to fall at her feet. "I'm here, and nothing ever happened to me."

She inhaled the sweet and spicy scent of the woman she desperately wanted, telling her rioting body to calm down. They were sharing nothing more than a hug between two adults who respected and loved each other platonically. But she felt her nipples tighten under her jacket, shivered at the tendrils of arousal that began to wind through her body.

Kai was stiff against her for a moment before she returned the hug, clinging fiercely to Chloe. "Do not ever, ever tell your mother about this."

"I won't. You see, I didn't even want to tell *you*."

The older woman met her eyes. "I want you to tell me everything, Chloe. Everything. I can't say I won't judge, but I promise not to fly off the handle or betray your trust."

"Okay."

Kai's breath stroked her neck, making her tremble. Unable to help herself, she wriggled against Kai, seeking relief for the ache in her nipples, between her legs. She heard Kai's soft gasp, felt her stiffen against her a moment before the older woman's hands dug into her lower back, convulsively clasping her closer and into her hips. Chloe's belly clenched hard, and a moan of surprise and excitement slipped past her lips.

Kai jerked back, her eyes dilated to almost black. She adjusted her jacket over her shoulders as her gaze flickered away, looking everywhere but at Chloe. "Now, where were we heading again?"

They continued on through the fair, but things weren't the same. Chloe was even more aware of Kai as a woman, of the lean length of her under her clothes, the scent of her, the way their bodies fit perfectly together.

It wasn't long before Kai asked her if she was ready to leave, and she gratefully said yes. On the mostly silent ride home, Chloe texted Zahra that she was leaving the fairgrounds. They drove back to her mother's house in the quiet intimacy of the car, the heat blowing out of the vents and making Chloe's cheeks prickle. They spoke of nothing important as Kai expertly drove the black Audi through the lamp-lit streets. Talk radio droned on in the background; the tires hissed over the road.

In the driveway, she wished Kai a good night before letting herself into the house, hugging her panda tight. She closed the door behind her just as her stepfather walked in from the kitchen with a cup of something hot.

Her mother followed behind him a few moments later with her own cup.

"Evening, Chloe," Duncan greeted her in his thick Jamaican accent. "You're back early."

Her stepfather, an airline executive, had met Noelle Williams when Chloe was six. The family story was that they met on a Tuesday and he asked her to marry him that Friday. He'd fallen quickly and hard for the single mother. Luckily, the falling had happened both ways.

"Yes, honey." Her mother glanced at the clock on the wall. "It's barely eight o'clock."

Her stepfather sat in his armchair and set down his hot cider on the coffee table, glancing briefly at the TV, which was showing the beginnings of some live talent show. "You getting old so soon?" His mouth lifted in a grin.

She smiled weakly back at him. "Just tired."

For some reason, she didn't want to tell them that it was Kai who had dropped her off. "Zahra ran into a friend at the fair. She's going to hang out with her for a while. I just wanted to come home and get out of the cold."

Her mother briefly kissed her cheek in welcome before sitting and stretching out her sock-clad feet to touch her husband's. She curled long fingers around her cup of cider.

"California thinned out your blood, honey, she said. "It's really nice today for fall."

"But really cold for California." She dropped onto the couch, at her mother's side. "What are you guys watching?"

Her mother named a show that Chloe had no idea existed. "Oh."

"So did you guys have a good time?" her mother asked. "If I'd thought about it, I would've bought tickets for all of us to go together this week. But I know that Kai had plans to go with another couple, so . . ." Her mother shrugged.

"It was great." Chloe forced a smile. "I probably ate my weight in junk food there today."

"Yes, that's Kai's favorite part of the fair too, but she won't allow herself to eat as much of that stuff as she'd like. Sometimes I swear she just goes to the fair to torture herself with things she can't have."

Chloe blushed. With her mother talking about Kai, it felt like the woman was there in the room with them, a hot and compelling presence that made Chloe's tongue heavy and her body melt. She stood up. "I'm going to take a shower. It's been a long day."

"Okay, honey." Her mother brought her cider to her lips. "But don't stay up there all night, moping. Come down and be social after your shower."

"But only if you feel like it," Duncan said, still staring at the television. He poked his wife with his foot, his way of cautioning her against babying Chloe while she was staying with them.

She left her parents to their TV show and went to her room. She ran a bubble bath and checked her phone. Saw there was a message from Zahra.

Glad you got a ride. I left the fair and am at Café Intermezzo with the hottie. Details later.

Good for her, Chloe thought as she slid into her bubble bath. *Maybe that's what I need, some hot young stud to make me forget about Kai.*

But as soon as the thought came into her head, she dismissed it. Another mediocre lover would not help her get over Kai. Probably just the opposite. Fucking someone else would only make her fixate more on the original, whom she could not have—a woman who did not want her.

Chloe sighed. She lay back in the water, allowing the heat and the bubbles to slip over her breasts, her neck. With the water caressing her bare flesh, that fleeting moment with Kai at the fair came back to her. Their bodies pressed together as Kai's fingers dug into the small of her back. The delicious ache in her nipples that had spread low into her belly as she rubbed herself against Kai, clinging to her neck, while the other woman's hips moved against hers.

Chloe's eyes flew open, and she shot upright in the tub, splashing water on the floor.

Her breaths came faster. In shock. In hope. She pressed a hand against her chest, feeling her racing heart. It wasn't just her. Kai had felt something too.

But what was she going to do about it?

Chapter 4

Third Sunday night dinner had been a tradition for Chloe's mother and Kai for as long as Chloe could remember. It was an evening when both women stopped whatever was going on in their busy lives to connect with each other over wine and good food. On the third Sunday of October, less than a week since she saw Kai at the fair, Chloe sat at her dressing table, nervously waiting for dinner to start.

She tapped her fingers on her thigh, dreading but also anticipating sitting across the dinner table from Kai. Although she still didn't know exactly what she wanted from Kai, she'd worried about what to wear, eventually settling on a spaghetti-strapped black maxi dress that draped over her braless breasts, skimmed over the shape of her butt and thighs before falling to the floor. Sexy, but not slutty.

She had been ready for dinner for the past half hour but had not been able to bring herself to move from the bench in front of her dressing table.

Her face in the mirror was smooth and calm; her hair freshly washed and groomed until it radiated like a black sun around her face. The only sign of her agitation was her lips, already chewed bare of lipstick and nearly raw from her teeth.

"Chloe, honey! Dinner's ready."

She chewed on her lips again, feeling a fluttering in her belly. She pressed cold hands against her thighs, trying to still their tremor.

"Woman up."

She said the words out loud as she glared at her reflection. She said them again until she was able to stand.

Finally, Chloe took a calming breath and left her room. She stepped into the hallway, feeling the familiar creak of the wooden floors under her feet, the smooth banister under her palms as she took her time heading downstairs.

The skylight above allowed in the bright half-moon, the glow from distant stars. She remembered sitting on those very stairs as a teenager, wondering what Kai was doing, dreading running into her with one of her lovers but at the same time desperately wanting to see her. Eight years later she was still feeling the same anxiety, torturing herself over the same woman. Maybe in another eight years she would have moved on from her obsession with Kai to find real happiness with another woman.

"There you are, Chloe. I called you for dinner ages ago." Her mother waved her into the room.

She and Duncan had dressed up for dinner, her mother in an off-the-shoulder dress of green velvet and her stepfather in a blazer and button-down shirt. They sat at the dining table, which was set for only three. Covered serving dishes sat in a neat row in the middle of the table, while candlelight flickered from the silver candelabra.

Chloe stood in the doorway, staring at the three place settings. "Where's Kai?"

"Come sit down," Duncan, an old-fashioned gentleman, said as he rose to his feet, waiting for her to claim her chair.

Chloe sat down across from her mother, her stomach churning with disappointment.

"She had to fly out for work," her mother answered. "There was some sort of meeting in New York or someplace that she forgot about. She didn't sound too clear about it, but I do know she said she couldn't be here tonight."

"That's too bad," Chloe said. She had dressed for Kai, had prepared to face her attraction for the other woman head-on. And now she wasn't even there. She fiddled with the knife near her plate. "Did she say when she'd be back?"

"A week or two. Although she did mention that she might end up leaving from New York to go to her overseas meeting at the end of the month."

Chloe drew a surprised breath. "That's a long time away."

"She has an apartment in New York, where she stays when she has to work." Her mother shrugged. "Don't waste your time feeling sorry for my world-traveling best friend. Sometimes I think she would rather be on the road than here at home."

"I don't wonder why," Duncan said. "Aside from you, there's really nothing here for her. She works hard and spends most of her time jet-setting to those hippie festivals all over the world." He took the cover from one of the serving dishes and began to make his wife's plate.

For the rest of the meal, Chloe tried to pay attention to what her parents were saying instead of to the dismay sitting in the pit of her stomach. Kai didn't have to be gone tonight. She definitely didn't have to go as far as New York. She was just avoiding Chloe because of what had happened between them at the fair. She swallowed, feeling sick, although she'd barely eaten a bite of what her mother had prepared.

The lobster penne with Gruyère and goat cheese was one of her favorites, but she stirred her fork in the food, her appetite gone.

"You're strangely quiet tonight, Chloe." Her mother watched her with keen eyes, the candlelight flickering over her soft cheeks and silver hair. "Don't you like the food?"

"It's wonderful. I just don't have an appetite tonight."

"You?" Duncan stared at her as if she'd grown two heads. "The one I usually have to fight for the last bite of anything your mother cooks?" He nodded at his wife. "Yes, something is definitely wrong with your daughter." His mouth twitched with amusement. "I hope it's curable."

Her mother's look narrowed. "You're not sick, are you?"

"No, no. It's not that. I just . . ." She pressed her lips together, not sure how much she could say. "There's someone I'm into. I'm just not sure if she likes me."

"Are you kidding? Of course she likes you. What woman wouldn't?" Her mother pursed her lips as a thought seemed to occur to her. "She is gay, isn't she?"

Chloe smiled weakly. "Yes, she is. I'm very sure of that."

"Then there shouldn't be a problem. If you like her and she's a lesbian, then of course she likes you back." Her mother gestured to Chloe with a bare fork. "She's not blind!"

"And you have a wonderful personality," Duncan said, chiming in to reassure her.

Her mother sipped her wine. "That too."

"She could just be intimidated by you," Duncan said. "When I first met your mother, I was so bowled over by her looks that I almost didn't approach her. Once I introduced myself and found out what kind of woman she was, it still didn't seem possible that she could ever care for someone like me."

"But here we are, seventeen years later." His wife leaned into him and squeezed his hand as they shared an intimate smile. "You should have something like this too, Chloe. Happiness like this is worth the risk."

Was it? It would be nice to think she ever had a chance to create something with Kai that would last for a decade and more. That fantasy tempted her, but what chance did it have of being fulfilled?

"The moral of our story is, you should go after this woman, and don't worry about your insecurities," Duncan said. "She probably has the same fears and worries as you."

"I doubt it." Chloe felt odd listening to her parents' advice on winning over Kai, although obviously they didn't know who she was talking about. "But thank you both for saying that."

Their advice was impractical for her, but for a moment, she allowed herself to wish that she could take it, that she could be a woman with a simple crush who could just go and tell another woman what she felt. But things weren't that simple.

Her parents seemed content with her response to their advice. They went back to their food, gently teasing her that it hadn't taken long for her to find a woman in Atlanta. Chloe stayed at the table with them, drinking from her glass of water more than eating but still enjoying their company and their love, which seemed to shine through everything they did.

The more she watched them, though, the more envious she became, wanting something like what they had for herself. The way they looked at each other, laughed, and had this effortless rapport with each other made her think achingly of Kai. Of what could be between them.

As she ate, she slowly formulated a plan.

When she forced down her last bite of food, Chloe put down her fork. She took a sip of water and wet her lips. "Can you give me Kai's address in New York? I have something I want to give to her."

Her mother rattled off the Greenwich Village address. "Can't it wait until she gets back?"

"It could, but I want to give it to her now."

After dinner, Chloe searched the metal bread box where her mother kept all the spare keys and alarm codes. Sure enough, she found a brass key ring with Kai's initials; four keys dangled from it. She made a note to write down the codes and get the keys copied the next day.

Chapter 5

Chloe rolled her suitcase through the long hallway, looking for the right door. The hall was endless, but brightly lit with artificial lights, the doors staggered on either side gleaming with the number nine and a letter. Soon she came to the apartment. She'd used the code to get into the building but abruptly lost her nerve when faced with Kai's locked door. She tucked the stolen keys into her purse and rang the doorbell.

She had to wait only a moment before she heard noise on the other side of the door, the sound of locks being undone. Then the door opened.

"Chloe?"

Kai stood in the doorway in a green tank top, tie-dyed harem pants, and bare feet. Her toes were painted a surprising orange, and her waist-length copper locks were loose around her face. Slight shadows smudged the tender skin under her eyes, and she looked like she hadn't slept in a while.

"Hi." Chloe greeted her with a smile, as if it was perfectly natural to show up unannounced on the doorstep of her New York apartment. "Can I come in?"

She suspected it was more from politeness than from any real desire to welcome her that Kai pulled open the door and stepped aside to let her in. "Of course you can." The "But what the hell are you doing here?" was clear in her voice.

Chloe bit the inside of her cheek, trying to hide her nervousness as she wheeled her suitcase into the bright and airy living room, which let in a view of the restrained bustle of Greenwich Village.

Kai had been working. She had papers in a neat stack on the leather ottoman, a mug of tea sat near the papers, and her cell phone was discarded on the couch, where she must have been sitting when Chloe rang the doorbell. The apartment was warm, the heat making it seem like Atlanta in the middle of summer. Chloe shrugged off her jacket, and Kai quickly took it from her to put it on the coatrack by the door.

"I know it's a bit of a surprise to see me here," Chloe rattled off nervously, turning to Kai with a wide smile she was far from feeling. Her stomach jumped with her apprehension, but she was determined to see this through. "I had a couple of job interviews here and figured I'd come by your place while I'm in town." She did have the interviews. Appointments she had arranged a few weeks prior but had moved up so she would have that as an excuse to see Kai in New York. "I hope you don't mind."

"I . . . I don't mind. This is just a bit of a surprise, that's all." Kai ran a hand through her locks. "Does Noelle know you're here?"

"I told her I had some job interviews, yes."

Kai blew out a breath. "Okay." Her gaze bounced around the perfectly neat apartment. "Excuse the mess." She shoved her hands in the pockets of her pants, hovering across the room from Chloe. "Can I get you something to drink?"

"Red wine, if you have it." It was barely two in the afternoon.

Kai hesitated for a moment before giving her a quick nod and heading toward the open French doors to the kitchen. Chloe bit her lip as she turned away, not quite believing she was doing this. After she had gotten Kai's information from her mother, she'd made arrangements the next day to move up her two New York interviews. A couple of days later, she was on the flight, then in the office with the woman running the first studio. The interview had gone well. She felt she had impressed the woman enough with her skills and her knowledge of the industry, completely focused on being the best potential employee she could be. The second interview had gone just as well, if not better.

But once she left the interview, her mind had been focused completely on Kai.

So, here she was.

Kai's apartment was a beautiful corner space with views of Greenwich Village. The wooden floors and white walls, decorated with original oil paintings of women, reminded her of Kai's condo in Georgia. Most of the women in the paintings were posed seductively, but elegantly, showing only a hint of a breast or a suggestive look over a bare shoulder. Everything about the space was warm and inviting. She glanced down the hallways on either side of the living room. They had to lead to the bedrooms.

"Here you are." Kai came back with a glass of wine. "Please sit."

"I'd like to stand, if you don't mind." Chloe hated that they sounded so formal with each other, but she didn't know how to change that.

"I don't mind at all. As long as you don't mind if I sit." She dropped onto the couch, her thighs sprawled, her curled fingers tapping gently against her knee. Kai seemed uneasy, confused.

Chloe took a sip of her wine, her gaze flickering away from Kai's sexy sprawl on the leaf-green couch. It was a full-bodied red, drier than what she'd normally choose for herself but still delicious. She licked droplets of wine from her lips before she turned to Kai.

"If it's okay, can I stay here with you while I'm in the city?"

This time Kai's pause was more obvious. There was a stillness to her body, though her fingers twitched on her thigh. Then she nodded slowly. "You can. The apartment is a bit on the small side, but you are welcome to everything here." Kai glanced at her suitcase. "You can have my room, and I'll sleep on the futon in my office."

Chloe held the wineglass against her chest. "No, no. I don't want to put you out."

"You're not. Just allow me to be a good host to my best friend's baby girl." Kai held up her hands. "I know. You're no baby, but you know what I mean. In Noelle's eyes, you will always be her baby."

"What about in *your* eyes?"

She looked uneasy at the question. "Does it matter what my eyes see?"

"Yes." Chloe crossed the room with the wineglass held carefully in her hands. "Yes, it does. Your opinion has always mattered to me, Kai." She stopped in front of the couch, standing in the tight space between the coffee table and the other woman's sprawled legs.

Kai held herself still for a long moment, saying nothing, simply watching Chloe's face, her hands palms down on either side of her thighs.

"What's going on here, Chloe?" she finally asked.

Chloe suddenly lost her nerve. She gulped down more wine and stepped away from Kai, feeling the other woman's eyes on her the entire time. She thought she was ready to ask the important questions, to feel out what, if anything, Kai was feeling for her; but the other woman had gotten to the essential question before she was ready to broach it.

At the window, she looked down at the street, at the passing yellow cabs, at the people lining the sidewalks as they rushed toward their destinations. Chloe cleared her throat.

"It's nothing." She put the wineglass down on the windowsill. "It was a mistake to come here." She turned and almost ran into Kai. She gasped and pulled back, hands flying up. She hadn't heard her move. Her fingers brushed the wineglass, and it tumbled to the floor. Shattered.

"Shit!" Chloe exclaimed.

Wine rushed across the pale hardwood floor, creating a deep red stain.

"Be careful!" Kai said.

Although she was the one who was barefoot, Kai swept Chloe up in her arms and stepped quickly away from the broken glass and rapidly spreading stain. Kai's arms were warm and firm around her, bringing her tight against a body that smelled of the familiar mixture of spices, a scent that made Chloe's tongue ache to taste.

She clung to Kai's neck, burying her face in the scented locks, holding on for dear life even as her insides throbbed with conflict. She didn't want to want her. This wasn't fair. Even though she had come all the way to New York to force the issue between her and Kai, she knew nothing good could come of it. Tears pricked her eyes.

All too soon, she felt Kai gently lowering her. Onto a bed, not onto the couch, as she had expected. Chloe drew back, tears falling.

"It's fine, baby. It's just a broken wineglass. Nothing important." Kai sat on the bed beside her, smoothing her thumbs over Chloe's cheeks.

"Fuck." The tears came harder, rushing down her cheeks and, she just knew, ruining her makeup.

"It's not the glass," she cried, hands digging into Kai's shoulders.

"Then what is it? Tell me," Kai said. "You know you can talk to me about anything."

Chloe abruptly pressed her lips to the other woman's. Kai froze. Her entire body went stock-still against Chloe in the bed. It seemed that even her breathing stopped. Then her mouth softened under Chloe's, and she kissed her back, hands curving around Chloe's neck, stroking her skin with skilled fingertips. Chloe trembled at the caress, her body melting as it sang:

At last.

At last.

At last.

She whimpered with pleasure and slid her hands into Kai's locks, pulling her closer. Then the other woman jerked back, her eyes wide with shock.

"What . . . what are you doing?"

"Shit!" Embarrassment flooded Chloe's face. "Nothing. I'm sorry. This was such a bad idea." She tried to scramble off the bed and go back to the living room, get her things, and leave.

But Kai held her captive on the bed, her hands firm on her shoulders. "Don't move," she said, eyes nearly black with emotion. "I need to clean up that glass." She got off the bed, looking confused for a moment before she went to her closet and put on a pair of sandals. She was shaking her head as she left the bedroom.

Chloe wiped at her cheeks with the palms of her hands. "What did you just do?" she asked herself furiously.

She sniffled, wiping at the tears, which refused to stop falling. She sat on Kai's bed—Kai's *bed*—with her stockinged legs stretched out across the burgundy and gold bedspread, her knee-high black boots stark against the soft sheets, and the already short skirt of her black dress riding up to her thighs.

Angry at herself, she slid off the bed and made her way to the bathroom. In the mirror, she was a mess. Mascara running, eyes red and swollen, lips chewed bare of color. *Shit!* No wonder she backed off when Chloe kissed her. Or was it because her best friend's daughter had tried to make out with her? *Shit!*

She cleaned up her face as best she could, getting rid of all the makeup and just biting color into her lips. Then she left the bathroom to find Kai. She stopped in the threshold of the living room at the sight of Kai going into the kitchen with a dustpan and broom. The knees of her pants were stained red with wine. Chloe bit her lip and stepped back. It was not like Kai to be so careless. Not at all. She must really be discombobulated. Completely outside her element. She waited until the other woman came back from the kitchen. This time, Kai had a spray cleaner and a cloth in her hands.

"Kai. I'm so sorry about this." She twisted her hands behind her back. "I didn't mean to . . ." She couldn't even say what she hadn't meant to do. The evidence of her premeditation was there in the corner, her suitcase, and even in the outfit she'd changed into after she left her interview, low bodiced and tight, despite the New York chill.

Kai only glanced briefly at her before she crouched over the clean spot where Chloe had spilled the wine, and sprayed the cleaner, thoroughly wiping down the area with the cloth, although no hint of red appeared on the cloth. She stood up.

"We should talk," Kai said.

Yes, they should. But Chloe didn't want to. What she wanted to do was run away and pretend none of this had ever happened. Pretend that her feelings for this woman hadn't been plaguing her for years and making her life one big avoidance. She took a breath.

"Okay."

She waited until Kai put the cloth and cleaner back in the kitchen and sat on the couch before sitting beside her. Kai scooted back, putting more distance between them.

"Tell me what's going on, Chloe."

She felt chastised and didn't like it. Immediately she went on the defensive. "You mean you don't know? You kissed me too."

Kai winced at her words, looking briefly ashamed. "I did, and I shouldn't have." She shook her head. "I could use my celibacy as an excuse, but there's actually no excuse for what happened a few minutes ago."

Chloe took a deep breath. "I've been in love with you since I was in high school, maybe even before."

Kai jerked as if she'd been slapped. She closed her eyes tight. "Don't say that. Please."

Chloe crossed her arms over her chest. "Then what should I say? That you caught me in a moment of weakness and I was just horny?"

"Fuck!" Kai jumped up and prowled to the window farthest away from Chloe. She ran her hands through her locks, her back stiff and unyielding as she stared down into the street. "Noelle is going to kill me."

"This isn't about her."

Kai turned around, her bright eyes haunted. "It damn well is. She's my best friend. You . . . you came out of her body. You are young enough to be my daughter too."

"But I'm not your daughter. I'm a woman, Kai. A woman who happens to want and love you very much."

"No." Kai shook her head, hair flying around her shoulders. "This can't happen. It can't."

"It already did." Chloe got up from the couch and started toward her.

"Stop!" Kai held out her hand. "Just stop right there."

Used to obeying her commands, Chloe paused. Kai abruptly left for her bedroom. Moments later, she came back dressed in Timberland boots, jeans, and a thick sweater. At the door, she grabbed her jacket.

"I'm going out for a while." She didn't look at Chloe. "Make yourself at home and have whatever you need. I have my cell on me, but I'll be back."

Then she left without another word.

Chloe fell onto the couch. She squeezed her arms around her stomach, trying to quell its butterflies. But the more she thought of the look on Kai's face as she left, the more regret burned at her and the faster the butterflies flew, until she felt like she had to throw up.

What am I doing here?

She didn't know what else to do. She hadn't thought beyond telling Kai her feelings. She hadn't known how the other woman would react, but she had hoped for something more than this. More than her anger and the pain in those beloved eyes. Her stomach cramped, and a sob hiccuped from her lips.

Kai.

Chloe felt like she'd just killed something beautiful and precious. Nothing would ever be the same now. Kai hated her. Her mother would blame her, and rightly so, for trying to seduce her best friend, who hadn't been with anyone in damn near two years. She cursed again. Then fumbled in her pocket for her cell phone.

Zahra picked up on the first ring. "How'd it go?"

"She hates me." Then the tears came.

They flooded down her face as she told her friend everything that had happened. The devastated look on Kai's face. Her anger. The way she hadn't even wanted Chloe to come close to her.

"She thinks that I'm some sort of conscienceless nympho who doesn't give a shit about family!" she cried. "I can't believe I kissed her."

It had been better when she had Kai's unconditional love, when Kai saw her as just a little girl to spoil and indulge. Now she had nothing except the older woman's contempt.

"Slow your roll, honey. You don't know any of that." Zahra made soothing noises through the phone. "Stop over-thinking these things. Maybe she just went out to get some cigarettes. You probably got her real hot and bothered when you laid that kiss on her."

But Chloe wasn't in the mood to laugh. She wanted to just cut her losses and leave the apartment. Pretend that she hadn't said any of those things to Kai. Allow the other woman to get back to how her life was before Chloe confessed her dirty secret and tried to tongue her down in her own bed.

"I'm just going to leave," she said finally.

"No, girl. What if she left without her key? Are you just going to leave her stranded outside her own place? That's not cool."

"Then what am I going to do?" She felt like an uncertain teenager again.

"Face things like a woman. If she doesn't feel the same way, then clit up. Face the facts and move on. You're not going to be in Atlanta for very much longer, anyway." The sound of traffic came through the phone, like Zahra had stepped out onto the balcony of her office to talk. "You did a bold thing. It's cool if it didn't work out. A lot of us don't bother to take those kinds of chances with our lives."

"But I didn't want it to turn out this way!" She went to the window where Kai had stood, and looked down onto the sunlit day. The brightness and the falling leaves mocked the way she felt, the agony and fear tearing her stomach to pieces.

"We don't choose the way other people feel, girl. We can only take risks and hope they pay off." Zahra sighed. "It'll be okay. Just come home as soon as you can. I'll make you a Hennessy and Coke, and you can cry all over my new Gucci suit." She made another soothing sound. "It'll be okay. It's not the end of the world."

Chloe sniffled and wiped the tears away with her fingers. "Okay."

"Now, go wash your face and change into something more comfortable. I'm sure those fuck-me heels and that tight-ass outfit you have on aren't the best to sleep in."

Chloe looked down at her dress, which pushed her cleavage up to her neck, and the high-heeled boots, which seemed more suited for a horizontal position. "You're probably right about that."

"Have some ice cream, or whatever it is you need to feel better. Then just apologize to her when she gets home. Tell her you made a mistake and ask her to forget about everything you said. Okay?"

Chloe winced at the thought of talking with Kai about the things she'd confessed. She dreaded facing her but knew she had to. Her mother didn't raise a coward.

"Okay." She pressed a palm to her hot cheek. "Thanks, Z."

"Of course, girl. I got you. Don't ever forget that." The sound of a sliding-glass door opening or closing came through the phone. "And when you get back, I'll hook you up with a fine-ass stud to fuck the shit out of you. After more nuts than you can count, you'll be saying, 'Kai who?'"

Chloe did laugh at that, a weak sound. "Thanks again for talking me down from the ledge."

"Anytime."

Chloe hung up the phone. Then she did what her friend had suggested, taking a shower and changing into her flannel pajamas. When she came out of the room and saw that Kai still hadn't come back, she didn't feel like eating anything, not even the Ben & Jerry's ice cream in the freezer. Instead, she climbed into Kai's bed and, exhausted by the weight of her own emotions, quickly fell asleep.

Chapter 6

Chloe woke up to the sound of quiet footsteps in the dark. Under the covers, she turned her head toward the doorway of the bedroom to see a tall feminine silhouette. She didn't move. Only watched Kai come farther into the bedroom and sit on the bed, sinking into the mattress with her scented weight. She felt the torment in the other woman, her unease. Chloe turned to her.

"Kai—"

The other woman's mouth quieted the rest of what she had to say. Chloe gasped at the feel of those warm lips and Kai's cool cheeks, which had been exposed to the brisk fall wind outside. She tasted like alcohol, like something hot and potent. Whiskey.

One night years ago, her roommate had brought some absinthe from Amsterdam for Chloe to try. The drink had been potent and hot, a surprisingly bitter burn, and Stacia had insisted that Chloe have it with a honey chaser. The drink had slid hotly into her belly, settling in it like sparks that caused a thousand forest fires. Kai was like that now. She tasted of both the bitter and the sweet. The honey and the absinthe sliding together down Chloe's throat, a heady concoction that made her open her mouth for more. More. More.

She trembled as Kai lightly brushed her lips across hers, a gentle tease, before pressing more firmly, delicate and determined. Kai licked her mouth, tasted its corners, her hands settling on Chloe's shoulders. Those hands were cool but quickly warmed as they moved gently over the flannel covering Chloe's skin.

Chloe parted her lips for Kai's tongue, and the other woman groaned, a tortured sound.

"Fuck . . ." She tugged the covers down to get more of Chloe. "I'm going to hell for this. I'm going to hell," she moaned against Chloe's mouth. "But, God help me, I want you."

Chloe made a glad noise, pressing herself even more into the kiss, into Kai's firm upper body, which was covered by a thick cashmere sweater. Kai pushed the sheet away completely, then unbuttoned the flannel pajamas as her kiss sweetly seduced Chloe, her tongue firm and hot, her skin soft and perfect. Chloe trembled, unable to believe that at last, she was getting to kiss the older woman the way she'd always wanted, that Kai was touching her with desire.

She gasped when Kai touched her breasts, her thumbs brushing nipples that were already painfully hard. Between her legs was a river, flooding with want and anticipation.

She whimpered as her body surged with sensation, her senses nearly on overload at the improbable that was actually happening: the dreamed-for moment of Kai making love with her.

"Oh, God . . ." She clawed at Kai's shoulders.

"Sh . . ." her lover murmured as she kissed Chloe way down her throat, her lips moving in a tingling path down to where her hands already tugged and pinched at Chloe's sensitive flesh, inciting her even more. "I'm going to make it so good for you." Kai bit her throat. "So good." She soothed the bite with her tongue; then her head dipped down.

Chloe cried out as Kai's mouth covered her nipple. Her tongue swept over the sensitive tip again and again while she squeezed and tugged at the other nipple. Chloe's sex felt too swollen to be contained. She shifted her thighs under the sheet, trapped in the flannel pajamas.

"Kai . . ." It was so natural to call out her lover's name after so many years of fantasizing about touching her, about feeling her mouth, her hands. Chloe threw her head back, gripping Kai's thick locks as Kai pleasured her with her mouth, teased her breasts and the sensitive nipples. Chloe quaked in the sheets, overcome by the sensations.

This was what it meant to not have an imitation of what she craved. Ecstasy rolled through her, and she shuddered, her body reaching its completion without Kai ever touching her pussy.

Chloe panted and sagged in the bed. But Kai didn't stop. She tugged down the pajama bottoms and slid her fingers into the dampness between Chloe's thighs.

Kai groaned with pleasure as she effortlessly found the swollen clit and stroked it. Chloe's desire swiftly rose again. She groaned and arched her back, her breasts lifting into Kai's mouth, her hips circling in the bed as Kai pressed and circled her clit. First a slow and languorous dance of fingers and sensitive flesh. Then a firmer caress, a finger under Chloe's hood. Harder, then faster, until a flush rose up Chloe's chest, a prickling heat, and she cried out again, shudders of orgasm shaking the bed.

"Can I get inside you?" Kai gasped the question against Chloe's throat.

"Yes!" Chloe widened her legs, and Kai slid her fingers deep inside. They both trembled.

"You're fucking amazing," Kai groaned. "Amazing . . ."

She settled her body over Chloe's, one hand sinking in her hair, gripping it tight, the other between her legs, sweetly fucking another orgasm into her, then another and another, building the sensation higher and higher, until she gushed her peak over Kai's hand and into the sheets. She screamed from the pleasure, her body a tight bow, all her muscles tensed and aching. Kai still fucked her, her fingers pressing, making a firm and beguiling motion against her G-spot, which stirred her hips again.

It was like Kai was making love to her for the first and last time. Giving Chloe everything at once.

Chloe panted as the sensations tripped through her.

"Wait . . ." She pressed her hands against Kai's chest. "I want to touch you," Chloe gasped. "Let me touch you!"

"You're so beautiful. . . ." Kai buried her nose in Chloe's throat, nibbling the side of her neck, her fingers making lazy strokes between her thighs, stirring through the thick moisture, then wandering back until they slid hotly against her rear passage.

"Oh!"

Chloe's fingers clenched Kai's sweater as the other woman explored her tender orifice, sliding in a gentle finger. Another finger caressed her clitoris, circling the sensitive bud.

"Kai!"

The finger at her rear moved deeper, moving subtly to the rhythm of the first, while Chloe's breathing changed again, the pleasure building with each movement of Kai's fingers on her, inside her. She had never felt anything like it before, her bottom stretched and opening hungrily to swallow the long finger, the knowing press and caress of her clit, a quivering pleasure.

Her breath quickened. Her nails sank into Kai's sweater while her lover's hands worked magic between her thighs until she was coming apart. Coming apart and screaming.

"Stop!" Chloe gasped. "Stop, please."

She pulled away from Kai, acutely feeling her nudity while her lover was still fully dressed. "I want to touch you. I want to make love with you."

Kai shook her head and pulled back even more, pressing kisses to Chloe's hands. She was breathing heavily.

With the orgasmic tremors falling away from her, Chloe could smell the alcohol even more on Kai's breath. The other woman drew back even farther.

"It's just this time," Kai said. "Just this once." Her hungry gaze swept down Chloe's body. "Ever since the night of the fair I've been thinking about you, thinking about touching you. It felt so wrong." She groaned. "But damn, you feel so good."

Chloe grabbed Kai's sweater in her fists. "Don't say that. Stay with me. Let me show you how much I love you."

But Kai took her hands and pressed them together. "You don't want me, baby. Not really."

Chloe stiffened. "Does that mean you don't really want me, either?"

"Fuck, I still want you. I want to taste and touch every part of you. I want . . ." She made a noise of frustration and need. "But this has to be it. There can't be any more." Kai stumbled to her feet and backed away from the bed. "Go back to sleep." Chloe could make out only the barest gleam of Kai's bright eyes in the darkness. "I'll see you in the morning."

She stared in disbelief as Kai left the room and closed the door behind her. Her body was satisfied. Thoroughly ravaged and drenched in the aftermath. But she'd wanted an exchange of equals. Not some bullshit encounter that Kai could write off, as if it had never happened. The more she thought about it, the angrier she got. She jumped up from the bed and stumbled as her weak knees nearly buckled under her. She clung to the side of the bed for a moment, then left the bedroom, still naked, to find Kai.

She didn't have to go far. As soon as she padded into the hallway, she heard the sounds of light snoring. She followed the noises and found Kai sprawled on her back on the couch, still fully dressed, one leg dangling on the floor. She looked . . . vulnerable. Unlike herself.

Chloe felt that ache inside her again. The feeling that she had done something to Kai, something that was wicked, something that the older woman did not deserve. Chloe remembered the words Kai had moaned against her mouth as she made love to her, the agony behind them.

I'm going to hell for this, she had moaned. *I'm going to hell.*

She didn't want Kai like that. Not so torn and obviously tortured about what they had done and about what she was feeling for Chloe. Sighing, Chloe took off Kai's shoes, put her dangling leg on the couch, and draped a blanket over her sleeping body. She loved Kai, but the last thing she wanted to do was hurt her like this.

Chapter 7

The light was too bright. Chloe turned over in the bed and away from the morning sunshine. The sheets shifted against her naked body, and she sighed at the sensation of the cotton against her bare nipples, her back, and belly. She moaned and settled deeper into the sheets.

"You keep making those noises, and I won't be responsible for what happens between us today."

Her eyes flew open to see Kai in the doorway. She had showered and gotten dressed, impeccably put together in dress shoes, black slacks, and a gray sweater over a white button-down shirt. Her hair was loose around her shoulders and framed her handsome, smiling face. She looked like she was ready for a meeting.

Chloe stared at her, amazed at the difference between this woman and the one who had stumbled out of bed last night, regretting everything they had done together.

"Good morning," she said tentatively, keeping the sheets over her breasts.

"Yes, it is."

Chloe frowned. "What have you done with the Kai from last night?"

"This is me, Little Bit. Just sober, unlike last night." Kai tapped long fingers against her thigh. "Take a shower and get dressed. I'm taking you to breakfast."

"I—"

"No arguments. Your bag is at the foot of the bed, and everything you might need is in the bathroom. You have forty minutes."

Then Kai left the doorway, her sexy, loose-limbed walk taking her down the hallway and toward the living room.

"What the hell?" Chloe stared after her.

But she didn't bother wasting any time. She flung the covers back and quickly made the bed before hopping into the shower. Even though she wanted to linger over her body, savor the sensation of stroking places that Kai had so recently touched, she was mindful of the instructions she'd received, and thoroughly scrubbed her body instead, leaving the savoring for another time.

Within thirty minutes she was dressed in her ankle boots, skinny jeans, and a red cowl-necked sweater. Her makeup was impeccable but her nerves were a mess when she left the bedroom in search of Kai.

The other woman was in the kitchen, sitting at the small dining table, drinking a cup of coffee and reading the paper. Kai lifted her head when Chloe came through the door. Her bright eyes darkened as they took in her outfit, her figure, her face.

"You look beautiful, Chloe."

This was the Kai she was used to. Controlled and debonair. Charming and unwavering in her pursuit of every sort of pleasure available to a woman. She was glad to see the uncertain, drunken woman from last night gone. But hadn't she been the one who had made love to Chloe? Hadn't she been the one who was out of control enough to take what she wanted?

"Thank you." Chloe cleared her throat. "Any more orders for me, Ms. Harrington?"

Kai's eyes sparkled. "Not yet. But it's still early in the day." She put aside the newspaper and drained the last of the coffee, then got up to rinse out the mug in the sink.

Chloe couldn't help but watch her slow, graceful movements around the kitchen, the press of her butt against the slacks, the long legs and the beautiful body, which were only emphasized by the slim-cut pants.

Kai turned around, her eyes still amused. "You like what you see?"

Chloe didn't bother saying anything but the truth. "Very much."

"Good. Are you ready to go?"

She was more than ready. Curiosity was eating away at her about what the Kai of serious talks and paternal distance had to say to her this morning that was different from what her lover had said last night.

"I'm ready whenever you are."

They left the apartment for a restaurant nearby, Chloe feeling simultaneously proud to be at the older woman's side and nervous about the reason for their conversation. In her slim-fitting slacks and three-quarter-length coat, and with her snapping gingerbread and mint eyes, Kai attracted more than a few second glances. Her entire look shouted power dyke, and her energy was so sexy and potent that it gave Chloe chills as she remembered what they had done together the night before.

At the restaurant, Kai opened the door for her, ushering Chloe ahead of her with a hand at the small of her back. From the outside, it was a cozy and unassuming place with an anonymous-looking set of glass windows, an innocuous sign on the door. But once they walked in, the place was gorgeous. Stone floors, old-fashioned Campari posters on the walls, a long and elegant bar, with a gorgeous tuxedoed woman smiling from behind it.

The tables were small and round, intimate, like the ones Chloe had seen in a thousand advertisements for European and African cafés. The walls were each painted a solid color, a deep yellow, ocean blue. The clientele was mixed, though mostly female, nearly a dozen tables filled with patrons, even though it was a Tuesday morning. The place smelled like delicious cooked things.

People glanced up as they came in. Chloe thought she saw envy directed at her for being with such a fine woman. Her cheeks warmed with pride and an awareness of Kai. The hostess seated them at a corner table, with a blue wall framing Kai. Two glasses of Perrier later, they placed their orders.

Kai took in the restaurant with a slow and appraising eye before turning back to Chloe. "You looked beautiful in bed this morning."

Chloe found herself blushing, remembering how it felt to awaken naked, the sun on her face, the sheets brushing her nipples as she luxuriated in the afterglow. Across the table, Kai's gaze was amused, in control.

This was the calm Kai, whom Chloe was more than familiar with. The woman who approached any crisis—whether it be Chloe's first car accident or being downsized at work—with a levelheadedness and calm designed to put those around her at ease while masking her own panic. This was also the shrewd corporate strategist who never blinked first.

"I'm glad to see you're so calm about this," Chloe said.

Kai chuckled softly. "The truth is, I'm absolutely terrified about what happened between us last night. But it won't do any good to ignore or avoid it." She leaned back in her chair, bracing an arm against the table's edge. "You were so responsive and luscious last night. I can't let that go without saying so. You deserve to know that I enjoyed myself and had a wonderful time making love to you in my bed."

Jesus!

Chloe felt her face roasting in the face of Kai's casual acknowledgement of their lovemaking. This was what she wanted, wasn't it? And she should have known that Kai wouldn't avoid talking about what this thing was between them. Her new lover was not a coward. Still, she waited for the other shoe to drop.

"Last night shouldn't have happened," Kai said.

The other shoe.

Chloe took a careful sip of her sparkling water, giving herself time to respond to that unfair statement.

"It shouldn't have happened," Kai said again. "And I have absolutely zero excuses for it. I have been celibate before, and I have never taken advantage of a woman just to get off after a dry spell. I have been drunk before and have never dragged a woman to my bed to fuck her just for my own satisfaction."

Chloe couldn't keep silent then. "You didn't drag me anywhere, Kai. I was already in your bed and waiting for you. And you certainly didn't take any kind of advantage of me. I was ready and willing to make love to you. I've wanted it for far longer than you've been celibate."

"Well." Kai's eyebrows popped up, and she adjusted her napkin in her lap. She sighed, seeming at a loss for words. But, of course, that didn't last long. "Your mother is not going to like this."

"Why do you have to tell her?"

"I'm not going to tell her anything. *We* are." Kai's eyes flickered like lightning over Chloe's face and throat before she looked up at the waitress, who had arrived with their hot drinks—a cappuccino and a hot chocolate. She waited until the woman left to speak again. "It's bad enough that I did it, but it's worse that I want to do it again." That smile of Kai's came again, a flickering and searing look that made Chloe's nipples tighten against the sweater, made that place between her thighs tingle with the first stroke of arousal. "Thanks for coming out to breakfast with me. I didn't want to risk falling into bed with you again by having this conversation in the apartment."

Chloe blushed again. Pleasure and amusement made her smile despite the gravity of their discussion. "It's not like you gave me a choice, Ms. Harrington."

"True. My apologies. Sometimes I can be a little high-handed."

And Chloe had never known that side of Kai. Not really. She'd known about the stern disciplinarian. The woman who bought her anything she asked for as a child. She'd even known the best friend who would stand by her mother no matter what. But this lover who took charge with casual and complete confidence was new to her. This side of Kai made her melt even more.

"Don't apologize," Chloe said. "I like it."

Kai shook her head. "And that's exactly what I'm talking about."

It was then that their food came. Chloe's broccoli and cheese omelet and oven-warmed wheat bread. Kai's buttery cheese grits with a side of eggs, which she nearly covered completely in hot sauce.

"So, what do you mean that we are going to tell Mom what happened?" Chloe bit into her buttery wheat bread, licking her lips from the slightly crisp outside, the soft and chewy texture just beneath.

Kai's eyes fastened on Chloe's mouth. She didn't say anything for a moment. Then she answered, "Just like I said. We need to face her together and tell her what happened. I don't want her to get the wrong idea or blame the wrong person."

"It was my fault," Chloe said immediately. "I was the one who came to New York and threw myself at you."

"But did you throw yourself at me at the fair too?"

No. That night at the fair had caught her by surprise. Yes, she'd wanted Kai for years, but that night at the fair she realized that Kai had wanted her too.

"Was that the first time you . . . ?" Chloe didn't even know how to finish the sentence.

Kai tilted her head, obviously debating whether or not to tell the truth. "Unfortunately, no. I've thought about you as a woman for at least the last couple of years. I was very grateful you were at a school all the way across the country."

"Thank you." Chloe smiled.

"For what?"

"For being honest with me. I've wanted you for so many years that I felt completely alone and wrong."

"Make no mistake. Because it's mutual doesn't make it right."

Chloe shook her head. "I don't want to believe that." Then she remembered how Kai had been last night, tortured.

I'm going to hell for this.

She sighed. "But I don't want to hurt you, Kai. Whatever you want is what we'll do." Even though it would kill her. At least she could get herself together enough to leave Georgia within the next month and be away from the source of her temptation.

"I brought this on myself." Kai lifted her fork but did not touch her food. "They are my own feelings, Little Bit."

"I'm not your Little Bit," Chloe said gently. "I outgrew that nickname a long time ago."

"I have to keep thinking of you as that if I'm going to release this thing. It's for the best. We'll tell your mother when I get back to Atlanta."

Chloe's heart thumped painfully at the thought of that conversation. She had screwed everything up so badly. The least of which was, potentially, the friendship between her mother and Kai.

She gently blew on her hot cocoa to cool it then brought the mug to her lips in time to see Kai's bright eyes devouring her in a way they never had before.

It was because they had had sex. It had to be. Now that the dam had broken, now that they each knew how the other tasted, it was going to be even harder than before.

Chloe put the mug down, licking at the corner of her lips to get rid of any errant traces of the hot drink. Across from her, Kai made a ragged noise.

"I think you're trying to kill me." Kai put down her fork and gulped down half her water. "And I think you're doing it on purpose."

Chloe smiled but shook her head. "I'm not responsible for your lecherous thoughts."

"And therein lies the problem." She put down the water glass and braced her arms on the edges of the table. "Chloe—"

"Let me stay with you for the rest of the time you're in New York."

"What?"

"Let me stay." Chloe put a hand around the mug of cocoa but did not lift it. "I'm not ready to face Mom yet. Not about this."

"But you have to." Kai's voice was firm.

"I know. But not yet. Please."

Her insides trembled at the very idea of it. How could she tell her mother, and Duncan, about the secret she'd harbored in her heart all these years? How could she have it exposed and treated like something dirty and perverted and wrong?

"Just give me a few days' reprieve. I'm waiting to hear back from my interviews. Maybe one of the jobs will pan out before you have to leave. Then we can tell Mom and I can move to New York. I don't want to stay in the house with her if she's going to flip out on me." She'd feel too guilty if she had to look at her mother's face, see the evidence of the friendship she'd destroyed.

"I'm not sure that's the best idea, Chloe. I've got to be here for another three days, and we'll be alone together the whole time. It won't be the safest situation."

Chloe propped her chin on an upraised fist, deliberately leaning closer to Kai. "I do have self-control, you know."

"But what if I don't?" Kai was staring at her mouth.

Heat surged up Chloe's throat, and she swallowed, then cleared her throat. "Okay. How about this? It can be like a simple escort situation. We agree now to the terms. No sex." She flushed harder as the words left her mouth. Just saying the word *sex* made her think of the other woman's hands on her. "Just like an escort. Like when I was in college. We can even draw up a contract."

Kai's face grew cold. "I'm not going to treat you like a whore, Chloe. That's insulting to both of us."

"It won't be like that." She cut into her omelet, giving herself time to formulate the best argument to convince Kai. "I want to escape for a while. You may need someone to get your papers together, maybe arrange for dinner with your colleagues."

"I don't know. . . ."

"But *I* do. Why don't we try it? I honestly don't want to face being in Georgia alone with this thing looming over me. Over *us*. I know it's cowardly, but just try to see things my way a little. Okay?"

Kai sighed, a torn look on her face. "There's a contract involved?"

"There can be. I can put one together if you like."

"No. Let's not do that. It makes me feel like I'm hiring you."

"But you are. And this way, you don't have to worry about losing control and trying to have sex with me." Chloe smiled gently. "I'd even wear a chastity belt if it helps."

"That wouldn't stop me from getting what I want, believe me." Kai cleared her throat and went back to her spicy eggs.

Chapter 8

Chloe and Kai didn't end up drawing up a contract, but they might as well have. When they got back to the apartment, Kai immediately set up the office as her bedroom, firmly putting at least that boundary between her and Chloe.

"Now that that's all settled, let's see if we can get back to some sort of normalcy," she told Chloe.

Kai stood in the living room with her hands in her pockets. The bright autumn light from the windows fell on her beautiful face, over the rippling length of her locks, the curve of her breasts in the buttoned-up shirt. Chloe couldn't stop her eyes from lingering on those breasts. The pulse in her throat tripped as she wondered what it would have been like to taste them, feel their tips harden under her tongue.

"We should probably go outside and do something," Kai said as she watched Chloe's face and the desire that had to be written plainly on it.

Chloe blushed. Yes, they needed to go outside for the sake of her sanity and this invisible contract of theirs.

Chloe had never been that much into sex. It was something she could take or leave. When she'd shared her virginity with Nicole Walker in college, it had been a nonissue, two young women sharing pleasure one night after a party. Nicole had been ravenous for sex, but Chloe had only shrugged, going along with the demands of her sudden girlfriend because what Nicole made her body feel was pleasant.

But she'd never truly *desired* someone before, until Kai touched her. With her, Chloe wanted more, wanted to do more, see more, wanted that explosion between her thighs to go on forever.

"And you're sure you don't want to reconsider this 'companion' thing?" Kai asked.

"I'm sure."

Kai sighed softly. "Then let's get out of here."

They left the apartment in search of New York in autumn. A train ride and a slow meander through the city took them to Central Park. There the fall leaves were in full glory, fluttering around them to the ground like pieces of sunshine. At the park, Chloe strolled at Kai's side under the bright leaves, her hands tucked into her jacket pockets, while sunlight lightly kissed her face and throat.

"Thank you again for allowing me to stay here with you, Kai. I really appreciate it."

"I'd thank you for not thanking me for being an enabler," the other woman said dryly. "You should be back in Atlanta, confessing our sins to your mother, not hiding out here with me."

"But I'm not hiding out." Chloe spun once, flaring her jacket around her hips as she gestured at the park and the people in it. "I'm with you, and we're strolling under the sun, where anybody can see us. Mom will know everything soon enough. For now, I just want to *be*."

"Right." Kai's look was a mixture of cynicism and amusement.

Chloe smiled. Despite the sensual tension between them, she was enjoying their walk. Having Kai at her side was a natural high. The leaves crackled under their footsteps, and the air was crisp, smelling like happiness. Someone nearby was roasting peanuts, and the scent of dying leaves drifted through the air. The park was the perfect blend of empty and beautiful, the leaves and other sights bright enough to bring out the strolling locals, but the tourist season at enough of a lull that the paths weren't so congested.

Chloe sighed in contentment. "How long have you had this apartment?"

"About six years now, give or take."

"Really? How come I didn't know about it? I came to New York at least half a dozen times while I was in college. My friends and I could have crashed at your place." She gave Kai a cheeky grin, knowing that would never have happened.

"I'm never in the mood to entertain children, Chloe." Kai's eyes flashed an unknown emotion.

"It's a good thing I'm not a child, then."

They stopped at a stall to get hot cocoa, Chloe buying them both a hot cup, which Kai accepted grudgingly.

"I thought you were my companion for the next few days," Kai muttered, taking her cup from the vendor. "Shouldn't I be paying for all your expenses while we're here?"

"I don't think we need to take things that far." Chloe paid for their drinks, then tucked away her wallet. "This is my treat to myself and a thank-you for letting me inconvenience you in your own home."

They started walking again, sipping their cups of hot cocoa.

"You're not an inconvenience, Chloe."

"And you're not a very good liar." She cupped her hands around the warm Styrofoam container. "I know you're uncomfortable with me here. For various reasons. I'll try to minimize the awkwardness as much as possible."

"It's awkward only because I want you." Kai's voice was a hot whisper, one that Chloe felt deep in her belly. "I've always enjoyed your company, Chloe. When you were a child and even now, when you're making my life far more complicated than it needs to be."

"Thank you for saying that."

Kai glanced at Chloe, her mint-ginger eyes haunted. "What? For confessing that even now I want to drop to my knees and give you something we both want?"

Chloe flushed with pleasure and arousal, gripping her cocoa tighter. "Yes."

She and Kai took the bridle path under the Gothic Bridge as bright yellow and orange leaves scattered on the wind around them. The edges of their clothes fluttered in the mild breeze.

Chloe sipped her cocoa, slowly coming to terms with the decision to tell her mother about what she had done to Kai. Seduced her, brought the tall woman tumbling down into sexual abandon with her. And what a tumble it had been.

Flashes of the night before came to her: Kai's hands cupping her breasts, lust-drugged green and gold eyes staring down into hers, tender fingers parting her pussy lips, then sliding, inch by inch, into her soaked cunt. Chloe trembled with arousal, happy she would have those memories until the end of her days.

She sighed and, unthinkingly, looped her arm through Kai's.

The other woman looked startled for a moment before she relaxed against Chloe. A sudden wind swirled leaves in the air, some catching in Kai's locks for a moment before flying away, the bright red and yellow leaves a fleeting kiss of color against her skin.

"You have something . . ." Smiling, Kai reached out and plucked a leaf from Chloe's hair. Her fingers brushed against Chloe's cheek as she untangled the leaf from her coils. She let the leaf fall but traced a finger around her ear.

Chloe shivered, unconsciously lifting her mouth to be kissed.

"Kai, is that you?" A woman's voice.

Kai's head jerked up. Then she smiled.

"I thought that was you!" The woman who had called out to her muttered something into the phone she had at her ear, then tucked it in the pocket of her shorts before flying toward Kai.

She threw her arms around Kai's neck, forcing Chloe to pull her hand away and fall back.

Kai leaned into the beautiful woman's enthusiastic embrace with a grin. "Adi," Kai greeted with the warm smile. "Good to see you."

Adi could have been a model. She was tall and had a graceful galloping walk. With skin like sweet blackberries and a brilliant white smile, she stood out like a diamond among the others strolling through the park. She had short natural hair cut close to her head, a regal neck, and a gorgeous body. She wore a slim-fitting black jacket, a scarf, and cream shorts over black tights that showed off mile-long legs. The cream and black wedges on her feet were precariously high.

"Girl, you look good!" She released Kai to pull Chloe in with her wide and infectious smile. "And you do too, honey. Whoever you are." She leaned in and pecked Chloe on the cheek. "You are gorgeous!" Her appraising gaze seemed to take in all of Chloe, from the toes of her high-heeled black boots to the thick kinks in her hair.

Kai smiled down at the two women. "Adi and Chloe, meet each other."

"A pleasure, darling." Adi touched Chloe's arm, then brushed a finger across Kai's cheek. "You look so happy. Is this a new thing or a seasoned love affair?" She looked at Kai as she asked the question but invited Chloe to answer as well. "I haven't seen you in at least a year and a half. Not since Black Pride."

"We're actually not together," Chloe said before Adi could go any further. "Kai is a family friend."

Adi laughed, throwing back her pretty head. Her teeth flashed in the late morning sun, and her laughter rang out loud and long, attracting more than a few stares. "If you two haven't fucked yet, I'll eat this entire park full of dead leaves."

Chloe watched, shocked, as color flooded Kai's cheeks. Who was this woman who could make Kai blush like a fifteen-year-old?

Adi laughed again. "Good for you, Kai. I'm sure your performance was stellar, as usual."

"I'm going to let you go before my face catches on fire, Adi." Kai shook her head, her cheeks still dark with embarrassment. "I'm never ready to play with you."

"Fine, honey. But you should come to the party I'm having this weekend. The bae and I are having a cookout on the roof. Bring your honey. We'll make her feel welcome, and you'll have a real good time." She kissed Kai quickly on the cheek, leaving a touch of her bright purple lipstick. "Don't tell me no." She slipped a card in Kai's pocket. "In case you forgot our address and number."

Adi squeezed Chloe's arm. "See you then, hot stuff." Then she was off, a strutting peacock on the path with her cell phone back at her ear.

"Oh my God!" Chloe stared after the leggy woman. "Who is that?"

"An old friend." Kai tucked Chloe's arm back through hers, and they continued walking down the leaf-strewn path. "I've known her for years."

"And you slept with her." Chloe raised an eyebrow.

"Once. Years ago, when I was at NYU."

At Chloe's narrowed look, Kai raised a hand, laughing. "It was just once, and just enough for us to know that it wouldn't work. She tried to hook me up with one of her friends about a week later."

"That's weird." Chloe shook her head. Since she had slept with Kai, she couldn't imagine trying to give her to someone else.

They continued down the paved path, passing a light trickle of people enjoying the late morning air, women with their children bundled up in strollers, joggers, groups of giggling teenagers who appeared to be skipping school.

"Do you think everyone can tell that we've slept together?" Chloe felt a shudder run through Kai's body after she asked the question.

"Shit," Kai muttered. "I hope not." She rolled her shoulders under her elegant coat. "It might just be Adi. She's very perceptive. On the morning after she and I slept together for the first and last time, she said that she would love to keep me but couldn't, since I was meant for someone else."

Chloe made a noise. "And ever since then she's been trying to set you up with random lesbians all over New York?"

"Pretty much. She insists she's just trying to help my woman find me."

Chloe bit her lip. "Do you think I'm that woman?" She held her breath, wondering what Kai would say.

But she said nothing, only glanced down at Chloe with an unreadable expression. Then she finally sighed a word and looked away to stare ahead at the path.

"Shit."

Chapter 9

Chloe woke up to the sound of Kai moving around the bedroom. The other woman was quiet, but Chloe heard the muted tread of her bare feet across the rug and the hardwood floors, smelled the oils she had recently smoothed on her skin after her shower.

She turned over in the bed to watch Kai, dressed in dark slacks and an unbuttoned dress shirt, slip beyond the bedroom door.

Since their morning in the park, Kai had avoided her as much as she could in the shared apartment, working long hours behind the closed door of her office, leaving first thing in the morning, before Chloe even woke, staying out past midnight some days. Even though Chloe knew why the other woman did it, her avoidance still hurt.

She lay in bed, staring at the ceiling for a long time, before she finally got up to tidy herself in the bathroom, then make her way to the living room.

Down the hall, she could hear Kai moving around in her makeshift bedroom. Within moments, she emerged, dressed for work in a gray pin-striped suit and a paisley tie. She had her hair pulled into a neat French braid. Tiny diamond studs sparkled from her earlobes.

"Good morning." Chloe yawned and curled her legs under her on the couch.

"Good morning, miss." Kai was so utterly calm. So handsome. Chloe felt her heart clench, but she kept the welcoming smile on her face.

Kai checked her watch as she straightened her tie. "I'm heading out to my meeting." It was almost eight in the morning. "I probably won't be back until late tonight."

As usual.

"Okay. So you'll be back around midnight?"

"Something like that." Kai disappeared into the kitchen. Chloe heard the sound of a cup being pulled from the cupboard. The trickling of liquid.

"Don't wait up for me," Kai called. "But make sure you're packed. We'll be leaving here tomorrow afternoon."

The three days in New York had passed more quickly than Chloe had anticipated. Part of her had hoped that they would stay for Adi's rooftop party, which was to happen the next day, Saturday. Despite knowing better, she'd imagined showing up at the party with Kai, the two of them acting like a couple, dancing beneath the Manhattan stars in their rooftop refuge. But that was a fantasy.

"I'll be ready to leave by then," Chloe said.

Kai nodded and went to drink her coffee at the dining table while she read the newspaper. Chloe sat back on the couch and allowed herself the luxury of slowly waking up, enjoying the silence. Beyond the windows of the apartment, the day was bright and getting brighter. She gazed at the light sparkling off the glass of nearby buildings, heard the faint hum of traffic nine stories below. Peaceful. *How easy,* she thought, *it would be to get used to this type of life. With Kai.*

In LA, things had been so different, wonderful some days, but also colorless. She imagined that life in New York, with all its seasons—brilliant falls, white winters, sweltering summers, and blossoming springs—would be a kind of heaven. If only she had a lover to share it with.

The sound of the newspaper brought her eyes back to the kitchen.

Kai folded the paper and stood up from the table. "The world calls," she said as she left the kitchen for the bedroom.

Soon she was back, smelling like toothpaste and draping a scarf the color of fresh papayas around her neck. The color brought out the hints of orange in her tie. She carried a light jacket over her arm.

"That's a great color on you." Chloe jumped up from the couch and picked up Kai's briefcase from the ottoman. "Let me walk you out."

She self-consciously tugged at the neckline of her flannel pajamas as she felt Kai's eyes on her, remembering abruptly that this was the same pair of pajamas that the other woman had tugged from her flesh before she kissed her, loved her, made her come to life.

With faint color in her cheeks, Kai turned toward the front door. "Are you taking this companion thing too far, Little Bit?"

"Just don't get used to it." Chloe gave Kai her briefcase with trembling fingers.

"That's a tall order." The color was still high in Kai's face, a deeper shade under her ocher skin, but a smile plucked at the corners of her mouth. "Even with everything that happened this week, I'm glad you came up. It's been fun having you up here with me."

The way Kai was looking at her, warm and hot at the same time, as if Chloe was everything that she had ever wanted, made Chloe ache to slide her arms around Kai's neck for a lingering kiss and send her off to work like a real wife.

"Go to work," she said, giving her a gentle push.

Kai hesitated for a moment before she pulled on her jacket and started down the hallway. "See you tonight, Little Bit."

Chloe paused in the doorway to watch Kai walk away, her long body graceful and feminine in the masculine suit, her hair brushing against the back of the jacket with each step.

"I'll have dinner waiting when you get home," she called out with an impish smile.

Across the hall, she noticed another woman in a doorway, kissing her man just before he left the apartment. How domestic and sweet.

The man strolled past her in the hallway. "Good morning," he greeted.

She nodded back at him, then watched him join Kai at the end of the hall to wait for the elevator. Kai looked over her shoulder, and Chloe blew her a kiss. She could practically see Kai frown, and she hoped that she would pay for her cheekiness later.

"Bye, honey." Chloe waved. She might as well milk the morning for all it was worth, since the next day she was heading back to Atlanta and would never be in this unique position again.

The elevator bell sounded as the car arrived. She waited in the doorway until Kai had disappeared through its doors before letting the smile slide from her face. The sadness came easily then. New York with Kai was over. Now it was back to her real life.

With heavy footsteps, she went back inside the apartment to pack up her things. She had almost finished when her cell phone rang. She didn't recognize the 212 phone number.

"Chloe Graham speaking. How can I help you?"

She sat on the bed and draped a blouse she was folding across her thigh.

"This is Isabel Ortiz with Generation Next Effects. This is in reference to your recent interview."

Chloe's fingers clenched the blouse, and her heart rate sped up. Generation Next was the New York studio that she wanted to work for the most, even though she'd hedged her bets with applications at five other studios around the city.

Her heart continued to pound as Isabel Ortiz told her she liked her very much as a candidate and wanted to offer her the position of full-time special effects makeup artist. Her mouth went dry at the offered salary.

A half an hour later, Chloe got off the phone after having set up a time to come in and sign the papers and start the process of working for the company. Her head was spinning.

She sat on the bed, staring down at the phone, running through the conversation in her mind. She would start a week from Monday. Her salary was even better than she'd hoped. She was officially moving to New York. She needed to find a place to stay.

"Oh my God." Chloe jumped up from the bed, a smile stretching from ear to ear. "Oh my God!"

She wanted to scream and share the news with Zahra and her mother and with Kai. At the thought of the other woman, she froze. *Kai.*

Did it make sense for her to go home tomorrow when she had to come back to New York in less than a week? Could she stay in the apartment while Kai was in Atlanta? What did that mean for the talk they were supposed to have with Chloe's mother? What did that mean for *them?*

She sank back onto the bed, her thoughts running away from her. When she lived in LA, she hardly ever saw Kai. Except for her college graduation, she had only ever seen the older woman during holidays in Atlanta. Once Chloe went to college, she and Kai never enjoyed the relationship they had had when Chloe was younger.

Most of that was her fault, she knew. She hadn't wanted to be faced with the temptation of Kai and her own over-whelming feelings. New York was closer to Atlanta than LA. How could she keep Kai at bay if she lived and worked so near? Not to mention that Kai had an actual apartment in the city, where she spent at least five days a month, ac-cording to her mother. But she knew family members who shared the same city but never saw each other.

Sadness clutched at her throat at the thought of not seeing Kai again. The fact was that she'd seen more of the other woman in the last couple of weeks in Atlanta and New York than she had in the past five years. And it had felt good. She knew she couldn't keep seeing her, though. Kai was torn and in pain about how things had developed between them. Chloe didn't want her to hurt anymore.

Yes. If she lived in New York, she wouldn't see Kai. Her mother's best friend would have to become like a family friend she never had time for. Like her uncle Frank, who lived in Rex, barely a half hour from where she and her mother lived in Atlanta, but whom she saw only at wed-dings, funerals, and graduations. He was like a stranger to Chloe. She didn't want that kind of relationship with Kai, but maybe that was the only way to get them past this.

She shook herself out of her stupor and called her mother.

When she answered, Chloe could tell she was in the kitchen, probably trying out a new recipe or creating something dazzling for one of her A-list clients.

"Hi, darling." Her mother sounded slightly breathless, like she had been lifting something heavy or wreaking havoc in the kitchen. "How are things in New York?"

Her mother was an amazing chef. But watching her in the kitchen was like observing a tornado, as she would spin from stove to plating station to fridge to countertop to deep freezer all without pausing. It was a manic ballet Chloe loved to watch.

"I got the job."

"What?" Pots clanged through the phone; then everything seemed to stop. "You did? Was it with Generation Next?"

"Yes and yes." Chloe blew out a breath, excited at being able to share the news.

Her mother shouted out in praise. "I knew you could do it, darling!"

"They want me to start in less than a week. On Monday."

"Oh." Her mother's voice pulled away from the phone as she spoke briefly with someone else. Then the sounds of the kitchen died away. She was walking away to find a quieter spot. "You just got back from California. Are you ready for that?"

"Yes." She needed to be. "I'm already here and wouldn't have to spend extra money getting back and forth to the airport if I stayed." She shrugged, although her mother couldn't see it. "I would just ask Kai if I can stay at her place until I find my own."

"You know that airfare is not an issue, baby. Duncan's flight benefits get you there for free."

"I know. But I think the sooner I settle in here, the better."

"All right. If that's what you want." Her mother sighed softly. "I'm happy for you, Chloe. But I'd be lying if I said I hadn't been looking forward to you spending a few more weeks here with me. After you went to California, I feel like I barely saw you."

Chloe didn't call her mother out on her exaggeration. With flight benefits, her mother had been able to fly to LA at least once a month to see her. But she knew it was different for her mother to go upstairs and sit on her bed for chats versus putting her life and job on hold to fly across the country every thirty days to see her child.

"I know, Mom. But you can always come up here and visit me. I'm a New Yorker now." She creased the edge of the comforter between her fingers, thinking of the decision she had made to stay away from Kai. She didn't want that to affect how often she saw her mother. She couldn't let it.

"We'll see each other, Mom. Don't worry."

They stayed on the phone for another hour, talking about her experience in New York so far, including seeing the city in all its fall finery, enjoying the streets, which were nearly empty of tourists, and sampling the food.

Chatting with her mother made her realize how long it had been since they'd had that sort of conversation, since they'd lingered on the phone to discuss whatever it was that came up between them, the weather, their feelings, how her mother's business was going. It felt good. It felt like old times, like when they used to picnic in front of the fireplace and drink wine.

There were a few times during the conversation when she thought about bringing up the subject of Kai and what the older woman meant to her. But each time, her courage failed.

Chloe hung up the phone with promises to see her mother soon and then turned her attention back to her nearly packed suitcase, which lay open next to her on the bed. As she folded the last blouse, she noticed a photograph on the dresser of Kai and her mother.

They were young, sitting on the front steps of a house, both wearing sagging jeans and backward ball caps. Kai was grinning at the camera, a handsome teenager with thick, wavy hair down to her shoulders. Chloe's mother wore her hair in cornrows and had her flat stomach bared in a cropped tank top. She had bright red lipstick painted on her sultry smile. They looked like T-Boz and Chilli from TLC, almost like a couple, especially with the baby who sat between them on the steps. Chloe.

She stared at the child between the two teenagers, not seeing herself, but the idea that she could come between these two women who'd been friends for so long. Tears burned her eyes.

Chapter 10

It was well after midnight when Kai came home. But Chloe was expecting her. Lit candles flickered around the apartment; all the windows were open to allow in the urban stars of New York City, the streams of light from passing cars, the whisper of traffic. A pot of apple cider sat on the stove, perfuming the rooms with the scent of apples, cinnamon, and cloves.

The living room was draped in shadow and dancing candlelight when Kai's key sounded in the door. Chloe waited. She handed a surprised Kai a drink, took her keys from her hand, and put them in the small wooden box she kept on the wall shelf.

Kai smelled like the outdoors, fresh and crisp, with a hint of sweetness, like she'd been to a hooka bar.

"You smell nice." Chloe tugged off Kai's scarf and draped it over the coatrack. Took her briefcase and laid it with care on the rack as well.

"What . . . what are you doing?" Kai stood frozen with her arms wide, the drink held obediently in her hand, as if she didn't know exactly what to do with it.

She stared around the apartment at the candles, at Chloe, who had dressed carefully for the night in a clinging red dress that bared an indecent amount of cleavage and stretched tight across her bottom. It was a dress she'd bought with seduction in mind, a dress that even she wouldn't wear outside the house. The stilettos she wore with it were equally scandalous. If shoes could scream "Fuck me now!" it was that pair.

Chloe unbuttoned Kai's jacket, tugged it off, maneuvering it around the tumbler of whiskey in Kai's hand. She turned around unnecessarily to put the jacket on the coat rack, giving Kai the full view of the red dress, rocking her hips with each step.

"I'm being a companion. What we agreed on." She took Kai's hand and led her to the couch. "Is whiskey okay? I can get you something else if you'd like."

The woman she wanted to be her lover again faltered just a few feet behind her, linked by the tether of Chloe's fingers, watching, Chloe knew, the sway of her ass under the dress.

"Chloe . . ." Kai's voice was hoarse.

With their hands joined, Chloe walked her to the couch, gently shoved her into its depths before kneeling before Kai. She pulled off her leather ankle boots, revealing thin black socks that clung to her slender feet. Kai's feet were warm in Chloe's hands, the bones narrow and pronounced. Chloe peeled off the socks and tossed them aside.

"Chloe. Stop." Kai swallowed audibly.

"I'm not doing anything," she said as she brought Kai's feet into her lap and slowly began to massage them. "You've had a long day. I'm trying to make you comfortable." Chloe pressed the heel of one foot between her thighs, leaning forward until Kai's toes touched her breasts. Her nipples, hard before, pressed like diamonds against the thin material of her dress.

"This is much more than that, and you know it." But Kai didn't remove her feet, only stared down at Chloe with dazed eyes, a hand still clutching the tumbler of whiskey, whose contents sloshed dangerously but did not spill.

"I'm seeing to your wants. Your needs." She pressed the heel even more between her thighs, releasing a silent gasp as it ground into her clit. "Don't you want me to do that?"

The bones of Kai's feet were delicate under her hands, almost like a bird's. A surprise since she'd always thought the other woman so strong, steel wrapped in brown velvet. Chloe used her thumbs to press into the soft flesh, the balls of her feet, between her toes, her instep, until Kai relaxed on the couch, her head falling back, her lips parted on a sigh. From the floor, Chloe looked up at the woman she loved. At her beautiful body stretched out on the couch, its strength, its perfection, its uniqueness.

Although she'd tried time and time again, she'd never been able to find another woman like Kai. It was time she stopped trying to duplicate this woman who'd captured her heart before she'd been aware she had one.

Chloe stopped massaging Kai's feet once she was completely relaxed, her breathing even and calm. She still hadn't touched her drink. Chloe put Kai's foot on the floor, on the outside of her thigh. Kai's eyes fluttered open, and she looked down at Chloe, her gaze bouncing away from the ripe breasts spilling from the scooped neck of the red dress. Her tortured gaze landed on Chloe's eyes.

"Chloe." Her voice was low, rough. "We talked about this. You know this can't happen again."

"I got a job here." She knelt with her hands in her lap, eyes downcast. "I'm staying in New York." She lifted her lashes to stare at Kai. "I won't be in Atlanta much anymore."

"This still can't happen, Chloe. For so many reasons." Her hand clutched the whiskey, and she finally brought the tumbler to her lips.

"I probably won't see you again," Chloe said, although it nearly made her sick to realize that could be true. "You shouldn't tell Mom what happened between us. I'll stay here and work. You go back to Atlanta on your own tomorrow and leave me here. By the time you come back to the city for another business trip, I'll have my own place."

Kai blinked slowly, her lips glistening from the whiskey. She looked dazed. "That's not realistic."

"What's not realistic is to tell Mom and not expect her to be upset. I don't want to destroy your friendship with her. It's better if you go back to Atlanta alone. We don't ever have to see each other again, and she never has to know what happened between us."

"And that's why you're on your knees, like this?" Kai gulped the whiskey again, wincing from the drink's bite.

Chloe flushed. How could she find the words to say that she wanted to taste Kai just once? That she needed the feel of the other woman's most intimate flesh on her lips, a feeling to carry with her for the rest of her life?

"Kai." She touched the legs on the other side of her, slowly moving her hands up to lean thighs, then narrow hips. Kai was frozen under her touch. "I want to make love to you. Just once."

Before Kai could deny her what she wanted, Chloe climbed into her lap and kissed her.

It was like the first time. Kai's surprise that their mouths connected. A stillness. Chloe cupped her cheeks and deepened the kiss, keeping control this time, then straddled Kai and breathed against her mouth, licking the irresistible firm lips until they parted. Chloe made a soft sound of relief and pleasure. Half the battle was won.

She sighed into Kai's mouth, her tongue tentatively exploring the hot space as cool hands crept to the tops of her thighs, merely resting there as Chloe explored her mouth, licked the tongue that met hers with growing passion. She melted as Kai kissed her back, arousal like summer honey between her thighs, her nipples tingling against her dress.

Chloe lifted her head. "I want this," she said. "This once." She reached for the buttons of Kai's shirt.

"Chloe, no." The other woman's lids drooped heavily over her eyes, and her lips were red and swollen from their kisses.

"Yes." Chloe grabbed Kai's hand and shoved it under her dress, between her thighs. "Yes."

A rumbling growl left Kai's throat. Her fingers began moving of their own accord, teasing Chloe's wetness, stroking her clit. Chloe bit her lip and shivered in reaction. She grabbed the bodice of her dress and pulled it down, spilling her breasts into the warm air of the apartment. Kai moaned again, a tortured sound, and latched a hot mouth onto Chloe's nipple.

"Yes, Kai. Yes . . ."

Chloe's hips moved as the hand played between her thighs, effortlessly finding the source of her pleasure, touching her with long and sure strokes, while a tongue licked her nipple, flicked it, circled the turgid point with warmth, until all Chloe could do was cry out Kai's name. She shuddered in orgasm and sagged against her lover.

But Kai's fingers still moved over her clit. They skated down to delve inside her wetness, stroking her deeply, inciting pleasure once again. Chloe hissed. She wanted to ride those fingers until she found bliss again, but there was something she wanted even more. She tipped her hips back, moving away until Kai's fingers slid wetly from her pussy. She shuddered.

Chloe slipped off her lover's lap and dropped to her knees between the spread thighs. She undid the belt, the pants, and yanked down the surprising black thong to latch her mouth onto Kai's clit. She was wet. The thong was soaked. Her clit was already rising up to meet Chloe's mouth.

"Fuck!" Kai's hands clenched her hair. "Baby, don't. . . ." But even as she was saying she didn't want it, her hips were moving, her pussy heading toward Chloe's mouth for more.

She tasted fresh. The heat and wetness Chloe had expected, but there was a sweet scent of spice, as if she had rubbed her entire body down with the oil she used on her hair. Spicy wet cunt.

Kai's breath heaved. She panted Chloe's name.

"Fuck, baby. . . ."

Tingling arousal dripped between Chloe's legs at the sound of her name on Kai's lips. Moaning, she slipped her tongue down for more wetness from the drenched pussy, clenching her hands on the muscled thighs, which tightened and released with each stroke.

She'd waited her entire adult life to be here, on her knees for Kai, her skin aflame with sensation and lust. She was in shock that she was actually getting to taste Kai, getting to fuck her with her tongue, getting to feel the slippery heat of her pussy against her mouth, hear her groaning breaths. But her body knew what to do.

Her tongue fluttered at Kai's moist opening, licking the delicate gate to her pleasure, while her thumb caressed the slippery clit. Her lover shuddered. She hissed and gripped Chloe's hair, yanking her tight into her cunt, pulling Chloe's tongue deep into her wet heat.

Arousal gushed over Chloe's tongue. Kai gasped and thrust her pussy against her mouth, fingers tightly clenching the hair at Chloe's nape. Chloe gasped from the pain but did not stop the movement of her tongue, did not pull her thumb away from Kai's thickening clit.

She looked up and saw the most beautiful sight of all: Kai with her head thrown back, lips parted, hands fighting to push aside the buttons of her dress shirt. Then she gave up the fight, yanking the cotton until the buttons flew across the room. She made a sound of relief, yanked up her bra to touch her breasts and stroke her own nipples.

"Chloe. You're driving me crazy!" she gasped. "I'm losing my mind over you."

She tugged on her nipples as Chloe slid her long tongue deep inside the heated wetness, sucked the swollen clit, undulating her tongue, until Kai was crying out her name and shivering. Her juices dripped down Chloe's chin.

"It's okay," Chloe whispered against the quivering flesh. "I've got you."

She held her mouth against Kai's pussy but did not release her.

More.

She wanted so much more.

Her body hovered on the edge of orgasm, wickedly close to achieving its ecstasy just from Kai's taste alone. She started moving her tongue again. But Kai fisted a hand in her hair and gently forced her head up. She dragged Chloe back into her lap, kissing her all the while, heat and sensation and a glorious explosion of lust between them. She unzipped Chloe's dress, tugged it completely off her body while they kissed, their moans rising urgently in the room. Then Kai's hands were on her bare breasts, squeezing her nipples, circling them with her thumbs.

She pulled her damp mouth from Chloe's. "I didn't get to do this last time. But I need it now."

She lay Chloe back against the leather ottoman with her feet braced wide against the couch. Something cold, like a glass paperweight, pressed into Chloe's bare shoulder. A pencil poked her in the side, and her head hung down on the other side of the ottoman. But Chloe didn't care.

Her thighs were spread, her ass hovered over empty space, and her pussy was bare to Kai's gaze. Candlelight flickered around them as Kai licked her lips, then leaned forward to blow against her pussy. She trembled at the cool breath. Then the hot tongue lazily licked her clitoris, a slow and languorous dance that pulled at Chloe's hips, inclined them toward Kai's mouth for more of that expert touch, the mere brush of tongue a tease and a torture and a pleasure. She felt so open. Her body was so decadently stretched. Chloe opened her eyes to see the room upside down. Candles burning, the lights of the city. Her past life blowing away like ashes under a cleansing flame.

Jesus . . .

Her hips pushed into the air, toward Kai's mouth, while her thighs spread wider and her body stretched more.

"You're so beautiful," Kai murmured against her wetness. "You taste what I imagine heaven is like."

Then she slid her tongue inside Chloe. Fullness. The slurping of juices as Kai tongue fucked her, her nose stimulating her clit, her body quickening even more.

"Oh! God!"

Kai gripped Chloe's hips, feasting on her pussy. They both moaned at each stroke of Kai's tongue, the sensations rising with Chloe's gasping breaths. Sweat rippled across her skin and her belly heaved as Kai licked pleasure into her. Chloe screamed with her eyes shut tight. She clenched her fists in her own hair, crying out, thrusting her hips into Kai's face. The tight heat soared inside her until it had no place to go but out of her pussy in a hot, gushing pinnacle of fulfillment.

Gulping sounds. Kai swallowing her cum. Then her world spun as Kai lifted her, tenderly put her on the couch.

"This is the last time," Kai panted.

"Yes." The tears slid from Chloe's eyes. "Okay."

For a moment, Kai hovered over her, indecisive. Her lips parted. "Okay," she said. "Don't move."

Chloe closed her eyes, feeling the tears rush down her cheeks, feeling like a fool for getting emotional when she was the one who had started this, the one who had wanted to fuck one last time before going her way. It had been even better than the first time, as she had gotten to touch Kai and the other woman had touch her too. Her body was still tingling in the aftermath of her orgasm, her nipples tight and ready again for Kai's mouth. Chloe shook her head, clenching her eyes shut and turning her face into the back of the couch.

Accept your own decision. Kai has.

Thinking about the lifetime she would have without Kai, she felt the hopelessness begin to descend on her. But a warm kiss at the top of her foot brought her eyes flying open.

Chloe gasped at the sight of her lover. She was crouched like a cat over her, beautifully naked. Her slender body was everything Chloe had ever imagined and more. Her hair was loose down to her waist; her eyes were heavy lidded in the candlelight. Her breasts were small, the nipples a deep brown and large, making Chloe's mouth water to taste them.

The dildo strapped to her was average size. A golden brown to match Kai's skin, the leather straps black and gorgeous against her flesh. The intent in Kai's eyes curled Chloe's nails into the couch. Her pussy twitched.

"I want to fuck you," she murmured as she kissed her way up Chloe's leg. "Can I do that?" Her voice rumbled against Chloe's skin, sending shock waves of arousal through her. "If you don't want me to, I can get rid of this. There are many other ways for us to enjoy each other."

"I want you to fuck me," Chloe whispered. "Please."

"You never have to beg me for anything, love." Kai kissed her thighs, delicately biting her as she nudged them apart. "Everything I have is yours. Everything."

Her hot breath steamed over Chloe's clit; then her tongue slid over her with slow stroking licks. Chloe moaned and widened her legs, watching Kai's face. Watching the way she licked her pussy, her tongue long and graceful through the thick hairs of her cunt, her mouth slurping as she found her buried treasure and sucked it into her mouth. Again. And again. The breath shivered in Chloe's throat as the beginnings of orgasm sparked between her thighs.

She gripped the arm of the couch behind her, arching her hips to shove her soaked cunt into Kai's mouth. She panted and moaned as the sensation built. She cried out, clawing at the arm of the couch, and then the feeling snapped tight inside her body.

She cried out Kai's name as she came. In the same moment, Kai rose up and sank her dick into Chloe's quivering cunt.

"Oh!" Chloe gasped. "Fuck!"

Kai's mouth covered hers, kissing her deeply, as her hips moved between Chloe's thighs. She was surrounded by Kai's smell, her hair, her body, her sweat, as they slid together, a slow and intense fucking. The dick moved inside her, raking up shudders of pleasure, building an urgent sweetness deep in Chloe's belly.

Kai squeezed Chloe's breasts to the rhythm of her thrusts, an easy and intense song of sex, like a drumbeat, a song Chloe had heard a million times but had never known the meaning of, until now.

"Kai!"

She called out her lover's name again and again, singing it in time to the magical song weaving through her. They came together like crashing waves. A symphony of noise and movement, flesh meeting flesh, that left them both breathless and staring wide-eyed at each other.

"Chloe." Kai touched her damp forehead to hers. But she didn't say anything else.

She held on to Kai, knowing what she felt, both tenderness and regret, not that their lovemaking had happened, but that it would never get the chance to unfold again. She threaded her fingers through Kai's locks, traced a line down her sweat-dampened back to the muscled curve of her ass.

"Make love with me all night, Kai." She whispered the words against her lover's mouth. "Let's just take tonight. Nothing else matters right now but us."

Kai stirred against her, lifting her head to look down into Chloe's face with her starlit eyes. She blinked. "You are the only one who matters tonight, love. We'll let tomorrow take care of itself."

She braced herself above Chloe with her palms flat against the couch. Then she began to move her hips again.

Chapter 11

Their night was long, a heated dance that took them from the couch to the bed to the floor, then back to the bed again. Their breaths and bodies came together over and over until the sun rose. Then, after they had taken a nap at dawn, Chloe reached for Kai, and their lovemaking began again. It was as intense as it was surprising. Kai's stamina was more than Chloe had ever dreamed. Her inventiveness. Her patience. Her willingness to try things that Chloe had always wanted to but never had the chance.

It was a dream of sex. Electric and never-ending, it left Chloe's body sore but still wanting more from every angle, every surface, with every kind of touch that both of them could imagine. Now she knew what the big deal was about sex. It was amazing and magical, and she wanted to do more of it. Especially with Kai.

But she knew that wasn't possible. Which was why the coming of the morning, the bright 11:00 a.m. sun, found her with tears on her face.

She opened her eyes to find herself lying sideways on the bed, her legs entangled with Kai's, the sun pouring over them from the large windows on either side of the bed. The covers lay heavy over them, shielding their bodies from the slight chill in the air. Her lashes were heavy from her morning tears, and she felt the dried tracks of them on her cheeks as she stirred. Kai's arms tightened around her, and she realized that the other woman had not been sleeping, had merely been holding her while she slept.

"I don't want today to come," Chloe murmured, snuggling into the warm body of her lover. She felt torn in two, saturated with both sadness and sexual satisfaction.

Kai trailed gentle fingers down her back. "But it's here. Let's make the most of it, no matter how it unfolds."

But Chloe closed her eyes, not wanting to hear that. Not now. Not after the amazing discoveries of the night. She wanted to run away with Kai. Never mind the decision she had made the day before. Now that she'd experienced the completion of their lovemaking, she wanted more. She wanted an even deeper connection. She wanted more time.

"Baby, it's going to be fine—"

The sound of the doorbell cut off Kai.

"Who *is* that?" Kai reached for her cell phone on the bedside table and squinted at its display. "It's not even noon yet."

Chloe stretched against the sheets and pressed a kiss to Kai's throat. "You know, some people have already done their entire day's work by now."

Kai muttered something about her work just beginning and climbed from the bed. She pulled on boxer shorts and a tank top before leaving the bedroom. Chloe curled up under the sheets, her bare body sliding into the warmth Kai had left behind. In the living room, she heard Kai's voice. Something in it made Chloe sit up and listen.

Seconds later, Kai rushed into the bedroom, her face pinched and cold. "Get dressed. Noelle is here."

"What!"

But Kai was gone again.

Chloe jumped up from the bed, hissing silently at the rush of cold air on her skin. She grabbed the first thing she found near the bed and yanked it on. Ran to the bathroom to brush her teeth and wash her face and hands. In the mirror, her face looked terrified. The hot water burned her cold hands and splashed all over the bathroom sink. Her fingers trembled as she brushed her teeth.

Her mother? Here? Why?

She frantically tried to remember anything about their phone call that said her mother was about to come to New York, but she remembered nothing. Only the tears and the guilt and the relief that she had decided not to say anything about her and Kai, after all. She shoved her hands through her hair, fluffing it as best she could. Her eyes were wide with panic. She stared at her reflection, trying to think of what to say to her mother, wondering if she could just stay in the bathroom until she left.

"Chloe?"

She flinched when her mother called her name from down the hall. Wild-eyed, she checked her reflection one last time, hoping there was nothing about her face that gave away what she had been doing all night.

Wiping up the water she'd spilled around the sink, Chloe delayed for a few seconds more before taking a breath and leaving the bathroom. In the living room, her mother was pulling off her thin leather gloves, saying something to Kai, who had her back to Chloe. She looked elegant and chic as usual in thick black leggings, riding boots, and a sweater that came nearly to her knees. Her thick gray hair was tousled by the wind.

"Surprise!" Her mother rushed toward her with a smile and kissed her cheeks. "I figured if you weren't coming back to Atlanta for a while, I'd just come to you. And I brought you some extra clothes for work. You know you never think about things like that."

When Chloe didn't say anything, she drew back, narrowing her eyes at her daughter. "What are you wearing?"

With the note of suspicion in her mother's voice, Chloe saw her plans for avoiding the discussion about Kai go up in smoke.

She glanced down at herself and realized she had on a pair of boxers and one of Kai's black undershirts. The shirt, clearly too small to adequately contain Chloe's C-cup breasts, was obviously not her own. And it was inside out.

Shit. "Sleep clothes," she said, unable to prevent herself from responding to her mother's interrogating tone of voice.

Her mother stared at Kai, who had slid the lock home on the door and stood facing the room with her arms crossed over her chest. She looked combative. And guilty.

"Why did you come out of Kai's bedroom?" Her mother frowned, as if she couldn't believe she was actually asking that question.

"Mom, I—"

"She's sleeping in there since I set myself up in the guest room," Kai explained.

Chloe squirmed as her mother narrowed her gaze at Kai once again, taking in everything about her best friend. Boxer shorts, a thin tank top with a clear imprint of her dark nipples beneath. Her bare feet, tousled hair. The constellation of hickeys on her fair-skinned neck and throat.

Her mother's voice went low. "Did you just lie to me?" She put her hands on her hips, staring at her best friend.

"Noelle . . ."

"You did. I know that look anywhere." She turned to Chloe. "What's going on?"

"I'm in love with her." Panic turned Chloe's voice into a squeak. But at that moment she felt she had to say the words, take that leap out into open space, and hope her love for Kai would save her.

Her mother froze. "What did you just say to me?"

"She and I w-were t-together last night," Chloe stuttered, before getting the words out properly. "I started it. I was the one who seduced her." She crossed her arms over her stomach, trying to quell its tremor.

Kai cursed softly before striding to the bar on the other side of the room.

"Don't move, Kai. Don't you fucking move!" Her mother's eyes were wide and afraid. They blinked quickly as she looked from her daughter to her best friend. "Tell me exactly what happened. Tell me right now."

Kai ignored her and grabbed a decanter from the bar. She poured a heavy measure of whiskey into a glass, quickly swallowed some of the liquor before turning to face her best friend.

"Things just happened. I didn't do this to hurt you, Noelle."

"Do what?" Her mother's voice was frantic. "What the fuck did you do, Kai?"

Despite what Chloe had said before, it seemed that she only now understood what her daughter was telling her. Chloe, her *daughter,* had just been having sex with her best friend.

"Chloe, go into the bedroom." Her mother's voice snapped with anger. Then she flew at Kai, slapping her hard. The sound was loud and echoed in the room. Her sweater jerked up around her hips; her hair was wild as she reared back for another slap. "What the fuck!" She slapped Kai again, and her best friend didn't try to stop her. "Kai. Tell me you didn't do this." *Slap.* "Tell me!" she screamed, the noise a wailing cry of sadness and betrayal. Her arms windmilled, mercilessly pummeling Kai.

"Mom, stop!" Chloe rushed across the room, but her mother shoved her firmly back. She stumbled against the couch.

"I said go to your room, Chloe. This doesn't concern you!" Her mother screamed at the same time that Kai ducked and backed away from a punch.

"It's okay, Chloe." Kai spoke with effort, trying to hold off her best friend. "Do as she says." A bruise was already forming on her cheek.

"I'm not a child!" Chloe righted herself against the arm of the couch but did not go toward them again.

Neither her mother nor Kai was paying attention to her. It was like her mother had transformed into that girl on the stoop in the long-ago photograph. Her lip was curled in a sneer, and her body was a slim and deadly challenge.

Chloe was truly frightened. Noelle Graham didn't seem like her mother anymore, but like a broken woman flinging shards of herself at someone she had once loved, someone who had shattered her completely.

She flew at Kai in a rage, slapping her friend in the face, punching her chest, arms, and anywhere else she could reach. Kai tried only to hold her off, to avoid getting hit again.

"What the fuck is wrong with you that you're fucking my child? She's only twenty-three, for God's sake!" Her mother was crying, tears running down her face.

"Noelle. I didn't hurt her." Kai's voice broke as her own tears began to fall. "I promise. I didn't mean to hurt you."

"Have you always been looking at her like that? Were you grooming her to be your sex toy this whole time?" Her mother screamed more obscenities, cried out each new scenario that occurred to her as she slapped and railed at Kai.

When her slaps turned into punches to Kai's face, her best friend grabbed her arms and shoved her back. "Noelle! Please!" Her face was tortured, lips trembling as the tears fell faster.

Chloe felt as if she was the one breaking apart.

"There's nothing you can say to me that will make this right. Nothing!" her mother raged.

This is all my fault! Chloe stared in horror at the fighting women. She had caused this.

"Stop it! Stop." She shoved her way between them, then gasped as a fist smashed into her lip. Her head snapped back, and she tasted blood. She stumbled against Kai.

Her mother gasped. "Oh my God!"

Everything stopped for a moment. Chloe's body dipped, and her vision wobbled. The next thing she knew, she was lying on the couch.

"Get the fuck away from her," her mother snarled. "I'll take care of her myself."

"But you're the one who hit me," Chloe muttered, putting a hand to her throbbing lip. Her fingers came away stained with blood.

Nausea seized her stomach. The sight of her own blood sickened her. But she saw that despite her words to Kai, her mother had moved aside to allow her best friend to put a damp cloth to Chloe's mouth. Her mother tucked a pillow under her head and smoothed her cheek. She sat down next to Chloe.

"I'm sorry, darling. I didn't mean to hit you."

Chloe put a hand to her head and turned away from both of them. "I'll be okay. Just don't be angry at Kai." She touched her mother's arm but looked at Kai, who now sat at the far end of the couch. "I . . . I was the one who started it. She didn't have anything to do with this."

"I'm sure you didn't force her to eat your pussy."

"Mother!" Chloe blushed so hard that her face hurt even more. She could not bring herself to look at Kai. "Please, don't say things like that."

"I'm afraid the time for being coy has passed, my love." Her mother closed her eyes and turned her head toward her friend. "Kai, for you, of all people, to do this to me . . ." A sob left her mouth. "This is the biggest betrayal. Even worse than when Evan abandoned me, leaving me to raise Chloe on my own." She drew a trembling breath and seemed to fight for control of herself. "Kai, when did this start?"

Chloe opened her mouth.

"No." Her mother squeezed her hand tightly. "I'm not talking to you right now."

Kai, her face still wet with tears, squirmed in her seat. She stood up and went back to the bar with her empty glass, but she did not refill her drink.

It was a long time before she said anything. Then she answered, "I didn't touch her until this week."

Chloe's mother hissed with angry impatience. "But when did you start *thinking* about her like this? Be honest. I need to know."

"It was the day we dropped her off at school in California."

Chloe strangled her gasp before it could escape her lips. *That long ago?*

Kai stood with her back to the room, her legs spread wide, hands braced against the surface of the bar. She looked delicate in the thin tank top and the peace sign boxers, her skin bleached nearly yellow in the morning light. Her shoulders were shaking as she spoke.

"Chloe was already moved in. You and Duncan were off somewhere, trying to find out about visitor parking. I waited with the truck in case the cops came over to hassle us for parking in front of the dorms."

Then Chloe *did* gasp. She remembered that day. She remembered it clearly.

She had just left her new dorm, feeling giddy at finally being in college and away from home. The sun was brilliant in Los Angeles, and everything smelled so different. The air. The trees. It felt like being set adrift in a beautiful foreign place where everything and anything was possible. And that day, as she walked across the lawn in her flip-flops, with her hair in wild twists and the new breeze on her skin, even her infatuation with Kai seemed different.

Kai was leaning against the large SUV Duncan had rented to take Chloe across the country. One foot braced on the ground, the other against the bumper of the dark green truck. She tilted her head toward the sky. Her hair twisted on top of her head, bound in a tie-dyed scarf, and her eyes closed as she savored the quiet she'd managed to find in the chaos of the campus. Her arms were bare in a white tank top, and a black strap of her bra peeked out. She wore cut-off jean shorts that were loose around her lean thighs and green Converse. Even now, five years later, that image of Kai was so clear to Chloe that she could have seen it only minutes before.

On that sunlit Los Angeles day, something must have alerted Kai to Chloe's presence, because she opened her eyes and smiled. Their gazes met across the small distance. Chloe remembered locking with the green and gold orbs, feeling a tightening in her belly, a melting and spilling over of all the love she had for Kai. The other woman's eyes fluttered away. For a moment, it was like she saw Chloe, really *saw* who she was, for the first time. Then Kai's gaze returned to her, startled, almost afraid, before it skittered away again.

"I saw Chloe surrounded by all the other college girls," Kai said. "Beautiful women with their booties out in shorts and little dresses. And I remember thinking how much better than all of them she looked. How beautiful and . . . sexy." Kai cleared her throat, then slowly turned around. She tapped the empty whiskey glass against the surface of the bar. "I left LA as soon as I could and have avoided her for the most part ever since then."

"Until last night, when you fucked her."

Kai sighed. "Yes, until this week." Her distinction made it clear that last night was not the first time.

"Fuck." Noelle shot to her feet like she wanted to attack her friend again. "Fuckin' really, Kai? Really?" Chloe had never heard her curse that much in . . . ever. She stepped away from Chloe, her footsteps stiff and awkward. "I don't . . . I can't even look at you right now. I really can't."

"Mom, stop this—"

"No. Noelle is right." Kai's face was wet with tears again; her stoic façade in ruins. "I'll leave."

Chloe jerked to her feet. "No! This is your apartment."

But Kai was already slipping past her. She came back from the bedroom within moments in the same jeans and sweater from a few days before. Her feet were still bare.

Chloe started to go to her. "Baby! Your shoes."

Her mother shot Chloe a poisonous look. "Get the fuck out of here, Kai!" she shouted, still staring at Chloe. "And don't come back until we're gone."

Kai's eyes darted toward the bedroom, where her shoes were, before she seemed to make a decision, grabbing her keys and rushing from the apartment barefoot.

"Mother! Her feet! It's cold out there." Chloe rushed toward the bedroom to grab a pair of shoes for Kai, but her mother blocked her way.

"*Fuck* her feet!" With her hands braced on her hips, her mother stared her down. "Tell me everything that happened with Kai," she said. "Starting from the very beginning."

Chapter 12

Chloe sipped her mimosa and uncrossed her legs, nodding along, as if she was paying attention to the story her coworker was telling the entire table. She hid a yawn behind her champagne flute.

It was Saturday, a bright summer afternoon in New York City. Chloe sat with three other women at a sidewalk table of her favorite brunch spot in the East Village. All dozen or so tables were filled with weekend unwinders, and the air sparkled with the sound of people laughing, the tapping of knives and forks against plates, traffic rumbling past on the street only a few feet away.

She'd been in New York for the past eight months, and she'd gotten to know most of her coworkers well. She spent time after work with the three she connected with the most. Lisa, a self-described man-hungry bisexual. Billie, a Trinidadian lipstick lesbian with a big dick complex. Dion, a German transplant who'd been trying to push up on Lisa for as long as Chloe had known them.

The eight months had been about more than just work. It had also been a time that Chloe had spent nurturing her relationship with her mother. She'd visited Noelle Graham every month and shown her that she was a woman grown enough to be in love with Kai, not the overindulged and unprepared child she often imagined her mother saw her as.

During those months, she'd frequently mentioned Kai to her mother, but Noelle had never wanted to talk about her former best friend. That hadn't stopped Chloe from trying to get them to reconcile. Just a few days before, she'd written her mother a letter, begging her to forgive Kai and laying out the reasons why it was better for the two women to be friends again. She had put everything in that tear-stained letter. Her grief over what she had done. Her love for her mother. Her longing for Kai, which she knew could never be satisfied.

Before she'd left for brunch that afternoon, Chloe had got a postcard from her mother. "Message received," was all it said. She put the mimosa to her lips, wondering what her mother meant by that.

Just then, the waitress stopped by their table to refresh their drinks. The bow-tied butch gave Chloe a flirtatious smile and a wink before moving on to another table. Everyone stopped what they were doing to give her the eye.

"Chloe, you have *got* to tell me how you always look amazing, even after working all damn night, then coming back at six in the morning." Billie pointed her glass of mimosa at Chloe. "Right now you look like we all didn't bust our asses in the studio until nearly two a.m."

Their studio was working on a science fiction TV show on a tight schedule, which meant long hours, lots of coffee, and far too much time with coworkers.

Chloe didn't bother to tell Billie the truth, that when she felt her worst was often when she looked her best. And the past eight months had been hell. Between pulling herself together enough to realize what she'd done to her mother's friendship, apologizing profusely to Noelle Graham, and even plotting to see Kai and truly apologize and face her like a woman, Chloe had had a rough time of it.

She gave her coworker a flirtatious smile. "You mean this old face?" Chloe tossed her imaginary long hair over her shoulders and batted her lashes.

"Billie's right. You are gorgeous every single day." Lisa glanced at her with a slightly jealous smile. "When you first started working with us, I was sure you couldn't keep up this supermodel glam. Now, almost a year later, you haven't missed a beat." Lisa pursed her thin bright pink lips. "Girl, you have been noticed."

The three women at the table examined her thick, shining hair, the white cotton dress that came to mid-thigh, and the quartet of turquoise necklaces draped around her neck. She knew her makeup was flawless. She'd seen to that before she left the apartment that morning.

"I don't know what y'all are noticing." She sipped her mimosa and fussed with the menu in front of her, uncomfortable under their regard.

"No worries, doll face. Pretty girls always make other bitches uncomfortable." Dion stirred a straw in her screwdriver and shrugged, then glanced around the sidewalk. "It's a law of the jungle or something." She stopped the movement of her straw when something made her pause. "Damn!"

"What?" Lisa immediately turned around to gawk over her shoulder.

Chloe, who sat next to Lisa, only sighed with quiet relief that their attention had turned elsewhere.

Dion whistled. "That is one *fine* mama jama."

Lisa laughed. "Mama jama? What are you? Sixty?" But when she saw who Dion was looking at, she lost her cool points too. "God. Damn."

Billie and Dion, who were sitting across from Chloe and Lisa, had the better view of whatever was going on. Billie nodded in appreciation. "She's not quite my speed, but she is *wearing* that vest and fine face of hers, surely."

Over the past few months, Chloe had gotten used to seeing some of the most beautiful people in New York. Models, actors, everyday women who probably had star-

ring roles in many wet dreams. Seeing women like Sanaa
Lathan or Samira Wiley was expected, and appreciated,
but it was no longer a cause to go crazy, like everyone else
at the table seemed to be doing.

"Come on, Chloe. Even you aren't too fine to check out
this gorgeous sista."

She rolled her eyes, annoyed that Lisa would say
something like that. But she turned around, anyway, to
see what they were all gawking at. Her eyes widened, and
she spilled her drink all over herself.

It was Kai. She stood at a storefront only a few feet
away, talking with someone whose back was turned to
the women's table. Yes, she looked incredible. Her thick
hair was loose around her face and rippled in the summer
breeze. She had on a peacock-blue vest, which was unbuttoned over a V-necked white T-shirt, and jeans that clung
to her slender thighs. Her stance—hands in the pockets
of her jeans, legs planted wide, head high, and chest
up—made the most of her already impressive everything.

Although she'd known that Kai was in New York, it
still startled Chloe to see her. Her mother, who said she
wasn't speaking with Kai, somehow knew that her former
best friend was in the city that week for work. When she
let that slip, Chloe took it as the perfect opportunity to see
Kai and lay everything between them to rest. If only her
mother had been able to come to New York, like Chloe
had suggested.

A nervous tremor began in her fingers.

She'd spent the eight long months crying and praying
and straightening her backbone to become the kind of
partner the woman she loved could one day see herself
with. With a plan and an apology in mind, she had decided to see Kai at her apartment the next day. The *next*
day. Not now. Chloe wasn't ready to face her yet.

She blushed and grabbed a napkin, dabbing up the wasted mimosa from her dress. The drink had immediately stained the white cotton yellow, plastering the thin material to her breasts.

Lisa snickered. "Is she *that* fine, though?"

As the women laughed, Kai looked up. Chloe felt her bright eyes on her like a rough caress. Then Kai's face shuttered to hide whatever it was she was feeling. The woman she was with turned around to see what she was staring at. It was Adi, the friend of Kai's she'd met in the park months before. She smiled and blew Chloe a kiss. Flustered, Chloe turned away to refocus on wiping the drink from her chest and lap.

You're such an idiot.

She had eagerly embraced her new life in New York and had tried her best to accept that for now, and maybe forever, she could not be with Kai. It was hard. She ached every night for the feel of the other woman's arms around her, for the sound of her laughter, for things they had not gotten the chance to share together. Though she knew there was a chance she'd run into Kai before she was ready, seeing her on the street just then felt like a punch to the stomach. Chloe reached for her water and gulped it down, trying to control her reaction but not quite succeeding.

"Damn. Is she coming over here?" Billie hurriedly straightened her blouse, fluffed her straightened hair.

She was. Chloe could sense Kai, could almost smell her coming closer in the hot summer air, bringing temptation and all the twisted guilt she felt over what had happened between them. Seconds later, she stood just on the other side of the divider between the sidewalk and the restaurant.

"Chloe. What a surprise to see you here." The women at the table gawked at Kai. She inclined her head at them before facing Chloe again. "Can we talk?"

Chloe muttered excuses to her coworkers, then stumbled to her feet, leaving the women staring at her out of blatant curiosity. At the exit to the sidewalk, Kai pulled the gate open for her.

As they left the restaurant, Chloe hoped that she'd remembered to pay for her share of brunch. At that moment, though, she could barely remember her own name. And all the words she'd thought and rethought about saying to Kai when she saw her again disappeared, as if they'd never been.

"It's good to see you, Chloe."

"Good?" She clutched at her necklace with cold, nervous fingers. "It's tearing me apart to see you here." She squinted into the sun, vaguely remembering that her shades were in the purse she carried over her shoulder. But then the thought flew from her head when Kai touched her arm, leading her around a set of Japanese tourists who were pointing up and taking photographs in the street.

"I didn't come to cause you pain," Kai said.

"I know. And I have no one to blame but myself."

Kai took her by the arms and dragged her from the stream of traffic and under a bright green awning advertising a deli. "Stop with this blame thing," she said intently. "It doesn't get us anywhere." Her hands tightened on Chloe's arms. "I'm as much at fault as you are, but it doesn't matter. It really doesn't."

The pain Chloe had kept inside her for all those months rolled up her body and out her eyes. "How can you say it doesn't matter when I feel like I'm dying every day without you?" She trembled in Kai's fierce grip. "I wish I'd never touched you. Now that I know what it's like and how things could be between us, it feels like torture. Fuck!" She gasped as tears scorched her cheeks. "It hurts so damn much."

"Shit." Kai pulled her into a clumsy embrace. "Baby, don't cry. Please, don't cry."

But Chloe was beyond simple tears. She broke down in Kai's arms, sobbing as if her entire world was ending. The tears poured hotly down her face, hiccuping sobs making it impossible for her to speak. She buried her face in Kai's warm throat and clung to her, trembling beyond control.

In the time she had been in New York on her own, she hadn't cried once. She'd kept it moving, fitting into the life she told herself she'd always wanted, slowly trying to build herself back up, although not quite succeeding. The fissure of sadness had sat inside her chest, a steady crack in her universe, but she'd managed to hold it together. Until today. She tightened her arms around Kai's waist, bawling.

Kai cursed again and gathered her closer. With Chloe tucked into the curve of her shoulder, she rushed to the edge of the sidewalk, through the crowd of pedestrians, and whistled shrilly.

Seconds later, a yellow cab pulled up. Kai quickly ushered Chloe into the back of the cab and gave the driver an address. Chloe couldn't stop crying. She sagged into Kai's chest, unable to halt the loud and ugly sobs that poured out of her. Kai stroked the back of her neck and made soothing noises as the cab bullied its way through the weekend Manhattan traffic. Soon it stopped, and Kai paid the cabbie, then rushed Chloe out and upstairs to her apartment. To the familiar couch.

Chloe cried harder and turned her face into the back of the couch, pressing her hot cheek into the rough cloth. All those months of holding on and being strong shattered, as if they had never existed.

Kai stroked her temple, her cheek. "Baby, everything will be okay."

"You don't know. You have no idea!"

"I have every idea," Kai said. "Every day I want to scream about how unfair all of this is. Finally, I find the woman I want to share my life with, and it's someone I can't have." Her fingers were gentle on Chloe's face. "Believe me, I have an idea about how much this fucking hurts."

The sadness in Kai's voice turned Chloe to her. Kai's face was a cool mask, but Chloe could see behind it. She could see the pain that Kai was holding on to and holding in.

Chloe touched that beloved face, tracing the tense muscles under her cheeks, the tight flesh over her forehead and under her eyes.

"I feel like such an asshole for what I did," she whispered, her words thick with tears. "And I know I did this to both of us. I should have just stayed in California and worked my shit out myself."

"No. This thing between us had to come to a head sooner or later. Even Noelle agrees."

"You talked to her?" Chloe's eyes widened. A tiny spurt of happiness bubbled inside her. Did that mean her mother had taken her advice, after all?

Kai nodded. "She called me a few days ago. I was shocked but so damn relieved. After thirty-plus years of being friends with that woman, she means more than the world to me."

"More than I do?" But she hated the words that came to her lips as soon as she said them. This wasn't a contest. This was about happiness and making sure that, whatever happened, Kai and her mother were all right.

"No. In a different way." Kai stroked the backs of Chloe's hands with her thumbs. "I love you. I've had to accept that it's not wrong. You're not a child anymore, and I've never felt this way about anyone else in my life. This is something I've been processing with Adi and with your mother, trying to understand what I feel and making sure that these things aren't going to harm Noelle."

"What did Mom say?"

"You should ask her yourself. I'm having dinner with her tonight." A smile drifted across Kai's face. "You should come."

Chloe struggled into a sitting position as hope for the women's friendship surged in her chest.

"This dinner is something private between the two of you," she said.

"What's happening concerns all of us." Kai's voice deepened with emotion. "I'm sure she doesn't mind. Besides, I think it would be good if you were there too."

Did Kai already know something about the impending conversation that she wasn't saying? Chloe clasped her hands in her lap. "You're right. We all need to put our true feelings out there and see if it's possible to move forward in a way that we all can live happily with." She nodded. "If Mom says yes, then I'll come."

"Good." Kai drew a breath and smiled again. "Her plane gets here in a few hours. I'm picking her up from the airport."

"Then we should have dinner here," Chloe said, making a sudden decision. "I'll cook."

"Are you sure?"

"Yes. I want to do something for the two women I love."

She stared at Kai. At the freckles across her nose and cheeks, the lush brown lashes dipping low over mutable eyes. The faint laugh lines around her mouth. Her mouth. For as long as she lived, she would love this woman.

Kai brushed away the new tears that tumbled down Chloe's cheeks. "I'm humbled by you."

Don't be humbled, she thought. *Just love me.*

But she only looked away from the penetrating eyes to her hands in her lap. It was overwhelming to see Kai again after so many months. The absence had eaten away at her so much that she barely knew what it felt like *not* to miss her. The pain was even sharper now, for she knew that she had to endure the separation and the raw feeling of loss all over again.

But damn. It felt so good to touch her again.

Chloe clenched her hands in her lap. "I'll see what's in your pantry, then go to the market to get whatever else I need. Is that okay?"

"That's more than okay." Kai put something in her hand. "Here's a spare key to the apartment. You can come and go as you like. I need to go out and take care of a few things."

Chloe suspected that Kai just didn't want to be closed up in the apartment with her.

"Okay. That's fair." She stood up. "I'm going to wash my face and get started."

She felt Kai's eyes on her but didn't turn around. The other woman said something, a soft exhalation of sound, just before Chloe stepped into the well-lit hallway and headed to the bathroom.

When she returned, Kai was standing by the door, keys in hand. "I'll be back later on," she said. "Make yourself at home."

Chapter 13

Chloe found only a few of the things she needed in Kai's kitchen. Understandably so, since this was her work space and a bachelor pad. After a quick visit to the nearby market, she returned to the apartment, turned on music to distract her mind from thinking about Kai, and began to make a meal for three.

When, hours later, Chloe heard a key in the door, she quickly snatched off her apron and stood by the kitchen sink, steeling herself for her mother's reaction to her presence in Kai's apartment.

"It smells like someone made an amazing summer feast." Her mother looked over her shoulder at her best friend as they came in, a strained smile on her face.

Kai carried a bag over her shoulder, something big and pink, obviously not hers. She looked nervous but happy. The door closed with a heavy click behind her. Chloe picked that moment to step from the kitchen so they could see her.

"Hi, Mom."

Her mother stopped and stood still. "Chloe." There was no surprise on her face, only a wary gladness.

They'd seen each other a couple of weeks before, when Chloe visited Atlanta for her stepfather's birthday. It had been a great visit, but Kai's absence had lent a somber air to the annual festivities, which she usually attended. Noelle Graham had been noticeably unhappy. That was when Chloe decided she had to do something other than wish for the two women to reunite. This response to her letter was even more than she could have hoped for.

"It's good to see you, darling."

"It's good to see you too, Mom." With a sob, she was in her mother's arms, eyes tightly closed as she clung to her.

She heard Kai move out of the living room and around the apartment to give them some privacy. Chloe pulled back. "I'm so glad you came."

"Me too." Her mother clasped Chloe's face between her palms, looking intently into her eyes. "Thank you for writing that letter, and thank you for not giving up on me." Her own eyes glistened with unshed tears.

Chloe nodded, unable to say anything.

Her mother sniffled and wiped at Chloe's tears, ignoring her own. "Now, let me help you set the table for dinner, or whatever it is that you need."

They set the small square table—it was perfect for two, but it would do for three—that sat at a window overlooking the street. In the summer evening, tourists and New Yorkers alike strolled in their shorts and T-shirts, the tender parts of their bodies bare to the warm breezes. The sun was not long from setting, and golden light fell into the kitchen like a blessing.

"Thank you, Mom." Chloe hugged her mother once more. "Go wash up, and I'll finish in here."

She couldn't stop the tears that spilled over as her mother turned away and left the kitchen. The two best friends were speaking to each other again. Her mother looked happier than she had in a long time. Kai was . . . still Kai.

Chloe wiped her face and blew out a calming breath. She had herself back under control by the time her mother and Kai sat down at the kitchen table.

After she married Duncan, her mother's appreciation for Jamaican food heightened. Now her favorite meal was the traditional dish called run down, a slightly sweet seafood stew made with fish or shrimp, coconut milk, tomatoes, and spices. In California Chloe had practiced making it, wanting to serve it to her mother on a special occasion one day. This seemed like the perfect occasion.

Kai, a Southern girl to the core, loved chicken and dumplings. And so Chloe had made the two dishes for the women, along with the Mexican corn bread they both loved.

"Oh my God. Is this what I think it is?" Her mother, seated at the table across from Kai, sighed as Chloe set her food in front of her: a wide plate holding two small bowls, one for each main dish. Chloe put the corn bread, cut into squares, in the small space in the center of the table.

"I made your favorites," Chloe said with a timid smile. "I hope you like it."

She'd never cooked for her mother before. Noelle Graham was an award-winning chef who had created dishes that literally made people cry. Chloe had always been intimidated by the idea of cooking for her, but she had wanted to show her love in a way her mother would understand.

"It looks incredible, darling." Her mother looked at the table, then at Kai. "Everything smells wonderful."

"Thank you." She placed an identical plate in front of Kai, served herself, then filled their glasses with the fresh peach iced tea she'd made earlier. Finally, she set a bottle of white wine and three wineglasses on the table for later.

She sat on the third chair at the table, draping a napkin across her lap. "Do you want to say grace, Mom?"

Her mother's chin trembled with emotion. "I think I'll let Kai do the honors tonight."

They held hands, Kai's cool palm against Chloe's left hand, her mother's hand in her right. For a moment,

Chloe felt the awkwardness of it. The woman she had made love to, whom she wanted to love for the rest of her life, was holding her hand at the same time as her mother. She bit her lip. Then her mother squeezed her hand, and the feeling of awkwardness went away. Kai began her prayer.

"We thank you, Creator, for allowing these two wonderful women into my life. I am thankful for having them at my table once again. Whatever may come, know that we are grateful for each other and all the happiness we've shared over the years. We live in gratitude for this meal, for our love, for being able to share both freely. Amen."

Amens echoed around the table before hands were released.

"Thank you." Her mother glanced at Kai.

The green and gold eyes were dark with emotion. "I'm the one who should be thanking you."

"Weren't either of you paying attention to the grace Kai said?" Chloe picked up her spoon and prepared to dig into the run down. "We're all grateful, so that's that."

Soft laughter rippled around the table.

Chloe dipped her spoon in the bowl. "I really hope you both enjoy this. You were in my heart the entire time I was cooking."

Her mother touched her hand, eyes again shining with tears. "I know, my darling. I'm sure it is wonderful."

"Don't be so sure. Remember that one time I tried to make Kai chicken and dumplings when I was in high school? It was so awful that she threw up right after she finished choking it down."

A smile tugged at the corner of Kai's mouth. "I think everyone remembers that day."

Which was why whenever Chloe offered to make a meal, the response was invariably a resounding no. With amusement, she watched her mother and Kai approach their dinner with cautious spoons poised above their bowls.

"I'll go first." Chloe put a spoonful of the Jamaican dish in her mouth. Just like when she had tasted it in the kitchen, the mixture of coconut milk, spices, sautéed onions, and tomatoes was fragrant and delicious. The shrimp, which she'd added during the last few minutes of cooking, was perfectly tender, perfectly seasoned, with just a hint of heat from the Scotch bonnet pepper she'd put in the dish.

The two women watched her face carefully as she chewed and nodded, giving them permission to eat their own portions. Not tasting her food while she cooked was a failing of hers while she was growing up. She had thought that since her mother was such a wonderful cook, culinary genius practically ran in her veins. Not at all.

"Oh, wow. This is amazing." Her mother's eyebrows rose in surprise. "Really, really good."

Chloe was grateful to see Kai aim her spoon directly at the chicken and dumplings. She spooned a large portion into her mouth, her face neutral but committed. Chloe saw the pleasure overtake the careful mask, her mouth moving as she chewed, a low sound of appreciation leaving her throat.

"Excellent," she said once she'd swallowed.

Chloe released a breath of relief. "Good. Success!"

"I see what you're doing here, love." Her mother had also taken her spoon to Kai's favorite dish, eating it with a smile of delight and, of course, surprise.

"I wanted to make sure I got it right this time," Chloe said.

"It's perfect." Kai's smile was warm and soft around the edges, as if there was something she was longing to say or do but didn't dare.

"Thank you."

But it was her mother who lightly touched her hand. "That's not what I mean. I appreciate the love you've put into making this meal for us."

The tears Chloe had sworn to banish for the evening surfaced again. "I love you both so much!" The words rushed from her. "I'd rather anything in the world happen to me than lose either of you." She batted her tears away. "But it would be even worse to see you lose your friendship with each other, especially because of me."

"We haven't lost anything, Chloe." Kai spoke carefully, tenderly. "We've been dealing with the situation. Noelle may talk a big game, but there's no way that I'm going to let her out of my life. Not ever." She put her spoon down in her bowl, glanced at both women. "I'm not going to minimize what happened. But the thing that I want to be clear about with you, Noelle, is that I love you like a sister and you're in my life to stay. I'm also in love with Chloe."

Chloe's spoon slipped from her hand and clanked against the edge of the table. Hot color surged beneath her cheeks, and a tidal wave of hope began to swell in her heart.

Kai continued. "But I would sacrifice what I feel so that you and I can have what we once did." Her lashes dipped as she glanced at Chloe. "And I think your daughter feels the same way."

"I don't think you should speak for Chloe on that account, honey."

"Mom, I—"

"It's all right, my darling. I know what you feel." They'd talked about it over many glasses of wine and many tears. "And I know I can't keep telling you to follow love while getting in the way of your journey when it makes me uncomfortable." She turned back to Kai. "This situation is a motherfucker. But we'll get through it. We have to."

The two women exchanged faint smiles, something tender and private, which made Chloe warm with relief. She went back to eating her dinner, deciding to leave the two of them alone together once she finished.

Her mother filled the three wineglasses on the table and put on a determined smile. "So, now that we've dealt with that, tell me, Kai, what's going on with the merger I've been hearing about all over the news?"

The conversation segued into business, her mother and Kai going back and forth about the merits of the merger versus the shit storm it was bound to release, and Chloe bringing a voice of reason to the discussion. Soon their dinner was finished; the iced tea nearly gone. Darkness danced between the city lights just outside the window.

Her mother daintily wiped her mouth and put her napkin on the table. "Okay . . ." She glanced at her dinner companions. "I think it's time for me to step out for the evening."

Chloe looked at her in surprise. "Where are you going?"

"Why? The last time I checked, I'm grown." She kissed Chloe on the cheek, then did the same to Kai. "You two need to talk. I'll see you in the morning." A rueful smile touched her lips. "Maybe even in the afternoon."

Kai jumped up from the table, accidentally dropping her napkin on the floor. "What do you mean, Noelle?"

"You know what I mean, Kai. I'm not going to stand in the way of my daughter's happiness, even if it means she wants to be with you." She crossed her arm briefly over her stomach and drew a quick breath, obviously steadying herself. "See you tomorrow."

Then she was gone, leaving them with the sound of her high heels against the hardwood floors, then the front door closing.

Kai stared at the empty doorway, her mouth slightly open.

Chloe was stunned. She could only stumble to her feet, grab at her wineglass. The dry wine sloshed in her mouth, slid down her throat. She took another gulp, blinking with confusion. She had been ready to give everything up for her mother's happiness with her best friend. And now . . . and now she wasn't sure what was going on.

The dazed look slowly cleared from Kai's face. "You're drinking my wine."

Chloe looked down at the glass in her hand, realized it was nearly empty, whereas hers was full. "I'm sorry. I—"

Kai kissed her. Chloe gasped and backed away, trembling fingers to her lips. "What just happened?"

"Noelle gave us her blessing." Kai pulled her close again. "She won't fight against us being together. And God knows, I don't want to fight this anymore." Kai kissed the corner of her mouth, her cheek.

Oh my God. This is actually happening. It is. . . . It is.

Chloe melted in the soft embrace, the glass of wine tilting precariously between them. Kai grabbed it, put it somewhere, continued kissing Chloe until her mind and body caught up with reality. She parted her lips, allowing the slow buildup of Kai's kiss, the heat blossoming inside her.

Kai's tenderness and urgency brought them to the bedroom. She lay back in the sheets and pulled Chloe down on top of her, kissing her, her tongue seductive and hot in Chloe's mouth. Chloe quivered, turning deliciously liquid with her lover's hands on her hips.

"I love you." Kai kissed her throat. "Be mine." Her hands slid up Chloe's thighs and under the thin dress. "I've waited so long for you. Please say you'll be mine."

Chloe lifted her head. Under her, Kai was a dream finally made real, her copper locks fanning out across the pillow, her lips damp and full. This was the woman who'd inspired her search for the perfect lover. The woman she'd always wanted.

"I've always been yours." Chloe lowered her mouth for another kiss.